nethergeist

NICK STEVENSON

RISING ACTION

Cover Illustration © **Nuno Moreira**
Distributed by **Blackstone Publishing**

ISBN: 978-1-990253-71-3
Ebook: 978-1-990253-73-7

FIC009020   FICTION / Fantasy / Epic
FIC009070   FICTION / Fantasy / Dark Fantasy
FIC009140   FICTION / Fantasy / Military

#Nethergeist

Follow Rising Action on our socials!
Twitter: @RAPubCollective
Instagram: @risingactionpublishingco
Tiktok: @risingactionpublishingco

To Tywysoges Petra

nethergeist

BOOK I

Dramatis Personae

Agathon City

AYILIA, Regent, House of Kiya, the Lord General of the X Gemina Brotherhood of Knights

Doge LERANG, parliamentary ruler of the Panchayat (government of Agathon)

Provost BARRIK, leader of the opposition

JACOB and LORELAI MILANDRA KELCREST, Ayilia's ex-lovers and citizens of Agathorn

JARRAK, Ayilia's mentor in her youth

MANNFERLAING, Doge's courtier

FIRST AGATHON DEFENCE GENEERAL SCHORNHAMEL, military leader during Ayilia's embattled youth

X Gemina Brotherhood

Captain AARON

Lieutenant KEMET, Ayilia's mentor

Second Lieutenant NESSAN

Private SOREN

Private KOFI

Private CALEB

The Pit

VESPASIAN, Pro Consul of The Pit

Captain STILGEN

Lieutenant REENA

FELM, Centurion

SULLA, past Pro Consul of the Pit

TUGOR, common soldier

BASTUBIC, common soldier

ZEAMUS, common soldier

GLECK, common soldier

TALOROUS, Centurion

Vespasian's Sythian Siblings (Generals of the Goat)
MABIUS

OTHO

VITALLIUS

Military Units of Nethergeist (Present)
LIFELESS, automated soldiers replacing the Imperial Carnivore Legion of the past

LUBBERKIN, giant, hairy creatures used to drag large weapons of war

Imperial Magi, Centurions, legionnaires, ballista operators, archers, slingshots, optios (communications)

Military Units of Nethergeist (Past)
IMPERIAL MAGI, sorcerers serving the Goat

WIRRAL, Imperial Carnivore Legion

WOLVERINE, Imperial Carnivore Legion

GOBLIN, Imperial Carnivore Legion

PROTO-GOBLINS, Imperial Carnivore Legion

VENSA, Imperial airborne demon

Asthen Magi Raiders of the Ascendancy
Commander BARRACKUS

Major SHEYNA

Captain ADIRA

Captain SKYRON

Captain LARS

Dust Tracker ANDROMEDUS

Private GORLAN

Private DAYLA

KRAYAL
Elder MAROUKISH

Elder AMATASHTAR of the Ahiram (a Krayal clan). Also, member of the nomad council convened in times of danger

Elder RETARI

Chief SEFTUS

Chief's Second JARONG G'LAITH

Others

THE GOAT (Abomination, God, Imperator, Undying One), Emperor of the Universe

REGALLION, the First Federal Administrator of the Outer Rim Prefecture zone X1

First Gryphon Sceptre AGELFI Bil'Hazen, a mage, an alleged Heretic of the Resistance and Ayilia's tutor

AL KIMIYA, alleged necromantic terrorist

CHRONICLER, storyteller

PROWLERS, Lifeless mounts which require little nourishment, if any

PHYSICAL FEATURES

SIRUS, MYRA, and DEMON, suns

NERO KaSeti, titanic world orbiting in tandem. Has its own moons

ZEINKARST, volcanic peaks north of the Agathon Stretch in the Rantor Ranges

GAUNTLET CLASP, tail end of the Zeinkarst

I'ANSANSIE LEAVES, used for tea

Points of Interest

THE UNCERTAINTY DOCTORATE, THE DISEQUILIBRIUM PARADOX OF SPITE, which details that vast organizations like the Imperium have too much weight and resource to support the moral bankruptcy of the eternal hoax of power and greed, and will consequently fall.

JI'NAA, the purest stage of being for any Magi, when soul, thought, and mind combine to create the ultimate being.

DEMON UNITS under DEMON MONARCH

SLACKEN, elite demon Vanguard

The HERETICAL BLASPHMEMERS OF TOOTH AND CLAW, demon advance

LEGION OF THE SWINE

LEGION OF THE UNJUST AND MOST CRUEL

LEGION OF THE SUCKLING PIG, led by War Wraith Ahriman

SCAVENGER CALVARY

AVENGER BLOODFEST LEGIONS

ANATHEMATIC COURT OF THE MOST LOATHED, demon court

"I remember the originals before Abandonment. My father used to deal with them; sometimes, he brought me to the Occupied Territories. He wanted me to understand from an early age what it's like. They were vicious, brutal. Remember, this was after the Treaty. Discussions were fraught—the Lifeless were always volatile, sometimes frenzied; they were nothing like the Pro Consul's recalcitrant brood who seem to hate him more than us. Occasionally, one would ... lose it, for no reason.

The X Gemina, our soldiers, are heavily armed, but I saw a berserker take out two of our men. It only took a moment, but what he did to them ...

Anything could go wrong, and it often did. One mistake, one sudden move ... they hate us; they loathe us. Every one of them is bred to believe in their calcified superiority over anything that lives, especially those who escape their rule, so they loathe us twice as much."

- Ayilia, Regent of the House of Kiya, addressing the human council.

CHAPTER ONE

DESCENT!

"**W**itch!"

The rock just missed her head. It would have struck her if there hadn't been a piercing flash from the gathering squall. The light caught the blur just in time. Even so, Ayilia barely spotted the intruder's shadow as he rushed at her through the gravestones. She reached for her broadsword instinctively, but it wasn't there. Hardly surprising. It was, after all, her father's funeral.

"You work for the Imperium!"

The man lunged at her. Ayilia dodged behind an ornate family tomb. The blade he'd pulled out clanged into the stone's edge with a slew of rock powder. The decrepit granite crumbled easily. Her hand grappled at the loosened chunks of rubble and old sand.

"You're the Goat's concubine!" His teeth were pearls in the light. "I won't let you sell us to the Lifeless!"

He circled the headstone, panting hard. She watched his eyes, not once taking her gaze away from their maniacal glint. He lunged again, but she ducked and smacked the stone shard she'd fumbled from the tomb into his scalp. He stared mutely at her, a spurt of blood checkering his puckered cheeks. As he slumped to his knees, Ayilia slammed her boot into his chest, and he fell backwards.

Two guards clanked into view, though not with the urgency her father would have expected had he still been in charge. She inhaled deeply, steadying herself. The rock lay near her feet, the man's blood still shining dully on the sharpest edge. One of the guards kneeled on the stricken figure and tied his hands with leather straps.

The other regarded Ayilia. "Ma'am ... you alright?"

She nodded.

"Don't know how he got through ..." The guard helped hoist the man upright. "We'll make sure it won't happen again."

Ayilia gave a curt nod, and they turned away.

"Like you care," she hissed, almost inaudibly.

Both intruder and guards disappeared. The cemetery was hers again. She mulled over whether to call in more soldiers, but decided the security of the cremation was best placed in *her* hands. For the hundredth time, tears began to well, but she was determined not to let the acidic stares of the waiting dignitaries outside have the satisfaction of seeing her grieve. She swallowed them back.

Ayilia could see her father's coffin. The arcane rituals demanded that she be alone for the part when he was set to burn, and she was almost grateful. The way things were going, being alone was safer.

In the ebbing light, the white-blue spires of Agathon city gleamed far below like freshly-scrubbed bone, the sea a silver slab against the brooding dun of the approaching superstorm.

Sirus, the red giant, was fading into scarlet obsolescence on the horizon beyond the graveyard's broken skyline. The star's tiny siblings, the twins, Myra and Demos, would soon follow. People watched in suspicion from the streets, piazzas, and shores, far beneath the plateau that housed the whitened tomb yard.

Tentatively, with tears threatening again to well, Ayilia approached the open coffin. She would have to be quick. She placed a shield across the chest of her father. It glinted against the tawny hue his hand. He lay there, serene, in a dark, green-gold tunic. An impressive Kestrel long sword, embossed with fierce Gryphons down the hilt, lay to one side.

He looked paradoxically healthy for a man who had been sickened to the quick by an incurable and mysterious necromantic virus, one that had lasted decades. His eyes were sewn shut, and his frame was a still spectre in a box. The pallbearers would lift his corpse onto the central pyre at the apex of the granite necropolis, and he'd burn brightly for the crowds. His death-light would flare into the coming night. He would burn for everyone; Ayilia would just burn internally. In that moment of darkness, she imagined the faces of the three people that once loved her: Aaron, Jacob, and Lorelai. If she didn't sort the newly elected zealots out, she'd be alone forever—or dead.

The suns disappeared behind the horizon in a final, blinding flourish, setting off the quartz in the shrines. The crypts were grim silhouettes, the corroded sea stained like blood. The dignitaries, courtesans, and nobles, the great and the bad, all waited. They leaned forwards, searching for facial giveaways, a ruin to wade in, garish mannequins under the clash of the clouds. Lightning broke the sky. In that moment, Ayilia caught the fleeting image of the approaching funeral lighter among the whitened crypts.

Her blood froze. This time, the tears ran hard and fast.

☠ · ☠ · ☠ · ☠ · ☠

The dignitaries shuffled impatiently outside the boneyard. Crestfallen, Ayilia smothered the signs of grief and looked up. The storm was growing into a violent one, just as the pyre was about to be lit. She wouldn't have been surprised if it stretched all the way to the Pit, hundreds of leagues away, and its witless, abandoned Consul. Either way, they didn't have much time.

"Ma'am...?"

Ayilia started. It didn't look dignified to jump, but she hadn't seen the guard coming. A tomb rodent suddenly bobbed off.

3

"You've disturbed the Time of Solitude!"

His reply was soft but brusque. "I was sent." Another flash of lightning. His face was hard, contemptuous.

"Without these customs, no matter *how* arcane they seem, I can't imagine what we have left!" She didn't believe it for a moment, but she had to say something. Even so, Ayilia heard her old mentor's voice growling from the darkness inside.

Play the game, Ayilia, or it will play you!

Old Jarrak could never shut up. Used to drive her to frustration, but she dearly missed him now.

"Sorry, ma'am," the man muttered, placing one knee on the ground before changing his mind and standing back up. After all, she wasn't her father. "It's the city council, the Panchayet. They desire an audience."

Ayilia took a deep breath. The man at the graveyard was the second person to attack her today, and now the newly elected jackals wanted in. The surge of rage inside masked her anguish, albeit fleetingly. She'd been preparing for this moment for years, for her father to finally give into the coma, but the pain was worse than she'd ever imagined.

The Panchayet's timing was appalling.

"Are they *serious*? Can't they at least wait till their marionette has burned her last parent, the only living relative she had left?"

"There's been a ... development. It requires your immediate attention."

She stared in heartbroken disbelief, desperate to keep her eyes dry. She refused to look weak in front of his merciless scowl. "I've spent my whole life at the council's beck and call. All I ask is a moment to mourn the only family I have."

Hesitation. The guard fumbled with his sword hilt, then looked up. His eyes betrayed cruelty that had been absent when her father continued to slumber in his delirium. His death should have meant her ascension—it seemed to have corroded the only authority she had left.

"I don't believe this can ... with all due respect. The council are gathered already, in full session."

That dread rose again, tearing at her soul.

There was a low growl of thunder. Again, she tried to mask her unease, but the growing strength of the lightning revealed the slightest expressions. "Impressive ... *full attendance*. Miraculous, considering the council must have had as much notice as me!" He looked mystified. She tried not to snap, but fear made her prickly. "That means no notice at all, or can they fly? Even then, they would've been late."

He stared back mutely. He was official Panchayat Honour Security trussed in baroque green robes, lustrous black chain mail, purple cingulum, and soot-dark trousers. The Panchayat emblem, a dove and a fig, were fastened into the mail. It matched her arm crest, a gryphon astride an image of the three suns. The beast represented the people, and the sun the House of Kiya, her family. Symbols had once been everything.

Ayilia smiled weakly to look authoritative. It was likely unconvincing. "I'll join them, but as they were notified well in advance of their nominal puppet, I hope I can be forgiven for delaying a few moments longer."

The guard's eyebrows came together as he mouthed the word 'nominal' to himself. The rain came. Patters of water speckled down their fronts. At the least, it would hide the tears.

"Please, could you tell them?" She smiled again with more success. "You can leave out the puppet bit if you like. I *just* want to mourn my father!"

He nodded slightly and made his way towards the shimmering city still visible below, now pinpricked with an adornment of lights. The council was already gnawing her waning rulership to the bone, and she'd only officially been regent half a day. The tombs lit up in bleached rows under the gaze of the squall. Grasses tussled against the soughing of a strengthened wind. As the flames consumed the penultimate of her bloodline, Ayilia held her hands to her face and, finally, loudly, allowed herself to grieve for real, bathed in a rain that only got harder.

••*•*•*

"*I love you.*"

Ayilia pivoted round on her saddle to stare at the mounted figure next to her. The horses were matted tendons of mercury, their shoulder muscles bunched like leviathans' fingers. Though this was now ten years ago, it still felt fresh, raw.

"*What did you say?*"

"*You heard... dimwit,*" *came the laughing reply.*

With that, Lorelai, eyes gleaming like moons, gripped her reigns and rode hard towards a weald on the edge of a league-high, white precipice overlooking a waxy, puce-coloured sea. Ayilia urged her horse through the silvered bark of the glade, past boulders patinaed with saffron sprays of rich lichen, and along the cliffs themselves. Lorelai remained ahead; she always did. Her form was haloed by rainbows thrown up by the salt spray and floating clouds of thick surf froth carried by the wind, even from that distance. It landed around them in bubbling clumps like creamy sorbet. Ayilia was an adequate rider, but Lorelai was the best she'd ever seen. On they rode, sending capricious coveys of shingle down the face of the rise in ivory shoals.

"*Enough ... God's sake, enough!*" *Ayilia screamed joyously, her eyes puckered with frantic mirth.*

Lorelai turned round, even as she rode. "*Why?*"

"*Why do you think?*"

"*Because. I'm a better rider than you?*"

"*You're better at everything,*" *Ayilia gasped.* "*I can ... barely breathe!*"

"*Okay then...*" *Lorelai said, voice tinkling.* "*Now that you've finally admitted it.*"

Lorelai slowed and let the panting regent and her equally gasping mount pull up beside her perfectly calm horse.

"You unbelievable..."

Ayilia didn't finish. Instead, she grabbed the woman's cheeks with urgency and thrust them against her own. They kissed passionately on their horses, the tidal breeze merging their flowing tresses. Eventually, Lorelai carefully pulled away, mouth moist from the other's ardour.

"I didn't know," *Ayilia eventually said,* "that you really felt that way."

Lorelai smiled. "It's been a while, hasn't it, since I've opened up about anything. But... well, that's something I just don't do. I'm sorry, I don't do... trust."

Ayilia looked down, her eyes soft tarns in a winter sunrise. "Don't be. I'm just not used to hearing it. I guess it goes with my ... situation. No one stays long."

"That's not quite true, is it?" *Lorelai replied.*

"Well, Aaron was an ass and couldn't stay long anywhere, even if it was a free mead factory, and Jacob ... never mind."

Lorelai frowned, her face becoming as hard as tin. Ayilia instinctively recoiled. She loathed that look. Lorelai's moods could switch at the drop of a hat. She could cut anyone off in the space of a heartbeat. It made getting close to her fiendishly challenging.

"That's just it, Ayilia. The truth is, as you said, people can't handle your role, and, if I have to be honest, neither can I." *She looked away as if embarrassed, but when she finally looked back, the hardness was still there. It was hardly surprising. Lorelai was a hawkshaw for the local constabulary. It wasn't a place that usually took on women, and she'd become as flinty as a basilisk's cuspid.*

"Ayilia, I don't want that kind of bull in my life anymore. This city's going backwards. The longer your father rots in his coma, the more narrow-minded they become. They think you're a witch, and they think your malady's a thaumaturgic hex. Heck, they're starting to gripe, utterly unjustified, of course, that you're as useless as Pro Consul Vespasian in the Pit despite all your hard work. There's even talk in the sweatshops of stringing you up. The more their fear grows, the crueller, more bigoted their taunts become. I can't watch your humanity get violated much *longer, and if I have to be honest, I'm getting weary of taking the flak myself just because I love you."*

Ayilia turned away. It was happening again. "I can't leave my father like this, decomposing alive in that bewitched hell, you know that. And I can't legally step down until he finally recovers, or..." She broke off.

Lorelai regarded her for a long moment, her mop of brown-blonde hair blowing in the breeze.

Ayilia said nothing.

Deep in thought, Lorelai carefully folded her arms around Ayilia and kissed her thick, black hair.

"I know," she whispered. "I know."

♀ · ♀ · 💀 · ♀ · ♀

The warlord came to. The lighting in the room flickered alarmingly. It took him a few moments to realize it was the approach of one of those cursed worldwide storms. Sentries faced him, features dispassionate as the stone of his seat. Their worn, dark, grubby skulls were nicked, their sockets piceous in the darkness. Embarrassingly, he'd drooled down his front. He was getting worse. Through the monastic prism of his ruin, the yearning to slip into darkness was aestheticized only by the same nullifying stupor that filled his days.

This time, though, something was happening. He could feel it in his marrow.

Lightning flashed again. The terrified warlord started and tried to pretend he'd been thinking. He knew the sentries hadn't been fooled. He coughed and flexed his fingers. Another stab of fear lanced his insides. Something bad, very bad, was coming imminently. He hadn't felt this petrified since childhood. Beads of sweat cloaked the parchment skin of his face. Though his lungs were knotted clumps of redundancy, he inhaled loudly to mask the fear. They made an odd sound in that cavernous room of strobing light.

Abandoned in an Imperial outpost that no one needed, in charge of a world that no one wanted, all Vespasian could do was putrefy. The Emperor Goat had left behind only a workforce of lifeless drones and broken soldiers that were slowly coming apart.

The Pit, his kingdom of decay, had become an underground catacomb of oxidized desuetude matching the other inside. It ruled a world of humes, a renegade species that called themselves "human," who toiled the dirt for him. The remaining few not under Pit control cowered in delusions of freedom in a coastal hole called Aga-something, and the Krayal, a destitute throng of reptilian miscreants who once covered the lands from horizon to horizon, were now confined to desolate rises up north. Once proud, they'd been hunted to near extinction before Abandonment, when the Pit thrived as an Imperium meta power. Under him, it was a citadel of rust while *his world*, slept without fear.

His ceremonial dirk suddenly slipped from his lifeless fingers. It clattered next to the armoured boot of a guard. In the heady confines of that space, it seemed comical. Pro Consul Vespasian came close to laughing.

"Sire...?"

The voice came from one of his guards. The warlord looked around, eyes wide. It was impossible to tell who'd spoken. In the dark, each looked exactly like the other. Fortunately, they spoke again.

"You appeared ... animated, liege." A thunderclap detonated overhead. What little remained of his skin nearly bolted for the exit. "Do you have orders?"

Vespasian recoiled as if stung. "*Orders*?"

"Beatings!" Another had spoken. Again, he had to look around. He managed to identify the speaker quicker this time.

"*What*?"

"There are no beatings, no executions. When we were part of the Goat's Imperium, they used to make examples. The old virtues are gone!" The rebuke was unmistakable. "You are Sythian; your *whole* family is Sythian! A *priceless* gift. Your kind are more puissant than the most powerful necromancer in the

Imperium, outside the Emperor Goat Himself. You should crush the humes in that city and disembowel the Krayal scaleheads in the mountains." They fixed him a murderous look. "*Not* merging into your seat!"

There was another clash of thunder. If the storm was a 'planet shaker,' the walls would soon start vibrating.

The warlord's malady-riddled face clouded. The thing had a point. Sythian sorcerers weren't just rare; they were beyond measure. Though they looked like people, they were, in essence, necromantic spores. Like potent nomads, Sythian DNA drifted through species over millennia, gestating and hibernating, until a hijacked host was transformed without warning into a Sythian Magi. The Goat had sought out these Magi, stolen them from a mother they never met, and made them lifeless. His siblings were lethal necromancers of extraordinary ability, but he was almost completely theurgically sterile.

There was another clap of thunder, and this time the walls did shake violently. Vespasian flinched, hands quivering.

Add cowardice to magical sterility.

He had to think of something to say before his moribund authority bit the dust. They might even demand that he declare war on that last human city whose name he could never remember. Loss of memory happened a lot lately, probably because he'd been in charge for near twenty years. Yet, the thought of violence made him feel both faint and physically sick.

"Before Abandonment, we had materials to repair our people and *fresh*, life-giving Ichor from the Goat, His very blood, to animate new ones," Vespasian garbled witlessly, voice trembling like a barnacled trumpet. "Now we have mulch to bind their wounds while the Ichor's gone rancid. I thank the underworld god if they don't fall apart passing wind!" His laugh was hollow, and he hoped for a response, but there was none.

The speaker part bowed, their bony brow flecked with barely concealed disgust. "Very good."

Very good, indeed. He'd gotten away from deciding for at least another week. He looked at his hands. In the piercing lightning, they looked almost as skeletal as his people. He had no heartbeat, as there was no working heart. His organs were as motionless as clay bricks. The marks on his wrists were still visible. Had he done that?

There was another crash of thunder, this time deafening. Lines of dust and mortar pattered down in furious drifts. Vespasian winced openly, total power and utter powerlessness mired into one. His normally neutered Sythian senses were kicking in. Whatever was happening, whoever was coming, it was today.

This was the last day when nothing would ever happen again.

Ayilia wiped her face vigorously, again desperate to hide anything that could be perceived as weakness. They feasted on that. At least she'd made the jackals in the parliament wait. If anyone attacked her again, she'd have a sword.

Her father's essence was part of the sky. They had seen the light of his fire right across Agathon City below. The storm was still in its infancy despite the rain. She made her way out of the tomb yard. A troop of listless city guards who waited for her with the captain exchanged sly glances, then followed. Any of the great and good who had remained in the graveyard to pay their respects to her father made way for her with icy graciousness. Little wonder the aristocracy hated her. She had tried to persuade the Panchayat's government to raise taxes on them to benefit the stinking bowels of the city.

She descended the spiral staircase leading to the city below as the downpour thumped. The graves at the peak of the imposing rise were a vagueness along the blurred horizon. At the bottom, a rippling crowd waited. For the most part, they were placid, but there were too many, so the barrelled-necked captain of the guard gestured towards an adjacent alley. It made sense. It led directly to the parliament and was free of onlookers. Nevertheless, Ayilia felt a stab

11

of trepidation, but before she could protest, she was unceremoniously shoved forwards.

There was a sharp flash of sky charge.

The lightning lit up more grey, wet faces within the dark innards of the cobbled road. Each had either a dirk or a long blade in their hands. She screamed a warning, but the captain couldn't hear; the chattering noise of the crowd had grown too loud. There was a scurry of bodies, a disarming clash of steel, and the captain went down in a fountain of blood, his throat a red furrow. The other guards tried to fight, but they weren't experienced soldiers and were immediately forced back. A slew of thugs poured from another door and cut off their exit. In moments, Ayilia and her guard would be overwhelmed.

Ayilia grabbed the captain's weapon and scanned the alley before thrusting into the centre of her beleaguered defenders.

"Quick, form a cordon around me. *Now!*"

Something in her voice compelled them. The ramshackle guard quickly backed into a holding position with a series of clanks and curses. The attackers continued tearing into them. The formation helped, but it wasn't enough. Ayilia let out a cry and pushed to the front, her sword an electric slash in the storm light. One of the assailants instantly backed off, their shoulder bleeding heavily. The others paused. Encouraged, Ayilia swung her blade again, and another attacker staggered off, gripping his side in pain.

There were still too many. She searched for an escape route but couldn't see one. A series of shouts issued from behind the crowd, and a swathe of armour crashed into view. Three assailants were cut down where they stood. The rest fled for their lives into the darkness, swiftly pursued by the new arrivals. Ayilia bent over, gasping for air, as the terrified guards around her gave a weak cheer.

The leader of the arrivals hurried over. He slammed his helmet on the ground and leaned over to inspect her, his bald, umber dome sheened by rain.

"*Regent*," he breathed urgently. "You alright?"

She nodded, still panting heavily. "Even by their standards ... this is a first...."

Kemet's fists flexed maniacally, eyes popping with disgusted venom. "It's the most blatant thing they've ever done!" His neck muscles twisted as he scouted around for more possible trouble. "Your enemies *always* preferred the darkness. This has to be Barrik. Now he's finally in power, and he doesn't give a damn anymore."

Ayilia wiped her newly-acquired weapon. It was of excellent quality and her favourite style: a heavyset broadsword, or longsword, with a double-edged blade, commonly referred to as the bastard sword. This was no time to think about the previous owner, who lay in the mud, especially since she'd just left her father's funeral. Raindrops as large as marbles rolled down her face, masking any sign of tears. It was so typical of Barrik to strike when his adversaries were grieving.

"It's going to get worse. This new government's dangerously militant. They won't stop till they corrode everything."

"This new government borders on fascistic!" Kemet gripped her arm. "You're not seriously thinking of going in after this? Most of our people are out in the Occupied areas monitoring the boneheads, stopping them from mistreating the enslaved. The X Gemina can't hope to protect you."

Ayilia tried to smile and simultaneously regain her breath. "If I don't, he'll get them anyway. Our only hope is to stop him from gaining the Panchayat's support or the Doge's. The Doge might be half man, half armchair, but he's not corrupt, unlike Barrik!"

"I'll send word to Aaron. He's at the barracks with what's left of our soldiers. Seems mine have vanished in running these cutthroats out of town, and you certainly can't go with these blockheads here..." His hand pointed at Ayilia's terrified-looking guards. "They're as hapless as beached smesh!"

She raised a brow, then placed her hand on Kemet's shoulder. "I'll be fine." Her voice sank to a whisper. "Besides, I think Barrik will wait until he's officially deposed me before he tries again."

She turned towards the shell-shocked guards. "Leave one or two of you with the dead and send another to get help. We can't just leave them lying there, even the thugs. The rest of you are with me." She turned towards Kemet, her face damp with water and pink smears of other people's blood. "We'll be seeing you later, won't we?"

Kemet smiled. "Wouldn't miss it for the world!"

Ayilia flashed him a warm but deeply uncertain grin and sheathed her blade beneath her belt. He watched her go, face a ruin of gaunt concern.

· · · · · ·

Two of the Lifeless guards huddled near the Pit's only interdimensional portal, covertly glugging illegal mead. The crime was punishable by flogging, not that the Consul enforced such things. Vespasian was soft, and they despised him for it as much as they took advantage of his oversights.

They stopped their thievery; something was wrong. The dark that normally concealed them had changed. It felt like it was reaching forward with iron claws. It was the night commander approaching, though this didn't provide them much relief. She hated them sharing a watch. The two had grown unusually attached, unheard of throughout the Imperium, but in the Consul's chaotic universe, anything was possible.

The commander stopped before them, frowning. "Not you, too," she hissed. "Fixed the rota so you could have a smooch again?"

Vernon had staggered to his feet to give a fumbled salute. "Ma'am, no. Just happened that way!" Hobart managed to kick the bottle into the dim recesses with his boot. His hand scratched his armpit furiously. Pit bugs were out in force tonight.

She glowered at them. Vernon studied the ceiling uncertainly, searching for an answer. "It's not like there's anything to report, ma'am; the gate ain't been used in two decades." He nodded towards the silent, foreboding form of the portal. "Nothing's coming through for another two decades if you ask my opinion."

"I didn't!" she snapped, eyes red flares in a pockmarked skull. Her thinned hair, a luxury among their kind, was chaos in the dim gloom. The commander turned to leave. "If I catch you two spooning again, hell's udders there's going to be trouble." She made a cutting action against her gullet. "I mean it this time!"

The moment she left, Hobart rose and stuck his finger up before catching Vernon in a huge smooch. "Screw her, pal. Let's break the good stuff out. Going to be a long night, and I feel like letting me hair down."

Vernon snorted. "You don't have hair!"

They laughed and thumbed at the liquor bottle Hobart swiftly retrieved. On the surface, they were a calcified mishmash. Underneath, they were no better. Hidden within their dirty armour and sagging rib cages, they were clumps of stitched guts and twisted sinew. Liquor seemed to do something special to people who couldn't feel anything other than the bite of bugs.

"Did you hear that?" Hobart growled, trying to pretend he wasn't afraid. "I hear something."

Vernon's eyes were pink smears in the half-light. They had little strength left. His skull was grubby, his stubby teeth black with decay, and the enamel corroded from booze. "You damn ass, there's nothing down here. No one *ever* comes down here outside that judgmental sow!"

Hobart flinched again, letting his grip fall from the other's knee. "It's coming from the bloody portal."

"Hell's teeth, fool." Vernon sighed. "You said it yourself—it's barely been touched in two decades. It's why we're *isolated*!" He rose and thrust a fresh bottle of foul liquor into the other's chest. "Got this special number on the black market only today. You could use it, you rotten sod. You look like—"

Crack.

They grappled for their rusted cutters. The sound had come directly from the gate. Hobart took a tentative step forward. His shaking hand reached toward the vast, silent lens. A glimmering split was scything from top to bottom within the confines of its ancient maw. The room was abruptly bathed in otherworldly light and the imposing frame of something terrifying.

"By all that's...." Hobart's hand, skeletal on the best of days, was a gossamer spindle against the moonlike glow. "Something's coming ... something's actually coming through the door!"

"Come back, dolt, we don't know what's there," Vernon called, then gaped. "What in all the unholy worlds is *that*?"

A powerful shape with burning eyes emerged from the portal's lens amid a fierce glint of diamond-hard metal. Without a pause, their clean blade swept Hobart's astonished head from his shoulders. As the bloodied lump bounced in wet puddles across the floor, the figure flung their sword at Hobart's gobsmacked companion. It pierced the point between the Lifeless's sockets, neatly rupturing his face into two.

Without a word, the figure picked up their weapon and stepped over the fallen shapes lying on top of each other. The chipped bottle gurgled its contents across the cobwebbed flagstones.

It was still in Vernon's hand.

"Sire?" Pause. "*Sire?*"

The dazed warlord looked up, his face frozen by an eye-numbing flash of piercing lightning. He was outside, perched on the top of the edifice that was his Pit, overlooking the ossified sands and stunted hangman trees that were his desert. Obsidian clouds broiled like twined intestines over a twister-dominated horizon.

"You risk much troubling me here," Vespasian indicated a tempest far from its zenith, "These winds would tear your skull off!"

"My liege, news ... *tumultuous* news!" The messenger quivered so much he risked flaking apart. Vespasian studied his spidery, stunted build blearily. By the intense look in his tangerine orbs, this was *the* moment of the wretch's non-life.

"News?" the warlord muttered, kick-starting his brain into action. His hair was fluttering so uncontrollably he looked more like a wild man from a lost weald than a worldwide ruler, no doubt. "Have they cracked the mead rackets?"

The messenger's eyes rolled. "No, he's *here*! He's back, they're *all* back, and they're here to *stay*!" The speaker's spittle congealed in a weal around his pockmarked mouth. It was like looking at a primeval froth in a crater. Vespasian found himself wondering how a skeletal puck with absolutely no feelings could shake. "It's *him*, sire; he hath returned."

The warlord inhaled to steady himself, even though he could no longer breathe. "Who has returned?"

"No more excuses now, no more respites!"

"*Who... has... returned?*"

"Your brother, Mabius!"

Fittingly, there was another clap of thunder. The back of Vespasian's skull rang as if someone had pummelled it with a multi-spiked sledgehammer. He wanted to scream but couldn't. He could see in the messenger's gaze something new and malignant. This news was a raging bushfire consuming his tinder authority, burning it to pellicles within the confines of the Pit.

"He's changed *radically*," the Lifeless gasped. "He commands the vanguard against those Heretic wizard-dogs! Hell's lugs, he was something imposing in the Pit, but now... *phew*!" He spat. Most of it was blown back into the messenger's face, but he hardly noticed. "The humes, their harridan queen and Agathon City, are finally going to be wiped from existence! Stupid, *dirty*, stinking *swine*, no more reprieves. They're going to get it and get it *hard*!" His fist slapped against his fragile palm.

"The last hume city?" the Consul replied eventually, voice faltering. His legs trembled. "What would my sibling want with ... Agathon?"

"Don't know," he said, shrugging. "He demands your presence. *Straight away!*"

There was a scurry at the door. The Consul turned. A skeletal figure, wrapped in animal pelts and corroded Imperial armour, pushed past the messenger. After a curt bow, he growled deeply: "I see you've heard?"

The understatement of the decade.

"Yes, Stilgen. Seems we have to be somewhere fast."

He glowered, then snorted. "I will take your side!"

Loyal to the end, even one that was imminent. Such a trait was as rare as a bloodless sunrise above the Pit. Vespasian decided nightfall was boundlessly optimistic. The rest of the Pit would already be switching sides—everyone knew who was in charge. Just like the old days! His legs shook so much he could barely walk.

She was young.

A garrulous man with big shoulders had outstretched his chunky hands for a hug. He was smiling at her underneath a silver helmet festooned with a ridiculous sprout of purple and scarlet feathers. He'd just returned from some important chinwag with the dead men of bone and tendon, and he looked happier than he normally looked. Even the desert gnats didn't seem to bother him. Surrounded by a gaggling clutch of self-important nobility, smug captains of industry, and his X Gemina guard, her father clearly expected her to run from her mother's arms and give him a public embrace.

Instead, she burst into tears.

Some of his retinue looked sheepish for their leader. It was meant to be a celebratory homecoming. But he just laughed loudly and bent to the scrunched face of the child, his eyes an exploding blister of laughter lines and weathered care.

"It's no problem, little one." He smiled, intensely proud of his one and only child. "If you won't come to me, I'll come to you."

"No ..." She backed away. "They're looking at us!"

Eyes were watching her. Even then, she was cursed. She could sense their hostility. Many thought she was adorable, but the small-minded among them scrutinized her with furtive distrust. A word was muttered when they thought she was out of earshot.

"Witch!"

They thought she had the 'evil eye.' They thought she could tell what they were thinking, and it made them fear her. Some said she'd grow up and put a hex on them, the city, even her father.

"Mark my words," some scullery worker had said, grimacing when she thought the child's back was turned. "She says things only an adult would. She has the hellion eye. Have you noticed how the weather changes when she's outside? There's a demon inside 'er, you knows. She'll grow up into a succubus and put an illness bout on her father! Mark my words!"

It stung like hell. It stung even more when the whispering spread to the city. All kinds of maladies were blamed on her. They started to hiss about her heritage, things she was only just beginning to understand. It seemed to make the criticism more potent, though she couldn't comprehend why it was even relevant.

"They're ignorant, Ayilia," her father said softly, leaning close so no one would hear. "People like us are lionized when things go well and demonized when things don't, but not for who we are but what we are. We're held to a higher standard than others. It's not fair, but we are a resilient family; we've had to be. Be strong, be yourself. Take ownership of your mistakes, but don't apologize for things that are not your fault. Such people secretly feel unworthy inside, so they shift their self-loathing onto others. We will prevail!"

He put his sepia-toned, thick-veined hands on her shoulders. "If this city doesn't get its soul sorted out, something will come for it. Its collective mindset, its fearful, hateful thoughts will come back and haunt it. The people choose their own fate, and they will blame all and sundry for it as, I fear, it will be a terrible one, but they are responsible, no one else."

Gently, the man the size of a bear picked her up and hugged her before placing a large kiss on her grubby forehead. He made sure his voice could be heard now.

"Been playing war games again, have we, my little Ayilia?" He turned to the others. "She's going to grow up and be the best sword wielder in all of Agathon." They cheered and laughed. He winked at her. "Aren't you, sweetheart?"

The girl took one look at his feathers and, without warning, yanked them from his hat. Satisfied, she threw them on the floor and scowled at her bemused father.

"You look stupid in those!"

He turned to the others, leaned his head back, and let out an uproarious laugh. The others joined in.

Ayilia smiled shyly and finally gave her father the hug he wanted.

The memory hit her with the force of a ballista's bolt. Ayilia winced and closed her eyes, still refusing to let the malicious revel. Despite being prepared, the level of her grief stunned her. This was the time they picked to question her.

The main piazza was unexpectedly busy. Once an armoury, it had been relocated during the reign of Elthelereed the Unbelievably, Stunningly Unfortunate. Ayilia could see stalls, wagons, crates, and barrels filling the dirty, straw-flossed flagstones amid smears of crushed tomatoes and the folds of discarded cabbage. They mixed freely with animal dung and the waste of the unhoused.

The crowd bustled, trying to catch a view. Some smiled, many frowned; one spat, though not quite in her direction. Muffled scuffling vied with disjointed comments, faces clenched with imagined slight. The rain was coming down in sheets. It ran off the surfaces in rivers and sprayed off the stalls. People, mostly concealed in wet hoods, were lit up by bouts of lightning. Ayilia and her soaked retinue were forced to halt. The gazes of the throng were glittering dagger points in the gloom. The masses swelled against the guard's armoured shores like an oil slick. The parliament was just out of reach, though she could see it gleaming above the twin waterfalls underneath the ominous cloud.

An older woman shot out a hand scarred by gruelling work. It gripped Ayilia's arm tightly. "I'm a seer," her voice husked intrusively from within a deeply frayed shawl. "Don't go in. Don't go in, Regent!"

Despite her grief, Ayilia tried to smile reassuringly. "It's just a formality."

"They don't want you!"

The host was overwhelming the soldiers. They hadn't sent enough. Agitated voices were beginning to rise.

"I'm sorry; I can't hear you!"

"You're not one of them," she rasped like a broken saw. "You sense things, I can tell! They can *smell* difference in that place. They can sniff people like us out, mark them for treatment." Her breath was foul, but her beady eyes flashed like dragon teeth. "Many still support you. You bring hope to those who have no voice, but those who do, are stronger." She gripped the regent tighter. "They have been poisoning your name for years, telling lies. They say you're a sorcerer! They want you gone!" The woman's grip was increasingly painful. "Someone who's lost his soul is inside. He only has eyes for power."

A guard shoved the woman aside. Though Ayilia tried to hold on, the seer fell back into the crowd in a flurry of beads and torn linen. People pushed forward, oblivious to the rain. Some patted her back, though many glowered with readily given offence. Her enemies had whispered against her, but that wasn't the only issue. Neither was capability. She already handled her duties unofficially without a hitch. The fact she was apparently 'barren' rankled. They muttered that she was bewitched by malignant sorcery like the one that struck her father, but it wasn't enough.

They even overlooked her heritage when it suited them. Sure, it was a problem, but her parents had been beyond reproach. Even the diehard meat grinders in the slurry quarters had grown to grudgingly accept them. What really soured the gamy hide of their disgust was her going it alone. They wanted a dutiful, parturient breeding machine steamrolled into acquiescence by a thick-skulled buck raised to misrule. The city was parochial, dangerously insular; the last free remnants of a human diaspora from an antediluvian war no one remembered, waiting for a cull no one knew was coming.

They'd become as narrowed-eyed as a burrowing ground murmel, a small, furry creature that only came out when starving, preferring to hide from reality the rest of the time. It didn't help that she'd harboured the delusion she could govern!

A voice from the crowd disturbed her internal wave of doubt. "Witch!"

Thrusting and hammering, the metallic leviathans of the Pit's machines belched toxins into the air so sulphurous, entire weather systems writhed in gaseous brumes between the churning pipes. On good days, the forked charge mischievously doled out shocks. On treacherous days, thickened cloud banks deluged them with acid or the deadly attentions of a passing smut devil, toxic twisters of smog. The Pit drones laboured on working the pinions and greasing the tines that kept the rigs thumping. It never ceased, yet the warlord never quite knew what they produced. Stilgen scowled at Vespasian's side, flanked by two troopers they hoped were still loyal. Furtive glances were thrown in their direction, and mutterings rose as they passed. Resentful indifference had become something else: ridicule.

Unwittingly, the scorn matched the melee surrounding the regent some leagues distant.

"They wait in the Forbidden Chamber, liege," said a sour-faced sentry. "They have been demanding your presence for quite some time."

"We're here, aren't we?" Vespasian swallowed. It wasn't normal for the security to display overt hostility.

All he could think was what a stupid name the Forbidden Chamber was—why were people summoned to it if it was forbidden? A bridge on pylons arced in a silver corona over a cavernous gorge ahead, its struts the vertebrae of an extinct beast. The crucified forms of hundreds of figures lined both sides leading over the rise and beyond.

Aghast, Vespasian approached the nearest, his hand reaching out as if to soothe. It was one of his Pit soldiers. Like all the Lifeless, his bone was thick enough to harbour a hidden circus of manufactured veins and tendons within, without which there would be no mobility. The dense rib cage, constructed to leave no gaps, and the armour covering it, was split wide open. His grey gutting spewed down his legs in twines, and the rest lay at his feet in still-steaming clumps. His once-red eyes were blank, and his stitched tongue lolled from a gaping jaw.

Vespasian's already pallid features went whiter still. "What is this?"

Stilgen shook his head. "Decimation!"

"Why?"

The guard had joined them. "Your sibling regards your people as ineffective, weak. Like you, my lord. He ordered a Decimation of one in ten." He nodded slyly at Vespasian's horrified face. "Common practice among poorly performing regiments. He thought you would be ... pleased at the assistance."

"By the undead god, that psychopath's taken out a *tenth* of my guard, a guard that would've switched sides anyway," Vespasian growled, sucking the air through cracked teeth. The Decimated forms above were a rictus parody of power and death.

"You're a Sythian just like him!" Stilgen hissed. "He won't touch you!"

"I'm infirm! To them, I should be hurling wayward moons at the Krayal mountains for fun, but all I do is shoot fat bluebottle beetles from the ceiling and *only* if they're asleep." He put a hand on Stilgen's shoulder. Though he was visibly quivering, Vespasian was overcome by something he hadn't felt in a long time. Compassion. "Go while you can, my friend. By the time he's done with me, you and any loyalists you can still find will be gone. No need to risk your non-life for me."

"You're his flesh and blood; he won't harm you," Stilgen spat, ignoring the chance to flee. "You and your siblings were *sired*! Everyone around here was stitched into existence on some factory line or grown in a vat. Sythians are *pricelessly* rare and astonishingly powerful. No Magi comes close, and that includes the Heretics!"

Vespasian smiled. "I'll be sure to remind him."

Stilgen's eye suddenly widened.

Swallowing back surges of overwhelming panic, Vespasian looked over. A plethora

of heavy footprints led away from the Pit's interstellar gate. Two hapless Pit soldiers had been butchered where they stood. Their severed heads watched in a state of almost comical shock from a flower of pikes beneath an alcohol bottle.

Vespasian gulped quietly. Damn, he was doing a lot of that lately. *Some warlord.*

They carried on, hands instinctively gripping the hilts of their blades. Rounding a bend, they abruptly stopped. A phalanx of immaculate armour waited, a militaristic porcupine of pilums bathed in scarlet banners and coloured standards. Blood-red capes draped behind shiny breastplates. The gold, double-headed standard was held aloft, proud Imperial defiance against a cowering universe. Their jutting helmet visors were clamped tightly shut.

Stilgen's eye was a crimson moon. "Stormkomers ... elite Kommandos! By all that's unholy, this is bad."

A Kommando approached him, a high-ranking centurion. Like a trapdoor spider's den, the visor snapped open. Tall and powerful, his face was a tight fist of tree-root sinews knotted within a strong skull. Vespasian and Stilgen recoiled instinctively.

"Pro Consul Vespasian, fallen Sythian and relegated demi-god?"

Despite his terror, Vespasian marvelled at the Centurion's features. Hard conditions required hard faces, and his ossified, naked brutality was the hardest he'd seen. Skull ridges fluxed and rippled in tandem to an inbred contempt. Living thralls had been known to experience involuntary paralysis on sight. Standing there, it wasn't impossible to imagine why.

"I think so ... I mean, yes!" Vespasian sputtered.

"You're late," he rasped. "You disregard protocol. You should already be in session."

Fear turned to red mist. This was *his* place, after all. "I arrived when it suited." He pointed at the floor. "I do what the hell I please, *here.*"

The Centurion stared blankly. His inexplicable ability to mimic breathing during moments of apparent displeasure was exceptionally unnerving.

"Do we have a problem?" the Consul asked, not so convincingly.

Silence.

Vespasian tried to maintain the bluff. "Two decades rotting in this darkest of places with no news, no contact with the outside universe is bad enough, centurion," he snarled, using the most threatening voice he'd practiced. It hadn't been frightening in front of the speculum in his resting chamber, where he spent a few hours a day regenerating his strength, and it wasn't frightening now. "But what particularly stinks is your attitude when you finally deign to turn up. You know who I am, but do you appreciate *what* I am?" Full of fantastical courage, the warlord jabbed his finger into the thing's chest to ram the point home.

Like a bolt of lightning, the creature thrust his glinting blade against the Consul's gullet. Cursing, Stilgen's fingers gripped his weapon. Vespasian stood transfixed. In a head rush, he gripped his ceremonial rapier, hoping to target the exposed spot at the bottom of the centurion's jaw. With embarrassing effortlessness, the Lifeless' leg kicked with the force of a battering ram into the warlord's equally ceremonial loins while his boned fist smashed into Vespasian's left cheek. The consul was hurled backwards onto his rear. Vespasian lay back, humiliated, a spreading liquid darkness around his head.

Just like the old days.

There was a sharp hiss. With miraculous dexterity, Stilgen's sword flicked the centurion's weapon from his grasp. It clattered across the room. The soldiers behind went for their spears, but the centurion immediately held up his hand. Fixing Stilgen with piercing scrutiny, he carefully recovered his blade. Gasping, Vespasian gingerly struggled to his feet, leaving his ruined pride firmly on the flagstones. His two guards watched silently, their last few strands of fidelity eroded to nothing.

The centurion towered over Stilgen. "Impressive for an obsolete model." His voice was sandpaper on glass. "I assumed you were as indolent as your master. I won't make that mistake again."

"I expect not."

"Don't tell me you learned such trickery in this cesspit!"

"I keep my eye in."

"So, it would seem." He leaned close, too close. "Howbeit, do not think sleight of hand suffices for what lies out there." His head gestured in the direction of the portal.

A legate emerged from the Forbidden Chamber, barely visible behind a troop of the heavy soldiery. The new arrival, decked in a spurious plume of feathery, brusquely pushed past the centurion to confront the consul.

"Pro Consul Vespasian of Etherwolde? You are perilously late. I have seen people filleted on the spot for less." Pointing at the Kommando, she added: "For his insolence, ten of his favoured spearmen will be garrotted." She beckoned them to follow before turning away.

The soft, malachite sheen of the Krayal's scales was invisible, even though the light from the setting suns was still strong. His brooding silhouette faced a landscape of ebony sprinkled with twinkling glass as though a passing giant had tossed them in a game of knucklebones.

As the three suns elongated towards the far horizon, electric charge began licking the dry ground with cobalt tongues. It happened only rarely, so this was to be cherished.

"Seftus...?"

The Krayal figure on the rise didn't answer.

At times like this, his troubles seemed distant, unimportant. Despite his renown for courage and his skill with a desert blade, Seftus was set apart from his people, considered "different" for preferring the company of males over the females of his species. For such warlike people (warlike because they had to be), such things were the stuff of specious gossip, even outright disdain. No matter what service he did, or the sacrifices he made, many never accepted him. Anger consumed him like gout. At times like this, the majestic solitude of such a sunset should never be disturbed.

He inhaled deeply and closed his eyes. The air hummed with crackling, naked power.

"Seftus?" Jarong's voice below was insistent.

Seftus tore himself away from the sinking stars. He looked almost human in the golden light. "What is it?"

The other stammered. "It's the Pit."

"You *know* this is my moment."

Jarong shrugged haplessly. Being slightly on the heavy side, many of his kind scorned him for believing he lacked fighting skills. Seftus had ignored their opinion and taken him in as his Chief's Second. As he, Seftus, was regarded as the Krayal ideal, at least on that front, albeit one with that dangerously volatile disposition, no one had argued.

Jarong's mouth shut tight as tiny vibrations spread into their boots. A piercing light bloomed in the distance. The Krayal flinched and covered their eyes as the horizon erupted into a boiling nebula of blinding fluorescence. For the humans, it was a spectacular phenomenon, one ignited by the sinking suns in convergence with wild thaumaturgy in the atmosphere left over from the time of the Ancients. Why the world was saturated with old magick, no one knew, but for the Krayal, it was the 'god light.' Seftus found it intoxicating. He never got used to it, no matter how fleeting.

"The Pit?" Seftus mumbled, transfixed by the receding glow as a hot wind covered them in a violent shroud of desert fug. The light flared brightly one final time, then dissolved into an infinite dot. "No one, but no one cares about that obsolete rust-hole anymore, Jarong, The Pit is as dead as the stiffs that inhabit it!"

It was one thing tolerating the humans, as Krayal and humes could barely stand each other, yet the days of hating the Imperium's forgotten outpost belonged to a bygone age.

"The elders have terrible news."

Seftus angrily brushed sand from his garb and faced his friend. "The Krayal elders have warned of that place before, yet still the worn-out sops of that old Imperial scab erode themselves into oblivion drinking, fighting, and gambling. Since Abandonment, the Pit is no threat."

The other was shaking his head, white as a corpse. "It is now."

Seftus regarded him with glittering, green eyes. Jarong, perhaps realizing he finally had his mentor's attention, spoke swiftly.

"They're back, Seftus."

"Who?" he snapped.

"The Imperium. They came through the Pit's portal yesterday to reclaim their property ... and this world!"

The stone dropped. Seftus' reptilian face froze in disbelief in front of his friend.

☠ · ☠ · ☠ · ☠ · ☠

"Little one," the voice hissed.

Silence.

"Little one," it called again.

Long moments passed.

"It's going to be alright."

She flew down a flight of finely carved granite stairs, past flaming torches and immobile statuettes of heroes, their purposes corroded with time.

"Trust me."

The voice scoured the room. The elements within the immense stone rattled in seeming sympathy. A gust swept the empty corridors, unsettling tapestries and rustling the sterile canvases of fading portraits.

"I see you, but you don't see me."

Her keep, was contaminated by one of those nighttime sprites. Ayilia kicked open the oaken doors and flung herself through earthenware kitchens. Giant wood-fire ovens and empty wash sinks lined the desolate rows beyond. Arcs of electric charge baked the scene with such staccato brightness they left rippling slashes on her retinas. She fled down twisting stairways to the cooking halls, tapering shadows branching like mangrove roots in all directions before skidding to a stop.

A shape lay sprawled on the floor. The girl approached with tentative steps. It was one of the late roster maids, apparently unconscious.

"You've grown; no longer Regallion's doom. What are you? Fifteen? More? Aren't you tired of running?"

She looked around but could see no one speaking.

"There's no redemption for those who are different!"

Mind numb with terror, she crashed through the servant's entrance.

"Accept your fate with gratitude!" More subtly, "Ayilia—let it go."

There was a fierce burst of lightning. She bolted for the door.

"No safety in the forests ... ha."

Ayilia fled into the dark gardens beyond, past statutes of vainglorious generals and sightless lions. They glittered like quartz in the punishing rain. Vaulting over the neat flower beds, she glimpsed another figure slumped on one of the metal seats, this time a gardener. He was also lost in a deep sleep, breathing heavily in the pattering, wet denseness.

"Still here, little one."

Blankets of rain sprayed her with chrome sheets. The heavens were bathing everything in alabaster brilliance. In the distance, a pinnacle glowed against swishing trees on the garden's periphery. Ayilia darted through towering hedges and passed bleached figures of lost warriors and once-earnest politicians. All stared lifelessly back under the forked charge.

Crash

A maelstrom of spiny foliage slapped against her raised forearms. The tower rose from the skyline like a god's spear, its universe the rain-lashed weald of thrashing movement below. Its imposing length shimmered into the infinity of the storm. Ayilia launched herself towards the hard, damp surface of the wooden door. There was a cracking of twigs and branches behind. Something was coming. Ferns and tall grasses parted violently as a powerful object scythed through the undergrowth.

"I'm coming, oh fake child of Agathon!"

The sound of the creature was a heretical noise inside her mind. She gasped and slammed the door's wet surface with both fists.

Click.

The latch turned. Terrified, Ayilia shot into the hallway and up a spiral staircase. It whirl-pooled to the ground. Something was bounding up after her in a disjointed lope. She ran to a door at the end of a bare corridor, gaze darting up at the achromatized blasts of power visible through a glass ceiling overhead, and slammed it shut after her. The room within was dark and quiet. It was filled with bookshelves. A single table stood in the centre, on which stood unlit candlesticks and rows of crumpled scrolls. A single, reclining leather chair faced a desk papered with blocks of dusty tones and rolled parchments leathered with age.

There was a dark shape in the chair. She tried to focus but couldn't. When it spoke, her blood ran backwards.

"So, I didn't imagine it."

Ayilia went rigid. There was a hungry pawing outside. "What?"

"All this time, for years, I thought I was losing the plot. The lonely voice in the void coming and going, calling to me ... astonishing!"

The scraping outside increased in urgency. She looked mutely towards the door.

The man shook the vague shadow that was his head. "That creature doesn't matter, not as much as you think it does!"

She faced him desperately. "It's going to kill me."

"Listen to me, Ayilia; it is Ayilia, isn't it? At least, that's what flashes through my mind. That thing is feeding off you; it infests you because you shine in the dark, even though you have no theurgy!"

She slapped her hands on the desk, eyes popping. "Then get it out of me ... please!"

"By the gods, I didn't even know you really, truly existed until just now. You must understand I'm not here in the flesh, and I'm already out of strength. The distance between us is shocking!" He looked as though he had already faded.

"You can't go!" Ayilia scattered the contents of the desk across the floor and tried to grab him, but her hand went through the void. The door cracked and bulged inwards. The disappearing figure abruptly rose.

"Get out, Ayilia ... Leave. I'll teach you how to deal with such things; I know how to reach you now. Just get out before it drills into your skull and does its best never to come out."

"How?" she sobbed, looking around frantically.

"Fear's only an energy. That thing feeds off that energy to gain strength, but you are stronger. You can fight it, but for now, you must ... wake up."

"What?!" she screamed.

He leaned forwards. "We're inside your mind. This is something you do, though I don't know how. You're asleep. Just ... wake ... up."

The creature threw its bulk against the wood. Panicked, Ayilia flew at the figure for support, but there was only emptiness. Behind, the door split down the middle. Crack.

She shot upwards, suddenly awake. The bed sheets were haloed with the wet outline of her shoulders. The skin on her back was soaked with sweat. Light was streaming through curtains billowing in a gentle breeze. Despite the beauty, all she felt was something waiting for her to drop her guard every time it got dark.

𝌆 · 𝌆 · 💀 · 𝌆 · 𝌆

Seftus glowered at the Krayal scout with angry astonishment. He wasn't in the best of moods. The heat of the northern ranges, their homeland, could do that to you. On top of that, some panicking youth was telling him that they were being invaded. Thank the gods someone around here had a level head.

"I tell you, they're Imperial! I'd say there are about fifty," the scout said.

"Impossible!" Seftus spat, quickly forgetting he was meant to be the calm one. "We haven't seen Pit boneheads in this god-forsaken desert for twenty years. The Pro Consul would *never* attack us. He's about as belligerent as a damp rag!"

The scout shrugged. "Yet, here they are."

Scowling with disbelief, Seftus leaned over the ridge and stared across the plains. A plume of dark dust was coming towards them at impressive speed beneath the vermillion skies. No living thing could ride so hard under the heat of the three suns.

"They'll hit Hangman's Throat on that course," the scout added. "Gullies here are death traps in a skirmish! Don't they remember anything?"

"Apparently not." Seftus waved at the pack of Krayal gathering on the high ground overlooking the ravine.

"Positions!"

Seftus brought his arm down. A creviced boulder tipped over the edge and crashed into the ravine below. The riders came to a skidding stop, scree shooting all directions from the hooves of the Prowlers, their massive, lifeless mounts. Another boulder closed off any hope of retreat.

"Fire!"

The gully became a squall of arrow and sling shots as a hundred Krayal let loose with everything they had. A dozen shapes crashed to the ground, armour clanging against the desert gravel. The rest threw themselves off their cornered Prowlers and took formation. They moved swiftly, disciplined.

Jarong joined Seftus, an intense sweat clamping his puckered face. "By the gods, Seftus, I've never seen Pit move like that." He paused to think. "In fact, I've never seen them move at all, well, um, not far anyway!"

"Good thing we're always prepared, then."

Seftus gestured to his warriors. A slew of boulders came crashing down. He could see crushed skulls, smashed torsos, and the splatter of yellow fluids below. Within the melee, a blurred knot of bone and metal fought on like dogs.

"Through those gaps ... Fire!"

Another wave of shot felled fighters with considerable success. Every time the unit repaired the gaps, additional boulders opened them up again, creating fresh targets for the shooters.

Seftus nodded. "The Consul's insane. Does he not remember how suicidal traversing those gullies are from the days when the Pit was active? They're boxed in either side; no hope of backing off to regather."

On cue, a massive Lifeless ran from the decimated formation and scaled the steep sides of the gully. Krayal tried to hit them with spears, but the angle was tight, and the thing was too quick. Unnerved, Krayal warriors rushed forwards, but the Lifeless smashed two to the ground with their shield, then grabbed another and hurtled him into the melee below. The hapless Krayal was diced by the surviving soldiers. Another was swiftly butchered where he stood, his head split in half.

Barking frantically, the assembled warriors hit the Lifeless with a wave of spears. Mortally damaged, the soldier stood glowering, shield and blade raised defiantly. With a strangled cry, a warrior lunged forwards and skewered the teetering powerhouse through the midriff with a jagged spear. Still glaring, the undead toppled slowly over the side. As they did, a Lifeless soldier below grabbed a pilum and flung it into the warrior's chest, tossing him a dozen paces back. He lay still in a rupture of blood, mouth open with shock. The other Krayal stared disbelieving at the gulley below.

It didn't take long for the arrows to finish off what was left of the Pit. Jarong, nevertheless, was stood open-mouthed. "How ... how did that ... *thing* throw that?"

"No Lifeless can do that," Seftus snarled.

He strode to the ledge and began to descend.

Jarong's eyes were as large as moons. "Seftus? Come back. This is madness."

"Follow me," came the disappearing reply.

Jarong scrambled afterwards, followed by a dozen warriors. At the bottom, he gingerly made his way around mounds of slain legionnaires, their skulls and necks cut by shot. A river of undefinable gore ran down into the centre of the ravine where most the powerful bodies lay. Seftus was standing over one of the Imperial troops. He seemed to be caught by a rock and was still animated. Tendons peeked from underneath the cracked surface of the crushed bone, the pink network of veins that drove the killer onwards. His left arm was pinned underneath the stone. Seftus whisked out his blade and shoved it against the Lifeless' gullet.

"What are you doing here? Speak!"

The creature laughed, then swore.

Seftus breathed and then repeated the question.

The soldier fixed his blazing eyes on Seftus and spat, hitting the Krayal in the forehead.

Slowly, deliberately, Seftus wiped the mucus away. "Do that again and—"

"You'll what, lizard guts?" He stretched forwards. "Torture me? I don't feel a thing. Kill me? I'm already dead."

The creature had a point.

Jarong ambled up, followed by the others. The Lifeless snorted. "Hell's blood; I thought you scum ate only the fungi you scrape from the rocks." Seftus thrust his head hard against the stone, but they only snarled. "Do it, scale-breath. Know that if my limb was free, I'd stick that thing up your reptilian—"

"What are you doing here? What do you want with our tribes?" Seftus' tone marked that he was done with these games.

The thick, skeletal mouth slowly parted in mirth. Jarong involuntarily shivered. "You imagine we are here for a motley nation of nearly extinct toads? You think these rocky plateaus hold anything of value to us?"

Jarong's features creased in thought. He looked down at the soldier. The other Krayal shifted uneasily around him. "This is a scout group, no, um, *a hunting party*. You don't want us; otherwise, you'd have brought an army to deal with the rises. Even a novice can see just how, well, how *dangerous* this terrain is. I don't think you thought about us at all."

The Lifeless's eyes gleamed. "The portly one has more sense than your whole storm of scum-suckers put together. Kill me now, or so help me, I will slit you all open where you stand."

Seftus regarded Jarong for long moments, then smiled grimly at the creature, a dark gleam in his eye. "How did I miss it? You're not Pit at all. Your uniforms are clean; your armour shines, and you're built like a trade wagon." He bent lower, and his lips curled back. "You're the off-worlders we heard of." He shook his head. "It defies belief. The Imperium finally returns to retake its renegade outpost and its suns-cooked world of yellow dirt and forgotten rust. Why? Since the Pit already owns the human helots in the Occupied Territories and since you clearly forgot we exist, that only leaves ... *Agathon*." He shoved his forehead against the thick brow. "What in all the hells would the Eternal Empire want with a city of crumbling brick stuffed with bitter humes on the edge of a lost desert?"

The Lifeless lay still but remained terrifying, then smiled again. "I told you to kill me."

His right leg slammed into Seftus' head, sending him toppling like a lead weight. With a guttural curse, the Lifeless wrenched his shoulder so hard he tore free of his trapped arm in a smorgasbord of tendrils. At the same time, he sent a hobnailed boot into the midriff of the nearest Krayal. Catching his falling blade in the process, he decapitated another as she leapt forwards. Her head clacked across the ground, leaving dark streaks in its wake. The yelling hit fever pitch as her fevered companions circled the heavyset, skeletal shape.

"Let's see the colour of your entrails, geckos," the Lifeless goaded, his features contorted into a saturnine leer. "Not so brave when there's no high ridge to ward you."

A figure rose from nowhere and thrust their dagger into the Lifeless' jaw-bone. The soldier gawped, then sunk to his knees.

Seftus, dizzy and spattered, heaved himself up and gripped the dying soldier by the neck. "Again! What ... are ... you ... doing here? What do you want?"

Something that could have been part of the Lifeless' mind was seeping across his well-scrubbed cranium. His eyes were watery with death, their scarlet blaze nearly blank.

"What do I want? I want you dead. I want all living things, all organics, dead! The era of the soulless is here. The modern age is witnessing the final takeover of all things that breathe, skulk, and defecate across the cosmos. We are coming, lizard, and when we do, not one of you will be left." He wiped gruel from his mouth. "This is the age of extinction."

CHAPTER TWO

HELL AND EARTH

T he voices bellowed pompously in unison. "Hear, hear!"

"I tell you, we have had *enough* of schism. Fact: the modern age belongs to undead. We belong to the undead universe. Thanks to treaty, the Imperium has provided a fundamental existence guarantee for our city and exclusion from the war. We're an insignificant, forgotten backwater with resources of no use to anyone. Outside Agathon City, the rest of humanity, and most this world, is run by that renegade Imperial outpost called the Pit. We are all that remains of humanity, or 'humes' as the Lifeless charmingly call us, and freedom is a fragile luxury. The rest of our kind are either under the Pit's rusting boot or official citizens of Empire, whose name I dare not utter, scattered throughout space. There is nothing we can do about it!"

There was complete hush in the hall, the rarest of moments.

"There has been a cosmological war in the stars for longer than records exist, and that, ladies and gentlemen, is a *very* long time indeed." The speaker paused for polite laughter. "During all that time, Agathon, our great city, has been excluded from this ruin. In antiquity, as one great enemy of the Imperium fell, another rose. The Goat has fought the royals of the majestic Interregnum, the Asthen Magi of the Ascendancy, and now the sorcerer Heretics, the leaders of the allied Resistance. For the first time in existence, *the first time*, the emperor will soon have no rivals."

Barrik, the Provost and head of the new government, let that sink in. It would be hard to get the watching parliament to reconsider decades of ingrained servitude to the obsolete puppetry of the city, the regency. Yet by the end of the session, the council would be feeding out of his hands. That aging witch of the nearly extinct House of Kiya would be spayed! Treason was still a hanging offence. His new masters would be very grateful.

"Think *hard*, councilmembers. Before, there was no inclination to finish off a remote enclave such as ours. Barely a few leagues beyond our walls, you will see our conquered brethren till the fields for the autonomous authority inside the Pit. This was a fate spared us when the Goat's armies stopped outside our gates all those centuries ago.

"And why did they stop? Trust me; it wasn't just our high walls.

"They stopped because of a catastrophic setback off-world against a then-vigorous Resistance. Though I passionately wish otherwise, that knife still remains thrust against our collective craw. Rapine, destruction, enslavement, and annihilation are a simple command away!"

Barrik paused briefly for effect. Other than one elderly member who'd dozed off some time ago, he had the Panchayat transfixed. No Provost had his skill in oration, and he would use it mercilessly.

Ayilia glowered quietly. She was sick to death of Barrik's espousing of his fanatical belief in the old ways, and she'd heard about Barrik's particularly ruthless streak from the workers at the skinning factories he owned. They whispered he yearned for the days of flogging, state-sponsored amputations, and even executions. Her position, freedom, and life were at stake. The funeral was a distant memory.

She scanned the room furtively. Banners of white muslin encompassed the lip of the horseshoe-shaped ceiling speckled with painted figurines. A ring of council guards held spluttering torches for reasons no one seemed to know against the whitened froth of the waterfalls visible through those grandly designed windows. They chugged and gurgled into hazy oblivion far below where Agathon's lights winked, despite the storm now safely outside, and Barrik's uninterrupted, continuous drone in front as he slowly closed in for the kill.

"The Eternal Empire is very different. In those pressing days, co-operation was demanded, and now it is *rewarded*. The emperor can afford to be generous. I doubt the Heretics of the Resistance can. Councilmembers, we live in an age when the rise of a Lifeless universe is simply unstoppable. The time has come to reappraise our habit of perpetual suspicion of *anything* that does not have a pulse or a heartbeat."

Warnings clanged inside Ayilia's skull like a ship's bell in a thunderous squall. The Panchayat were hanging on his every word. The only face not remotely intrigued was the lone sleeper. He'd drifted off into the deepest slumber possible without actually expiring. Provost Barrik took his rimmed spectacles off and peered at the assembled peers intently, his balding plate wet and shiny with sweat. It, and the rest of his face, lit up like a death mask every time the lightning flashed. A deathly silence awaited his continued speech.

"The Heretics have not once consulted us. Even after Abandonment, when the Pit was stripped of its abled-bodied butchers for the distant wars, not one person came to us to either enlist our help or explain the Resistance's great plan. I ask you: why should we see our land desecrated for *their* off-world struggle? Things have changed from the day when our people first arrived as refugees on this world. In those days, the Krayal were the top dogs here, or should I say ... reptiles?"

A brief eruption of laughter echoed through the chamber hall.

"Now look at them! These proud desert warriors have been driven into the arid north, where only a fragment of their once great tribe ekes out a pitiful existence. For them, there was no Resistance triumph within the stars above to divert Imperial soldiery away!"

Barrik's body shivered. It was almost sexual. He'd waited a lifetime for this. Every single one of the gormless dolts gaped at him like boiled smesh in a seafood factory. Time for the kill! Time to lay the finger of blame on that spoilt sow and see where the sands of fate took her. It was disgusting she believed she had the right to rule alone, even more disgusting considering her family. The last governments should've insisted on her forced wedlock to an aristocrat or captain of industry or clapped her in chains on any charge that would stick. He'd spent his whole life working for recognition. The aristocratic flotsam in the chambers hated self-made people like himself, and he loathed them back, especially as they'd overseen a remorseless erosion of Agathonian virtues.

"The regency guides us during times of tension, but their distrust of the Lifeless has become a culture in its own right, a worn-out glove that no longer serves its user. Has the lust for defiance turned into a self-fulfilling prophecy? Will this narrow-minded attitude become the epitaph of a collective grave that does not need to be?"

The room broke out in applause. Faces turned to look at Ayilia accusingly. She was the anachronistic barrier to a peace that could not exist, not in the way they wanted it. Their faces stretched with faux hope in the half-light, looking as garish as porcelain mannequins. She sat there, mouth drawn into a thin line, staring stonily ahead.

Barrik held his hand for silence, and the hooting faded into hushed expectation.

"Most of us are already in feudal servitude to the wayward Pit. Such co-existence *already* makes us collaborators." Some voices rose in disagreement, so he raised his louder and thumped his podium for dramatic effect. "The damning truth is that if we rely on the few forces we have and an old scrap of ageing Treaty paper, we won't stand a chance, even united with our conquered brethren in the Occupied Territories!" His beady eyes scanned the audience nakedly. "The off-world Resistance is defeated, spent. Ladies and gentlemen, we have *weeks* left."

The hall let out a uniform gasp. Barrik pressed on, eager to ram his point home. "We have heard Imperial troops have returned to reclaim their property and this world with it. We have even heard that the Goat's legions have *retaken* the Pit." Despairing eyes again swivelled towards Ayilia. State puppet or not, she was assigned to warn the chambers of possible threats, not the other way around. "I ask the regent what exactly is the problem with a closer relationship between us and an organization beyond our wildest understanding?"

As the room seemingly exploded, Ayilia bit back furious indignation. She was the political felon holding truth to hostage. People once hung for less.

At least Barrik was done his tirade.

She rose uncertainly and began to make her way through the muttering throng. The room was a glittering cluster of sparkling eyes as sharp as cut diamonds. It was hard to make progress from the isolated seating they had allocated her. Members of Barrik's political party were taking their time letting her pass.

Maintaining an air of controlled calm, Ayilia exited the seated area and made her way to the dais that Barrik was over-graciously vacating. With a start, she noticed that the head of state, Doge Lerang, was already there. Ayilia's powers were largely honorary aside from security; his were anything but. He was so infirm the state would be better run by a rooster. His fine robes only amplified the ossified frame it cloaked. As a result of his confusion, Ayilia was forced to hover beneath the plinth.

Barrik's teeth shone like steel knives.

"Well, umm, thank you, Provost," Lerang said falteringly. "Umm, that was the official position of the newly appointed council administration. I must confess, it's the first time we've heard about the calamitous fall of the Resistance and the Pit's alarming ... reactivation." He shot Barrik a dark look from beneath bushy brows. "The idea of reunification with the Imperium is going to be ... how should I put it, controversial? I assume that's what you mean?"

Lerang glanced unsteadily at Ayilia.

"Well, without further delay, it's now my great pleasure to officially welcome the new appointment to the historical, hereditary role of regent of the last free human city anywhere in charted space." Lerang regarded her properly this time. "She is the titular head of the Panchayat and the Lord General of the X Gemina Brotherhood of Knights. We welcome her appointment, even if such a thing is under the worst kinds of loss." She took a step closer, then stopped. He *still* wasn't done. If he wasn't such a fool, she'd have suspected he was in on Barrik's game. "As you all know, ladies and gentlemen, over the centuries, the legendary House of Kiya has provided military guidance to Agathon and its domains. It is no disgrace to say few, if any, of us could possibly hold hope of her emulating the insight of her father."

Damned unwittingly.

"Honoured members of the Inner Sanctum, I present Ayilia of Kiya and of Agathon."

Light applause rippled through the room and faded quickly. Ayilia took the podium. From there, the hall looked massive. When the murmurs stopped, the only sound was the soft churn of the waterfalls as they fell a quarter of a league below where the city slumbered. The storm appeared to be passing, at least for now. Moonlight shone through the great glass ceiling in dagger thrusts, eerily mummifying the watchers. They looked like hollowed-eyed spectres, undead senators.

"Firstly," she said as clearly as possible after a slight cough, "let me take this opportunity to thank the Doge for his kind words. Secondly, may I heartily thank the Panchayat and its Inner Sanctum and all the citizens of our city who have taken the trouble to wish me well on my ascension. I can say it means more to me than you can possibly imagine." More applause came. Despite the unsettled faces, her sentiment was genuine, and they knew it. "The highly

42

unorthodox situation of my father's mystery coma has meant I have been unable to officially take over his duties for a very long time. Unofficially, I've had the opportunity to lead numerous military expeditions into the Occupied Lands, to ensure the relative wellbeing of our compatriots there as stipulated by Treaty."

Her voice trembled momentarily. She cleared her throat. "But may I *remind* the Provost that I do not wield real power, not without the council's say. The Agathon Defence Force and the Panchayat Honour Guard, are independent of anything I can do or say. The regency's X Gemina soldiers cannot impose policy, only defend it."

Silence.

"What matters are these disturbing revelations. Council members, if these rumours about the Pit are true, we are playing with fire if we gamble our hard-won freedoms against a universe-wide organization that knows only the most rabid hunger. I've *never* opposed diplomacy, just the repercussions if things go the way I suspect that Barrik wants them to."

An audible mutter rose from the room, but whether it was sympathetic was impossible to say. Barrik's smile was frozen. His spite had a chilling off-world stink to it. "What exactly can we hope to achieve by redefining our relationship with this cosmic super-power? Why highlight our irrelevance to the attention of its unspeakably malevolent mind? Why offer the Goat concessions he did not request, or has he already made requests of his own? Why would the Empire come *here*, the edge of nowhere, when there is so much still to do off-world?" Ayilia's eyes darkened. "Have they offered you something, Barrik?"

She would recognize that look anywhere: guilt.

With dilated pupils and lips speckled with tiny dots of salvia, he leapt to his feet so fast that his chair was left spinning on its legs. "*Witch*—you want us to join the Resistance." A cacophony of voices rose in support. These were no ordinary hecklers. The Doge tried to silence them, but he couldn't stifle the growing abuse tossed at her from around the room. A man was screaming something about her lineage to her near left.

Barrik had regained his composure. Looking slightly sheepish, he sat again.

Gritting her teeth, Ayilia raised her hands. For long moments, it looked like she would be ignored. Fear, doubt, and grief all vied with the black hound within, urging her to run. She gripped her hands together as tightly as possible, hoping no one could see the trembling. Fortunately, the hall quietened. Breathing deeply, she addressed the hall with as much authority as could be mustered.

"Witch or not, I never once said we should join the Resistance, not once."

A man stood. "You don't have to; you're a Heretic puppet."

Three members smirked, though there was genuine disquiet among the faces of the opposition. Ayilia beckoned to the council guard. Though most stayed where they were, another ominous sign, four came forward. The man quickly sat down again.

"I've been called a Resistance sympathizer before," she growled in a voice of cracked granite. "I am neither a Heretic puppet *nor* a puppet of the Imperium, unlike, perhaps, others." She shot Barrik another look.

The man on the left still wasn't done. Seemingly unable to control himself, or perhaps having been paid a little too much, he thrust himself to his feet and started ranting so loudly that a flock of slumbering birds outside burst into flight. "Liar! You're their stinking whore. You want to lead us to ruin. You want to sell us out to the goddammed Resistance and that withered Heretic pimp of yours!"

Voices rose in horrified consternation. The red-faced Doge rose and yelled for the guards. They plunged into the melee and grappled with the heckler.

With a sudden grunt, he shoved them away, then pointed directly at her. "Lock her up! *Lock her up!*"

Spluttering, the purple-faced Doge shouted for quiet. Barrik smiled broadly. The chambers eventually calmed, and guards dragged the man away, but the atmosphere remained dangerously volatile.

Shaking visibly, Lerang turned to her. "Regent, only if you feel able, please continue, though I am deeply regretful to say, through no fault of your own, time is acutely pressing."

Ignoring the smugness on the Provost's features, Ayilia nodded and gripped the podium with whitened knuckles. Though many in Barrik's party were unable to comprehend the depths he'd sink to take control, they were the majority in the chamber now, and he had their full support.

She had maybe the night to fight or run.

"Have any of you any idea what they're like?"

Perplexed glances.

"Have any of you *ever* met one, talked to one, fought with one?"

Silence and puzzled looks.

"Have any of you watched a colleague, a friend, *butchered* by one, in front of your eyes?"

The Provost glanced anxiously at her, then at the audience.

The Doge's face was creased with confusion. "To whom are you referring, Regent?"

"The Lifeless!"

She nodded at the room and the stupefied expressions looking back. "I'm not speaking of the clapped-out drunks we're used to, those usually found covered in mule waste. I'm talking of the boneheads the Pit *used* to have, the ones that almost wiped us and the Krayal off the face of this planet, that have apparently returned!"

Barrik rose, chest puffed out with an extra helping of feigned indignation. "I protest at the language deployed and the outright—"

"Shut up," she hissed. "*Sit down.*"

He gawped like a bug-eyed fish on a hot pan, so she hissed again, "You had your turn; sit down, or I'll get someone to sit you down!"

Someone sniggered. Probably the previous Provost.

"I remember the originals," she continued, "before Abandonment and before Treaty. My father used to deal with them; sometimes, he brought me. I guess he wanted me to understand what it's like from an early age. They were vicious, brutal. Discussions were fraught. They were always volatile, sometimes psychotic; nothing like the Pro Consul's recalcitrant brood who seem to hate him more than us. Occasionally, one would lose it, for no reason." Ayilia quietened. The veins in her hand flowed with ice. "The X Gemina are heavily armed, unlike our main forces, and I saw a berserker take out two of our men. It only took a moment, but what he did to them ..." She winced. She hadn't talked of it in years. "My father split their skull down to the neck. Anything could go wrong, and it often did. One mistake, one sudden move ... they hate us; they *loathe* us. Every one of them is bred to believe in their calcified superiority over anything that lives, especially those who escape their rule, so they hate us twice as much."

The Provost's natural lobster hue was now a fetching alabaster.

"What Barrik actually proposes is *occupation*: Lifeless thugs on every corner, mass killings, no self-determination of any kind. Those in power would be rewarded: a good estate, a Senatorial post in the lower house. *All* of you would be pigs in a pen—*we* will be the new dead!"

A slew of men entered to take up positions along the back. They wore plain jerkins, no regalia. Barrik's militia—an astonishingly serious development. Another door opened, and another half dozen came in. One thrust a document towards the sentry chief. His face grew confused as he read the orders and reluctantly left the chambers along with the council guard. Barrik's eyes were twinkling points of naked intent. That last night of freedom seemed hugely optimistic.

The Doge rapped his desk for attention. He stood, checked his pocket chronometer, and shot Ayilia a stern look. "This is all very insightful, Regent, but right now, we need your proposals, a negotiating stance." An aide passed him a cup of water, which he gratefully guzzled, his layered throat bobbing up and down like a leather ball in a wet sock of crinkled cloth.

"If I thought for one moment, Doge, that we could leave it to the Provost, I wouldn't be speaking. I would even be offering my resignation willingly, not because of what I am but what I want *us* to be. Ironic that the historical oversight that is my role is all that stands between our existence and something infinitely worse than the comatose occupation beyond our walls. If Barrik has his way, the future will be a place where even his wealth and self-satisfaction count for nothing, a time when the living envy the dead."

"What can we do?" a council member spluttered from amidst the sea of hard eyes. "Surrender is all we have now that the Imperium's back and the dying Resistance is no longer able to divert their killers!"

Ayilia gripped the podium so hard the old wood creaked. "Flight!"

Silence.

People strained closer, assuming they'd misheard. She repeated it. "A new era, a new human diaspora. We did it before, and we can do it again. Our ancestors fled here from distant Imperial slavery, made Etherwolde their home. We can do this again, someplace further. There's a small, hidden portal somewhere in the north above the Krayal's mountain ranges. A ... source once told me. The Resistance's Heretics can help us find a new home. There are hundreds of thousands, maybe millions, of interlinking portal routes threading their way through the voids. The Imperium built their Pit around the only known gate on this planet, but I can find out where the other is; I can guide us. My source can help!" They watched as she pushed her hair back behind her ears. A few white strands caught the soft sheen of moonlight. The quiet was electric. "By the time our messengers have ridden to the Pit and back a dozen times negotiating our 'surrender,' we'll be gone!"

Her voice petered out. The room erupted. Whether it was too much reality or not enough didn't matter. They were screaming. They were standing, screaming at her. All but the defeated minority, who'd remained seated, their faces visibly crushed with the hard dawn of the new order. Barrik had flung himself from his already battered chair. Slamming his fists on the podium, he bellowed so close to her face that she was flecked with alcohol-infused spit.

"Let's be brutally honest, your family line dies with you. And there has never been a female head of the order, and, frankly, this is exactly why. Instead of supporting our *legal* right to strike a bargain with an Empire that has shown us only tolerance and respect, she wants us to run like sand rats." He turned to the chamber. "Council members, let's rid ourselves of this traitorous farce once and for all. Grant me the powers now, and I will see it done."

Cries of, "Lock her up!" reverberated again through the hall. Scarlet-faced members were shouting at her or each other.

Engorged with political puissance, Barrik turned gleefully back to her. "I *always* said you were a witchling, a dark thrall. People like you should know their places, like in the old days. The Empire's threat made us equal, but trust me, that won't happen again!"

Ayilia's fist slammed him in the mouth. He went down like a hock of ham and rolled off the plinth, leaving splatters of red in his wake. There he lay, staring moon-eyed up at her, his trembling, pink palm holding a gashed lip. The blood gushed through stocky fingers and down his ornate garb.

Barrik's militia needed no further encouragement. As they approached, she kicked the podium at them, then leapt down and executed a perfect double turn as she brought out her weapon. Her broadsword arced across their chests. Two men immediately doubled over, clutching bleeding torsos. She kicked the feet out from under another and hovered over him, blade above her right shoulder. "Those two will live, but I can't guarantee I'll be as unlucky with you." Ayilia swished her blade venomously. "If there's one thing I'm good at, it's this."

Taking his cue, he scuttled backwards, followed by the others.

Shouts filled the cavernous halls. Council members filed towards the doors, faces bereft of entitlement. Barrik's cabinet, with impressive haste, had already made their way off the plinth. Chairs, papers, and grand styluses were scattered everywhere, the grandeur of state laying chaotically in all directions. The braver members of the militia drew near, albeit with a little hesitancy. Cornered, Ayilia circled slowly. For the first time in an age, uncertainty left her. It wouldn't last, but gnawing, never-ending rage gave her a strength she hadn't felt in years. Its corrosive energy flowed through her arms and sword like an electric charge. Her weapon twanged acidly in the half-light as she held it in front of the guards' alarmed eyes. Barrik exhaled loudly, consternation carved into his bloodied features. Glowering at his guard, he gestured furiously. "For the love of God, what are you waiting for? She's just a woman!"

A small, short-haired goon crashed forwards, his rapier coming down hard toward her skull. She blocked it with a loud grunt and kneed him in the stomach before smacking the metal across his forehead. Red splashed her hair and skin. Two more guards lunged at her, but Ayilia felled them with a double swipe. When they lay bleeding at her feet, the others paused, faces frozen with strained tension.

Ayilia glanced up at the frightened figure of the Doge. "Is *this* how it was meant to be, your honour?"

"Guard, *hold*." Lerang, his face twisted in horror, turned to Barrik. "This *is not* what you promised! No violence, no bloodshed. Hell, this is a catastrophe!"

The Provost whirled on him. "This is the new reality!"

"Killing the Regent of the House of Kira? Selling us out to the Goat? This was *not* part of the bargain!"

"No one can stand in the way of progress, you aging fool; you should know that." The militia began advancing again. "Pretty weapon, Regent. Kill all you like. You'll still be in pieces when you leave this room." With impressive alacrity, Barrik grabbed the Doge by his robe. "Your honour, either we bargain with whatever leverage we have, or they take us anyway."

As he began to lead the older man away, the Provost looked back. "Well, finish her off!" The wary militia began to close in again.

A jarring series of thuds halted their movements. The jittery militia, now the only other people left in the chambers, turned. Six X Gemina soldiers stood by the main door. Barrik's men warding the exits lay on the carpet next to them, only some with life enough to groan. Everyone froze.

Ayilia breathed a sigh of relief and lowered her blade. "What the hell took you so long?"

Kemet stepped forward and unsheathed two battle axes. "Sorry, ma'am, couldn't find Aaron, again."

She frowned. "Did you try The Prancing Cock?"

He smiled sheepishly. "No time." He glowered at the militia. "Didn't think these goons would strike until the session had ended!"

She smiled grimly. "Ended a little sooner than most of us expected."

A snow-faced Barrik shoved the Doge through a far exit, then turned back one last time. His voice was unusually soft, but they could hear every word.

"You really are a witch."

She grimaced. "So, I've been told."

"In case you need reminding," he spat, jabbing a finger. "Your toy army's out in the Occupied Lands far from here doing sweet nothing, monitoring the Pit's inebriated boneheads, also doing nothing. I suggest you crawl off into the desert while you still can." There was a tense pause. "Assuming you survive this lot, the best cutthroats the city gaol could find."

He was gone.

Some of the militia looked at the heavily armed Gemina and decided they weren't the best kind of cutthroat after all. They quickly followed the Provost. Those that didn't, regretted it. Kemet charged to Ayilia's side, knocking half a dozen guards from his path, while his soldiers made a beeline for those further back. The fight was brief, leaving scattered bloodied figures motionless on the ground. Ayilia moved to see if any could be saved, but Kemet put his arm out.

"Don't bother."

She swallowed. "I've never killed before, not something that actually lived. Tonight, I killed three people." She regarded the guards, plus a fourth nearby. "I don't think that woman's getting up either."

"Then thank the fates it took so long." Kemet regarded her levelly. "Time to go."

"I can't."

He squinted. Ayilia brushed her shaking hands along her tunic, trying to get rid of the blood stains. "I must see someone. Only got word he's back on the way here. Hell, it's been a Goddamned age."

"You jest, right?"

She shook her head, her mind simultaneously wired and dazed by the horror of violence. He sighed, knowing full well she wasn't going to be talked out of it. "The Provost's right about one thing—most of our people are hundreds of leagues away monitoring the oppressed. We'd be heavily outnumbered even if they weren't, so we absolutely don't stand a chance now, X Gemina or not." She patted his arm. "I won't be long. Get the others ready. I'll see you at the barracks in a few hours at most."

Chapter Three

FALL FROM GRACE

The knot of bristling spears and shimmering staves hunched on their mounts in the cobalt half-light, resembling more a large, neon porcupine than a battle group. Drifting flakes of snow-spotted hair and brows with glittering, glassy baubles. A stream of planetary giants spilled across a gilded skyline above their heads. So arresting was the sight that it seemed a stove of lambent flame had tipped its fiery guts across the gelid void. A rising planet dwarfed the sorcerers' silent silhouettes like a vertical cliff-face, its imposing arc a canvas of gaseous ribbon.

Though the mildly toxic atmosphere stung their lungs, the soft veneer of their Magi shields repelled the worst of the acridity. Each fighter gripped a sorcerer's mace. The freshly activated weapons hummed against the soft patter of the snow. Mounts, sable pits of impatient energy, huffed, rolling dark eyes.

From their positions into the distance, a spread of lights was sent, spitting and flaring. Powered by thought and sheer willpower alone, each thaumaturgic beacon lit the way like a floating torch. It might be the last time they could be so brazenly visible. Soon, the enemy would be everywhere. Barrackus knew he was the only one who really understood what was at stake.

One chance left.

NETHERGEIST

The Asthen Magi Raiders of the Ascendancy shifted anxiously amid the tangerine mists as they eyed the interstellar gate a quarter-league distant. There would be no turning back. As far as they knew, no Asthen would have gone as far as they were to go, should they enter that silent, timeless portal waiting for them. Freshly discovered, it would take them deeper into the Abomination Goat's Imperium than any Raider had gone before.

The prospect was terrifying.

Barrackus' cry went up. "For death!"

The Raiders pounded in unison towards the argent lens of harnessed puissance among the dark rocks ahead. Like all portals, it was a spatial borehole into infinity, a funnel through the quantum veldt. It would burrow through space and the ditzy slew of stars within before joining the breath-taking network of cosmic walkways that formed the portal universe. Like quantum rope, the network stretched outwards to apparent eternity, maybe even the neural event horizon of the vanished builders themselves, the Ancients.

Or so the theory went.

The Ancients were long since gone, and though vast, the network was said to have an end. Nevertheless, Barrackus shook his head in marvelled bewitchment. To all extents and purposes, these empyreal conduits through the interstice skein of absolute nihility were indestructible. He'd heard his own hard-boiled veterans mutter in hushed whispers about how the Ancients had discovered terrible realms where only the damned existed. He, their commander, had laughed. So did Major Sheyna, his sidearm, but then, she openly scoffed at most things.

"What does it matter?" she had said. "The fools wiped themselves out one way or the other; why the hell should we care about the Ancients when we don't even know their names or what they looked like?"

He looked over at her now, but she was fixated on the path ahead. As they rode toward the strangely unassuming object, Barrackus wondered if the nagels, or storytellers, didn't have a point. He'd seen chroniclers lean forwards and hiss through vermillion teeth how the Ancients unleashed a demonic realm so chaotic and maniacal that it ended their dominion forever, leaving nothing but a sigh of imprints in decayed stone to mark their passing. And, of course, their indestructible portals.

Barrackus snorted out loud, but no one heard it above the pounding of the hooves.

It was clear that the god-like shits had either ascended to something greater in their smug mightiness or they had inadvertently destroyed themselves altogether. Though he lacked Sheyna's inner toughness, he wasn't a person who gave into old fisher tales, superstitions, or the gossip of the weak-minded. There was nothing mysterious involved at all.

The Ancients were scientists, and somehow, they'd scienced themselves out of existence. What mattered was the here and now.

In defiance of their veneration, he led his task force towards the gate, in a direction that would either change their lives for good, or end them.

❦ · ❦ · ❦ · ❦ · ❦

A shadowed, behemothic figure sat impassively on a throne hewn from fossilized bones on a colossal, dried tongue of scarlet rock. Behind them reared the massive stone head of a mighty deity, the lava from vents beneath giving life to the burning light behind each eye. A network of vast, curled horns tapered down the back of its cumbersome cranium and ribbed neck into the floor below. The god of the undead.

Vespasian had forgotten it even existed.

An imaginative spread of femurs, clavicles, and backbones cluttered every square cubit of the voluminous walls, juxtaposed almost artfully with gilded shields and the nightmarish plaster casts of faces of slain foes. They were mostly Krayal, but there were humans too. Clusters of cracked soldiery lined every periphery, heightening a sense of claustrophobia. A guard stepped forward, flipping a red cape aside. Overhyped with Ichor, they hovered close to Vespasian's face until the centurion barked a command. Reluctantly, they stepped back, withdrawing powerful skeletal fingers from the hilt of their sword. Normally reserved for cavalry and, in this case, mostly ornamental, the Spatha blade was still as lethal as the standard gladius the regulars wielded.

The drone of the bloodsuckers hung in the air, a little surprising considering that there was no one with blood to suck. Vespasian realized something profound and yet so utterly obvious that he was amazed it hadn't occurred to him sooner. He hated it all! He hated the troops with their heavy skulls deliberately bred into demonic expressions of disdain. He hated the fear and the power. He hated himself most of all, and his aversion to violence. Or was it cowardice? Something his kind detested more than even the living.

Mabius' nearly seven-foot, pitch-black silhouette filled the room. The collective stares of his hatchet men bored deep into the Consul.

He could stand it no longer.

"You're back."

It was an incongruous thing for Vespasian to say after two decades or more, but he couldn't think of anything more appropriate. If Vespasian had a working heart, it would be pounding in his ears. He'd heard humes describe this sensation. For the first time, he understood what it really meant. A soft knock came from the floor. With a jolt, he realized that it was his knees knocking together.

"Vespasian!"

The rumble was so deep that the very molecules of the ground seemed to reverberate. Vespasian flinched. Surely, time must have mellowed even *him*?

"The years roll off the very edge of the universe itself, yet despite the consummation of so much time and so much opportunity, not only do you remain stunted and necromantically dysfunctional, I see you are still also quite the wretch."

What to say? "I watch what I eat!"

It didn't seem to go down well. Mabius' shape seemed to darken.

"What does this say about you, Vespasian? What does this say about you when you represent the Imperium's interests on this ass of a world but do nothing but decay at the same rate as the rancid rind of this hole?"

The two Nethergeist underlords faced each other in a dark alley of blade and bone. The tension crackled with charge. For the first time in an age, though that corrosive fear was still firmly in control, Vespasian suddenly accessed a deep well of necromantic theurgy he'd thought was gone forever.

"Brother, I have faithfully served the Undying One without question, without complaint, even while stuck here forgotten and discarded on this godforsaken dust bowl on the furthest side of the Outer Rim." He tried to steady the quaver in his vocal cords. "No one has asked of me or visited; nevertheless, I kept the Indigenous species under firm control with dying resources and a dying hope as currency. Consequently, the Resistance has been dissuaded from moving in and harvesting an entire world for their war." He straightened his shoulders. "Without being asked or aided, I have served the Imperium well!"

At his side, Stilgen flexed his fingers around his weapon. The undead god, whose name the Consul had forgotten, stared at them with eyes of the deepest red. The volcanic fissures underneath must have heated up lately. He wiped his brow feverishly, forgetting it had been decades since he could sweat.

"Vespasian!"

"Brother?"

"I think you're spinning me moonshine, brother, clappy-happy hogwash!"

"I have done *everything* demanded."

"*Demanded.*" The underlord glowered, bathing in the insidious atmosphere he created. "You have done nothing except fester in myopic delusion within the fetid stench of this aphotic, dulse-encrusted cistern. Don't talk of how your mighty Pit has clung on nobly against the feckless barbarians of the Resistance on this barbarous excuse for a land, not when you talk of free humes and those oleaginous knots of reptilian gristle in the mountains." His finger was jabbing the air repeatedly as he ranted. "The truth is, you were simply abandoned with an agrarian subspecies of organics, and you did nothing. You are truly the scum on a derelict sluice, and you shame the rest of us by rotting unfettered while we strive."

In the space of a few non-existent heartbeats, Vespasian had been comprehensively degraded. The whole Pit would know. His mouldered power base would be irrevocably flushed, and his reputation waited to greet it. He shot Stilgen a glance, but even his loyal friend could only look down.

"Mabius, my missives were returned with orders from Viceroy Myrian to keep quiet or face being, how was it put again, 'torched.' What are we?"

Mabius thumped his fist on the throne arm so loudly that a furred creature with a blue, fathered tail shot into a far hole with a high-pitched squeak.

"What you feel, care, or think is immaterial. If Myrian is involved, thank what passes as your deity that your reproductive organs remain attached. Life is cheap, Vespasian, especially yours. If you had any sense, you would've slunk off into the void like the inebriated purloiners and torpid filchers you purported to govern." He leaned closer still. "And in case you haven't understood, I am calling you the family runt."

Flickers of Mage Rage funnelled along the skin-caked sticks that served as Vespasian's emaciated fingers. For a brief moment, indignation replaced terror. "My abilities have *nothing* to do with this, Mabius. Disability doesn't—"

"By the gods, have some pride. We are a warlord Geno, an exalted DNA diaspora crossing from star system to star system, flesh to flesh, until our nomad chromosomes erupt gloriously unannounced from a host's unwitting body. Spare me the blathering chicanery; you are neut and unworthy of the charitable tolerance of others."

Stilgen swore and unsheathed his blade, but Vespasian gripped him tightly. "Remember what you said about another day," he hissed.

"Do you know how long it's been since the last Sythian spore decided the political and cultural climate was right for emergence, when our seed could be free from fear and persecution? Well, do you?"

Vespasian's eyes flickered. He felt something he hadn't felt in an eon: true and genuine anger. Minute darts of black fire stroked the contours of his irises. His fists clenched and unclenched. Forgotten Magi sparks trailed down each hand towards the floor.

"Far too long! It's perilous to be a Sythian despite our might. We have an entire family of them, yet the eldest, that's you, is a thaumaturgic impotent! Oh, you can fling coloured lights across a room or give flame to a screaming vagrant's skull, but that makes you little better than your average vat-bred Magus."

Something went off in Vespasian's mind. Mabius' eyes widened with anticipation. The crowd was howling, lusting for mob justice. Overpowered by the excess potency of Ichor, one of Mabius' soldiers rushed at the hapless warlord, blade spinning. The Consul raised his fist and shot a dart of obsidian flame through the centre of their head, sending their teeth through the back of their skull. A deafening cheer went up until the blur of a weapon cut the air and smacked him across the forehead. The wayward Sythian unceremoniously hit the hard flagstones, a pool of fluid circling outwards from the gash. Enraged, Stilgen flung a dirk at the soldier, but their shield parried the nicked blade into the darkness.

Mabius held up his hand, and the others froze. Stilgen stood between as many of them and the Consul as he could. Vespasian rolled over and applied flickers of black flames across his face. The parchment skin was welded uncertainly back into shape, and the cracked bone beneath fused into an unwieldy scar. He hardly cared. It joined the medley of nasty welts from childhood. He rose to a standing position in a stupor. With a series of groaning cracks from the throne, Mabius reared to his feet. The red gaze of the under-god framing him was shadowed into oblivion. A ripple went through the crowd as they sat in awe of the Sythian's immense theurgy.

"A true Sythian would have immolated that soldier before the weapon even left their hand, then given flame to most their comrades in the same act."

The Consul tried to focus. "Tell that to their friend—"

"You always let us down, Vespasian. You let us down at a time we could have been irresistible, all-powerful. Together as a mailed battering ram of unbridled puissance, we could have done prodigious, spectacular things. We would have grazed the emerald perimeter of the macrocosm with nothing but our will to power us. No longer would we dance to another's bloodless tune—instead, we could have ruled this Empire as a family, without that Great, Imperial Ass—" Mabius cut himself short and scrutinized the room. Reassured no one had noticed his blasphemy, his voice softened.

"The Resistance's anemic leadership is finished. This is the age of an undead galaxy, perhaps an undead universe. The time of sentient life, that which depends on a working heart, is finite."

The soldiers let out another cheer.

Mabius smiled. He gestured for silence, then pointed towards the Consul, his arm silhouetted by the stone god's cerise hue. Though he and Stilgen stayed where they were, their two Pit guards quickly stepped back, petrified eyes darting in all directions.

"By now, brother, you should be harnessing the towering potency that exists in every blade of grass. By now, you should be siphoning its atomic brilliance throughout the seared contours of your immolated soul. You should be directing its choleric ire at whatever you care to choose, destroying our enemies wherever they skulk or intimidating our friends whenever they scheme.

"Vespasian, your barrenness is an insult, and I cannot see any reason for permitting this pitiful sham any longer! His Imperial Highness has tolerated your decrepitude long enough; it is simply an ... affront."

A cry of fury went up from every killer in the room. Stilgen scoped the room defiantly, weapon poised, but it was a futile gesture.

"No more chances. Brother or not, your time is past, long past." He beckoned towards the centurion.

"Crucify him."

The undead soldiers stared back, nonplussed. The giant's fist closed tighter.

"Are you deaf? I said crucify him!"

The baying crowd surged forwards. A host of powerful hands grappled a mortified Vespasian while Stilgen was overwhelmed where he stood. Their two guards had finally done what they always wanted to do and fled. No one paid them any attention.

Chapter Four

ANIMUS

V espasian was led unceremoniously to a wheel across a small, rusted, iron bridge spanning a room of derelict scoria. Facing him was a vast, scarlet mosaic of the undead god framed by a labyrinth of horns. Mabius looked down at his stricken brother and gestured at two soldiers. They approached, holding wooden mallets and long nails.

Vespasian's eyes widened. "Brother, you don't need to do this."

"Already done."

The soldiers grabbed his right wrist and strapped it tight. He tried to tug it away but couldn't. With an enormous effort of will, Vespasian blasted the strap with an impromptu burst of flame. There was a howl of startled voices, but the material was tough and wouldn't melt. No matter how hard he wrenched against it, it held fast. Completely at the mercy of an all-consuming mania, he lunged forwards and tried to bite the binding apart, but instead, a loose tooth went pinging into the molten slag. The warlord slumped back, utterly spent, to the sound of derision and laughter.

"Wait ... *please*!" he called.

Mabius' expression remained fixed. "What would be the point?

"I can be useful. It doesn't take the mind of a great alchemist to realize you're only here because something's happened. I can help. I never left. I know this place better than anyone else."

"That is helpful?" The low voice was a scarred menace.

The Consul nodded earnestly, trying to impress.

"Did you know, under cover of darkness, my people have been coming through your portal unchallenged, unnoticed?" Mabius leaned closer. "Did you know that while your Pit slumbered in its pitiless stupidity, my intelligence officials went to the blasted lands to negotiate with the new government in Agathon, or that soldiers covertly entered one night and crept past the sleeping guards? Did you even realize one of our Sythian siblings, Otho, was leading them, or that the old Imperial port below the hume city was reactivated in preparation for a surprise sea invasion to bypass their walls?"

Gobsmacked silence.

"How can you or your punks help me? If you were not also my flesh, the nails would have already sunk into the mephitic spew that is your hide, long before we left you here."

"You want the humes?" Vespasian's eyes were rolling in gut-wrenching dismay. "Why would you want them? There's been no trouble in nearly two decades! We were far more concerned with the Krayal!"

"Hell's udders, Vespasian, the Imperium has more to fear from the gnats in this accursed room than derelict races that do not know they have even died!" Mabius glowered for long moments. "Of course, we didn't cross the boundaries of the visible cosmos for this planet-wide sewer and all the festering quidnuncs inside, but whatever our reasoning, it is still too late for you."

He nodded at the guard, who leaned over and put an iron nail against the Consul's wrist. Decades of fear and frustration poured down his face in grimy tears of oily murk. Openly disgusted off-world troops spat in his direction.

"Wait ... tell me. Tell me what you want. How do you know my insight won't be any use unless you give me a chance?"

The guard looked up at Mabius for orders.

A poignant silence fell abruptly. No one had seen a Sythian killed, let alone executed. In fact, few had seen one at all, let alone one that was visibly whimpering.

"Mabius, you've come for *something*. Whatever served as your spies in the last few weeks or so *won't* scratch the surface of what I know."

The crowd became restless for violence, for something that might mask the self-loathing void inside they all shared. The centurion barked furiously for quiet, even flailing at a Lifeless with his whip. Facing the stricken Sythian again with a dark look, Mabius growled. "Everything comes to you?"

"Despite appearances, there was some kind of order here; I know *everything* that went on."

"You wish for mercy in return?"

Vespasian leaned as close as the straps would let him. Even as he talked, he felt pathetic. "Yes! Release me, and you'll see how necessary I am."

The giant paused. Every passing moment was an eternity.

"Vespasian, you are a weak chink in the armour of our order. If I cannot rely on your puissance, I most certainly cannot rely on your judgement."

"What? What do you mean? Come back!"

Vespasian stared mutely at the guards and the room. They watched back intently. When Mabius gave a signal, the mallet went down with a hollow thud.

The Consul had thought the childhood beatings he had endured were a lesson enough in pain, but those were was nothing compared to this. When they smashed the nail into his other wrist, his screaming stopped, and he passed into welcome oblivion.

The darkness moved and coalesced into a tall shape. Slowly, a figure emerged and approached the crucified warlord. What could be seen of his armour glinted.

The worn, dark green pelt of a Fa-Torg, a rare, primitive beast native to the Core, was flung across his shoulders.

The guards departed. The room was empty.

Vespasian was still on the wheel, wrists congealed clots of black. His opaque eyes widened. He tried to speak, but his mouth felt like it baked sawdust. The figure lowered his hand and soothed the warlord's throat with onyx flame.

After some moments, the Consul managed a rasping gasp. "You've come to save ... me?"

Vitallius's piercing grey eyes scrutinized him. "No, my brother. I came to ease you on your passing." He fleetingly closed his eyes. "You *must* perish, you realise that don't you? One day they'll come for the Sythian brood, they always do. We must be ready, alert. We *cannot* depend on the runt of the pack. This sort of thing always happens. It is the very culture of power. Why cling to a life you don't want and doesn't want you?"

Vespasian's head thumped back against the wood. His lank hair was wet with the wounds the soldiers had given him.

"All your life you pushed Mabius too far! Why, Vespasian? You're not even a warlord; you never were. You're just a glorified quill-pusher that's too weak to even flog his own people!"

No answer.

"You may be the elder, but Mabius has eclipsed us all. Your development remains ... " He looked away as if embarrassed.

"Say it."

"You are ... as stunted as this subterranean netherworld. Understand his disappointment. He needed you; *we* needed you." Vitallius swallowed. "Hell, Vespasian, you are *Sythian*—whole civilizations would fall at your feet and worship you. Your thaumaturgic infertility is *still* more potent than the best vat-reared Mage coin can buy. You cannot believe the amount of Ichor the Goat uses just to make *one* Mage. Why did you rot so, Vespasian? No one is impressed!"

The dying warlord attempted a shrug, but the blood only flowed faster. Vitallius rubbed his chin. "They sensed trouble." He looked away as if searching for the words. "You don't mistreat your workforce; you don't execute prisoners. Hell, I don't even know if you even *have* prisoners!" Vitallius brushed his brother's blood-soaked hair back. "I don't know how to say it, brother, but you're too ... nice!" He looked away again, deep in thought. "You've missed so much. I have seen Mabius swot heroes aside with a flick of his hand. They say one day he is going to be stronger than Pharsalus of yore, our greatest general!"

"Seems like Mabius found his true vocation in life," Vespasian grunted. He inhaled deeply, filling his necrotic lungs with air they couldn't absorb. "Personally, I don't think self-actualization will solve his issues."

The other didn't smile. "You should have made yourself indispensable with the precious time allotted, Vespasian. That way, your value may have stopped sinking like a corpse in a bottomless pool of piss." Vitallius put a gentle hand on the warlord's weakening shoulder. "They will drag you outside the Pit as a public warning. You will die watching the suns rise and fall over your own lands; a beautiful but slow death.

"Perhaps there is a place in some hell-hole afterlife for us somewhere, for those that once lived before the Goat thieved our young lives from us. If so, save me a seat.

"Until then, farewell, my sad, obsolete brother."

Twenty Years Ago

"Ayilia, *please* ... show yourself!"

There was no answer, but it was patently obvious the child was behind the chest.

"My dear, there's no other way. Events rage like ship-eating tempests at sea."

Ayilia looked up from behind the large wooden casket. She was in the corner of the highest tower in the Keep of Kings overlooking the bay. Slowly, the twelve-year-old stood up. Though her clothing was faded, especially the ready-wear brown trousers, one thing gleamed like new: the light side-arm she always carried at her waist. Low-level thunder growled sporadically among a brushing of grey clouding in the distance, edges tinged with yellow. Within, a Jacob's ladder as fragile as silk shed its watery rays onto a pallid sea.

Jarrak breathed in. Understandably to him, Ayilia was still crying.

"Again, I am most *terribly* sorry." He sighed, desperately trying to find the right words. He was a man who didn't do words well. "I oversee your safety now, at least until your father recovers. Hopefully, this peculiar malady won't last. I have good people, *loyal* people who will help him and you. You already know Kemet. I only promoted him recently. The X Gemina, also, will never leave you, though God knows where that name from. There are many among my generation who have not forgotten the regency's ancient liberation of our people and the trek across the great void to this distant haven in the skies."

She didn't budge.

Hardly a surprise.

Her father had just been stricken by a mystery phage some swore was magical. Her mother was already gone, and there were no relations of any kind. Guilt swelled against the flinty shores of his ex-soldier consciousness. He was handling this all wrong. By all that was foul, this announced meeting with that otherworldly thug Regallion was one of the worst things to have to force someone so young to do.

"Ayilia," Jarrak said, bending. "Come here, child, please."

Reluctantly, she came out and placed two small hands in his outstretched grasp. She'd known him for all her life and trusted him for good reason. He would defend her with his life. Underneath his aging gruffness was a heart of polished gold.

"Your father intended you should be guides, not kings. You are not alone. It is *we* who are alone without you and the experience of your lineage."

One small hand fiddled with her sword. A blade always made her feel comfortable in times of stress.

"No one expects anything, Ayilia, it's just a role, and the Panchayat is loyal. You'll be as old as me by the time you take over, and that's a long way away." Jarrak's weathered head with his whitening hair was framed by the brooding squall. His eyes and its grillwork of weathered lines were lit up by flickers of faint charge.

"What if my father doesn't recover?" She bit back tears.

Jarrak's tortured face clouded further. "He will."

"But if he *doesn't*?"

"Well, even though that's *not* going to happen, if he doesn't, we'll all simply share the burden until the day of ascension, until you're old enough to do the job on your own."

He marvelled at her resolve, the secret strength helping her keep it all together. He doubted she knew just how strong, how unique she was, was both a blessing and a curse. People didn't always like different. If anything, they seemed to be growing ever more intolerant of anything that differed too much. "Your father's faculties are temporarily diminished, yet his body still thrives. Every physician in the land, every quack with a leech, has been through his doors ..." He trailed off hopelessly, yet she nodded. He scratched his thinning hair furiously, again lost for words.

There were already whispers. They said the mystery sorcery that laid low her father had afflicted her, too. Someone in the keep was leaking stories about her being a 'witchling.' Fortunately, the Panchayat government wouldn't let the rumours get far. She should be safe, as long as the Heretics off-world kept the Lifeless meta power at bay, the city's paranoia was manageable. Fear was the worst enemy. It made them hate anything remotely different.

Ayilia glowered with resentment. "I *don't* want to go. I *don't* want to meet her."

"There's no other way; I'm sorry. It won't take long. And I'll be there the whole way."

Shooting him a savage and defiant stare, Ayilia abruptly turned and walked through a side door out onto the ramparts. The cinereal rolls of cloud were ominously thick. Jarrak joined her, his loose garb fluttering in the breeze. He imagined faces the colour of spilt blood swirling and wisping in the nebulous vapours, their pitch eyes studying the city with arctic intent. They stared for long moments without talking. After letting her digest the situation for as long as he dared, Jarrak looked down at her with sad but determined eyes.

"This Lifeless lord Regallion appeared without warning. She's trying to take advantage, Ayilia. She knows your father is stricken. She wants to exploit that. The people are in a panic, and the council is confused. Her timing is intentionally terrible."

It wasn't helping. "I don't know what to say to a dead woman."

"You don't have to say anything. You are regent elect, not regent. I'll do the talking."

She shrugged her pitifully thin frame; she was trying to be nonchalant, trying to hide just how nervous she was. It only made his heart break the more.

"Why do the Lifeless bother with us at all?"

"Ha, why indeed, Ayilia," Jarrak replied quietly. "Some think they fear us for reasons so ancient there is no record left. I personally think they cannot abide a place that is not painted their colour on their universal map."

"Maybe they'll run out of paint?"

He laughed long and hard. "Maybe."

Ayilia paused. "The Magi should save us. Why don't the Magi save us?"

Jarrak swept his hand across his balding head. It felt terrible forcing a child to meet a person who belonged in a grave, but there was no choice. Time was in short supply, yet he wanted her to be ready. "The Resistance is up against the undefeatable. Our territorially irrelevant pinprick of free humanity thrives because the Imperium is too busy fighting, and *that* is the Heretic's gift to us."

Ayilia narrowed her gaze. "I think this dead man cares only for himself. I don't think he's here because of his super-large Empire. I think he's here 'cos he wants to be a king!"

Jarrak inhaled sharply. There it was again. Most of the time, she was in another world; then, out of the blue, she said something that knocked him sideways. He floundered for a reply but, not for the first time, his mind was blank.

"I won't leave your side." It was the only thing he could say.

She squished up her nose but said nothing.

☠ · ☠ · ☠ · ☠ · ☠

With a feeling of dread, Ayilia followed Jarrak down the white stone steps dusted with powdery mildew. They crossed a large courtyard patterned with clumps of bitter blue wisteria, one of the many species that had piggybacked a path to the new world on the coattails of the human diaspora. Squads of soldiers paraded in the distance while court administrators hustled folios with exaggeration in order to seem busy. Outside the reassuring confines of the keep, wrights, bright smiths, and chaise makers toiled obliviously within the bowels of the industrial quarters while chiffoniers, tuckers, and tanners took charge of fresh stock. Much of it was from the Pit's lands, their Imperium labels still visible.

The nearby tanneries always made her retch. The stink of fleeced hides and thick oils pervaded the yards, barely out of sight. Some years ago, when she was even younger, she'd slipped Jarrak's ever-watchful eye to hurtle playfully down a dark passageway and found herself facing a bent building strung with raw pelts. Inside, there was a succession of dugouts slopping with rank-smelling fluids. A worker had emerged with a wagon groaning with cow heads attached to a stringy net of vertebra. She'd bolted, screaming, into Jarrak's arms.

"Ah, little princess, you have seen much, but in this world, it is already not quite enough," he'd said.

She'd sobbed. "Why do they hurt the animals?"

His taut face creased. "One day, you will govern these people. You will learn they are not here to be judged by those who have much but to be understood, for so many have so little."

"*I don't care!*" She'd gasped, furious. "What's that red stuff in the holes in the ground?" She glared at him. "Please tell me."

His face grew red, and he looked away from her briefly. "Well, the hides are soaked, pounded, and scraped. Those pits are full of lime and, um, urine because ... well, it helps the process. Eventually, the hides are salted and made ready for cutting."

"They stink!" she said, holding her nose. "It's cruel."

"Animals don't think like we do; they don't care."

"Of course, they do. We make ourselves no better than dead men by doing to them what they do to us." She wiped her eyes. "Aren't we like that, compared to the Lifeless?"

Jarrak had silently stared at her. She never forgot that expression of dark astonishment.

The Great Hall and its weather-lashed gargoyles welcomed all official visitors. The fact they never had any didn't bother anyone. Theoretically, everyone was equal in the sprawling commercial and social hub of the city where the hall was situated, but none more so than the wealthy burghers.

Ayilia and Jarrak entered completely unnoticed.

Bored Yeoman stood with a clack to attention as they passed, the noise startling a visiting tourist family. Ayilia could make out a tall figure flanked by two fierce centurions. Impressive feathers crossed the tops of their helmets. They were clad to their jagged teeth with clanking weapons and red capes made of expensive materials rather than the usual hessian garb. The overlapping metal rings hewn from hard iron were replaced by smart, aureate breastplates. A network of shiny medals was interlinked by metal chains ran along their fronts.

Ayilia and Jarrak regarded the visitors silently. The child fought an overwhelming urge to turn back. More than ever, she couldn't stomach the beings of violence waiting for them, for her most of all. The fear was so crippling she wanted to cry. She shot Jarrak a pleading look and was greeted by the kindest smile she'd ever seen the old general manage.

"Don't despair, little one," he whispered, eyes twinkling. "These idiots are just bullies full of self-importance, masking the most fragile of personalities. Their egos are stretched so taut it doesn't take much to pop them."

Her face creased with corroded doubt. Every part of her yearned to see her father come into the room, make that great big smile of his, and then stride over with supreme confidence to whatever Imperium vassal waited. He'd sort them out; he always did, and he made it seem effortless. Even the toughest automatically respected him. He always got his way.

"I don't think I can 'pop' them, Jarrak. In fact, I think I'm out of pop!"

"If anyone can, Ayilia, you can," he replied gravely. "Honestly, you have more of your father within than you could imagine! Every time I see you, I swear he's there in everything you do. Trust me; you're ready." He flexed his fingers animatedly, almost defiantly. "Actually, when you get going, I don't think they'll stand a chance."

The tall Imperium figure regarded them. A luxuriant black robe embroidered with devil skulls and studded gems was draped across her shoulders. Her face had proper skin—visibly taut, pockmarked and parched—a sign of presumed importance. A mat of tendons worked under the veneer of her weathered hide, but it was her eyes that captivated Ayilia, as they approached. Not for this Lifeless the usual daggers of red. These sparked a fiery blue.

"Regent Elect—so sad at the news," the Lifeless hissed, part bowing, once they were within earshot. The voice was softer than the usual off-world accent.

Ayilia tried not to swallow, but it was impossible. The thing literally towered over her. She felt hopelessly inadequate. The Lifeless' eyes consumed every flicker of emotion on her face and in her trembling gaze. "I ... thank you, for your personal ... er, condolences at this—"

"Of course," she snapped. "Now that the pleasantries are done, I should notify you that I am accompanied by two legions respectfully located just outside Agathon's borders. I think you are aware of the ramifications of your father's illness for this last remaining slave city you represent!"

Jarrak flinched beside her. The thing had taken over the proceedings from the start. The dark-blue veins on Jarrak's hands bunched dangerously; Ayilia wondered whether he was considering if decapitation was a better form of diplomacy. "My lady," he said, deeply agitated. "This is the Honourable Regallion, the First Federal Administrator of the Outer Rim Prefecture zone X1 of the Nethergeistian Imperium!"

"The First Federal Administrator of the Outer Rim Prefecture zone X1 of the *Everlasting* Imperium," she snapped.

"I'll be sure to make a note," Jarrak growled. "Miss Ayilia, this hall is too open for the sensitivities involved. We have a side room for this kind of thing."

"There is nothing delicate about this." Regallion snorted.

"Please come this way, your—"

"Regallion will suffice," she said after a pregnant pause. The vicious blue of her gaze took everything in. "It has been a long trip to this backyard. You cannot imagine how tiresome it was avoiding the Sythian pups they're rearing in that Imperial cesspit they fittingly call the Pit. By the undergod, they've no idea what they're breeding there!"

Jarrak's face was impassive as he led them away. Ayilia followed in a daze, unnerved by the visitor's audacity. None of them had treated her father that way. They entered a small, panelled room often used when the city had been important. Regallion's guards waited outside, much to her relief. The presence of such massive creatures was electrifying.

"Let's cut to the chase, little sister. Your rump state's existence is an outrageous affront," Regallion said the moment they were inside. "Your progenitor's removal from state affairs presents the ideal moment for reunification."

Direct and to the point.

Ayilia stared at the Lifeless, dumbfounded. None of the other officials had been this rude to her father. To her astonishment, some of her fear began to evaporate, replaced by something else.

Chagrin.

Outside her arrogance, there was something else about the resplendent giant that lurked within those diamond-hard irises. Despite her unnerving presence, Regallion seemed oddly desperate. A small swell of courage bubbled up in Ayilia. Her breathing calmed, and her senses abruptly focused on every facial expression she made.

"This farce should *never* have been tolerated," the Lifeless continued, oblivious to Ayilia's realization. "The subjects of this enclave were never given the status of freedmen. Do you understand what that means? You are and always have been nothing more than escaped thralls." Jarrak made to say something, but the thing didn't give him the chance. "Notwithstanding, my legions will occupy every administrative centre, nodal point, and military installation. We will occupy the barracks of the tiny force known as the X Gemina and the regular regiments who form the considerable bulk of the city's armed forces. Imperial diktat will be implemented with extreme prejudice. The migration of all humes into the greater collective, off-world, will take place, uninterrupted, during the coming decades. Prepare yourselves."

Ayilia shook her head. Not only had her nerves vanished, but she found herself experiencing another emotion altogether. Rage. "That's it? You've come all this way just to say *that*?"

Outraged at what she'd heard, she turned to look at her mentor, but he shook his head firmly before glaring stiffly at the Lifeless.

"Regallion, on what grounds do you justify this naked aggression? Our peoples have been trading partners for centuries. Resources are scarce on this world, but our nominal fidelity to the emperor has always been strong." He grimaced slightly as if he'd bitten his tongue. "Why jeopardize a profitable relationship that's worked for both our peoples for so long?"

"*Relationship*!" the thing grated, her rasp echoing off the wooden veneers. "The concept is meaningless. Your ruler is neutralized by a necromantic pathogen. Your city is ours. Your sapling dictator will submit to our will and bring her people with her."

"I'm *not* a ruler, *nor* was my father," Ayilia snapped, her voice high in that small room but firm. "We haven't ruled for ages because my father says it's up to the people!"

Regallion's beady, sapphiric gaze bored into her own. "Without her witless begetter, she is politically sterile at any age in this place. I won't degrade myself by addressing the fly-infested, claw-wound that calls itself the hume council. It is her role to bring them to heel. Believe me when I say there will be a lot less blood-shedding if she co-operates, hence the courtesy of my visit."

Ayilia frowned, her mind on overdrive. *She was bluffing.* "You think the council will hand itself over to me?"

"The Nethergeistian dominion recognizes only the head of the X Gemina as leader. Your skulking council cannot lead their genitalia into a whorehouse backwards; they will do as you instruct, and the city will follow!" She paused unexpectedly to check Ayilia's reaction. "In matters of survival, the people instinctively turn to the regency; it's ingrained. Historically, we deal with and recognize no one else. Refusal is not an option!"

Jarrak opened his mouth, but Aliya spoke with an authority that surprised the both of them. "Unacceptable!"

Regallion looked like she had been struck. She clearly didn't expect that, not from a youth. The Lifeless official leaned close, her rasping tones as gelid as the sough of a hangman's lever.

"You would violate my ... the Imperium's protocol?"

"The Treaty forbids it! It's written in blood on the legal stuff, the ... parchments. The dead can't take our lands without us saying it's okay, and, as we do not say it's okay, then it's not okay. Sorry, but your journey's been a waste of time, especially as I don't see any of the Pro Consul's officials with you."

Most definitely not her words. They poured out of somewhere. God, she was trembling again, but there was no going back. She fixed him her most important stare, even though her mouth was as dry as a hangman's gullet. "You *are* here with his approval, aren't you?"

The Lifeless' ossified, skin-challenged skull was a picture of hatred. Her bony finger jabbed at Ayilia.

"*You*! Inbred whelk! Don't force me to bring my legions to your door. You think your city of fleas and dust won't soil its breeches and let them in the absolute moment they appear? Well, my little tyrant, *do you?*"

Jarrak was apoplectic. He strode over and thrust a scarlet face bulbous with rage into Regallion's. Shocked, the Lifeless official took an inadvertent step back. For the first time, Ayilia saw into her non-soul, and it consisted of cold blankness. Regallion was nothing more than a good, old-fashioned charlatan.

"She's got you there, Lifeless. Your actions are not only illegal but, seemingly, unauthorized. Why is there no Pit presence here? It's unthinkable that Pro Consul Sulla would give you free rein. Did you tell him porkies, Regallion? I mean, if you did, he won't like that. Not only does he regard this world as his property, but he would also have a cut of everything." Jarrak leaned closer. They could have been kissing. "You did cut him in, didn't you?"

The mini calculations racing through that unblinking, cobalt look were unmistakable. After long moments, she went ice calm. "How will it help the hume slaves under your father's care in the Occupied Territories throughout this desert world if you antagonize what we are? More importantly, what we would become if refused?"

Ayilia, despite her diminutive size, held her own. "Simple! We're allowed to be here—you aren't. No one's going to get angry 'cos no one knows you're here. You're doing this for yourself, Lifeless, not for the Goat."

Regallion's reply was as rude as anything she'd heard in any barracks, but she didn't flinch.

Jarrak, on the other hand, went white. "*Leave!* We've already heard enough from your stitched-up flap of flesh you think parades as a tongue. Get out before I call the guard."

Regallion turned towards the door, then halted. Losing all remaining vestiges of diplomatic pretence, her thin lips curled. "You are a venal race of self-entitled flotsam on the brink of a sewer you should never have been allowed to leave. You stink of sweat, oil, and fat and are *nothing* like us. Like an infectious pestilence, you simmer across worlds, fouling them with your pollutants and soil-consuming greed. Parasites continuously consume the flaying moulting from your wet, fetid hides; Lifeless are always clean." Regallion gathered the splendid folds of her robes. "I pray for the day we force you to serve this universe, not ruin it."

She was gone. The stomp of the soldiers followed in her wake. Jarrak hurried out of the room, shouting at the hall guard to escort the Lifeless from the city. When he returned, his face was molten anxiety.

"*Holy God*, I've *never* heard one so young talk to a soulless with such ... certainty. Honestly, Ayilia, I thought for a fleeting moment you were someone else."

She grinned despite herself. "She wanted to take out our city!"

"She still does!"

"We have to act, then."

"What do you mean?"

"Father used to talk to me about what to do in an emergency. He used to drill it into my head." Her eyes were pools of pain. "We must mobilize the city guard and the army."

"We can't fight proper legions without your father, Ayilia. We need to notify Sulla and get the Pit to kick Regallion's bony trap back off-world."

"It'd take too long." It was like watching someone else occupy her body. "Send someone to the council and tell the government they must call the guard. Our Gemina will help their soldiers be brave on the walls."

Jarrak froze as if shell-shocked. "We need to discuss this *first*, Ayilia, especially if he's really on the make."

"My father told me about officials like her. They get into huge debt bribing their way into important places like the Senate. Afterwards, they get their money back robbing their areas dry. If they don't make it, they're ruined. Please, Jarrak!"

If he closed his eyes, she sounded at least a decade older. There was a sudden series of raps at the door. They looked up, startled. The door opened to reveal a messenger flanked by six city guards.

"Ma'am? The Panchayat and the Doge request your immediate presence. A scout reports Imperial legions are deep in our hinterlands."

She looked at Jarrak. "Get the X Gemina, please. Then meet me on the walls."

Chapter Five

The Ascendancy Fights Back

The shockwave rattled their ears like kettle drums in a raging hurricane, even as their forms metamorphosed into streams of liquid light. Each burning river gently melded into a mosaic of miniature suns, shining bonfires in the vacuum. Moiling and broiling, the collective mesh of atomic brilliance rushed towards the gate's exit at breakneck speed.

The Asthen Magi Raiders were through the portal.

The quantum maelstrom extinguished the moment the portal's iris grated shut. A new world awaited them, a world of dim light and onyx rain.

"Incoming!"

The Asthen Raiders, still steaming from the jump, looked towards the warning. A firestorm of shot approached their position. Someone fell, consumed in a cloud of spitting flame. Darts of black-orange fire began to fill the skies.

"Ambush!"

Coruscating energy bolts cannoned towards them at peak ferocity. Lines of dimly lit Imperial phalanxes bristled in the distance. Amid the cacophony of rising shouts and curses, an Asthen battle cry hollered in the darkness.

"Carnivore legions, regroup!"

The Raiders jerked into formation. In the distance, lines of darkness were approaching. Someone was shouting.

"Imperium! Looks like Wirral! *Shields up.*"

Barrackus leaned to peer through the thick curtain of rain. Definitely Wirral, the berserker beasts the Imperium preferred as their frontline. They were closing fast. Divisions of armoured shapes crashed forward, drugged to mania by battle lust. Attack diamond formations were grouping with Imperial sorcerers at the apex. They were firing ruby heat into Asthen energy shields. Two to three Raiders lay eviscerated at the foot of the gateway, sightless faces seared charcoal.

Eyes wide, Barrackus sent serrated mage shot at a knot of necromancers heading the nearest formation. A sorcerer collapsed, followed swiftly by their companion. Streaks of super-heated charge came screaming back. The glow of their maces arced in the darkening light. His Magi shield whiplashed into shimmering light around his arm, and the shot split into cobalt embers on impact. He returned fire, hitting another.

Angry cries erupted from the accompanying phalanxes. Heavy ogres with flailed chains beat the armoured Wirral as hard as they dared without killing them. Imperial optios were flitting between the lines, waving their wax tablets of high-ranking orders at the legates. They shouted louder at the giants with the chains. The war-crazed legionnaires, driven psychotic by mistreatment, ploughed on, but a single Wirral stopped to face its tormentor. With a grunt, it rammed a weapon into their forehead, shattering it into pink pulp. A lusty cheer rose from its companions, and the other chain wielders quickly stepped back.

Armoured Wirral sprang from the ranks, legs reversed backwards, towards Asthen lines, their hoary feet pounding the ground in great clouds. Crimson eyes flashed above multi-jawed faces. A plethora of cone-shaped shields and giant nicked cleavers were advancing on him, held by powerful arms. Trying not to lose his nerve, Barrackus roared at his troop. The Raiders hurriedly dismounted, staves raised. Their energy shields haphazardly merged to create a single, crackling barrier of rippling puissance. Combined, it was an astonishing riot of roiling colours as it absorbed and repelled incoming sorcery.

Major Sheyna pushed through the lines to join him. They'd fought so many times over the years that not a word was needed between them. The two commanders pumped round after round of plasma at the charging shapes. Blurred figures flared and fell, leaving mounds of smoking metal and flesh, seared sockets watching their own demise.

A collection of Imperial Magi targeted Sheyna directly. Dropping to her haunches, she fired everything she could through her stave, dropping them where they stood. Enraged, a second unit took aim. She tried to fire back, but the stave spluttered weakly. With cold horror, Barrackus realized her energy was dangerously low. He lurched forward in a vortex of thaumaturgic fire, flinging it in the enemy's direction. The stunned beings were atomized into fluttering particles. Something clicked inside. Unable to contain himself, he rammed flaming charge at Mage after Mage, until every visible necromancer was burning furiously in the gloom.

Barrackus collapsed next to the breathless side arm.

"You ... all right, Sheyna?"

"Outside my sense of self-esteem, I'm fine," came her brusque response.

He helped her up. They were breathing heavily, their faces wet with rain. Still red-faced at her perceived weakness, she brushed him off.

"Not like you, Commander, to take risks, but thanks." Her eyes flashed. "What the hell was that stunt you pulled anyway? Some new trick you've been hiding? Where'd you learn to do something like that?"

Pretending not to hear, he shot another glance at the rest of the Raiders. They were doing what they did best, working together as a single, mobile killing machine. "They're nearly done, already. The Wirral are powerless without Magi protection."

Sheyna snorted. "Shame there are so few of us then! If the Asthen weren't leading this motley alliance of races, the Imperator would've won a long time ago." She hawked on the damp earth. "Our allies would've been wiped out where they stood, they're as magically neut as mud worms!"

"Be fair; Wirral are very dangerous!" He breathed with a wry smile. "Anyway, it's not the fault of our allies that they weren't born with our gift."

"May as well not be born at all, for all they're worth. We're too few to beat the Abomination on our own."

Unable to think of anything to say, he grunted noncommittally and pushed his way to the front. Even in defeat, Wirral usually kept coming until they were in pieces. It was critical to take out the decision-makers. On his cue, the entire company targeted the legates, sub-commanders and chain drivers, all those in power. Within moments, the dangerously uncoordinated Wirral formations began to buckle, then unravel. Volley after volley of Asthen charge laced the smoky sky, shredding the dissipating battalions into fiery rinds until the dying turned to hundreds and fear touched thousands.

Despite outnumbering the Asthen, many of the Wirral were turning to flight. Gesticulating wildly and with hope suddenly soaring, Barrackus hustled a hit group of Raiders onto their snorting mounts and charged the disintegrating melee. After an extremely rapid and somewhat terrifying dash, the desperate force rammed the forward lines at the exact point where the wilting battle groups harboured its officer seniority. There was a savage roar from the Wirral on impact, and they were ruthlessly crushed into pink shreds of bone and tissue by the heavy hooves. The officers seemed to vanish altogether.

Barrackus swallowed back a knot of disgust at the gore, but it was swiftly replaced by an immense surge of relief. The Wirral began openly fleeing in huge numbers, almost all Imperial control lost. The time it had taken to rout them had been extraordinarily brief, even by typical Asthen standards. Despite his revulsion at the manner of dispatch, he felt proud. His people could take on almost anything, within reason. Fighting an entire army was not what hit-and-run units did. His eyes began to mist, so he quickly rubbed them dry with his battle-filthed sleeve.

❦ · ❦ · 💀 · ❦ · ❦

Meanwhile, Sheyna, in true indomitable fashion, grabbed her mount to follow when the sky violently ruptured into a fleeting volley of black shot heading directly at her. She threw up a weakened Mage shield for protection, but a heavy iron arrow slammed into the side of her helmet with a vicious thud. There was a piercing dart of pain, and her sight distorted into white streaks. With a furious curse of magnificent proportions, the warrior slumped, frustrated, into the swamp of mud, spit, blood, and the rank feces of the dead. Struggling for breath, she, much to her own disgust, felt herself passing out.

The force propelled her into a whirling history of faces, places, and people at breath-taking speed in a dream-mare of stark imagery slashed with thaumaturgic potency. It propelled her through the spinning canopy of her mind's eye until she was back in that rural orphanage of misery on her home world, the place where she'd spent most of her childhood surrounded by trees straight out of poems and dark fantasies underneath the silence of rainbowed moons.

She hid in the trees. They were places to escape the beatings and the betrayals that filled her with fury every day of life. Her species wasn't always as enlightened as they believed. The sough of the multi-hued bows in the cool, long summers swarmed with shimmering winged-horns still made her soul swell. They were bittersweet tears, bittersweet memories.

The trees only survived for a year, but they dwarfed a whole continent with thick folds of oxidized leaves and fruits of livid flame. The sight was so enriching, her youthful spirit sometimes soared above the fleshed cage of her body and ascended over the bonfire of scarlet lustre, over league after league of flaring light. She couldn't do it now, but the isolation in those stark rooms of fear sparked her being into something utterly alien, something that was free.

The clinquant forests had passed across her burning corneas; alive, visceral, vibrant.

It was all so brief.

The rain-slashed horror of the battle returned with a jarring bump. Her eyes flicked open. Despite the gore and noise, the memories drove the bitterness on. Unlike her captain, she was made of forged platinum, where Barrackus, despite his skein of impressive power, Barrackus had a soul of glazed powder. Sheyna sometimes found herself despising him for it. She'd never had the luxury to wallow in self-pity. Watching him fight, he looked like a stray god visiting its wrath on the wayward, but she sensed that soiled softness within that would kill them all one day.

She faltered through mending the wound on her forehead with tendrils of healing charge, then summoned her mount with a mind command. On Barrackus' urging, Raiders began to form attack squares, still shielded by their azure barriers. Return fire from the now chaotic Imperial archers; their arrow shot, lit by fire, crisscrossed the air in blurs, creating an eerie porcupine of glittering chaos underneath the twilight veldt. Sheyna rode after them, head seething. Already on this raid, they'd made kills that would sting the Imperium from the balls of its feet to the Great Ass at the centre, but the commander was still too cautious.

Grabbing the reigns of his mount, she brought them both to a standstill in the howling rain. "For God's sake, Commander, *haste*. There could be reinforcements on the way!"

"Can't—we're going to need everyone. It's madness to lose lives when we don't have to, or can't afford to."

She swore, trying to wrestle back some measure of composure. Her head was throbbing even though the wound was gone. "Have you given any thought to why Wirral are guarding a portal in some derelict crap yard? They're *not* natural guard troop."

He turned to her, his voice low and measured. "We had to face them sooner or later."

"Come on. These are hit Carnivore troops; they make the worst guard. There is something seriously wrong with this portal, Barrackus, which means we should be turning back *before* the cavalry's called."

He shot her a black look, then beckoned a fighter over. "Adira, form a wing on my left and get the shooters behind. I want shot, arrow, and stave fire to kill off what remains of their resistance without committing fighters!"

"Aye."

As Sheyna shook her head, Adira went to bawl at the troop. Raiders began to form four battle groups, three in front and a fourth behind, combining all the heavier firepower into one. Fear rippled through the few ranks of Wirral remaining ahead of them on the field. Again, a large number fled. Clearly, their Asthen reputation preceded them. Sheyna stared, her antagonism temporarily forgotten. It was nearly done. Just a few hundred Asthen had come through the gate. Now thousands of Wirral lay slaughtered in the sodden, smouldering mud. The Ascendancy would hail this a triumph, but that feeling of wrongness pervaded.

The firing began, and what were left of the Wirral fell quickly. On cue, the Raiders gathered as one on their mounts and made a beeline for the silent gate in the distance. Black clouds shed watery bricks of rain. Crystalline rocks, translucent and sharp, broke the skyline in hunched shoulders under the rippling shimmers of forked lightning. Occasionally, Sorcerer Magi would appear riding among the inky outcrops firing venomous charge in their direction. They were also quickly felled. For a split second, Barrackus caught the sight of his face reflected in Sheyna's vertical irises, still fiercely pumping with adrenalin, and wondered not for the first time if the plan was insane.

He tried to reassure her, but instead clapped his hands to his head. The pain was intense this time, impossible to hide. After a deep groan, he sent a calming elixir of gentle flame directly into his skull, and it quietly receded.

"Shit's udders, Barrackus, not again?" Sheyna asked, screwing up her face. "By the gods, Commander, they've been *increasing* ever since we embarked on this death run. You hardly ever had a sorcery-paralysis episode before, now, they're all the time. Remember what that old soothsayer said back home before we left? This mission is *cursed!*"

He tried to pass it off with a laugh, but she only glowered more, resisting the temptation to punch him off his mount. A messianic look gleamed softly on his dirt-streaked face. "No, blessed, more like. This mission has meaning ... this is going to count. Somehow, I know it, Sheyna!"

She said nothing.

The rocks appeared ecchymotic in the dank light, their beige tone discoloured with purple and black splotches. Set against the haunting grimness of their surroundings, the portal of silvered stone half a league off seemed surreal. Even as they drew near, the Asthen could see it was enmeshed within a series of pillars and intertwining struts gleaming dully in the pouring wet. It was the most alluring cosmic door they'd ever seen, and it was in the middle of nowhere.

If Sheyna's gaze was dark with suspicion before, it was jet black now.

Carved serpents, creatures, and sea goddesses twisted in ecstasies of pain and demonic hunger on its pristine surface amid a blaze of ornate fountains, broken urns and tortured statues. Every shape shimmered languidly into focus only when the viewer's eyes flitted away. Whoever had carved this was a genius with a clearly unfathomable brain. Barrackus scrutinized the gate guardedly. There was something disconcerting about it. The Ancients were undoubtedly the creators, no surprise there, but there appeared to be some kind of golden device on the edifice's maw.

"Keep your thoughts on your mission, Raiders," he muttered gruffly. "Leave the madness of what you see to the minds that crafted it!"

"Aye," Sheyna added, her skin turning as jade as a radiated skull on a sun-baked stone. "This scrawl has no bearing on what we do here."

Barrackus nodded. The gate's design was a mystery for a different time. He beckoned toward the watching troop. "Andromedus, over here. We have another exotic door that needs some of your love."

A hefty, middle-aged warrior ambled up, rivulets of rain coursing down his face and battle gear, jowls undulating beatifically in the wind.

"Ignore the texts, Andromedus; they're just mind tricks to divert the attention of the uninvited, maybe the dangerously uninitiated. That gold device there looks like a Magi lock belonging to the Ancients, one I've never seen the likes of before. It's got to be powerful to lock us out of a gate, and it's going to need our best dust tracker and walking master key."

"Umm, that's something you don't see every day." Andromedus bustled forwards and placed an ear gingerly against the gold, almost demonic-looking mechanism. "This isn't Ancient; this is Imperium! Definitely a protective barrier."

"By all the lights in all the skies, how the hell can the Empire block an interstellar portal?"

Andromedus swallowed, but his tone suggested he was repressing a surge of impatience. "The good news is that blocking a gate is nearly impossible, at least if the lock breaker knows what he's doing, and I do. The other good news is that such high-quality locks are just *so* resource-intensive; they're as rare as dragon eggs. It took the skill of an Arch Mage to produce this, and it would've taken literally decades to craft. The sheer intricacy of the innards alone defies any science I've seen. To weave the incantations into the metal and then watch them grow like some kind of empyreal shrub would have taken an extra two to three decades." He shook his head. "Not even an Arch Mage could do this; no one could!"

"But you can break the lock quickly, right?"

"Aye, I think." He scratched his neck. "As to the second part of your question, I don't have a clue!"

Andromedus worked feverously. The rain came down hard. Riders dismounted and formed an armed semi-circle around the door. All was deathly quiet, save the slap-sizzle of falling water.

Adira came over and placed a gentle hand on Barrackus' elbow. "I'd say we proscribed a beating of such proportions on the Wirral; there isn't too much left to worry about now, sir."

"I'd rather not hang around, all the same." Barrackus sighed. "Once we jump, the initiative will be ours again. We have the best dust tracker in the Ascendancy—he'll mask our progress!"

Predictably, Sheyna was far from convinced. "This squall-cursed hole was swarming with Wirral, Commander. The Abomination's Imperial Trackers will be right up our—"

He shook his head. "Think, Sheyna, the number of gates is just staggering. There are hundreds of *thousands* of funnels available to us right this moment and possibly *millions* more throughout charted space and beyond. Outside the Imperial's Core collection of hub worlds, they can't ward them all, and we cover our ethereal footprints like no other."

"Sorry, but that's bullshit, Barrackus!" She failed to hide her impatience, not that that came as any surprise to either men. "Hit and run; that's always been Raider discipline and that's because it's always worked. Going so deep into Empire without an extraction strategy is suicidal!"

Andromedus shot them a dry glance. "Honestly, I blame the Uncertainty Doctorate, the Disequilibrium Paradox of Spite. It says vast organizations like the Imperium have too much weight and resources to support the moral bankruptcy, the eternal hoax of power and greed, and will consequently fall." He laughed hollowly. "If you ask me, it's a load of goblin balls, as the galaxy's already waited an eternity for that to happen!"

Sheyna tried to mask a grin, despite herself.

"Sir, they're coming." A man appeared on Barrackus' right.

"Already?"

He scanned the dark grey hillock barely half a league away. Its summit was a hazy white, backdropped by bleak terrain. Barrackus clenched his jaw. He could just make out movement. The tracker was waving his palms frantically over the lock's symbols. The flesh on his face sagged from the effort.

"Time's nearly up, Andromedus."

"A moment longer."

Barrackus turned to the pale-faced messenger. "I want a carpet of living fire between us and whatever crawls down that ridge. It's our turn to set the parameter of combat."

"Aye, Commander."

Andromedus looked up, caked in sweat and rain from the tempest. "I'm there, I think—it's a complex, psychic locking mechanism of the worst kind. We must be on the verge of something major; this is once in a thousand generations kind of security. The imprint is high-level Nethergeistian; top official access only. Your intel's hit shit-gold this time." His eyebrows came together, then rose as high as they could go. "Hell's intestines, we're talking the highest command entry possible, short of the Abomination Goat Himself!"

"Can you get us in?"

Andromedus placed his ear against the device. "I'm guessing this gate's a nexus to many places, *special* kinds of places. I've not encountered such tunnel signatures before." He looked up, eyes glistening with possibilities. "It's a potential microcosmos within the main network, totally separate from any lore we're aware of, an alternative netherworld of funnels. Who knows where we'd end up!"

Barrackus thought hard. The intelligence covered undiscovered routes on the backend of known pathways but nothing about a universe within a universe. Andromedus hadn't finished. "This isn't our usual hop, skip and jump either! These are super portals so cyclopean they have, to our minds at least, an infinite number of exits and an infinite number of entrances! In reality, they have physical limits, but compared to our standards, these are astonishingly scary."

"Numerous worlds and places, simultaneously ..." Barrackus looked sick. "What the hell were the Ancients up to? Why has the Imperium placed such a unique lock on it?"

"Let's stop making love to the damn thing and break it," Sheyna spat. "Otherwise, let's lay waste to other motley assholes. Either way, do something!"

He tinkered furiously. "I just need to work out how to turn the proverbial key and go through. Umm...."

"What does 'umm' mean?"

"This locking device was installed *long* before we arrived, Commander; correction, long before we even *knew* we were arriving!" He peered closer. "In fact, I'd say we likely gave the Wirral as big a jolt as they gave us."

Barrackus' mind was burning on overdrive. They'd hoped to piggyback their way to Imperial Command Central using the hidden conduits Asthen intelligence had discovered. To wipe them out in one go could theoretically put back the war for centuries. The Asthen war Seers had confirmed it. No one had said anything about wild frontiers, alternative universes, or super portals. A commotion broke out in the ranks. He looked up. An assorted array of hedgehog spikes were superimposing themselves upon the crest of the ridge, growing into a restless sea of bristling spears, dark snouts, and ribbed helmets.

The major whirled on Barrackus. "I knew there was something wrong! Why the hell are so many Wirral here? What's beyond that dumbass portal?"

Ignoring her, the commander sunk to the level of their crouching tracker and hissed in his ear. "Time's no longer a commodity I can supply, my friend."

The tracker's face was glistening before such impossible wonders. "Unbelievable, the residing incarnate invoked directly into the locking mechanism refuses to budge. It's an Imp too, a diabolical elemental. Trust me; this is unprecedented." He scratched his rear. "No one can block a gate for long. The Ancients designed it that way. Static within their infinitely powerful funnels always ends up unblocking anything in the mouth. This is unheard of!"

A wall of lambent fire rose from Asthen lines towards the coal skies. A series of dirty, orange balls ruptured among the seething sea of Wirral. The light illuminated the watching Raiders in brief, violent flashes. Barrackus' regarded them pensively. "Adira's fireworks will give us some more time, but not much."

"They've slowed," Sheyna whispered. "Momentarily."

Barrackus swung on his hapless lock picker. "It has to be *now*."

"Neutralised the elemental outer security ..." Their tracker was dismantling the gold exterior as he talked. "A misbegotten childhood can teach more in the way of Magi hacking than your average archive. Attempting a touch of psychometry with some good ol thaumaturgic sextant scanning. Should trace us a path."

The Asthen fired non-stop now. "Just break the thing and go!"

"Where, Commander? We've never charted this region before or used a portal like this. If we screw this up, could we end up the arse-side of a black anti-star. We could end up literally anywhere."

"I don't care if we end up in the Abomination's back passage—this new army's three times the size of the last."

Brilliant pinpricks of flame raced into the void, causing untold damage to the defending host. The collective Asthen shield was up. Still, clods of ash and dirt fell in a dark shroud around them.

Crack.

Barrackus and Sheyna whirled, but this time the noise came from the portal itself. Unintelligible symbols along the sides of the lens radiated in cyan scrawl as the limpid pool of its mouth suddenly blazed into an infinite speck. The

Imperial lock over it fizzed brightly. A miasmic entity screamed within the mechanism before its clockwork innards exploded across the mud in a puff of smoke. Within moments, the lock was a Lifeless grey.

Andromedus laughed with relief. "Lock's bust, and the portal's opened. We're in."

"Brilliant, Andromedus," Barrackus said, though his face remained serious. "Why are we waiting? Set a course."

"Terra firma, frankly. I want us to avoid landing in an alien sea or inside a star. These funnels are ancient. A planet might not exist anymore, courtesy of a solar flare or something. We might transport into naked space, a vacuum. You get my drift?" His face was a cloud of sweat, but an excited gleam never once left his gaze. "The atomic passageways are more layered than the topping on a Magi wedding cake—I've *never* seen this kind of stuff before. The target's echoes are quantum-etched in the ether, but they vanished the moment the gate opened, so we have to triangulate a fresh path ..." He sat back, immensely pleased with himself. "Done! If Imperial Command Central was easy, a unit would've toasted them an eon ago."

Stilgen stared across the boundless horizon of cinnamon plains, dusted with rust-coloured sand and the white gleam of bones. The desert beyond the Pit baked quietly under the three suns. The stunted growths that posed as trees were timber headstones in a desiccated sea of grit. Dry charge rumbled in the background. The storm had finally died out, but the atmospheric electrics could still have days left of life.

He approached the crucified figure on the giant wheel.

The Consul started, sensing company.

If what served as blood could stop welling in bubbling spittle around his lips and nostrils, the view before him might have been considered picturesque. It didn't help that his left eye hung down his cheek on scarlet threads, or the disconcerting fact it still had vision, giving him unwitting views of his guts slipping down his legs from a sword gash in his abdomen. It collected into dirty coils on the ground, not that he needed it since the day the Imperator had given him, and his siblings, non-life. That same eye saw the figure looking back up at him, juxtaposed with his other vision from the good eye. Tears ran down his grimy face. Intensely embarrassed, the failed necromancer burned the wetness away with what little was left of his gift.

"Don't ... give me ... your pity."

Stilgen nodded gravely. "I have nothing left inside to give."

"News?"

"We are to ride out liege, imminently."

"How... many?"

"Enough for the task."

"How many... remain loyal?"

Stilgen paused. A breeze tousled his worn pelt. "A Pit battle unit, though they had no choice. They are the ones to ride out. I guess it's loyalty of a kind."

"No ... choice?" Vespasian sighed and scanned the horizon through bleary streaks of mist. For the first time in a century, it seemed awe-inspiring, infinite, but death did that to you. The pain had been considerable, but he'd eventually suppressed it. The nails, however, refused to melt even under concerted fire, understandable really, considering just how weak he was. "You've come here to tell me ... something other than just hearsay and gossip, Stilgen! I ... I doubt they would have let you out ... otherwise."

Stilgen snorted with bleak amusement. He scowled towards the Pit. "Permit me the gossip first. What I've learned seems to shed considerable light on why the off-worlders returned here in the first place. It's skull breaking, quite beyond all realms of belief!"

Vespasian raised a brow. "Try me."

"The sources are unreliable."

"Spit it out *please*."

He coughed. "The Al Kimiya's back."

Vespasian flinched. Overhead, a dry crackle of lighting lit his decimated features. "The serpent's back? Impossible. The thing's just a legend, the prattle of the weak-minded."

"It's not only back, but it's apparently after the gizzards of its old adversary, the Unholy Emperor the Imperator Goat Himself. Hence the sudden reactivation of the Pit as an Imperial outpost."

Vespasian's mouth gaped. An odd blackness slowly crept down the darkness of his dying mind. "Here ... on this very world?" His head clacked back against the wood. Something fluttered and landed on a strut next to him. A vulture that had plagued him earlier was back. Without hesitation, it tried to peck his dangling orb. Horrified, Stilgen clambered up to shoo it away with his blade.

"It's not actually *here*! Apparently, its egg has been visualized by the Emperor Himself in a trance quest, but He doesn't know where. It'll stay that way until the energy of the birthing's escalating puissance ensures it can no longer remain camouflaged from His all-seeing sight. The Goat thinks it will attack Him a second time." Stilgen repeatedly looked back, his regular paranoia on overdrive. The sense of threat seemed to magnify with every passing moment. "Not only has the emperor foreseen the return of the Al Kimiya's rabid eidolon, but so has an assortment of Imperial soothsayers and schnooks that counsel Him. We cannot discount it as myth, yet."

Vespasian closed what was left of his sight. He felt his being darken. Try as he might, he couldn't quite do the one honourable thing left to him and die. "That winged serpent, there's not a farg's chance in hell it'll slaughter the Goat.

The bastard slew it countless millennia ago. I can't imagine what it thinks it can achieve the second time if it's back."

A small pack of bluebottles had begun to swarm around his lank hair.

"Significant others outside the Imperium share the same foresight. I do not believe this is a coincidence."

Vespasian, with a degree of evil intent, studied the buzzing insects. Something had landed and laid eggs in his facial wounds, and the larva were already feasting on the necrotic tissue. He could feel them squirming within the trailing mess that was his innards.

"The Heretics?"

Stilgen nodded.

Vespasian shook his head with incredulity. "Now I know this universe is nonsensical. What would *they* want with an Imperial myth?"

"A shared enemy, a powerful reason for an alliance against the Goat!" Stilgen's non-living guts tightened. They were making a habit of that lately. "Many among the living, like the Heretics, also share the tale, but they call it a Phoenix. It's some kind of fire-phantom that also rises from past destruction; hence, perhaps, the comparison. It is not the same creature, but there are overlaps."

Vespasian didn't reply. A weal had erupted to one side of his forehead, and a pair of bugs began crawling down his cheek. Despite his revolted expression, Stilgen didn't move. Instead, he regarded the crucified Sythian with a steely gaze, watching him intently as the warlord summoned the last reserves of thaumaturgic potency and tried it on the insects. Eventually, the forms were immersed in a blue tinge. They began to tumble onto the orange earth below as black confetti.

Stilgen's mouth hardened. "I would slit Mabius' neck for this." He turned away and walked back towards the entrance of the Pit, returning with a spear with a wet cloth on the end. The Consul instinctively flinched as the cloth was raised to his mouth.

"It's mulch, the crap we eat. It will hydrate you, too."

"A little late ... don't you think?"

"That's what I came to talk about." He lowered the cloth, then dug the spear's end into the sand. "I have been arguing your case with your other sibling, Vitallius. He seems to have had a change of heart. He thinks you can still be of value on a world they have shunned for decades. After, admittedly, some persuasion, he's agreed to let me cut you down to join the mission."

All that could be heard was the sighing of the breeze and the buzz of the flies. More vultures were beginning to collect on a rocky crag nearby. They watched the dying figure with beady, unflinching stares.

"What for? What could I do? And what do they want to do here on a world forgotten even by the god of all undead gods?"

Stilgen's jaw tightened. The suns were coruscating the land with wave after wave of heat. Even for those without life, it was uncomfortable. "You must eat. That's the price you pay for knowledge. If you still want to die, I ..." He choked briefly. "Once you know, I'll assist you, if that's what you want!"

"A promise?"

"A guarantee."

The Consul looked up. The birds looked back. His face grimaced in a pained smile. "Cut me down first, then I'll decide."

Stilgen shook his head. "If I cut you down, that means you've consented to come."

"Okay, tell me, what could the mightiest organization time itself has ever seen be doing with a cesspit like Etherworlde? Is that what they call this world? I think I left part of my brains back there."

"The regent."

Vespasian's good eye popped. "The Imperator of all things sent His most powerful necromancers with crack legions to take out a single hume? They came *here* to kill the powerless puppet of a forgotten sprawl on the edge of nowhere on a world no one's heard of? Why?"

"The emperor has come to believe that she might have acquired insight."

The other snorted in disbelief. "Into what? The mead rackets I've failed to put down?"

"He thinks the regent has clues that might lead Him to the Al Kimiya's hatching spot."

"By the gods, He has gone insane!"

Stilgen lowered his voice, even though only the vultures could hear. "Seemingly, she witnesses things in dream states. The emperor is desperate to avoid running the gauntlet of the Al Kimiya's apparent re-emergence, so he plans to slaughter it in its shell while it slumbers."

"They think she's a soothsayer, a *hume*?"

"It defies belief!"

"Nearly all life is necromantically sterile! Our own Magi are manufactured using the Goat's oh-so-precious Ichor. Sorcery is impossibly rare. If the Goat thinks she can detect this winged insurgent, then she has become the most priceless being in the universe." Suddenly, their world was at the centre of all things. "The price of our help in this lunacy?"

"Vitallius believes we may have a chance at banishment. An acceptable alternative to ... this!"

"And the job?"

"Otho, your other sibling, covertly came through with rapid advance forces as soon as the Goat learned of the regent's supposed abilities." Stilgen kept his voice conspiratorial. "Otho's scouts apparently made contact with the new government in Agathon, a really unpleasant bunch but, for him, fortunate timing. They are working together to take her alive. If they fail, Otho will cut off all exits. They are, even now, surrounding the entire region, leagues out, even as far as the Krayal mountains up north! There is a hitch, though, a wild card involving an old ally of the regent."

The Consul nodded mutely. "That old Heretic! The one that used to ward her when she was a sapling."

"I believe his name is Agelfi. The people I talked to think he'll try to warn her in person. If true, it's potluck who gets there first: Otho, or the clapped-out old Magi."

The other felt a sense of dread. His mouth was unusually dry. "If Otho's already on his way, what the hell do they want of us?"

"Vitallius wasn't exactly forthcoming." Stilgen grinned. "However, a Pit trooper was talking to a machine drone, who was talking to a morgue drone, who was talking to one of those newly arrived killer monoliths, while it was happily haranguing one of our gruel handlers from the mulch kitchen for dropping a bluebottle ratatouille on its boot. We are to go north to cut the regent off, stop her potentially liaising with the Krayal in the mountains." He whistled quietly through his thin lips. "If she flees in time!"

Despite his pitiful state, Vespasian's face creased in astonishment. "They *hate* each other! The Krayal hate the humes for making that Treaty with the Imperator, leaving them to be driven into the rises when the Pit was active. They'll as likely skewer her as one of us!"

"Things have got a lot more interesting," Stilgen replied. "Certainly, worth me cutting you down for!"

"And if we fail?"

"I haven't quite rotted on my ass all these years we've been isolated here," Stilgen said, failing to mask a dry smile. "There were times I was ... busy!"

"You'd vanished much of those years!"

"I thought a day would come when the flotsam skulked back." He stroked his dry chin and regarded the drier land. "You think this desert is arid, but there's another, far more arid, hard south. The Krayal call it the Widow Maker. Regardless, no one goes there, and not just because it's hot, but because there is nothing there to go for, or at least, so I thought."

At this, the threat of impending death receded. The warlord would have held his breath had he any to hold. "This is going to be interesting."

"I did vanish, but mostly within the library archives. Some of the tomes there were stolen from ancient Krayal tribes back in the day, all of whom were wiped out along with their knowledge. No other records remain anywhere else in this world, and no person has bothered to access these records since they were taken." His voice dropped so low the other barely heard. "Liege, there is *another* gate … in the Widow Maker. At its heart, at the centre of a shallow salt late. It's small, but it's there, and no one alive knows it exists except us and a handful of trusted aides. In truth, the records involved were so buried in scrolls, so decomposed that I wouldn't have found them had not a smuggling rapscallion called Breasal helped me. That guy could find a fart in a gas factory with his eyes closed and his head inside a soup pot. I mean, I wouldn't trust him as far as I could spit, but the gate is there; the only thing is we don't know its exact location. But send a scouting party to the co-ordinates, especially with the rapscallion, and we'd have it in weeks, maybe sooner!"

Long moments passed before Vespasian finally spoke. "Listen to me, carefully, because I don't want to ever say this again as even the sand has ears here." He leaned lower, as close as he could. "Never speak to anyone of this again, not until we have to. No one must know, and those that do must forget. That piece of real estate might be the only route to survival we have, as the Krayal will not let us use the other one while the Pit no longer belongs to us. Make sure Breasal and the others are posted at accessible points in the Occupied Territories, so they will be available should we need their help at short notice.

"You do understand, old friend? You must speak to no one about this, not even me … not until there is no other way." The warlord swallowed, then leaned so close the wood beneath his nailed wrists creaked. Fresh fluid began to flow. "Do … you … understand?"

"Aye." Stilgen's voice was gruff.

"Good; you can let me down!"

Her father bent and readjusted the handle on Ayilia's sword. Though short, it was as sharp as any blade his guard carried. "Like this, Ayilia. You hold it like this, sweetheart. It's quite simple as these things go."

"That's stupid," the child squealed, face red from effort. "I can get a better hold if I hold it the way I was holding it."

The swordsmith, Ayilia's sparring partner, smiled at her father. He winked back, brimming with pride. Surrounding them was the keep's inner courtyard. No one could see them here, other than two guards by the inner entrance, both of whom were thoroughly enjoying the child's training sessions. These were a regular occurrence. She trained every moment she wasn't studying.

It was her idea.

"Honey, just try it once," he said, his great paw manipulating the child's hands across the haft of her blade. She resisted at first but gave up and tried it his way. At that moment, Jarrak bustled from the kitchen side door, munching on something he'd nicked. It looked like an apple. On impulse, Ayilia diverted her eyes upwards above his head to a small triangular window. She could just make out the shape of her mother looking down. Her mother never laughed, a strange thing when you thought about it, as rarely a day went by when her father didn't wear a massive grin on his face, but that day Ayilia imagined the tender hints of a smile on her mother's lips as she silently watched.

Jarrak came over and greeted them. "Ayilia, don't let Jaden get away with it this time. You always let him win and you're already better than him."

The trainer smirked, a polite one but a smirk all the same. Ayilia wasn't listening. Jarrak was trying to pump her resolve up. He had the most faith in her of them all. It's why she loved him almost as much as her father. He was the grandfather she never knew.

"Jarrak, tell them. My way is better than this stupid way Dad wants."

Jarrak held up his hands in mock surrender. "Ain't up to me little 'un. You got to show them."

Her father pretended to be stern, but she could tell he was delighted. "First, we try it my way, the best way, tried and tested for centuries. It's called—"

"I know, I know, the Blood Hawk Grip."

"Excellent!" Her father looked up. "Jaden, let's go again."

There was a clash of steel, and Ayilia immediately lost her hold. The blade clattered to the ground. She was overwhelmed by a boiling swell of frustration.

"See, I said it doesn't work; why won't you believe me?"

Her father sighed, shoulders shrugging. "Very well, have it your way, though I suspect you didn't try hard enough."

Energized, Ayilia grabbed the blade off the ground and pointed it at Jaden. He grinned and levelled his in return, looking up at the others knowingly as he did.

She knew he would do that.

With a sudden lunge, she flicked the weapon out of the startled man's hands and held it at his throat, though she could barely reach it.

No one said a thing.

Then the whole courtyard erupted in raucous cheers, even Jaden. Her father gave her the biggest hug, enfolding the girl in his powerful embrace.

Once she'd hugged the life out him back, Ayilia set herself free and proclaimed with a triumphant grin, "See, I was right." She thought carefully, then added, "From now on, that will be the Ayilia Hawk Grip."

As Jarrak, Jaden and her father burst out laughing again, the shape of her mother moved quietly away from the window.

Ayilia stopped mid-stride and buried her face in her hands. Images were sweeping up into her mind like storm fronts. The memory of that day had struck her from nowhere, a cutter through the heart. Though it'd been one of a multitude already, this one hurt like hell. The harder she tried to suppress them, the more emotionally bloody they got. Even by the standards of most bastards, Barrik was the worst. He could've at least given her a few days to grieve before the council meeting, but he'd made sure she was as emotionally stunted as she could possibly be.

Ayilia rubbed the tears away using a grubby sleeve and hurried on. Even though Agathon's spires were particularly beguiling that night, time was short. The ancient quarters, the Rjansi, remained unchanged. Its narrow passageways, eroded stone gutters, and sloping, tawny roof were covered with a weighty hush as layers of human history converged on her senses. It nullified the sounds of mewling cats and stinking bilge water flushing down decrepit drainage ducts.

A babble of voices made her halt. People were pointing, but not at her. The moon was forged of yellow fire. She inhaled involuntarily, realizing it was 'that time.' The stones around her transformed into an auriferous shimmer of molten tin. Soft terracotta waves rippled along the housetops as though their molecules were fluctuating petals of quantum light. In sympathy, the quartz lighthouse by the quayside ignited like a candle. It covered the bay in spreading rings of photonic brilliance.

Though a regular occurrence, no one knew why it happened. Many muttered it was wayward sorcery left in the universe from the time of the Ancients. Whether wild sorcery from the past was involved or not, it was a trick of the light. When the sea turned a livid ochre, those watching burst into spontaneous applause as they always did. The phenomenon vanished as abruptly as it began, and the city was hurled back into inky oblivion.

Ayilia put a tentative hand on a wrought iron gate with peeling, black paint. With a furtive look backwards, she stepped from the small piazza into the even smaller courtyard of a tower. The atmosphere thickened. She drew in the sweet scents of the climbing plants with tender familiarity. Ferns and creepers hung from straining trestles tousled with the fleshy, exotic blooms of off-world orchids. A flood of cream-winged butterflies flitted around her head before darting toward wild bushes of alabaster roses. Feeling more relaxed, Ayilia put her hand on the oak wood of the door.

Instantly, heavy bolts slapped from behind the wood and it creaked open. It *knew* her. Things really hadn't changed.

She climbed the solid, iron stairs. At the landing, Ayilia wavered. It had been quite some time. The utter lack of notice was bizarre, even for the old Heretic. She'd received his message literally on her way to the Panchayat.

It had been short: *drop everything and come.*

The urge to turn back while her life remained even remotely predictable grew almost irresistible.

"Ayilia, come in," boomed a voice.

Too late.

She took a breath and walked into the dusky room flickering with firelight. Candles blazed from transparent urns hanging mid-air from various corners. Agelfi sat facing her in a grand, old chair. Bookshelves, surreal paintings, graphs, spirit compasses, and stellar gyroscopes lay scattered across antique tables. Pelts belonging to animals he'd found dead in the woods kept the cool stone floor tiling comfortable while tapestries and curtains draped across every part of the wall. A striking, blue mosaic of elemental protection dominated the ceiling.

Ayilia faced him uncertainly. Her breath came heavy, wrought by a storm-front of emotions and a fair degree of tiredness. It had been so long since the last visit, it was overwhelming. To say the passage of time hadn't affected him was a lie, but he still looked vibrant. The extra lines added texture to the warmth of his smile and the compassionate furrow of his brow. Soft, green tinges were growing around the edges of the shock of white hair. All the while, he regarded her with rheumy, cat-like irises.

"I've wanted to catch up with you for *years* Agelfi, years, and now you're here, your timing's, well ... horrific. I think I made a mistake coming."

"Nonsense. No timing's worse than no time at all."

She stared at him, nonplussed.

He beamed and gestured to her usual seat. Even the sight of that flooded her with poignant flashbacks.

"Please, my dear, sit. Let me make you some tea. I've brought food if you want some?"

She rubbed her knuckles. The memories were so strong. It was almost impossible to look at his compassionate face and stay neutral. "Thank you, First Gryphon Sceptre Agelfi Bil'Hazen, for seeing me, but most of my people are hundreds of leagues away monitoring the Occupied Lands. I *have* to reach them, not that there'll be enough."

Agelfi snorted, highly amused. "*Please* don't call me by ridiculous titles no one uses anymore."

He stood, bustled over, and gave her a welcoming hug. She resisted at first, then gave in. With that, the pent-up well of despair and loneliness took hold with a fury. There was nothing she could do. Agelfi was one of her childhood mentors, and despite her determination not to break down, great, marble-sized tears rolled down her cheeks one after the other. The sobs were violent and humiliating. It wasn't just a day but an adult lifetime that went with it. She'd no idea how much time had passed—you couldn't tell in that place—but eventually, he gently eased her into her seat. After checking she was okay, he then collapsed gratefully back into his chair and shot her a beaming grin.

"For a start, there's *no* such thing as Gryphons or the magick they carried; it's just a dumb symbol my rather insignificant race gave those they regard as learned scholars. I think it gave them a sense of the grand!"

Ayilia gritted her teeth. Now that she'd purged her tears, for the moment, her attention turned back to the matters at hand. She tried to resist the temptation to see if Barrik's thugs were skulking in the streets.

Agelfi was already in full swing. He did that. What he was trying to do was guide her from the embarrassment she'd feel at letting her guard down. It'd been the same as a kid. She truly hated to show weakness. "True thaumaturgy is intrinsically pure science, triggered by those naturally symbiotic with the particles in every element. They are so very few of us, Ayilia, yet *still* the Resistance thinks I'm too old to be useful anymore."

"I'm sorry."

"I'm delighted. You have no idea how it pleases me, to be free."

Ayilia blew her nose on a rag she then hid up a sleeve and stared at him wide-eyed. "It does?"

"Yes, it means I am here to help you, when you need my help more than ever, even though, for both of us, time is short."

"Agelfi, there's nothing you can do unless you've an army to back you up, but I don't see one, unless it's hidden in the larder that somehow you've always managed to keep running."

He made to stand, but she gently shook her head. "Sorry Agelfi, I shouldn't have come."

"Wait." He held up a hand and gave a mournful smile. "We've been here before, haven't we? Once, decades ago, I taught you to fight night terrors and the elementals that came to feed on your despair. It's not the first time I've appeared when you needed me." His bushy brows creased with concern. "You have never left my mind; you are not and *never* have been alone. I've checked on you from time to time but always covertly. Couldn't have an old Resistance insurgent drawing attention to you, could we?"

Ayilia grinned sheepishly, feeling better. She held her hands to the fire and sucked up the flickering warmth. "I never doubted it, but unfortunately, the timing is belated."

"The Provost is dangerous, Ayilia, but he is the least of your concerns. The threat of him pales in significance compared to what I am *forced* to tell you." Agelfi fixed her with the kind but intense stare he used when something was critical. "I have incantations woven into the tower and garden. If Barrik's people so much as approach, they'll regret it." He tapped the side of his head. "Not quite as infirm as some think, I wager."

That familiar chair was as comforting as ever. She found herself sinking into its worn, soft folds. Agelfi smiled again. "Perhaps I'm the one who needs reassurance, Ayilia. There is turbulence on the seas ahead; a mighty necromantic squall is ready to take from us all that we cherish, and I don't just mean the catastrophic collapse of the Resistance. Please understand, I barely made it here myself."

"An auspicious start." Ayilia gulped. "But I'm truly sorry. The last thing I want is for you to be in danger because of me. Thank you for coming."

He flashed a grin and brushed back his long mane of white hair before fumbling with his beard.

"My mind's all upside down, Ayilia. You know how it is."

Agelfi had forgotten to offer her tea, but Ayilia knew that would be remedied halfway through some diatribe.

She sunk further into her seat. The leather crackled like the burning firewood in the grate.

"I would've written, Agelfi, but, well, I didn't have much to say. Truth be told, I was actively considering transferring the last of my duties to the Doge once father finally ..." She trailed off.

"Why would you do that?"

"I'm a ceremonial lamppost, Agelfi. What the hell does a modern society need with me?"

"It's not as modern as the times we inhabit, Ayilia!"

"Eh?"

"Negotiation gets my vote every time, but there is collaboration here, or should I say a sell-out."

She leaned forwards. "So, I haven't cracked up!"

Agelfi retrieved a log from a pile of wood nearby. With precision, he flipped it onto the grate, where it was immediately engulfed in a halo of flying embers. A succession of crackles filled the room, which already flickered with dancing shattered shadows. "The Imperium is behind this, yes. I doubt a backstabber like the Provost would have the courage to do these things on his own. By this, I mean dominate the Doge *and* usurp the only person actively protecting the rights of the city's freedoms and the enslaved outside your walls. That's the irony of your times, Ayilia."

Her hand flexed involuntarily. "How long's that scurrying rat been working for them?"

He regarded her evenly. "We will talk of such things presently, but, as you say, time is pressing. Before I go on, I wanted to say just how distraught I am about your father. He was *truly* a good person, like your mother, in her own way."

She gave a vigorous shake of the head. "I'm not."

He flinched but held his tongue.

"The last few months, he was suffering terribly. No one was able to lift the thaumaturgic virus or whatever he was infested with. Death, honestly, was his only way." She tried not to choke. "That's for another time. Right now, it's all about Barrik and the city." Ayilia sighed. "Honestly, the most rewarding times have been diplomatically kicking some sense into some Lifeless, usually very inebriated, asses. I almost felt sorry for them; their Ichor's old and rancid, their bones bent and worn." She rubbed her hands closer to the fire, feeling chilled. "Treaty permitted me to check on the humans under the Pit's control throughout this world, and that's taken up much my time." She smiled wryly. "I guess our dud warlord in the Pit made it easier. I mean, it might help if I'd ever met him, but he just doesn't seem interested in repressing people. I know the Pit's gone renegade, but we could almost give him a seat in the Panchayat; he's so useless."

Agelfi snorted in amusement and abruptly heaved himself to his feet with a wheezing grunt. He was noticeably slower than the last time they'd met. Hardly surprising, considering the time gap. "Again, I'm sorry, Ayilia. When I last saw you, there was such ... hope." He wandered in a slow circle, arriving back at the spot he had just vacated. "Things are graver than I've ever known. I am viewed with particular venom within the Imperium, paradoxically the only people who still take me seriously. My compatriots tolerate me, but in my undeniable dotage, I have become an irrepressible eccentric. It would be fair to say that I'm not always as accurate in my forecasting and strategies as my once formidable reputation would suggest. That's putting it lightly. Many even regard me as a serious liability."

"That's outrageous."

"Don't be, not for me. I still have friends and *some* influence. In many places, the elderly are tragically considered as relevant as mouldy mud-fish. In my case, they have a point." Despite her shocked expression, he laughed. "Some tea? Yes?"

He made his way to the oval-shaped space adjacent to the living room that he claimed was a kitchen before tinkering with pots and kindling. Ayilia tried to focus on the fire, but the iron grate was suddenly dark. Disturbingly, the wood was gone too.

"I don't see a fire, Agelfi. Where'd it go?"

"Oh, gone out?"

Understanding snapped in. "A Mage blaze. Those logs weren't real, were they?"

"I wanted the effect to be welcoming. In truth, it saves trees and doesn't take any energy on my part." He closed his eyes, and the hearth whumped into life again, along with the heat. "There, that should do it. Remind me if it starts to go again. Are you hungry?"

"No, thank you." Ayilia smiled, soaking in the heat.

"I have some crushed I'ansansie leaves fresh from the Renttor Edges for tea. Rare too—a slightly nutty taste, but deliciously refreshing. I don't seem to have brought any others, so I hope it'll do."

"Perfect."

Agelfi reached for some ceramic pots decked with white feathers and faded ribbons. He then shoved aside a dozen packets of what looked like spices and seeds before thumbing at a small pouch of leaking herbs. Muttering at the lack of proper containers, he started tinkering with a battered kettle already boiling on a lit grate.

"People like me are clouded in wayward spells, Ayilia. Sometimes it seems to change even our appearances." Returning to the living room, he put her drink carefully on a side table that pre-dated their city. A flaming bird was painted on its surface, along with a fiery arc of wings and a dark shadow holding up a protective hand. When she looked up, Agelfi had already sat.

"It begins," he whispered gravely. "Why I'm here. You're in desperate danger, and it's not from the squalid intent of this new council. I'm afraid the anti-forces are gathering, and this time they've noticed Etherwolde, humanity, and, more importantly, they've noticed *you*. The Goat has noticed *you*."

Ayilia stared at him. She put her mug down and sat upright. Something far off was howling, but it might have been the insidious and growing malaise of her mind.

"And I thought Barrik was a problem."

His hand shot out, blocking her attempt to rise. "*Ayilia, please,* you *must* hear me out. It's for your sake, not mine."

Ayilia's eyes flashed. She was that defiant child again, but this was too much, straight after the day from hell. "If you wanted to fill my head with crap like this, you should've come sooner." She wiped her face for the umpteenth time with the back of her tunic. The action caught his attention. Looking up, he noticed the dark flecks of blood across the sleeve and sensed the miasma of death hovering there. "Agelfi. I just need to gather the few Gemina left in the city before the Provost sends his *infinitely* larger army to round them up. It won't take long to get the authority he needs, and I've no allies left."

"You're free to leave, Ayilia, you know that." He withdrew his hand. "But you *will* regret hearing the truth from a foe rather than a trusted, life-long friend, even if much of my protection was often done remotely."

Ayilia leaned back, trying to mask her frustration and a deep, malingering fear. "You're talking of those damned dreams, aren't you? That was some time ago."

He nodded. "It's not so much the content, more the ability that goes with it."

Her hands tightened on the chair's handle. "I don't understand what that even means."

Agelfi tweaked at his beard. "Listen, Ayilia, it's best if I gave you some background, starting with the Resistance. Trust me—you'll understand. It'll only take a moment."

She said nothing, but she knew her face was a peculiar fuchsia.

Agelfi kept his voice as level as possible. "The Heretics are a mutual alliance of leaders who wield exceptional, but extremely rare, levels of ability. The desperation of our times means that almost all those gifted with sorcery end up in charge of the secular alliance of races, loosely termed the Resistance, in a war pitting those that live against those who cannot. They are governed by the Pynx, the leader of the Five Hundred. I know I told you this before."

The room had darkened. The shadows were long and blurred, hangman fingers that spread out in all directions. She barely noticed. She was in a personal nightmare.

"You have no trace of sorcery," Agelfi continued, though the flatness of his tone suggested that he was acutely aware of the distress Ayilia was in. "Hardly surprising as, perhaps, one in ten million or so has any hint of thaumaturgic perception. Nevertheless, it didn't stop you from entering dream states *only* accessible to Magi as a child. That's shocking enough, but the fact you had the skill to call for help using modes of communication only at the disposal of super adepts astounded me. Your unwitting signals were how I first encountered you, despite the incredible distance at the time."

Agelfi drained his cup and put it down. The fire had decreased, but he didn't seem to notice. He was rustling in his deep pockets for something. A whole manner of objects came out, but not the object of his search. Ayilia nodded towards a pouch by his waist.

"Your pipe's always in there."

"Oh, obliged." Delving within the sack of cloth, he pulled out the pipe, followed by the pungent scent. "See, context is everything—without it, you'd never have spotted the pouch."

She smiled despite the growing sense of doom. "I spotted it because you always keep it there!"

"That's where context comes in. All done." He stuffed the leaves in the hollow and lit them with a flick of his hand. "If you're a good enough Mage, the toxins stay in the pipe."

"Is that possible?"

He winked. "I hope so, or I'll get that hacking sickness and keel over for good."

The dark behind him was a cobweb of tight patterns. The stars glittered through a far window but, for once, they were dim. A hostile breeze teased the frayed curtains. It was impressive how little dust there was, considering how long the place had been empty.

"Ayilia, the emperor has the power of insight and it is vast, deep, and beyond *all* measure. This gives us a being overwhelmingly more powerful than anything the known universe can imagine. That includes any Arch-Magi, the Sythians, the Asthen Ascendancy of millennia back, the even more ancient royals of the Interregnum, and all the others who fought against Him or, for that matter, for Him."

Ayilia needed to go, but it was impossible. Her curiosity burned as ferociously as the day Agelfi first turned up. "Does that include the Ancients? They always fascinated me the most."

His eyes narrowed. "With good reason." His furrowed concern bored into her skull. He was training her like he used to, to fight for her life using knowledge as weaponry. "This enigmatic super-race ruled benignly across the arch of existence. They hewed from the quantum firmament the intricate network of indestructible tunnels and portals that connect all inhabitable worlds, moons, and stars. They knitted entire stellar clusters together, and so much more. One day, they grew so powerful that they are said to have built a link to another domain entirely, discovering realms of bristling energies, even of pure thought. Then it all went hideously wrong."

She leaned closer. "What happened?"

"They are alleged to have tunnelled into a demonic domain so wicked, so secret, so pernicious, that they vanished. Hard to say, as the emperor has wiped all records. True knowledge, after all, equals true power. Others say that they were so engorged on necromantic arrogance that they wiped themselves out in a fit of titan pique. No one knows other than, perhaps, the Goat."

Ayilia's hands were clammy, yet her brow was ice. Though the tower never once stopped feeling safe, the foreboding was almost impossible to ignore. "What about the Sythians bred in the Pit?"

"*Why?*" Agelfi's reaction was so sudden she started.

She shrugged apologetically. "Don't they fight for the Goat?" Her eyes darkened. "Are *they* the reason you're here?"

He looked flustered. Not only had his eyes widened, but his hands involuntarily clenched. The room was a powder keg of tension. "Hell, if only I could've come sooner." He shut his eyes and dragged deeply on his pipe, presumably ensuring nothing harmful went in. "Never trust them Ayilia, *ever*! The Sythians of yore were sought after as Magi fighters of immense ability in the wars between the Imperium and its many conquered adversaries of antiquity. *Every* single one of them served the Imperium, though no one knows why. They have no race, creed, or form. They are nothing but a cosmic spore that passes from host to host, obsessed with their own survival. Thousands of years of generational dormancy is nothing to them. One day, without a flicker of warning, their DNA erupts and engulfs a hapless carrier. The combined entity, the host and the spore, at the time of birth becomes, in essence, a fully-fledged Sythian. Notwithstanding, the DNA strand *is* its true form. It is the perfect parasite."

She tightened her fists. "Some kind of sentient virus then, an eternal, cosmic blight that stalks the flesh of the unwitting?"

"Precisely ... I look at them as a thaumaturgic bacterium of infinite capability. The truth is, no one, perhaps including the Goat, has the skills to detect them while dormant. They could literally be in anyone!"

Ayilia regarded her empty mug, lost in thought. Agelfi bustled over to get the kettle. He came back and filled the cup. Being unusually thirsty, she quickly drained it.

"General Mabius and ... his family," she fingered the handle of her mug, "All of them exploded onto the scene at once after all this time, though it didn't quite work out for the Consul, of course." Ayilia looked up. "Why choose *this* time to emerge?"

"Why indeed?" He watched her with sparkling orbs. "Is it a decision made by the collective consciousness of their Geno over the tidal flux of time?? Or is the *blip* of emergence something planned? I doubt we'll ever know. Needless to say, the emerged being exists only for a fraction of the time of their overall existence."

There was a hanging silence. Ayilia rose and parted the curtains. The streets were dark and deserted; outside, a lone cat stalked along a branch of low-level guttering. Agelfi watched patiently.

"I doubt they know you're here, but I've numerous guardian incantations in the stone," Agelfi said gravely before futilely repeating himself. "I should've come earlier."

"For God's sake, Agelfi, it was *never* your responsibility to look after me, but you did it from the other side of charted space. Without you, they'd have sectioned me in the local booby-hatch long ago."

He laughed heartily. For a fleeting moment, the tension was dispelled, but the dark soon seeped back. Agelfi sent a pipe cloud of smoke toward the ceiling. For a heartbeat, she saw demonic faces staring. They disseminated among the vapours, though traces of their baleful eyes lingered. "You recall the stories I used to tell you, Ayilia, of a winged avatar? Of how it possessed so much power that it threw it full force at the Goat Himself?"

"The Phoenix that isn't really a Phoenix?" Ayilia's brow arched in puzzlement. "I remember you said the Al Kimiya was a deluded insurgent and that no one knows if it's actually a bird or a basilisk. Didn't the emperor kill it an eon ago?"

"He thinks it's back."

Ayilia stared at him, expecting him to laugh, but he didn't. "A joke, surely?"

He slowly tapped his pipe on the side of his chair. "The Goat believes it has *already* returned."

She shook her head mutely. "Can't He just kill it again?"

"He's trying to as we speak. He's trying to locate its birth site, its actual egg, and destroy it before emergence. I think the Goat fears it's more dangerous than the last time. Only the creature's destruction matters now, before it rises as some fiery killer from the ash of its historic failure. The Phoenix is undoubtedly mythical, but the Al Kimiya is not. Blast."

The fire had gone out. Despite the unseasonal bite to the air, neither had noticed. Ayilia watched grimly as he shut his eyes and lit the flame again, but the once welcoming yellow blaze was only a cool blue. "Agelfi?"

"Ummmm?" He was still tending to the fantasy flame.

"Why are you really here? I thought you might help me with Barrik, but it's already too late, isn't it? Even you can't fight the city's army. Why is the Pit being reactivated? More importantly, why do you think the Goat has noticed my dreams? It's asinine!"

The wizened enchanter shifted uncomfortably, then threw some more make-believe wood in the fire's direction. Suddenly, the room was a warm, lit-up mosaic of dancing crevices and shimmering shards.

"There was no warning, Ayilia, nothing. Then, someone came into my rather dishevelled study and ..." He drifted off again. Ayilia let him think. "His name is, well, it doesn't matter; suffice to say he's a highly skilled Resistance practitioner. He comes in, and he says, 'they're after your friend—in Agathon.' Of course, I was taken aback, and I wasn't the only one. Within the blink of an eye, or so it seemed, the whole institute hears of it and is talking about us. It seemed to go as dead as a tomb yard every time I entered a public place." He paused and fumbled for a kerchief and wiped a damp brow fervently. "This adventurous claptrap regarding Kimiyas, Sythians, and Phoenixes hadn't entered my mind literally for ages; suddenly the talk is of all three."

She waited patiently, despite not exactly feeling patient.

"All the charts came out, all the mathematical counters, and the fiercely bearded soothsayers and their grubby feet—why can't they wear proper shoes once in a while? We had haruspices, augurs, and a vaticinator with a missing ear. Even though he prophesizes things to come, he couldn't see the worktop blade that took his lobe out while carving a wooden gnome for his garden water feature. Unexpectedly—and these people never see eye-to-eye—they came to an agreement."

Ayilia dry swallowed. "Care to elaborate?"

"They discovered the Goat Himself, the most powerful necromancer since the Ancients themselves, actually *picked up* the signature of such an egg. He believes it contains the living spirit of His old enemy, our Al Kimiya. He has sent out legions of scouts to claw and paw the earth for the faintest hint of its spawn site and destroy it with the most extreme prejudice."

Agelfi inhaled. She avoided the smoke this time, just in case even it and its devil faces were working for the Imperium.

"When the apogee of the creature's birth approaches, it will become so potent it—" He coughed and regarded her with rheumy eyes. "What I'm trying to say is, the piercing light of the Kimiya's thaumaturgic puissance will ignite across the empyreal firmament and be visible to the Goat's infinite sight, but only *just* before birth. Whether His goons will reach it before it emerges is a moot point, but to track and obliterate it beforehand is highly preferable to them! Our best seers tried to see it too, to sense if the shell's location is visible yet, I mean."

"*And?*"

"And they sensed ... something."

"*The egg*!"

"An egg!"

"But *the* egg?"

He shook his head in bewilderment, face ashen. "A shell with extreme power. We don't, of course, have the emperor's vision. Needless to say, if even He cannot pinpoint its exact location until it's nearly fully lit up like a cosmic beacon, we can't either."

A fissure of ghostly exhilaration flashed through her mind. Perhaps they could still save her city with the help of this Kimiya! "What are your people going to do about it?"

"Something is being done right now!" Agelfi sounded irritated, defensive, and, most disconcertingly to Ayilia, scared. "We're sending groups to search for it, and each group will have a Seer heading it. It is entirely possible they'll only be in time to see the Goat's henchmen hack its head off with a rusty cutter or even get butchered first, which is highly likely."

The despair returned. False hope could do that. "Sorry, but let them have the damned bird!" She stood, raising her hands in front of her. "I want to stay, Agelfi, really, but it's clearly more urgent than ever that I round up the X Gemina while we have time."

Agelfi regarded her from the chair with black eyes. She'd never seen him so unnerved. He leaned forwards, slashes of fear in the feline slits of his gaze. "The Resistance believes this thing is the only hope we have left, Ayilia. An alliance with it might tip what's left of the scales in the favour of all living kind, *including* your city." He puffed slowly and carefully. "We have to have a presence, a guardian cohort if you like, at the spawn site. If we don't care enough to even show up, then why should it care, you understand?"

She was barely listening. A realization struck softly, like a feathered spear through her mind's inner eye. Horrified, she gaped at him.

"The fool ... He, the emperor, thinks I can see this bloody egg, doesn't He? He thinks I can personally track it down just because I get paranoid nightmares and access woebegone realms where only lost Magi go." Ayilia clumped her head against the cool surface of the wall. "All I want to do is help this asshole of a city, but this ..."

Agelfi's mouth had opened like a craggy gorge, but he shut it the moment she turned. After a while, he spoke with a calm, gentle voice. "I know you'd rather be saving your people, Ayilia, but right now, I'm only concerned with your protection. The Imperator's been searching for hidden visionaries for decades to spot this Kimiya. Hundreds of thousands have been infected with the use of an information thaumaturgic virus by secretive Imperial agents to sniff them out. In your case, I'm guessing the Imperial lodestar was a certain Regallion."

"That bonehead from my youth?" Ayilia wanted to punch the wall now. "You think she infected me with some sorcery virus? To read my mind?"

"We don't know, but if so, in your case, it's a good thing." Agelfi spoke so animatedly his pipe had discharged most of his tobacco onto his lap. "You would have come up clean. Whatever gift you have is natural, undetectable. It would have shown you had no Seer abilities at all. My own people even now think you're a hopeless waste of time, for the same reason."

Her voice almost choked off. "The emperor's seen me, though, hasn't He?"

"You must leave, Ayilia. *Tonight*. You can't help this city. It has wilfully decided to hand itself over. It is a tomb of thralls now. There are thousands of regular troops, just a handful of Gemina." He brushed back his head again, lost in thought. "The emperor won't take 'I don't know where the bloody bird is' for an answer. Forgive me for being blunt, but once He has taken you, He will peel the bony carapace from your mind and extract everything He thinks you know, and it could take Him weeks to do it. Only a miserable death would save you."

She shot him an ironic glance. "I was happier with Barrik."

Quietly, he added, "If you're still here at daybreak, Barrik will have you strung up as a traitor. Or, he may have your hands nailed to the entry of the chambers." Agelfi's face puckered with earnest concern. "Get out of here, Ayilia; go north. I have friends in the Krayal Badlands. Ask for Elder Maroukish in the purple highlands—they all know him. Tell him you are my friend. The Resistance knows of an ancient, forgotten portal toward the Arctic. Barely anyone knows. It's what I use instead of the Pit's. You and your troop will be escorted there. It's tiny, but it will take you to a derelict moon. If I am not there, I will have instructions waiting. The Resistance is defeated, but not yet eradicated. If there really is something inside your mind, they might still help all of us, including your city. If we fail, it barely matters."

Ayilia couldn't believe it had come to exile or death. Her eyes moistened. Her granite surface of protective cynicism, created by her father's illness and a rabid council, threatened to crack. There were no words left.

"Ayilia, the truth is that if you leave, your people will be fine, for now. Their ultimate hope is this damned thing, whatever the Kimiya is." He shook his head and ambled to the kitchen. Fumbling with the kettle, he poured a lukewarm tea. Outside, the cats began yowling and an angry voice yelled out a window at them to shut up. Agelfi went to a table and began looking at some discarded scrolls. "Been a while since I looked at these. I've left this place to the orphanage. I'll miss it terribly and our long chinwags here back in the day, but I have an instinct that tells me I'll not be back. Old age creeps up even on Magi, you know." Before she could answer, he lifted his finger. "But you do have something *enigmatic* that has nothing at all to do with Mage craft. Without theurgy, I believe you have somehow, inadvertently, picked up this winged assassin's shell and that simple, unobtrusive fact, makes you the most wanted being alive."

She stared at him eyes bulging, features contorted with sudden fury. "I have picked up nothing."

❦ · ☠ · ☠ · ☠ · ❦

She'd accepted yet another tea, consequently answered several calls of nature, then developed a healthy 'hunger bug' and devoured some perfectly preserved condiment on rye husks. She suffered another explanation of the Uncertainty Doctorate. She listened, glazed-eyed, but managed to nod at the right times. What the older man was really doing was giving her time to think things over, and she was thinking hard.

"I think the Asthen Ascendancy of antiquity called it the Disequilibrium Paradox of Spite!" Agelfi announced.

"I see ..."

"To survive, the organization in question would need to dispel more energy just to stand still than be could ultimately supplied. Yet, we have an impossible, Imperial society that does not obey the law of universal physics. Perhaps that explains why the Goat is so concerned with this fire demon."

"*Agelfi!*"

He looked up.

"I still wake up drenched in sweat, and wayward sprites still violate my dreams. I can drive them off, like you taught me, destroy them if I have to, but somehow I attract them like flies to ..." She trailed off. "I have no awareness of a pretend Phoenix, an Al Kimiya, or an egg, and, I'm sorry, but I don't think I ever will."

"I understand."

He sat and drew a long soothing sip from his hundredth clay-baked mug of tea. "There is no choice. I know the Krayal and humans loathe each other, but they also know me, and that's crucial."

Agelfi's pensive face darkened further. "Ironic, the hatred on this desert world eclipses anything that goes on in the universe beyond, Ayilia; it's a scant wonder a Lifeless cosmos finds it so easy to break in." He coughed again. "My dear, we are going to send Seers to find this shell, but should they fail, and they probably will, your mind might be our last hope. I've always felt you were different, and now that the emperor senses it, I am more convinced than ever." He smiled wanly.

Ayilia shot him a look of grave amusement. "A bad day just became a bloody nightmare, but you're always right!" She went over and gave him a hug. "You're my mentor and one of my oldest friends, and I will always be grateful." She grimaced. "I'll send a message to the soldiers in the Occupied Territories, let them make provisions. I'll only take the ones in the city, without familial connections, which won't be hard as waifs and strays are the only kind the Gemina attracts. By dawn, we'll well be on our way up north to enjoy the bitter hospitality of the Krayal."

She turned and walked reluctantly to the door. "Stupid question, but you *are* coming, right?"

He shook his head. "Ayilia, I didn't realize until I got here your city was about to hang you, and some weeks or so ago, I didn't know the Imperium was going to hunt you. I have the most urgent business in the Resistance and I *have* to go. If I am late, they will not help you." He paused, staring off into the corner of the room. "However, I did pop in to see the Krayal elders in question on my way here, and everything has been arranged. All you must do is get out of the city and take the hidden back paths you know so well. If I don't meet the Resistance to confirm arrangements, it'll be too late to integrate you, as they are literally on the move, and even now it might be too late."

As she walked out that door, for the last time in her life, the dark finally seemed to engulf her. She took a deep breath, fighting back a surge of sadness, perhaps even grief. "I missed you, old friend," she whispered. "I've missed you more than you could possibly know. Please be there ..."

She left.

❦ · ❦ · ☠ · ❦ · ❦

Someone was watching her. She was certain. She was in danger. The experience was fleeting but deeply unpleasant.

A shadow darted at the end of a deserted market square.

Fighting gnawing anxiety, she pushed through sheets of colourful but ghostly batik fluttering from rows of deserted stalls. The dark safety of the tower was no longer visible, though the shape had cut off any hope of retreat. The lone woman hastened down a maze of interconnecting passageways without looking back. A night bird squealed overhead in the distance as something scurried under a rotten fence.

Pots and wooden boards stacked against sandstone bricks passed in a blur. She stumbled, sending everything clattering against a mouldy grate. A voice growled vehemently from an upstairs window. Incongruously embarrassed, despite her safety being at stake, Ayilia hurried on. Though she could see nothing in the murk, someone was following her.

Veering down a tiny side street amid a labyrinth of sagging, timber houses and grim cul-de-sacs, Ayilia collided with a network of low-level lines draped with wet sheeting. They tangled hopelessly around her neck and arms. The silhouette of a well-built man appeared at the street's entry point where she'd just been.

Cursing, she scrabbled at the lines with her hands until a dank pair of bloomers flapped across her face. The man took a step forward. Still, she couldn't move. A heavy-set woman with a flickering lantern shoved her bedroom window open with some force and fixed her a venomous glare.

"Who's there?" she hollered, her voice piercing the calm night with some force. "My fella's on his way down, scum!"

"I am?" a voice behind exclaimed in disbelief.

"Yeah, go get him, Reg," she ordered.

"I need a mo' to put my strides on."

"Go without them, you worthless turd."

"Don't call me that. Call me anything, but not that!"

Ayilia could hear them bellowing at each other as she struggled free. They quite clearly had already forgotten the reason for their bickering. She considered getting her blade out and finishing off her pursuer, but two more joined him.

There might be a whole mob.

Ayilia grunted loudly and desperately tugged the lines free from the wall in a puff of debris. She threw herself down the constricted streets, knocking bent rubbish cans over in an ear-splitting crescendo of scattering metal. The resounding echo pounded ahead of her, prompting a series of faces to lean from an assortment of gibbous windows with a further stream of colourful insults. Disconcertingly, the three shapes had become five, maybe six. Agelfi had been wrong. High noon was no longer reserved for daybreak.

Ayilia ran now with precision. With the street out of sight, the district became silent, deathlike. Rows of blue-white doors and shutters were closed tight. They passed her at a dizzying rate, but she knew the route inside out. So quick was the pace that the keep's bleak outline was in touching distance in no time.

After quickly scrutinizing the roads ahead for an ambush, Ayilia beelined towards the nearest side gate. In the distance, a giggling couple wrestled with a rattling medley of keys outside a door. A row of grain carts passed to her right. She unsheathed her blade, feeling immediately better at the dim glint of its alloy. An older man turned a corner and regarded her with a hostile frown, then shuffled on. Bats flitted in frenetic waves across the sky. A dog barked. She could hear footsteps following. The keep, dark but welcoming, loomed high. The thick, furry conifers running outside its walls were as still as the hilltop graveyard.

There was no sign of the guard, but the side gate was finally in front of her. Fumbling a chunky key into the lock, she twisted the handle hard, but it refused to open. Panicked, she tried again. It clicked. A ripple of relief ransacked her body. The gate opened with an explosive creak.

Someone shouted indistinctly nearby.

A blur of shapes rushed toward her. Fear vied with fury at being cornered outside her own palace. Ayilia whirled, her blade a neon sheen in the half-light. A man cried in pain and staggered against the others, then hit the ground. Dark blood pumped across the flagstones. Caught off-guard, the shapes gawped as she swished the cutter back and forth, the whites of her teeth gleaming manically.

"Not so easy now," she growled. "Try that again, and my shiny pal's going to make swine meat out of you."

The group gawped in the half-light. Hands sweating from adrenalin, Ayilia backed through the gate and slammed it shut with her foot. They rushed her, but she stabbed the blade through the grill, and another yelped.

"Stop!"

The shapes looked round. Ayilia, her foot wedged against the base of the gate, fumbled with the key until lock gave a satisfying second click. She closed her eyes for a fleeting moment again, immensely relieved.

"Piss off ... all of you!"

Her eyes flitted open to see a court official standing outside the gate, one of the Doge's courtiers. Four special constables were at his side. The attackers hurried away, carrying their severely injured friend. Another was holding an arm which shed blood like a watering can. The official didn't take his gaze from hers.

"Regent?"

As she was breathing heavily, she could only nod.

"I came to give you a message."

Ayilia sheathed her sword. "A message? I was nearly killed!"

"Those were Barrik's thugs. Been out scouring the city for you. There you are, out all alone without your X Gemina."

"Not quite alone ... check out the blood discolouring the soles of your expensive boots." She rubbed her sweating face, wet as a puddle. "What do you want, Mannferlaing?"

He regarded her with eyes as grey as chipped flagstone. He seemed to be wearing his council garb, though the only thing she could see with any kind of clarity was the shine of his balding dome. "We have a final chance to save your city, Regent. It's all up to you."

Her eyes narrowed. "I'm listening."

"The Doge's special constables are taking control. The Provost has been sent home. Most of his thugs have been dispersed. The Doge is patently alarmed at the extent of Barrik's treachery. He wants to bring all deliberations with the newly arrived Imperium into the public arena. To do this, the Doge needs your consent and your backing. As you know, it has to be verified by leading council members. They have been gathered in an extraordinary session, and they await you."

She snorted and leaned close to the grill. "Why should I believe you?"

The official delved into his pockets. Out came a wad of tightly sealed papers and the Doge's official ring. Around them, the city slumbered. Although her life had been in the most extreme jeopardy, it was like nothing had happened. A lone dog started baying to be let in. Someone inside cursed mildly and opened a door. There was a flash of lantern light that briefly lit the gate and the impassive stares of the men watching, then they were engulfed again in the bluey black of the night. For some reason, she noticed the gate's spokes were peeling, rusted. She made a mental note to tell the caretakers in the morning, before realizing that morning was a luxury she might not have.

"His word! Upon this rests his entire reputation. You know this." The man gave them to her. "You've known him for decades before he was even elected. If you do not attend and do this thing, officially, the Provost will regain control as he still heads the government and the main army. The city will be sold out. Within weeks, maybe days, Imperial predators will march in through our unwarded gates. Barrik will hunt you down to the ends of the deserts, and his new friends will help him."

"And they want to see me *now*?"

"Tonight, or Barrik will defy the Doge's orders perhaps as soon as daylight, by manipulating the council and thus, the city. A council that, need I remind you again, he has full control of.

"If you let him do this, you let him assume full control of the destiny of our people ."

Chapter Six

IMPERIAL ARTIFICE

"Ayilia."

The sleeping form stirred, looked out the window at a day that was still too early, and pushed the hand from her shoulder.

"Ayilia ... honey!"

When she finally turned to look up, Kemet's eyes were nearly popping out of his head. Ayilia worried he might rupture something. "You want us to go *north*? You want us to ride to lands ruled by cutthroat scavengers who trust us as much as recycled hog waste? You got this information from that Heretic *after* Barrik tried to kill you? If that's not bad enough, and it is, you now plan to see the fumbling Doge in the *same* building that Barrik tried to kill you?"

Ayilia chucked her sword onto a nearby counter and slapped a worn-out military belt across her waist. She stood by the fireplace in the barrack's mess hall and thrust her shoulders back while meeting his eyes. "That about sums it up. We can stop Barrik in his tracks with Lerang's help. The Doge is panicking. He thinks Barrik's gone too far, but we have to meet tonight before Barrik's powers kick in."

He shook his head. "Hell, Regent, you've got a death wish, going to that wizard in his sinister belfry of secrets *and* planning to return to the chambers in one night. No one wonder Jarrak's no longer with us. You wore him out."

She flinched inside at the name. "It's not a bell tower, and it's safer than here." Ayilia shook her head angrily. "Kemet, you don't trust any sorcerer, and you trust Agelfi even less. Besides, I needed you here at the barracks getting what's left of the Gemina ready."

"So that we can knock swords with the scaleheads up north?" Kemet held up his hands, his face a mixture of disbelief and horror, before stalking in circles around the room. "What about the bulk of our forces? You'll leave them in the Occupied Territories watching the local stiffs piss themselves on grog while we planet-hop into the middle of a dying war?"

"If the Doge and I can get Barrik banned, I won't be leaving anyone. If we fail, you and Aaron need to be ready, unless you think our few score Gemina here can take out several thousand regulars."

"It's one thing to go out into the desert rounding up our pals, but to go into Krayal Badlands looking for a miniature portal no one even knew existed with only our handful *here*, all the time praying they won't slit our throats once *there*, is madness." His pace quickened. The floorboards were beginning to creak. "We can't just abandon the city?"

"The city's abandoned *us*. Anyway, as I said, I'm going to—"

"Oh no." He paused and glowered at her; the shiny dome of his head silhouetted in the candlelight. "You're not going there to get diced in that political tomb above the waterfalls in the dark alone."

Ayilia rubbed her face and stared back blearily. "I'll have Aaron. He may be challenged by social niceties and by the simplest of tasks that involve what you and I call a brain, but he's a great soldier."

"He can't put his britches on without destroying half the room and cursing the gods for the time spent destroying it."

"He's also your best friend and my command second."

"Aye, but I'm still coming."

"Kemet ..." She looked out the window, wondering how to put it. She could see the blur of her troop in the dim light packing gear onto horses. "I don't want you to come with me tonight or, for that matter, off-world if we do leave. You have family, for God's sakes."

"That's all sorted." He walked over and sat in the chair opposite. Though his eyes had misted, there was defiant determination. "My wife and daughters are already on their way to my cousins down south. They're joined by the few Gemina who have social skills and families. The Imperium will never find them there. Their villages are in a series of gorges stretching hundreds of leagues in the middle of nowhere; they're impossible to trace. To be honest, it's the safest thing for them regardless. They were half expecting something like this since the new government was elected." He swallowed. "They always knew I was married into the service, and they will be fine. I can save them by getting you to the Resistance."

Ayilia emptied a jug of water into a mug and drained it. "How many can ride?"

"Perhaps sixty to seventy, if that. Barrik's timing is appalling." He turned to look out the window, eyes creased with concern. "And I'm *still* not happy about the Krayal. They still regard us as land-grabbing colonists all these centuries on."

"The enemy of my enemy and all that ... plus the fact Agelfi's already arranged it should do the trick," Ayilia muttered unconvincingly as she buckled on her sword. She sensed his heavy stare on her as she flexed her hands. "The Pit, back in the day, almost drove our Krayal friends to extinction. It's just as much in their interests if this Al Kimiya succeeds as anyone else."

"If you ask me, they're just a bunch of dirty, anti-social reptiles with an attitude that stinks—they hate everyone."

"Hell, Kemet, you sound like Aaron."

"I am his best, *only*, friend."

"The Krayal were the ones that invited humans here in the first place. We were just a despised bunch of nomads on the run. By anyone's standards, we should cut them a load of slack. Anyway, Agelfi's says they're okay, so that's enough for me."

Before Kemet could answer, a voice piped up.

"Regent, thank God you're back. They were looking for you in the keep." A blonde woman in her late twenties appeared at the doorway, pushing boxes and pennants out of the way as she strode in.

Ayilia began tugging on a pair of armoured gloves. "Who was searching for me, Nessan?"

The young woman bit her lip. Despite her relative inexperience, as far as seniority was concerned, she was already fourth in command of the X Gemina. "Council officials working for the Doge. Apparently, they urgently want to speak with you."

"Get me two fighters. Please, get them quickly, Nessan, as I'm about to leave. The night's rapidly escaping us."

Kemet tried to protest again, but Ayilia was too quick. "I've known Lerang for decades; he's telling the truth. If the Heretics want this screwed up fire-bird, let them have it. The Goat's apparently so chronically obsessed with it that it's essential we steer well clear of it. With the Doge on our side, we can recall the Gemina and play for time with the Imperium, while we weigh up our options."

The door was kicked open, and a second figure entered the room. He pushed what was left of the boxes over in his haste. Traditionally framed, his face could at times be regarded as good-looking, when it wasn't crimson with shock, anger, or disappointment. Reliable when calm, which was nearly never, he ran on raw emotion. This was no exception.

"Ayilia, what the *living shit* is going on? I was already on my third bottle of low-level Prowler piss when someone tells me to mount my horse in the middle of the night and ride it into off-world Resistance oblivion. Apparently, we're to join those stave bashers and their failed war, just at the point the Imperial boot descends on their collective craws. If Soren's put you up to it, I swear I'll take this bottle and insert it in places he's barely aware of, and I'm not talking his ass."

"You heard?" she said, smiling wryly. "That didn't take long."

"You told the quartermaster you needed supplies for a year, not the usual weeks. You tell him we're fleeing this dust hole to join the Goddamned Heretics." He waved the half-full bottle. "Tell me this is just hogshit, Ayilia, so I can down the rest of this rat-killer in deranged peace."

"I hope you can make it, Aaron."

"I knew it." Swaying slightly, he flicked back straw-coloured locks from a skin mottled red with mead.

She shook her head at the irony. Considered unemployable, he'd eventually been shuffled from the regulars to the 'stiff monitors' of the X Gemina by a Panchayat who did not have the guts to tell him he'd been sacked. To everyone's disbelief, he'd proved surprisingly adept. Nevertheless, Ayilia had been distraught at his appointment. Years back, he had been, as the gossips cruelly put it, her first 'hump-junkie.' It made no difference to them that she'd mistaken the summer-long 'relationship' for something meaningful.

She acted swiftly, speaking before Aaron's jaw, which was where Kemet had sworn he'd once seen his mind, had time to work further.

"The Provost tried to kill me. Agelfi is back and told me that the Emperor Goat thinks my dream terrors can track a not-so mythical, wild beast with intense power, before it hatches and tries to kill Him. The Doge believes we can stop Barrik, but it has to be tonight. If we fail, we'll have to take the scant few Gemina and hope the Krayal will lead us to a secret passage off this world, up north. Once there, we'll help the few Heretics not nailed to a wheel in the Imperial Forum, find this monster ... then the Goat has us all executed, probably via crucifixion." She flashed a smile. "Coming?"

Aaron's drink-rubbered expression said it all. "I thought it'd be worse."

"I'll take that as a yes."

Ayilia walked to the wall, wrenched a ceremonial shield off in a cloud of dust, and strung it across her back. "If it all goes wrong, Kemet, we'll re-join you outside the city gates. If it turns out fine, then we won't need you at all. Make sure the guard at the gate is amenable to our unauthorized departure."

He nodded sternly. Aaron, however, had rediscovered his wits. "Wait, you're only just back, and now you want us to see those rancid, onion-smelling, ostentatious, gilded, teat-sucking, governmental skull-humpers at *this* time of night? How the merry hell wasn't I told?"

She tried not to smirk. "I'm telling you, now—let's go."

Aaron halted, face puce. "No one told me I was going to fight on an amphora worth of the sweet stuff." Both hands at his mouth, he crashed through the doors towards the latrines. Even from where they stood, they could hear him throwing up repeatedly like a gull's dying caw. At that point, Nessan re-entered the room and shot them an apologetic, pained look. "He needs a little longer."

Kemet, grinning ear-to-ear, turned and gave Ayilia his widest beam. "Guess I'm hired after all."

$$\text{\textbullet} \cdot \text{\textbullet} \cdot \text{\textbullet} \cdot \text{\textbullet} \cdot \text{\textbullet}$$

The glittering city was wrapped by a scarf of cool mist the colour of rust. It wreathed in and out of the white spires with diaphanous luxury. The gushing rage of the double waterfalls fell in quartz magnificence into a storm of froth far beneath as the stairs of the grand spiral staircase twirled silently towards the Panchayat council chambers overlooking everything.

A sudden surge of dread struck Ayilia.

The inner foyer was deserted. There were no locked gates, no nocturnal watch, no artisans on out-of-hours repairs on the walls or frescos.

She swallowed and motioned her group up the stone steps. The two X Gemina, Soren and Caleb, followed like stalking panthers, as did Kemet, bleak suspicion haranguing their haunted eyes. At the top, the four surveyed the passageway ahead. Flickering oil lanterns threw dancing knife cuts against their silhouetted forms.

"This isn't right," growled Kemet, sotto voce. His tendons were knotted like river rope around his taut neck.

She took a deep breath. "We'll go at the first sign of trouble. If this is a trap, we've bought the others critical time to get ready."

"That's the plan?"

She winked. "I like to keep things simple!"

The group slowly passed down the marbled halls towards the function rooms above the main parliamentary chambers. Broad swords were belted, while double-headed halberds and short, light spears were strapped along their backs. Kemet had brought his personal war hammer instead of the double-headed axes favoured by the Gemina. Their footfalls echoed in the oddly quiet halls. The passageways were dimly lit, the atmosphere dense and unwelcoming.

Panic played cat and mouse with Ayilia's gut. Had she miscalculated? Through a dry throat, she murmured, "Change of plan. I've seen enough."

"Not so soon, Regent. In here."

Although the voice was soft, its unexpected arrival in the monastic silence cut like buckshot. A man stepped out from behind the luxurious drapes of the spacious offices facing them. Her heart skipped a dozen beats. It was Barrik.

"Provost?"

"No, no, please; no need for formalities here. Anyway, it's Provost Elect, though that's largely academic now. Barrik will do."

"I should cut your pipe!"

"Always the man of judgement, aren't we, my trusted Kemet, the faithful sidekick. It's how it should be. I assume Aaron's too inebriated to join us?"

"I should show just how a faithful sidekick treats people like you." Kemet stepped forwards clasping his hammer.

Barrik grinned, though Ayilia could tell it was forced. Kemet could do that to you. "By all means, bash my scheming brains across these polished floors, but hear me out first, please." He turned into the ornate reception area just beyond. "It's far more comfortable in here."

Ayilia muttered something at Caleb.

He nodded, then began scouting the exterior rooms adjacent to the corridor.

Kemet and Soren waited tensely.

She leaned close and whispered. "Stay *very* close to the exit. Be ready for what the manuals call an organized retreat."

Kemet snorted in amusement. "You mean run for our skins."

She sent him a mock frown. "I believe I just said that."

They entered the room, eyes scanning. The scouting trooper returned with a 'nothing there' shrug. Both Gemina took positions by the exit. Encouraged, Ayilia went further in, followed closely by Kemet. Barrik's face creased with concern.

"Please enter. What threat am I? Take some seats next to those gilded ornaments. They are extremely comfortable, only the best leather. To think humanity scratched like beggars throughout the stars. Now we've created such glorious ostentation and filled the deserts with olive groves and sweetly scented herbs." He indicated to one corner. "Please, Regent, take that side sofa by these lanterns and exquisite porcelain vases."

The group remained fixed on the spot. Barrik's eyebrows arched.

"I know we didn't get off to the best of starts, especially considering your warmer relations with the outgoing administration, but we can always try again in the interests of our people."

Ayilia swallowed scorn. Her right hand subconsciously stroked her so familiar blade. "I came for the Doge."

Barrik rubbed flecks of spit from noticeably wet lips. His face shone with perspiration. "Must be important. After all, you've been preparing to leave in the middle of the night with *all* your few remaining heavies." He shook his head. "I must say this is a first. This city's never been completely emptied of X Gemina before. Could leave us exposed."

"To *what*?" Ayilia took a step forward. "Haven't you done the deed with the Imperium?"

The Provost's expression was a picture of discomfort, but he masked it with another stretched smile. "Nothing's been signed. We don't yet enjoy their protection."

"Where is the Doge, Barrik? Tell me now, or I'll do something I won't regret."

Barrik regarded her thoughtfully, then leaned back in his seat. His cumbersome fingers fumbled for a silver pipe, which he proceeded to light. It took five strikes, and he dropped at least two matches. She could see his hands shaking even from where she stood. "Threats and more threats, but if that's how you want to play it, Regent, so be it." His orbs gleamed metallically as his pipe finally flared. "Rest assured, the Doge joins us ... imminently." The smell of charred leaf filled the room. It was nothing like Agelfi's tobacco, though Ayilia hoped it might at least kill him. "Regent, your ancestors handed power over to people like me. You do understand that, don't you?"

Her nerves screamed at her to leave. "Living anachronism or not, I *was* ready to vote myself into oblivion, Barrik. It does not give you the right to barter all our hard-fought rights away, rubber-stamped by your well-financed goons." Ayilia looked around. "Kemet, let's get out of here; the whole thing's a trap."

"Wait!" Barrik leaned forwards, spilling tobacco across the plush seats. Cursing, he brushed them away. Tiny burn marks marred the gold-green fabric. "You should know that I summoned those self-same 'goons' *back* to the chambers despite the bloodshed you left behind and took quite a few of the council with us. We've already passed the laws giving me executive powers in their entirety. I confess it was gratifying not having the opposition there, but somehow, they were not invited. A highly unorthodox way of gaining control, but effective, wouldn't you say, and it means I don't have to wait for *months* of council due diligence." He was almost laughing. "I've had you removed. You're no longer regent. Your position is held in abeyance until further notice. From what you've just been saying, I'm guessing you're probably highly relieved to hear it. If not, I have a feeling we won't be hearing your shrill protestations about the 'protection' of the people for much longer, anyway."

Blood drained from Ayilia's face. "You can't take emergency control without my approval or the approval of well over three-quarters of every single parliamentarian elected. That's something you blatantly don't have, even with your majority."

The Provost leaned forward in his seat, the dank, oily sweat on his forehead a harsh red smudge under the light. "Unless, of course, the Doge *himself* puts forward the proposition."

"He wouldn't."

"If he's convinced the very security of our people is up for grabs, he would." Barrik's saturnine grimace filled the room. "Especially if the blade is sharp, Regent."

Pushing Kemet's protective arm out the way, Ayilia lunged at Barrik, fear and rage burning like jaundiced fireworks inside. "You extremist bastard, you've spent your whole twisted life hating everyone around you for your own lack of worth, replacing it with power and naked aggression." Her dagger thrust against his throat. His windpipe gulped against the hard metal. "God's teeth, tell me why I shouldn't stick this cutter right through your spite-filled neck."

Barrik half-screamed and pushed back against the seat to avoid the blade. A pitiful, squalid, but expected response. She hovered over him, almost paralyzed with venom.

Kemet put a firm hand on her knife-wielding fist. "Regent, crawling sewer-shit like him is not worth staining your soul. If you murder him, the city won't take you back. We can find the Doge and put this right before the sun comes up." He forced her hand down. "Trust me; you'd only regret it."

"If I was going to do it, he'd already be dead," Ayilia spat.

"We're gone." Kemet motioned to the two Gemina. "This rat comes with us!"

"Wait." She moved her blade so it aimed directly at the point between the terrified man's eyes. "Not without Lerang. You forced him into this, and I'm taking him with us." The tip of the blade dug into Barrik's skin. "Where ... is ... the ... Doge?"

Barrik edged around the seat and backed gingerly away. With precise, careful steps, he crossed the room to an impressive pair of oak doors.

"You want the Doge, I give you the Doge."

The doors opened with a low growl. A tall figure in a side room flanked by a platoon of militia stood looking at them. Their steel-ringed armour shone from beneath a red cape. The soldier stepped into the room and the light. A Lifeless. Their heavyset skull burned fiercely with the scarlet glare of their sight. Their strong, skeletal hand held something red and clotted. With a contemptuous flick, they tossed the bloody object across the floor, where it bounced with a thud and came to rest by a grand table. Splotches of gore trailed across the floor from a spool of artery just about visible in the murk.

"Behold the Doge," Barrik exclaimed triumphantly.

No one moved. Soren almost retched against the same sofa Barrik had singed.

Kemet put a hand on his shaking shoulder. "Not that I fault you, but not now."

The soldier's eyes were wet. "Not seen anyone beheaded before."

Barrik snorted. "Ha, the fearsome X Gemina, as they really are. They've only dealt with the Consul's dregs up to now, so we can't be too hard on them." He had his confidence back. He beamed garishly at Ayilia despite the blade still being in his face. "You wanted to succeed your father as a symbol of our people?"

Ayilia moved back from him.

"Ah, good, perhaps we can sort this out maturely."

She said nothing. Kemet roused Soren and Caleb. They silently formed a crescent behind her.

"I'll give you this; you've made your mark. You surprised all those who thought it a bad idea for such a witless role to be filled by a female. An unwed female at that and one from, historically, the wrong part of town, but they still hated you all the same. So, don't feel bad; there was nothing you could have done."

Ayilia shot the others a look. Kemet twitched a brow in response. The provost hadn't noticed their silent exchange, too busy making derogatory remarks.

"Millennia of war and struggle, Regent, and all that's happened is an eternity of death across the fellowship species that look like us! We can't ever win. The realms of the living have finally given way to the age of the Lifeless. Had we only accepted the Goat at the start of all things, but it takes little hindsight to acknowledge the opportunities were there for the taking before the bitterness took its toll."

Ayilia slashed her sword, cutting the air with easy strokes. "You speak of avoiding death, but what you've consigned us to is a living death, one in between the grave and the meat house."

The Gemina began backing away.

Barrik's teeth shone, sulphuric in the light. An unobtrusive, political garment hanger had morphed into something almost satanic. "They want you, Regent. They want you so badly it hurts." He watched them greedily as they neared the exit. "They don't care much for this city, but I must deliver *you*. I might even get an official posting in the Imperial Core itself. So, you see, you can't leave."

Shuffling issued from behind them. The hallway they had entered from was filling with militia belonging to the Provost, the few who had not fled. "There're too many, Regent. Shame your man failed to scout upstairs. I've already alerted the city's armed forces, courtesy of my executive authority. They will not serve you now."

Ayilia glanced towards the rear windows overlooking the piazza outside. The twinkling lights of the city glimmered indifferently beyond. Kemet and the guards took the hint and began to move over.

"Going somewhere, people?" Barrik smirked. "Plenty more behind me! You're surrounded. A great pity what's in your skull must be preserved, but that doesn't count for the rest of you, so don't try anything."

A figure in the shadows pushed impatiently into view. They dwarfed the Provost. "I've had enough of this," they said, scowling. "Your role in this is over, Barrik." They strode forward up to her, their face encased by a dark iron mask and a hybrid maze of antlers on either side. Kemet shifted the hammer to his left hand and unsheathed his blade with his right. Ayilia held her ground, her mind whirling.

A handful of Lifeless shapes in red robes abruptly thrust aside the hapless parliamentary militia and joined the giant. Barrik's mouth slackened. Red-faced, he whimpered up to the tall shape. "Our lord and master, the Emperor Goat, would not want her too damaged and may appreciate my expertise in all things human. I also know the ways of this city, a *critical* advantage considering your army is not here yet."

The warlord ignored him and confronted Ayilia. "Come!"

The Gemina were nearly in position. Ayilia gripped her blade tightly. "Why? The Pro Consul has no authority here."

"Pro Consul *Vespasian*? Ha! He hasn't the authority to mount a hog, let alone rule this carcass of a world."

Necromantic puissance fissured in white embers from between the giant's fingers. "Aside from that Imperial Arse at the centre of all things, it is my sibling, the Lord Mabius himself, who requests your attendance. My name is Otho. I can bring you whole or just your mind. Trust me when I say I have the wherewithal to do either, while the Goat has the skill to read it; it's your choice." His voice deepened. It seemed to jar the atoms in the floor beneath Ayilia's boots. The Lifeless sentinels fidgeted restlessly, glowering fiercely. "I know of the Mage Agelfi. Forget that mad monk's warnings. Even the Heretics tire of your mentor's ageing whine. The night has eyes even if you do not, and it most certainly was watching you."

Kemet had had enough. "Intolerable! We are *not* coming, not now, not ever."

Aaron would have been proud. It also gave her the chance to back up. Otho was not impressed, however.

"You talk far too much for a lackey, hume!"

The Sythian whisked out a pair of cruciform blades and flung them at Kemet. The man barely managed to duck. They hissed overhead and hit the floor in a trail of silver sparks.

Ayilia saw her chance.

She imagined Otho's smiling face concealed behind the mask. She imagined that smile freezing beneath its iron cladding as the dirk she'd surreptitiously slid free flashed across the poorly lit room into his exposed throat, with his guard and Mage shield down. She imagined time slowing.

It seemed to do just that.

He roared.

Though the dagger disintegrated, dark fluids flooded down Otho's neck. Cursing loudly, the Sythian enclosed the gash in a blinding flare of healing Mage fire, but the wound remained life-threatening. Simultaneously, half a dozen heavily clad legionnaires rushed towards the Gemina, accompanied by human militia, though a significant number held back. The Gemina sprung at them, blades arcs of light against the enclosing melee. The off-worlders ploughed through the tables and chairs, tossing them out the way as if made from match-wood, fleetingly letting their guard down in their urge to close the gap. The humans saw their chance and slashed the skulls of the first two before they could wield their cutters. The bulky bodies were propelled forwards by their momentum, their craniums spilling across the polished floor.

Their companions paused in disbelief, their features a picture of chiselled malignity. Barrik's hired hands, meanwhile, had frozen ingloriously to the spot. Two legionnaires hissed like basilisks slumbering on a warm rock whose tails had been inadvertently trodden on by a one-eyed ogre. They raised stubby swords. Soren and his friend were rapidly overwhelmed with a breath-taking array of flailing arms and glinting metal. Steel sheered against steel as the elite human fighters were forced remorselessly back towards the window.

Kemet landed a kick into the chest of one of the nonplussed militias, sending the man into his companions. True to form, most quickly fled, but two that didn't were cut to the ground. Another legionnaire rushed him, sword and shield raised. He whirled, hammer ready, but the Lifeless was too quick and strong. Her blade hit Kemet's own so hard he was tossed across the bodies of the two men he'd just felled. The soldier went to skewer him, but a sweaty-face militiaman gave out a sudden cry and rammed his halberd through her unguarded spine. Enraged, she swivelled on her feet, tearing the weapon from the stunned man's grasp and hacking it against his head. Disgusted, Kemet lunged to his feet and smashed his war hammer onto the creature's head while her back was turned before shielding his face from the pink explosion. She slumped across the dying body of the loyalist militiamen.

Mustering in almost fanatical zeal, Kemet swung the hammer in angry, lethal circles, sending human militia flying in all directions before lurching at the Lifeless facing him so he could rescue his men being savaged by another. With a hollow shout, he smashed the weapon so hard into his shield that it went skidding unceremoniously into a grand chaise lounge, knocking a frilly, pink lampshade over his uncomprehending skull. Before he could rise, Kemet swung the weapon into the legionnaire's midriff, sending white liquid plumes across his boots. He was left stunned, however, when the creature kicked him backwards and leapt nimbly to his feet, blade in hand, the gorgeously crafted, tasselled shade still covering his head. Flustered and disorientated, Kemet lunged again, but the Lifeless' sword blocked the blow. At the same time, his left fist slammed the Gemina directly in the forehead. Kemet was sent reeling backwards into his comrades.

Soren wasn't best pleased. He and Caleb were now almost pressed against the window's ornate frame. "Hell's nuts, boss; we can't handle ours, let alone yours!"

Kemet grunted a biting curse and tottered almost comically towards his adversary, his face wet with blood. Desperately winded, however, he collapsed against the still-grand chaise lounge, realizing, with a fair degree of horror, that he didn't have a chance. Mercifully, two more loyalists turned on the remaining militia, who were close to overwhelming the regent. The effect was immediate.

Within moments, their combined force sent the rest of them running for their lives, leaving the others in dark streaks on the floor. The loyalists immediately rushed Kemet's badly damaged legionnaire with their sumptuous headwear, but swerved with terrifying alacrity and floored them with their shield. Cursing maniacally, Kemet parried off a rainstorm of blows, but the Lifeless' strength forced him back, step after step, until there was no more room to retreat.

Soren's bloodshot eyes rolled. "Not you again."

"Can't believe that my last sight's going to be your ... pallid arse!" Kemet growled.

Ayilia had been fighting off nearly half a dozen militia single-handed. Her arms ached, and her hands were slippery with sweat and blood. There were wounds in places that she didn't know she had. Inhaling deeply, she ran towards the unaware legionnaire, kicking a small table aside as she did before slashing her broadsword down their right shoulder. Instead of falling as it was supposed to, the apoplectic creature elbowed her in the head and sent her to her knees, nose spurting red. With a last, cavernous groan, Kemet sidestepped and raised his blade against the distracted slayer. In an immensely gratifying manner, the head went flying as their heavy cadaver crashed to the earth in a shred of ossein and clunking armour.

Exhausted, blooded, but hugely relieved, Kemet raised his weapon at a wounded soldier who had risen uncertainly to his feet and who most certainly wasn't loyal, but Ayilia blocked his arm and barked at the man to run. He did.

"These are *still* our people," she said before helping the two loyalists up and instructing them to follow suit. They were far too wounded to be of any help.

She turned to the still-present provost. Barrik's eyes devoured her with pathological hunger, his hands clasping and unclasping a ceremonial stylus with vehemence.

Soren and the other guard were still fighting for their lives. With another urgent expletive, Kemet threw himself across the carnage toward them, swiftly followed by Ayilia. On the way, Kemet's foot caught on the body of an Imperial soldier lying on the floor in a mesh of sulphur-white, artificial gutting, and he nearly fell. Simultaneously, Caleb turned wordlessly around, his body sliding apart in sticky, bloody slabs.

With a howl of outrage, Ayilia was the first to drive her sword through the Lifeless' metal-clad torso, just they were about to dispatch Soren the same way. He swept furiously round and struck out with his gauntleted fist, but Ayilia ducked and thrust her blade deeper into his midriff with a loud and disturbing cracking of ribs. Defiantly, he managed to hawk a knot of manufactured phlegm in her face as a final act of spite before the glare turned to blackness.

Ayilia recoiled, then wiped her face clean before throwing Kemet a hearty grin. "I've had worse!"

He smiled grimly, then slumped against the walls next to a stunned Soren, breathing heavily. Ayilia tried to stem her bleeding nose at the bridge with her fingers as best she could.

No one spoke for moments. Everyone was too spent. She took in the forlorn sight of her dead Gemina. In that flashpoint of grief, she imagined Jarrak's grizzled face. He had explained on dozens of occasions that the only way to combat the lethal power of Lifeless opponents was the tight, mailed thrust of a disciplined unit. Always avoid direct dog fights, he would add. Avoid them the same way you would avoid "all the fires in all the hells," and under any circumstance, don't give them the chance to use their strength. His diatribe always ended with his favourite, most maddening, and most nonsensical phrase, "Otherwise, no one that lived was going to win, and no one that lost was going to live!"

Still grasping his savaged neck, Otho continued to flame the rents together like molten tin. As he did so, his body tightened with renewed vigour. No one had hurt him like this before, and he swore bloody revenge once the wound was staunched. A line of Imperial fighters formed a row behind the still-stricken Sythian. Looking entirely unruffled, they silently drew their swords. Any remaining human guard foolish enough to think Barrik was still in charge had melted away. A second file of Lifeless soldiery emerged from the room behind the oak doors. There was no way out; every exit was blocked.

Kemet arched his brow. "Orders?"

"Tell Soren to do what I'm going to do, though he won't like it." She leaned closer. "Otho's in charge here, not Barrik."

Kemet nodded, still wheezing. "He's a Sythian and a live one at that, unlike our good old Consul. He can take us all where we stand once he's finished healing that nasty nick." He folded his brow, wryly. "I've no idea how you sneaked that in, but nice play."

She swallowed back a blood clot, ignoring the nausea that went with it. "With killers like that, he won't have to even bother with us."

Barrik cocked his head. "Planning something?" He presented her with an exaggerated bow. "Is the honourable regent finally going to come quietly, or will the rest of her men be butchered too? No turncoat militiamen are going to save you out of the blue this time. Think quickly, Regent; my friends won't take any prisoners now that their so-called blood is up."

Ayilia inched further away. The others followed suit. Barrik's beady eyes didn't miss a beat, so she flashed him her very best, full-toothed smile. "You want the puppeteer that pulls your strings to peel my skull apart for a map that probably doesn't exist? Not going to happen, Provost, not just yet."

"I was hoping you'd be this stupid."

"Here I was thinking that you wanted me alive."

"There are various degrees of life, Regent."

A barely recovered Otho shouted a warning, his hands already flaming suns, but he was too late.

Ayilia nodded at the others, turned, and propelled herself through the stained glass windows in an explosion of twinkling shards, haloed by the Sythian's energy charge screaming overhead.

The drop wasn't far, yet she landed with a heavy thump on the piazza overlooking the glimmering city below. Staggering upright amid a descending rainstorm of glassy fragments, she backed off into the darkness, blade raised towards the window, boots cracking loudly on glass. The other two Gemina sprawled in undignified tumbles nearby, within clouds of glittering debris. Stumbling haphazardly to their feet, they swiftly took positions on either side of the central fountain with its ancient mermaid lounging upon a pile of books of law. Ayilia almost laughed. It was intended to symbolize the freedom and responsibilities of ethical government, though she couldn't recollect what the mermaid meant.

A heavy shape landed with finesse before them. As they uncurled, Kemet flung an unstrapped war axe from his back into their fleetingly exposed neck. They hissed acidly as the blade made contact, the wound deep and fluids fast flowing. They staggered against a large ornamental tree for support, where they were bathed in a beautiful shroud of white petals.

"Bonehead should've landed a little further away," Kemet muttered.

There was a crash as the Lifeless' companions did exactly that. One's foot went straight through a stone birdbath, where it remained solidly stuck. They slammed their leg down to wiggle it free but only succeeded in ricocheting a stone sparrow into the head of their companion. The others regarded the humans through bloody eyes, then gave a hollering, soul-jarring shriek in unison and charged. The one with the birdbath followed suit with lumpy strides, though some paces behind.

The harsh clattering of heavy weaponry was interspersed with resounding clangs of Kemet's other axe. It ruptured a nocturnal stillness normally challenged only by the churning of the waterfalls.

With sharp cries, minotaur bats abruptly took wing in blurred flitters. As the Gemina retreated towards the falling waters, the crystal dome that encompassed the seat of government came into prominence with impotent grandness. The stone chambers, hallways, and private offices of the officials and council members were quiet and now henceforth pointless.

"Here, now!" Ayilia screamed.

She and the Gemina rushed to a line of ornate railings at the piazza's periphery overlooking a vast drop below, leaving bloody droplets in their wake. The main entrance was, at least, an unnerving one-league down. The waterfalls were roaring loudly nearby.

"Down argue."

Soren shook his head pitifully.

She grabbed the man forcefully. "*See that?* That pylon has notches. They're big enough for our boots but too small for them—we can scale down. I've been here a million times, and I know the layout inside out."

"I don't like heights."

"I've *never* liked heights, but you're still going."

A glazed look of mild terror rolled across Soren's eyes. "It'll collapse."

"It supports the whole damned thing. The waterfalls are *redirected*. Don't tell me you thought this was natural?"

Kemet bellowed for them to hurry. Red slits were erupting over his body from a flurry of glinting blades. He was in danger of being skinned on the spot. Ayilia thrust Soren angrily over the edge, courtesy of an armoured boot. The Gemina yelped like a pup, then flung himself across the divide, clinging to a strut opposite.

"Kemet! Jump!"

She jumped into the fray long enough to relieve the pressure so the bloodied man could fling himself in exhausted relief over the rails. As she turned to go, something went off in her head. Time seemed to slow, as it had when she threw that dart into Otho's throat.

The churning waters ground to a crawl, and the bats hung mid-air like bleak decorations on strings. In that momentary delirium, she felt the unassailable, indomitable power of Otho as he prepared to flail Mage rage at her exposed back. She caught a glimpse of Barrik's globular features working into a sweated flux at the far window, looking for all the world like a bulbous caecilian but without the charm. If she got away, his precarious credit with the Imperium would be irrevocably shattered.

He was a dead man perspiring.

For that alone, she was determined to live.

Flashing a grim, blooded smile in Barrik's direction, Ayilia backstepped over the railings as the Sythian's fiery shot rocketed nearby, followed by the unmistakable shape of the birdbath. Muted curses in undecipherable Nethergeistian accompanied her downwards. Her fingers clawed at metallic indents so rusty that they crumbled like scabs beneath her fingers. Hands immediately reached out and pulled her inwards. Swinging her legs over an iron parapet, Ayilia landed uncertainly before her blooded men, weapon tightly gripped in her left grasp.

"I thought you'd be right behind us, Regent—hell, I was just about to come back up."

"I *was* right behind you," she wheezed.

"You place too much stock in your swordsmanship," Kemet muttered, reminding her of Jarrak yet again. "Those things are killers—they could rip a man apart with their bare fingers."

"I'm not a man," Ayilia said in gruff amusement. She patted her blade before sheathing it. "And they'll only rip us apart if we drop these."

Soren was gingerly bathing his wounds in water from the deafening falls and tying strips of ripped tunic around the worst of them. A look of permanent panic stained his face. "They'll get to use their fingers soon enough and just about everything else. I know immersion in water pisses them off, but we're pretty screwed if we stay, and worse if we go. They've got us cut off."

Ayilia found herself smiling. Soren was a good fighter, but he lacked the one thing the Gemina relied on most: courage. She had promoted him because other than Aaron, Kemet, and herself, he was one of the best sword-wielders they had. It had helped somewhat that he wasn't groggy on grog.

"We're not dead yet, Soren," Ayilia breathed. "I learned something while stuck here half my life, being lectured to by the wind-bags back there."

"How to give speeches?" Soren asked, perplexed.

"Yes, we'll just blab our way out." She scowled at him in disbelief. "No, the escape route. The dilapidated, cobwebbed one they never use, in case of fire or attack! It takes us down an internal metal stair the other side of the waterfalls."

"Handy," Kemet said. "But they will consider it soon enough."

"Then we must be quick before they find their way through this churn. Come on!" They followed Ayilia as she made her way to an oxidized maintenance door close to the thunderous froth of the waters. With enormous effort and three to four hefty kicks, she finally forced the rusted object open. After bolting it shut, they pounded through the bowels of the edifice with its grand stairs and defunct parliament above, their boots clunking loudly in the dark silence. Ayilia avoided the main thoroughfares, instead taking them down dim passageways to the auxiliary administration offices, then down worn steps at the back to a wooden side door.

"Locked!" Kemet bellowed.

"It's always locked," she muttered. "After all the fun and games, it slipped my mind."

Kemet pushed past and flung an axe. The mechanism shot off sharply, cracking against a wall before jangling loudly to the floor.

"That'll do it," he grunted, clearly still in some pain.

"It also has the worst woodworm. Sometimes, it pays to have inefficient government." Ayilia kicked it open, and they burst into the semi-dark in a tempest of dust. She led the bloodied duo, and they knocked over crates, iron tripods, and stand-alone lanterns in their haste. A pair of stiff inner doors were busted open in much the same way as the others. Candlelight streamed through from what appeared to be a crescent-shaped room. A thundering clamour of armour cascaded across the walkways on the level above.

"I thought we were in the backwaters here," Soren whined. "Who lit the fecking candles?"

Ayilia shrugged, exasperation overtaking fear. "The caretaker?"

"Perhaps they'll think we took the front way out?"

"If they had no brains ..."

"They don't. Well, not living ones anyway."

She exhaled in an attempt to mask rising panic. "They'll have it covered, Soren."

"So that's a 'no' then, in regard to taking the front way out?"

Ayilia grunted noncommittedly and took them through and down into narrow corridors hewn from naked rock. Echoes pinged from all directions. Raised voices and threats mingled with the sounds of pursuit. Ayilia flattened herself to a wall to listen, then peered round a corner, hoping her memory was still accurate. Sure enough, it was, except for a full complement of armed militia waiting by the stairs.

Kemet, sweating profusely, regarded her quizzically. "More?"

"Human! They're not Barrik's men. They probably don't have a clue about anything all the way down here. In fact, they shouldn't be here at all. Copy what I do."

His dark hand gripped her arm. "Not wise!

"Anyone got any ideas? I'm certainly listening."

The heavy thunk of Imperial soldiery approaching left little time for debate. He shook his head. She nodded, sheathed her blade, and pulled her tunic, greased with wine-red blood, as straight as possible. "Good as new. Alright then, take my cue."

Sweeping around the bend, she walked purposefully up to the startled troops gathered by the only escape route available and raised her hand in a relaxed, languid salute. Kemet and Soren hurriedly followed suit. They looked more like highwaymen than X Gemina. The guard drew their weapons with a collective hiss.

"At ease," Ayilia said.

They stared uncertainly but didn't move. "There's been an attempt on my life. We only just made it. The others have them cornered upstairs, but the main exit is blocked. I'm going for reinforcements. You *must* cover us; the entire city is depending on you."

Sounds of approaching chaos filled the space: clattering and people shouting. Noises were rising from the lower levels too. They were going to get cut off. There were around twenty soldiers blocking the exit, too many to bypass, especially in their weakened condition. Mind whirling at light speed, Ayilia confronted the commander face to face. His expression was hostile despite his pallid complexion.

"Have I not made myself clear?" Anxiety made her voice twang, but it didn't seem to register with the guard. He was more concerned with orders. "I am your anointed regent, and I am *demanding* your assistance."

Though his voice was gravelly, there was a slight, nerve-induced stammer. "I must ask you to remain here." He nodded at one of his troops, who immediately ran off down the walkway. "We've had *implicit* orders to detain you. You can't leave; rest assured, the Doge will quickly sort it out."

Then came a series of crashes. A door slammed against the wall as the killers spilled into the lower level, though still out of sight.

Ayilia fought to control a raging urgency. "The Doge is dead. The people I am going to have arrested are the people who killed him. His head is still several levels up, gracing the floor of the grand offices he used to work in. The people who ordered you are the people who assassinated him. I am next. Do you understand?"

The man stared in mute horror. She repeated the question.

He gave a curt nod.

The sounds of pursuit were shockingly loud.

"You are an appointed official of this government. I am the senior military advisor from the House of Kiya and head of the ancient order of the Gemina. That makes me the nominal head of that government. You have a duty to enforce the security of all members, and that specifically includes *me*. I also am empowered to direct you during times of extreme emergency, and this is *precisely* one of those times. With the Doge gone, there is no one more senior than me in a military emergency. With such authority, I am *ordering* you to stand aside and offer your sword."

He stood facing her, trembling visibly. A ricocheting succession of ear-splitting crashes indicated their corridor had been breached. He tried to speak, but she immediately cut him off. "You have been misinformed, soldier. It can be sorted in the city, tonight. I can go nowhere; there is nowhere to go. It happened before, *remember*, or have you forgotten Regallion? Do you want them to get us this time round?"

"I ..."

"Move!" she yelled.

The man froze. Taking this as her cue, Ayilia shoved past, closely followed by the others. Kemet glowered at the guard as they passed; Soren blew a kiss. For two short, conflicted breaths, the man stood, deeply torn. As the glittering Lifeless soldiers swung into view behind, he turned and followed.

"Ma'am! Ma'am. I cannot allow this; the orders were indisputable." He thumped his chained hand on her shoulder. "Ma'am!"

Kemet swung his elbow into his face, sending him to the floor. Two others were also sent sprawling as Soren and Kemet lashed out with expertly timed blows on their helmets.

Ayilia raised her broadsword and aimed it at the others. They backed away.

Soren shot her a sly glance as they began to sprint toward the exit. "Didn't know you could fart piss?"

She shrugged haplessly. "Nor did I."

"Stop them!" roared a lumbering, skeletal powerhouse in a guttural cry that reverberated in the confined walkways. It slammed through the dumbstruck guards, sending them scattering, and seven more appeared behind.

Steps flew past in a blur as the human renegades careered down the emergency stairwell, banging into walls and railings and sending forgotten tapestries and unlit candle holders flying. Minds set to automatic, they flew downwards, arms and legs blurs of movement. A dream sequence of walls, faded pictures, and drapes passed in a blur. The approaching exit juddered around the edges, such was the speed of their flight. With absolute disbelief, Ayilia saw another contingent of befuddled militiamen warding it, turning to face them.

With the roar of a man who'd had just about enough, Kemet exploded into an armoured ball of mindless fury. He avalanched into the terrified group, tossing them in all directions. They were even more conflicted than the guard above and immediately fled into the dark, their weapons strewn in all directions. Ayilia and Soren thumped after Kemet and smashed into anyone still tottering in their path before slamming the door shut after them. Swinging wildly in all directions with no intent of serious harm, or at least of killing anyone, they bolted away and clambered unceremoniously over the governmental boundary wall. Only when they reached the outer gateways and the main central avenue of the city did Ayilia glance back.

Nothing.

Chapter Seven

BREAKOUT!

K emet came to a skidding halt. Bathed in an extra skin of congealed sweat, dirt, and blood, he looked closer to the afterlife than the people he'd just been fighting. Soren was still running, except it was more of a drunken trot. He wavered like a little boy coming last in a school sack-cloth race.

"Soren," Ayilia gasped. "We've left them ... far behind, at the perimeter."

The fighter stopped and bent over, both hands on his thighs. "Don't ... believe it."

"The Lifeless don't want to be visible in the city, not just yet. Every route will be cut off soon, though. We have to go, *now*."

"What's the point? They're the undead. They can run for ages—it's why they're called the Lifeless and not the 'slightly-alive' or the 'not-quite-finished-off-yet.'"

"The others will be waiting with supplies packed and horses ready, but we have to be quick, as the new government will be after us too." She snorted without mirth. "Ironic. The city falls to a coup by the same people already running it."

Soren straightened, eyes wide. "Hell's elbows, the army backed *you* when Regallion dragged her undead bony ass up to our walls. They can do it again, mobilized or not!"

Ayilia wiped her gloved hands down her ruined tunic. She preferred to keep her palms dry to grip the blade she'd used in anger more times in one night than in her entire life. "We were in charge then. Barrik was, briefly; now it's Otho. He doesn't even need our insidious lithography industry, the city scandal rags, to back him up with boneheads like that on every street corner. As for our esteemed army, they just tried to butcher us back there."

Though he was still panting, Kemet grimaced. "*Screw the army*! Remember when their officers came to the annual Festival of Spring, four years back? They ended up eating all the ritual offerings before the speeches had even started, then brought it up all over the last Provost, along with their root mead! I hated them. I'd rather invite a stiff to the next one than most of the grunts in the regulars!" His eyes gleamed with conviction. "Seriously, they have better table manners."

Ayilia wasn't listening. "Tell me I'm not imagining things!"

Kemet and Soren looked up. The latter whistled with admiration. "Where the hell did they find Prowlers?

The red eyes of the Lifeless mounts were unmistakable even from that distance, but they couldn't see the riders clearly.

"Those things can go forever on just a little gruel. I'd swap horses any day for their dead alter egos. They must have jumped some legionnaires while we were in there."

The Prowlers were nearer now. Even in the pitch black, something didn't seem right.

"Not so sure about this," Kemet said softly.

"Not our boys then?" Soren blurted, scratching his butt a little too forcefully.

"No, Soren, the trap's not only been set; it's already shut. The whole city's falling." Ayilia replied.

Kemet's brow arched. "They must really want you bad!"

They began to run again, ducking and weaving between the labyrinth of narrow alleyways until the blurred shapes on Prowler-back were no longer in sight. Eventually, Soren started to complain about his wounds with some justification, but Kemet, also heavily wounded and dangerously spent, politely told him to shut up. The reply was righteously indignant.

"With all this grief you give me, you're lucky I'm around to save your butt, *Commander*."

"Soren, you forget that I'm normally the patient one. It's Aaron who sits on everyone's spine and whines."

"Except at you."

"I'm his friend."

"I don't know who comes out worse."

"Alright, kids," Ayilia snapped, endeavouring to motivate legs constructed from dough. "We're at the rendezvous now."

☻ · ☻ · ☻ · ☻ · ☻

The city's walled ramparts were close. To Ayilia's immense relief, the portcullises were raised, and the gates were open.

It only meant one thing.

Aaron had persuaded the guards to allow the Gemina to pass on "emergency business." Clearly, Barrik's men hadn't reached the walls yet. Maybe the Provost would be gibbeted from them by daybreak. She smiled with grim satisfaction at the thought.

A shout came from behind her, followed by a chorus of charging hooves. She spun around. The Prowlers had spotted them.

The Gemina ran the opposite direction, clearing the inner Peace Gates, the symbol of 'friendliness and trust' between an inadvertently freed colony and its adjacent master. A row of onyx statues nearby honoured a siege lifted only by the violent resurgence of the Heretical Resistance in a last-ditch effort to eradicate the Empire. It was now an overgrown monument, an overlooked tribute sprayed with bird droppings. They hurriedly crossed the bridge overlooking an almost empty but glimmering moat, but there was no sign of life.

Aaron wasn't there!

Soren cursed. "Aaron's stitched us up. Just as we're about to be run down by Imperial tree trunks on four-legged gargoyles."

Kemet regarded him with something like disappointment. "You can get cut down on the run if you like, but I will die facing them." He shot Ayilia a glance. "I assume this gets the seal of approval?"

Ayilia could only shrug. "Do we have a choice? They're too fast."

Prowler hooves were hitting the cobbles with such venom that stones shot like bullets in all directions. The lead rider charged directly at her, its mount's orbs miniature supernovas.

Ayilia raised her sword.

An achromatic shoal of darts hummed overhead, impacting the towering riders heavily. They toppled like gypsum mannequins in a series of resounding crashes as their mounts veered off at sharp angles. One tried to stand, but waves of arrow and slingshot filleted it where it stood. Head daubed with fluid the hue of pitch, the Lifeless sunk to tjeor knees and then face with a quiet thud.

A familiar figure came running towards her, lost in a vortex of wild, flying hair and curses, his handsome features predictably contorted with splenetic redness.

"God damned Lifeless goons in our city. It may have turned to crap, but it's *our* crap, and they've no business riding those red-eyed turds all through it like it was their personal privy. Maybe they're as strong as renegade gods, but nothing can withstand a hail of Gemina shot like that, I swear, *nothing!*"

"Aaron," Ayilia tried to look annoyed but was too relieved to make a realistic go of it, "Where is everyone?"

"Here, where else?"

He nodded towards the nearby foliage outside the walls, all the time fighting back his mop of billowing hair that, in his haste, he hadn't tied back. Amid the riot of gold and red, she caught glistening silver. She hadn't noticed just how much he had these days. It suited him. "Can you believe we saw *more* of those things threading their way to the Panchayat, Ayilia? We were so freaked out that we were actively debating coming back to get you, despite your orders. They're not like the withered Pit dorks we've grown fat on here; they're the real thing and as life-threatening as one of Soren's—"

"Don't go there," Ayilia interjected, sheathing her blade. There was a motley smear of bloody marks on her skin, but she was too spent to scrub them off. "God, am I glad to see you, though." She shot an anxious glance back at the city. "However, we have to leave while we can."

"*Leave?*" His mouth dropped open. "What about Agathon, for God's sake, Ayilia? I know we're pitifully low on numbers, but once we rouse the barrack grunts and the government's dozy apes, we can scourge these knuckle-scraping zombies from every rat-stained cul-de-sac before suns break. We can't just abandon our people."

"They've abandoned us," she retorted. "The regs are already under Barrik's control, courtesy of some mightily unfortunate emergency powers, and *he* is under the Pit's control, courtesy of a Sythian lunatic called Otho. Until Otho kills him, that is, which has almost certainly happened already."

Taking a deep breath, she faced Kemet. "Take Soren, find Nessan, and prepare for immediate departure. We're right behind you."

They nodded and hurried into the dark in the direction that the Gemina firepower had come from.

She turned back to Aaron. "What happened to the gate sentries? Don't tell me the Imperium killed them?"

"Oh, those lusty hogs." Aaron shrugged.

She furrowed her brow and squinted. "You didn't?"

"Kill them? *God no.* The guardS are trussed up in the guardhouse latrine where they're happiest. That's what you get for denying us our right to pass."

She smiled despite herself.

Encouraged, he went on. "Still doesn't explain why these stiffs are sticking their gleaming craniums into our business all over the city. Hell's shuddering colons, it's a *blatant* disregard of Treaty."

"It's *us* they specifically want, not the city, Aaron."

He crossed his arms over his chest. "I'm not going to abandon it all the same."

"It's why we must go. You know, to avoid the inconvenience of being butchered in our boots—which won't help anyone. We ride out north. If we make it through the night, I'll tell you exactly what's at stake here. Until then, please, you just must follow."

The rose-speckled skies brightened into bloody smudges of menacing puce. Shadows stretched the silent group of fleeing humans into skeletal fingers. Ayilia deliberately traced the main roads. Despite the extreme danger, everyone understood speed was critical. Distance was their friend, at least until daybreak proper. Ayilia also gambled on something else: the flawed brilliance of their adversary's arrogance. To the Imperium, she was the toothless descendant of escaped helots bereft of experience, and that suited her to the ground. If nothing else, they'd underestimated her.

It also revealed just how poorly everyone perceived her, even the vast, Lifeless, meta power of the Imperium.

The gently sighing spruces were giving way to olive groves and white-grey eucalypti. Early morning scents rose from glistening roadside flowers, pristine in the first moments of dawn.

Am I really worth this sickening bloodshed?

To take a city on the edge of nowhere was an outstandingly futile waste of Imperial resources. To take it out because of a powerless puppet was beyond any definition of cruelty. The only positive was that Barrik's head would surely be joining the Doge's. Ayilia had toyed with resignation for years, even before Lorelai had left her. She closed her eyes and inhaled deeply.

Flashes of Lorelai's hair strewn about her chest as they lay next to each other in Ayilia's bed, and the sweet smell of her skin, an intoxicating mixture of local berries and hawthorn cream mixed in the apothecary stalls in the markets, nearly overwhelmed Ayilia. God, she had been obsessed with that woman. The urge to enfold her in the tightest embrace and, more importantly, to be enfolded, was overpowering. The regency was her legacy, but it was also her cross to bear, as it left her lonely for someone other than the Gemina for company. Now, it was being taken from her by political personalities as ethical as a rancid god. Her fists curled and uncurled repeatedly on her reins.

Her father would be sickened.

What had she done but submit to roles constructed by others for the benefit of the spotlight? The last thing the world needed was another half-dimensional political clown. The only thing time she'd flared into a living symbol of resistance came at Regallion's expense, and the Lifeless had been but some burnt-out official. All this since her father's funeral, literally the day before. She shook her head, allowing herself to become lost in grief and bitter anger.

The damned Lifeless had assumed she'd be the biggest push-over in human history! With the help of their human collaborators in the parliament, the newly activated Pit had infested the centre of government with Lifeless berserkers. Though the 'lame duck female' that was the regent had helpfully flown a roost that no longer cared, it nevertheless had been an expert takeover. Had Mabius, with all his raging, necromantic puissance been there, she would've been a goner, but Otho should have been enough. He was, after all, a Sythian too. Though it was still a close call, at least that would irritate him.

She smiled to herself, but satisfaction couldn't begin to take the pain away.

"We need a decoy."

"Eh?" Ayilia looked up.

"We need a decoy!" Kemet repeated. He'd surreptitiously drawn alongside her horse with his own. "The longer we stay on this road, the greater the chance of being overtaken. In fact, it's a certainty."

"Aye," Aaron said, pulling up on her other side. She felt politely ambushed. "Bloody bastards have Prowlers, too."

"Already on it," she replied. "We'll send a rider ahead with some spare pack animals. They'll leave a false trail for quite some way. Hopefully, if there's any pursuit, they'll follow, even when we've forked away. There's a hidden divergence around here I haven't used since I was a kid."

"Can they mask the tracks of the entire unit, though?"

Ayilia flashed a hollow smile. "We're in orderly file, aren't we, Aaron? Our tracks are as narrow as Barrik's neck, should they hang him. It should do."

"That's why you insisted on two-a-breast!" Kemet said, eyes gleaming. "We just need a volunteer now!"

"Cymar Hookhand is ill," Aaron said. "Stupid git drank too much, and he has a fever. If that wasn't enough, he claims his piles are acting up."

"Again?" Kemet growled. "I know it's no laughing matter, but they seem to be acting up every expedition we take lately."

"I suspect it has something to do with beakers of swamp whiskey." Aaron grinned. "He's been on it a lot lately!"

Ayilia didn't know whether to laugh or cry. "Okay, Cymar is perfect then. He's hardly going to be much use to us on the run until he sorts himself out anyway, is he? Tell him to take the loose mounts in ... that direction?" She pointed towards the horizon, due south. "By nightfall, he'll hit that remote Gemina outpost on the purple plains. It should give the credible impression we're beefing up both our supplies and numbers. Of course, it's nowhere near where we're going." She leaned up in her saddle to squint. "I'd say the hidden track's around here somewhere. I'm betting everything on the fact no one knows about it, certainly not the Panchayat anyway. They don't get much further than their local top-class, state-funded watering pits. If the sweepers do their usual job, our tracks off-road should be invisible."

◦ · ◦ · ☠ · ◦ · ◦

158

The group watched with grim expressions as Ayilia rode around the verge of the road, prodding the dried shrubs with her blood-stained blade for the path. It had been decades, but she claimed it was close.

After a few minutes, she hurriedly rode back to the others. "By the way, tell Kymar to spread the word to our people throughout this world that there's no point in resistance yet. Those that want to start again in the new order of things, that's fine. Those that don't, can go and wait it out in the mountains or go down deep south where your family is, Kemet." She paused, fighting back surges of fierce emotion. "If we don't get back in twelve months or so, then they'll have to make their own minds up."

Otho was likely so close he could smell the stink of their sweat, but even if he had guides from the city, it wouldn't do much good. The Gemina always kept the operational details of their past manoeuvres quiet in case the Pit's tottering grunt brigade caught wind that they were coming. As far as she was aware, no one had used the track since her father brought her decades ago. Jarrak had known, of course, but Jarrak was dead.

Her chest constricted yet again in pain at the memory of a past now completely eviscerated. Though she hid it well, her mouth was nothing more than a tight, bloodless knife cut.

What of Mabius, the superbeing of superbeings? The heat and lack of sleep were feeding her paranoia, but was he close too? Otho's strike unit was small and light; it had made sense to deploy it first. Mabius' was likely much larger but significantly slower. Her stomach lurched with he growing certainty that everything Agelfi had told her may just be true.

Lurch.

There it went again. Her enemies said she was nothing like her father. They said a woman couldn't lead. Here was her first proper war, and she was already in full flight, like the gutless, fraidy-cat milksop the back-bladers always hissed she was. Once, her insides would've ridden out the aridness of any desert, the worst tempest at sea, *and* ingested the most noxious roots in the field. Now, she wondered if it had been better if she had laid the false trail instead of Cymer.

Ayilia stabbed furiously at the foliage, looking for signs. The track was within touching distance; it was all coming back.

The Imperium was squeezing out every ounce of blood to find out where this cosmic serpent, the Al Kimiya, was spawning. They didn't care what it cost, how many lives were lost, or the devastation incurred. They wouldn't stop until its empyreal footprints in the so-called welkin vault were traced and the thing butchered. In a universe so upside down, so twisted back to front, it was almost no surprise a human, incapable of thaumaturgic ability, was to be used to track a beast that had too much.

Gulping back the need to throw up over her already ruined boots, Ayilia impatiently beckoned at the sweepers. The track, if it could be called that, lay among thick gorse directly in front of them. All traces of passage—the sweet-smelling horse muck, every broken twig or flattened blade of grass—would seem to continue on the road as before. Cymar's decoy horses, providing his condition held up, would leave no break in the hoof prints. By the time the pursuit reached the outpost, Cymar and the guard there would have vanished, and Ayilia's merry band would have done the same down this track. That was the theory anyway. Unless they brought dogs.

Dogs! She cursed under her breath, then almost laughed. The Pit had no animals alive or Lifeless capable of smell, while the city's dogs were so well fed and underused that they could barely find their way out the gate. She doubted Otho's advanced unit would've even considered hounds in the negligible time they had to prep. There would be no dogs. The sweepers had some peppered herb that harmlessly but effectively blocked the most persistent canine snout. In fact, it could block any snout.

Time to think of other things.

☠ · ☠ · ☠ · ☠ · ☠

Wispy scarves of discoloured vapour shrouded suns the hue of curdled blood. The Gemina quietly unfurled their weathered capes from small cloth packs to lie on. Others gathered over tepid tea, as sizeable, smoky fires were out of the question. A lake, its surface the contour of polished mirrors, refracted their silence with a solitude all its own. Though no one seemed to be following, the troop talked only in a light murmur.

Ayilia took a deep swig of tea. They had made it from the cold, clean waters of the lake. It washed down some unappetizing jerky they'd eaten, leathery rind sparingly garnished with old peppercorn. The dust on her face from the day's ride had dried into jungled canopies of ruptured lines. Despite the warmth, she huddled in her cape on the dry soil, staring at the thick fronds of a nearby plant, pondering whether it was a strain of cactus. The tears rolled again. No one seemed to notice, but even if they did, she didn't care. Her father had rotted for decades with the thaumaturgic virus. She should've been better prepared for when his time finally came, but the pain only got worse. Not only that, but other memories came flooding back on the jagged spine of the hurt.

Decades ago, when she was in her early twenties, she'd found a handful of butchered workers in a field's water system and a party of nonchalant Lifeless auxiliaries nearby. The pallid faces of the slain stared back up at her out of the ditches that their own blistered hands had dug. These were the wilder days, when the Pit's unexpected isolation was raw, uncertain. Days when Sulla's rule had been passed to the new Consul, Vespasian, who was still no more than a footnote in his own non-existence.

Ayilia had kicked up an official stink. Unexpectedly, the Pit had immediately complied. They'd removed the soldiers from all duties, even having them 'decommissioned' on a permanent basis, Imperial lingo for 'scrapped.'

This new Pro Consul clearly hated bother.

It wasn't enough. She had considered going the whole hog; she had considered liberating the human colonies once and for all. However, the Panchayat refused to authorize armed insurrection, and the Gemina were simply not numerous enough to even dream of trying. When Agelfi had quietly mentioned that it might bring the Empire back like a rat up a sewer pipe, her hopes tasted their own death. She'd got used to acting under restricted circumstances like everyone else, including, it seemed, the Consul. It was hard to tell who was the puppet and who was the master, but that was the way everyone preferred to keep it. If the Goat returned, there would be no winners. Jarrak had popped up with one of those sayings no one understood, "Why fight to wrestle more privilege from a fiefdom indifferent to a power they don't actually wield?"

Or was it Agelfi?

She quickly buried that thought, but it made her realize one thing—this new Pit, since Abandonment, was as muzzled as she was. Despite the rumoured suicidal decline of the Consul, some of his local chiefs in the field were, initially, another matter. Arrogant, self-important, they could self-aggrandize till the suns went down and came up again. These vipers were the ones to watch. One regional tyrant had created his personal slave plantation replete with beatings, torture, and lashings so frenzied that the witless victims were left as dead as the guards. They were the ingredients for one hell of a shit storm. These were the days before inaction, when shortages and liquor rotted already rotting brains and inertia had sapped the willpower to dominate. Fuming and terrified, she'd hurriedly gathered all the X Gemina and wiped out the whole outpost as they coiled in the Lifeless version of light slumber. She could still see their bony fingers stained with the blood of their victims as they lay there truly dead, their twisted tongues hanging out like slugs.

The Consul had issued orders to his subordinates to preserve the peace, but one or two local hotheads had reconsidered their fidelity to a Pit administration, viewing the Consul as going 'soft' on the female helot. They wanted her head. In a state of managed panic, she'd approached an older, more stable Lifeless governor in a nearby sector. She'd offered them the only thing they cared about: the acquisition of the fertile province of the garrison she'd slaughtered. Ayilia had leant close to their bony carapace and delicately whispered, in the part of the skull they used to hear, she would support their claim. It was her right as regent, a complicated by-product of Treaty.

Baleful orbs ablaze with greed, they petitioned the Consul, told him the hotheads were planning sedition against the state. Ayilia was their official witness. The other governors were promptly hauled up and executed by the Consul.

They'd never had a problem again, not in that sector. The governor simply got richer and, unbelievably, fatter; seemingly an impossible feat for an undead.

☹ · ☹ · ☠ · ☹ · ☹

That night Ayilia slept the sleep of a traitor. Nightmares flitted with ungodly speed across the backs of her eyes, but within her mind, there was only the faint imprint of culpability. The dawn tinted the horizon with scarlet cuts. Almost imperceptible wisps of crimson cloud swiftly faded as the blinding suns rose one after the other. Their morning rays speckled the boughs of the groves, haloing the long, waving grass with a soft shimmer. Buzzing insects and magenta butterflies frisked on the pinpricks of flowers. For a heartbeat, she felt glorious. Then, the feeling dimmed like a candle burning out its wick.

They rode on.

The suns were high, and the horses were steaming. Steam coiled over their rich, dark coats. A stream trickled through hills specked with wild olives, staggered at intervals along the ochre earth. By late afternoon, the trees had dispersed into a series of broken trunks, each the epicentre of a network of tapering roots. Nessan rode halfway up the column monitoring everything that moved, clanked, or clinked. Aaron let out the occasional curse, seemingly at nothing. Clammy sweat, itchy dirt, and star-burn had put him in the mood from hell.

"Ayilia, time to stop. Nags need resting."

She lolled her head over to him, wearily rubbing her neck as she did. "We need the high ground. There we can see for leagues in all directions, and the Dreamveldt is nearby too."

He wiped his face impatiently. "I don't like risking the mounts unless we have to."

"We won't know if we must or not until we get to the ridge. There are three different routes we can take once there to evade whatever's hunting us."

"How can anyone be hunting us when this route was meant to be secret?" He held his hands up in resignation at her answering glower. "Okay. But don't forget I call the shots should they start to lag. That's how we've always done things."

She screwed up her nose in wry, irritated amusement. "You know you can put me straight when you need to, any time."

He grunted something unintelligible.

Ayilia leaned over in the creaking, hot leather saddle weighed down with weapons, provisions, and bags and shouted back at the column. "We are not going to stop. It'll take a little longer, but I promise we'll get to rest properly when the time comes." She paused. "Nessan, did you get that?"

"Aye, ma'am!" hollered a distant voice.

She turned back and stretched. Aaron swatted a fuzzy blue fly in a bout of pique, and it splattered in his eye. He let out another curse. Kemet's head was turned to the west, scrutinizing the foliage. He hadn't relaxed since they left. The three commanders rode together at the front silently until Aaron began cursing the insects.

Herbal wreaths smothered the reaches of the approaching rises with smears of velvet. Icinthias, rockamist and beech helm, Indigenous to the land, vied with lavender, rosemary, and other imported strains. Most had remained precisely as they had been before replanting. Others had mutated into startling hybrids, such as the spiny acanthus now garishly splayed with brilliant explosions of indigo blue and scarlet. Butterflies and brightly splashed insects flitted languidly within the gently stirring canopy of rustling colour, despite the remorseless heat.

Ayilia looked at her now bare arms; they'd already darkened in the suns. Her black hair, with its wisps of silver, fell in unkempt tresses. She sighed and tugged at it with barely concealed futility. She'd murder for a chance to wash and then soften it with nutmeg oil spiced with the sweetly-scented bells weed from the southern spring plains.

She sighed, again imagining putting Barrik's head on a spike before Otho did. Somehow, it always cheered her up.

CHAPTER EIGHT

ASTHEN YESTERYEARS; UNDEAD TODAYS

The small unit presented a dark smudge against an expanse of orange scree. They thundered toward the arid horizon on their Prowlers, who were oblivious to the scalding desert. Their minds were fixed on the imposing peaks ahead. The days were a blur, their nights without slumber. Meals were sporadic, Imperial mush, but that was non-life. What leaves the few trees had left loitered on hangmen branches. The semi-dead atmosphere was enough only for an ecosystem on the very edge of existence.

Vespasian led the charge, his recently crucified frame visibly scarred and maimed. From time to time, his body wavered, threatened to fall. Stilgen would lean over and thrust him back. What the Sythian understood as pain was gone, but his body was a wreckage of lacerated slashes. The shimmering sentinels of the mountains had barely moved in the distance. Even for their non-souls, it was getting painful. As they began to despair of progress, the ranges finally leapt forwards as an obstructive haze cleared around the faint peaks.

The Lifeless machines of sinew and muscle effortlessly supported the heavily armed soldiers. Their Prowler hides clung tightly to their titan bones, like shrunken shrouds over pumping cogs. So powerful were they that the living sought them as much as the dead. Miniature whirlwinds scythed across a sky made of mountain and vapour. The panorama was so striking that Vespasian inhaled deeply into lungs that could not work and marvelled. The dizziness returned, and for the hundredth time, he slumped in his seat and began to fall.

☠ · ☠ · ☠ · ☠ · ☠

Aaron steadied his horse on the brow of the hill and surveyed the panoramic valley below. "We're here!"

Ayilia and Kemet joined him. Though the slopes were hardly mountainous, they could see for leagues across the dips and plains beyond with stunning clarity. Villages and hamlets nestled serenely among rolling wealds and the patchwork quilt of barley fields. There was no sign of danger.

"Unexpected," Kemet murmured with an edge to his tone. "They should've boxed us in and cut off all hope of escape. I can't see anything moving at all!"

Aaron's suns-damaged face regarded him quizzically. "How can they cut us off when they don't know what route we took?"

"They know where we're going."

"For all they know, we double-backed south."

Kemet gave it some thought before noticing how silent Ayilia was. He always noticed. "Why the long face, ma'am?"

"Look over there."

Their expressions remained blank. "Nothing!"

"Exactly! *Nothing!*" Bitterness boiled up in a wave of pent-up emotion. "I lost our last city, and for what? Nothing! We should've stayed, given them a fight!" Kemet and Aaron shot each other wry glances; nevertheless, she couldn't stop herself. "We weren't worth chasing; no one came at all. It's a ruse all along;

take our people out with the minimum of fuss, leaving more soldiers for the off-world front. We *must* go back."

Kemet shook his head, dislodging faint clouds of dust from his shiny dome. "If we'd stayed, we'd be meat chops by now, and you'd be their thrall to the detriment, apparently, of the whole universe; not that I understand any of it. Don't forget, *both* Barrik and Agelfi believed in this stuff, and they're on different sides."

Aaron shrugged his shoulders wearily. "If you want my opinion, screw the lot of them!" He took a deep swig from his pouch. "Let's face it; they didn't think we'd even get out of the boozer in time, let alone vanish. So, let's let our hair down and relax at least tonight. The only way they'll cut us off is if those Lifeless butt-bashers have been this way before, and that I *seriously* doubt."

"He's got a point." Kemet yawned. "This path's so dead it doesn't look like ants have used it, let alone people."

"That's because ants aren't that stupid." Aaron took another swig of water. "The size of that invasion shocked the hide off our collective buns back there, so it's okay to be a little rattled. Soren must have voided himself ten times over when he clapped eyes on that fleet."

A cold dread descended. Ayilia's head shot up. It felt as though something long buried had slapped her across the face. "What did you say?"

Aaron looked nonplussed. "Soren has weak guts?"

"The *fleet*! As in a fleet of ships?" Ayilia replied disbelievingly. "Exactly *what* fleet are you talking about?"

Aaron flicked back his hair as though he'd been struck, brow furrowed in stark amazement. "Back there in the city ... surely, you saw it?"

They stared at him, dumbfounded.

"You couldn't miss it so high up in the falls. I mean, I assumed that was part of the reason you folks were so publicly soiling yourselves coming to the gates?"

Kemet's brow creased. "We were too busy keeping our heads attached to our spines to notice anything other than the dozen stiffs chasing us on Prowlers! There was no time to see squat, even in the chambers."

Ayilia's throat clenched. "Aaron, truly. We didn't see anything."

"Gnat's blubbing teats!" Aaron swept his fingers through his locks in astonishment. "We saw an entire fleet of obsolete scows sail serenely, as you please, right up the harbour. No port cannons were fired; no warships sent to give them a hug. From my viewpoint on the gate tower, I saw platoon after platoon of freshly armoured boneheads disembark on the quays. We were frantic with worry until you showed up on the tip of that stiff hunting party."

"A fleet," hissed Kemet. "*Of floating junk.*"

Aaron shrugged again. "Must have come up from the disused dockyards deep south. It's not as though the Pit has a navy, and there wasn't time to build one from scratch. Not one of the fortified sea defences opened; not a peep."

"The defences were stood down." Kemet scowled. "Our government mongrels sold us out and then laid over to have their well-fed tummies tickled like a pickle."

"Most of them won't be so well fed now." Ayilia inhaled sharply. "Otho must've gone straight from the first ship in his urgency to intersect us, probably *way* before the others arrived. Talk about timing."

Aaron cursed in wonder as he heroically fought with hair, now in a spate of rebellious chaos. "The clapped-out fleet must've been behind schedule. Remember, it was way past bedtime by the time you showed up from that old wizard's lair."

"Aye," Kemet grunted. "Hardly seems it, but a spot of luck all the same. Had they arrived earlier, the Panchayat would've been rammed with them. As it was, Otho only just made it before us with one shipload."

Aaron was seemingly at war with his wayward follicles, pushing his hair this way and that. His eyes shone with savage fury amid his glowing burn. "The others were probably busy infiltrating the city, neutralizing a guard already neutralized by their own incompetence."

"The city is fine for now," Kemet said softly. "Aaron's right: we should try and get some rest."

"Okay," Ayilia agreed. "Barrik will rot in hell, though. If the Imperium doesn't send him there, I'll find a way. You can count on that."

Kemet smiled acidly. "Oh, I think he's already well on his way, Regent."

$\cdot\ \cdot\ \cdot\ \cdot\ \cdot$

Achromic worms of writhing light crawled in zigzagging patterns across the portal's circumference as the Raiders threw themselves in. Someone yelled at them to hurry. It had to be Sheyna.

Barrackus stared in silence into the gate's howling maw as more dark forms stepped towards the fiery portal. On the brink of infinity, their silhouettes shone as tangerine auroras of astonishing virulence. He thought he saw them fleetingly smile before vanishing into the thing's throat, each suddenly a billion sparks of quantum fireworks. Barrackus grinned. Turning back to the remaining Raiders, he gestured them to follow, then stepped in himself.

Hiss.

Somewhere far away, the exit gate they'd targeted began vibrating. Its lens shimmered before rupturing into azure brilliance. Gyrating fields stroked the contours of a spacious room beyond irradiating outwards from the vortex.

Hiss.

For fleeting moments, the exit convexed. The bulge of light juddered then plumed violently into a silver cloud of Asthen Raiders and mounts. Muscles bunched against the unexpected harshness of the landing, and voices cried or cursed. Fingers, numbed with delicate films of portal ice crystal, groped for staves. The armoured centipede of broiling figures breached the glittering threshold onto the floor, ready to kill whatever was waiting beyond as the photonic whirlpool behind.

Abruptly, it closed.

A grinding screech resounded in the room as the lens blanked out, and there was silence again.

A mount snorted. People began whispering. Someone barked orders.

Sheyna again.

Asthen shooters immediately took positions behind the vanguard. The area around the portal was filled with impatient animals and fidgeting warriors. Soft steam from the quantum chaos of the funnel rose quietly from the bodies of each heavily breathing shape. Raiders aimed their thaumaturgic maces in all directions, expecting an ambush, but all that could be seen was the faint glint of something gold in the distant darkness. Most of the sorcerer maces were re-holstered, but the few heavy-duty veridian staves they brought with them remained cocked. Veridian staves were another class of defence altogether. Each was attached to special crystal containers on the fighter's back; each was connected to transparent tubes through which pumped highly volatile tannan juice. The juxtaposition of the liquid with the holder's carefully wielded necromancy could eviscerate anything or anyone on the spot.

Swiftly dismounting, the steaming commander bee-lined toward the team leader, Lars, and surveyed the scene.

"Are we secured?"

"Yessir."

"Enemy?"

"No sign of opposition, or life, for that matter. Seems we're alone."

"That's debatable. Keep monitoring all the same. Adira, can you give cover?"

"Aye."

Barrackus patted Lars on the back and made his way to Andromedus by the exit portal. The Dust Tracker was already crouched over its controls, working intently. The bulky figure delved through a case of assorted plasma tools and removed some metallic divining rods liberally splayed with mathematical symbols. As he waved them across the now silent, infinite doorway, the rods started glowing. Barrackus watched him for long moments.

"Anything?"

The other pointedly didn't look up. His excitement was gone, and his shoulders were slumped. "Nothing. We're either truly alone in this lost universe of portals, or they've camouflage abilities *way* beyond Asthen technology."

Barrackus inhaled slowly and held his breath for several moments before continuing. "I don't think things are quite that bad."

There was only a grunt for a response.

"I assume you're trying to plot a way out; gain some distance from that mother of a gate we jumped back there?"

Andromedus rubbed his face. When he answered, his voice was soft but held an edge. "That portal we entered, the one surrounded by Wirral, is the problem. We jumped into oblivion without proper prep, at least by my standards. The first place it took us to had almost no oxygen—it was so old and disused—so we had to re-jump almost immediately, again without preparation." He got a dirty cloth out and wiped the grime from his face. "The static interference caused by illicitly jumping so many people in one go is stopping us from trying again right now. It's the same problem we always face, of course, but this time we're lost because, as I said, I did no prep."

Barrackus bent to his knees to hiss sotto voce. "We *have* to leave, old friend. Not only are we off target, but hanging around in massively powerful, inter-spatial wildernesses like this invites almost certain sanction."

"Don't you think I don't know that?" Andromedus rasped icily. "But illegal piggy-backing on Imperial signals causes horrific static for units numbering more than half a dozen. It's going to take a while for this gate's disturbance to subside. I can't navigate in this white blindness, not until the fuzz has died down." He finally met Barrackus' stare. "Look, Commander, we could jump legally, but that would immediately alert Imperium Trackers. They'd intersect us within heartbeats."

The commander was lost in thought. "I thought it *was* possible to blind jump during a static whiteout. We haven't always waited for it to clear like this."

"Oh, it's possible alright, providing you don't mind ending up inside a sun. We've said this before. Gates are indestructible—it'll go right on working even in the heart of a star, if that star happens to have swollen and consumed the world the gate was originally standing on." He snorted. "Maybe you fancy appearing at the centre of an Imperial polo match or a very nicely run gulag. It could take us to the realms only demons are said to hunt. That's the rub; if you don't want to risk a very probable death, we wait until the static clears. It's impossible to navigate and plot a course otherwise unless we do it on official channels."

Andromedus leaned back and scratched his butt, as he had a habit of doing these days. Perhaps it was the stress? Barrackus' lids flickered, but he held the other man's gaze. It was important to let the Tracker work his frustration and stress out at his own speed. "Sorry, boss, it's either stay here and wait, or travel openly, and that just wouldn't be advisable. We'd be lit up like a firework. The network officials could bring down another ten thousand Wirral on our collective bones with the crack of a cosmic whip, or maybe worse."

Silence reigned as Andromedus continued to tinker away with the device. Soft blue lights pulsed from his instruments. Barrackus straightened. People were milling around taking defensive positions, but eyes flitted hopefully in their direction. Decisions needed to be made.

"Understood," he said, eventually. "I've done this long enough, destroyed things for long enough."

Biting his lip, the Tracker looked up. His voice was pinched and tense. "Well, maybe that's where we get lucky, Commander. Inconvenient though this static is, it *masks* our signal just as much as it ruins navigation. That's why unofficial travel is so illegal. No one can see a damn thing in the fuzz! Normally, I prepare a flight plan in advance so that I know where we are. Generally, I'm in charted space if I can't, so I *still* know where we are. That means we can jump as many times as we like, even in a whiteout. All that counts for squat in a spatial void such as this, one that has never been mapped, at least not by us!" Andromedus cleared his throat. "We are so blind right now; the only thing I can tell you with any certainty is we are far from charted space."

Barrackus regarded him evenly. In full flow, Andromedus was suddenly only too happy to press his point. "If there's good news, it's that I scrambled the controls on the Wirral gate before we jumped. It means they couldn't lock onto our coattails, our signal if you like, before the gate closed. I mean, let's face it, they were *that* near—they could've seen our cosmic wind even in the static." The Tracker involuntarily sniggered, then immediately reverted to his stony glare. "It's more than likely Imperial Central Command will think we beat a hasty retreat to our own lines, like any self-respecting unit would this deep. That gate was big enough to find a funnel elsewhere. Instead, we went into forbidden territory, and now we're here, *two* jumps in. I don't need to mention, however, they still haven't cracked our stealth techniques—that's something." The Tracker's mouth tried, but failed, to crease into open satisfaction.

"Good news all around then." Barrackus turned to go.

"... not quite."

The commander paused. He'd heard that tone before. "I think I've had my fill of news, good or bad, for one day."

"Then this won't help. The enemy may not know where we are, but we have no idea where *they* are; by this I mean our target." He bared his teeth. "I lost whatever dubious intel approximations we had just getting us out of that static storm before we were ripped to bloody chunks. That's why no one ever jumps into a knowledge void, Commander, let alone an *unparalleled* enigma like this."

People stopped shuffling. Every ear was tuned to their conversation. Barrackus felt them watching like moon hawks. "Surely, there's something here you can extrapolate for guidance. Instructions? Maps? Something in the controls even?"

"It was one of the first things I checked." Andromedus flicked grimy hair from his forehead. "I've *never* seen such an astonishingly exotic gate; we have three in a row. What the hell domain is this?" His hammy fists clenched in anger. "It doesn't make sense, but according to these schematics, I think the gateway's master controls are located roughly a league from our position, down that way." His throat constricted. "This place might be high-class Imperial, but the layout's down to the Ancients, so you can thank them for the decor. I'm pretty sure that's what these controls are indicating, unless I've gone completely zippo."

Barrackus choked. "You want me to sanction a scouting party to some nebulous point one league away? *In this realm?* We may as well string ourselves up!"

"If there's something out there capable of harming Asthen scouts, Commander, they're just as capable of harming us. Besides, this fuzz's so bad it'll likely be days before it clears, and I can't risk another blind jump. Until then, we're completely lost, and to be honest, even if I get my bearings, we'll probably still be lost!" He wiped his clammy hands vigorously down his arms. "Regardless, I *must* have access to the primary controls, or I can't penetrate the static lock-out. If you don't send the scouts, we either wait two days and hope that no one shows up or risk a jump into the heart of a singularity or the emperor's bidet."

Barrackus glanced at the milling troop. "Primary controls it is, but it won't be a scout party; it'll be *all* of us. We're not going to get separated in the heart of a sub-space nightmare that's not on any charts, in the armed bowels of the Imperium."

Andromedus nodded and heaved himself to his feet, grunting with the effort. With highly-controlled purpose, he began putting the tools back in the box. "Okay, boss; not much I can do here anyway." One after another, the devices went into his bag as though each was a work of art. When done, he fixed his worn eyes on the commander. "Right now, the warning is going out across this side of space that there's a Raider hit force in town, the most lethal of the lot.

Command Central, our target, has never *once* been located, let alone attacked. Maybe we should cut our losses while we can?"

The other gritted his teeth. "You worry about the targeting; I'll worry about the target." He leaned close, and the Tracker flinched. "Right now, there's half a dozen fellow units out there, decoys all. They won't go nearly as deep, but it'll be enough to send the Imperium's best legions completely the wrong way. It's *imperative* that we camouflage our footfalls before they realize we're already halfway up their backsides instead of halfway home." The Raider Commander turned and strode away.

"To think I gave up having a family for this," Andromedus sighed to himself.

As Barrackus shouted at the troops to ready themselves, boots stomped past Andromedus. He looked up to see Sheyna storming toward the commanders with Adira close behind. Uncharacteristically, Sheyna hawked across the shiny, hard floor, a habit she always detested in others. She had to be in a particularly foul mood.

"Don't tell me, Barrackus, that we're lost. What's the point of all this funnel-jumping crap if we're going to get screwed with each twist we make off-grid? All that shit about that demon-infested lock back there ... *please*." She also detested people who swore. She found it cheap and vulgar. The fact that she did it all the time seemed to be utterly lost on her, but her mood was really terrible. "It stinks of tavern gossip. If Andromedus has a trace, why can't we just follow it?"

Barrackus shook his head. "Sheyna, look—"

"It's alright; most people can't get their head around Dust Tracking," Andromedus cut in, moving to her side.

Sheyna frowned at him but didn't berate his interrupting. She might be another aristocratic arsehole, but she wasn't like the others. She wasn't like anyone Andromedus had ever met. The more time he spent in her company, the more he noticed the majestic way she handled herself. She was magnificent.

Andromedus tried to explain. "I was just telling the commander, Sheyna, how empyreal pinpointing in the dark is still an undefined art. Some call it magick, but it's simple quantum divination. Every particle influences another; every cosmic fingerprint leaves its trace as information somewhere in the atomic calculus; it's just a matter of following that trail. If we tried some highly controlled mini jumps, six bodies at a time, say, the disturbance would be minimal because the mass is minimal. I estimate—"

"Estimation being the main problem here," she cut in abruptly. "We can't file a flight plan, and we have *considerably* more than 'six or so' fighters. I'm not stupid, Andromedus; most of the destinations are dangerous, but we don't have time or the luxury to advance in pigeon steps, either. In plain Asthen, we're buggered."

"It's better than being utterly screwed," Barrackus murmured.

"It's better than getting poked in the ear by an Imperial trident, but that doesn't help us much!" Sheyna retorted.

Andromedus tried not to let his smile deepen. He felt a strange pleasure when he saw Barrackus had noticed.

The Tracker spoke quickly. "What I wanted to say, ma'am, was the more we jump, even if they're all shock-inducing emergencies like this, the more we fill in the background dots. It gradually gives context to a dark and unknown area."

"For the love of all that crawls, growls, and defecates, just admit we're lost! If this mini-universe of covert portals is so damned special, why haven't our esteemed leaders back home seen them lit up like supernova on their projections?" Sheyna raised her shoulders in exasperation. "Why do people like us have to risk our guts filling the blanks in? I want to blow something up, not crawl in a cosmic sewer."

Andromedus swallowed. By those heathen gods of yesteryear, she was a goddess! "Our erstwhile boffins couldn't see a red giant in their own eyeballs, even after it went off. We're in a completely different kind of space, maybe another dimension altogether. One intricately woven *within* the atomic framework of the interstellar network itself. I need time!"

"I wish our people had travelled more," Adira mumbled unexpectedly. "Before the wars reached our systems."

"That's what being insular gets you," Sheyna said without bothering to look at her directly. "Now we reap the benefits of being historically parochial. Millions of portals, and we stayed put waving our flags of self-entitled isolation!" Her eyes bored into the Dust Tracker. "Just get us out of here, Andromedus. Science or sprites, use what you use; I'm not bothered." Looking decidedly unimpressed, she stalked off, angrily gesticulating at fighters to get into position.

Barrackus watched her go pensively, then turned to face his Tracker. "Okay, it seems discovery is apparently the consequence of whatever decision I make. You are sure the passage ahead and not those two is the one to take?"

"Aye."

He frowned. "Any particular reason?"

Andromedus raised his brows in mock surprise as though the answer was the most obvious thing in the world. "It's the main one!"

Barrackus didn't respond.

"We're not in an armed fort, Commander."

A junior officer bustled over and spoke into Adira' ear. She looked up. "Skyron's taken an inventory of lost equipment and drawn up a casualty list, sir. We're ready to take on anything that might be lurking further inside if that's what we're doing."

Barrackus nodded. "That's what we're doing." He straightened his armour, still glittering with portal ice, and approached the waiting troop. Perspiring, the Tracker hunched over, packing his tool kit into a military backpack. A shadow fell over him: Adira. Maybe it was the weariness, but he regarded her with mild suspicion.

"Problem?"

"Well ... no, well yes ... I was wondering?"

"What?" he snapped a little more gruffly than he intended.

"How did you know this place was even habitable when it doesn't exist in any known record? Don't tell me you guessed?"

He smiled. It felt strangely pleasing to be the only portal hotshot literally in this part of the universe. "Biosphere conditions are often invisible pre-jump, Adira; however, the Ancients breathed the same crap we do, so most destinations should still be habitable. Fortunately, the Imperium *also* breathes what we do, so to hit an almost airless world is astonishingly irregular, to say the least." He snorted. "At the end of the day, the odds were better blind jumping in a knowledge void than becoming the filling in a Wirral sandwich. But I wouldn't dream of doing that again unless I *absolutely* had *no* choice." Andromedus slung the pack with a loud thump along his shoulder and stretched. The stress was doing his back in.

Adira wasn't quite done. "This world could've been another trap, though?"

He rolled his eyes. Something about her grated. Compared to Sheyna, she was wan and insipid. "Adira, we're further in than anyone's been before, now is *not* the time for rookie naivety."

Adira's face reddened. "I'm not one of them, you know; I was born a commoner too. I had to fight to get where I am like just everyone else, so you can stuff your self-appointed smugness up the next portal we meet."

She stormed off. Andromedus shut his eyes and clacked his forehead against the gate. "My family would've left me anyway."

"Attack Formation Juna," Sheyna's rich and throaty voice rose from a distance. "This is a completely unknown prefecture, so look sharp."

❧ · ❧ · ☠ · ❧ · ❧

Barrackus and Sheyna led the way. Though the major officially reported to the commander, she had become, to no one's great surprise, largely autonomous.

Only the stupid or the ignorant risked her ire; it was easier to let her get on with it. The fact that she was the best Second in the entire Ascendancy was an undeniable help. Captain Adira, the Third, followed, co-ordinating the heavy firepower of the veridian wielders, their packs sloshing with lethal tannan fluid. The Fourth, Captain Lars, brought the main body. Lastly, the rear guard was headed by Captain Skyron, the Fifth. The mounts were being led separately behind the unit. Moving through the tunnels mounted on such huge beasts was clearly not practical.

The passage had widened into a copper-hued, stannic expressway decorated with archaic script of unknown origin. Diagrams juxtaposed with text were both beautiful and unnerving on the walls. Neat, tidy, and metallically precise, the golden vista hinted of splendour and undefined threat.

Barrackus' wiped his hand on his already-grimy tunic and straightened the war armour in a futile effort to stop it rubbing against his neck. He turned to Sheyna, but she was first off the mark.

"I know—goddamned hot."

"Too hot to hack a Wirral's head off." The commander shot a glance back at the troop. "Adira?"

"Yes, Commander?"

"Keep the shooters primed. Weapons might slip in this heat. Their support could be critical."

"Way ahead of you, boss."

He smiled. She smiled hesitantly back, then immediately dropped her eyes.

Sheyna brushed delinquent strands of hair off her forehead with an irritated swipe of her hand. Somehow her chestnut locks still looked pristine despite the violence, heat, and the static-charged interstellar hikes. "Tunnel forks off ahead, Commander. Which one do we take?"

Two routes jutted off in opposite directions. A third extended ahead into blackness. Despite the curves, the corridors maintained their steely hostility.

"Left. Always left at junctions here."

Both commanders turned to face the speaker. Andromedus had joined them, again. When Barrackus asked him to explain, he looked puzzled, as though the answer was obvious to anyone but a fool.

"That's where the signs point."

☠ · ☠ · ☠ · ☠ · ☠

Once their Dust Tracker was expediently ushered back into the relative safety of the unit, the commander sighed inwardly. Besides his techie's prickly manner, something was disturbing him at the periphery of his heightened psyche, but it was impossible to say what. Sheyna's eyes were darting like wildfires; she was clearly uneasy, even by her standards. The intertwining tunnels ahead were unblemished by anything the corrosion of eternity could throw. Nothing moved.

Maybe the worry was misplaced?

Attack and retreat, slash and burn, speed and death: these were the Raiders' specialties, their calling cards. Years of rapine destruction had wrought as much ruin on their collective souls as the charnel factories, garrison outposts, winding supply convoys, and military citadels they'd vaporized. In this war, blood came in all colours. It left a rainbow's worth of butchery on their blades, and it was set to get worse.

He'd heard whispers that something quite different was coming, something the Abomination was planning. Rumours and prattle were normally things he left to the weak-minded, but this was different. The Imperial beast legions were to be phased out. Unreliable, dangerous even to their own side, the replacement of such highly volatile troops was long overdue. What blew Barrackus' mind was what was to come.

Automatons.

Armoured death on two legs!

No heart, no life, no soul. It beggared belief. No one knew outside the Ascendancy's top brass, but out in the field, people picked things up. The authorities did what was best, what they always did. They treated the people as children, a resource to be manipulated. The population was to be lied to and infantilized. So much for civilization. The future would be an armoured cadaver with its organs tapered together by iron clamps and its fake guts welded into place by industrial flame. No one wanted to know.

"Ahead ... *there*," one of the scouts gesticulated.

"What is it, Gorlan?" he asked.

"I can hear something ... sounds like machinery. Can't quite tell, sir."

"What do you think?" Sheyna whispered when Gorlan was out of earshot. The side arm's face widened in surprise when he didn't answer. "You *always* know what to do, Barrackus, and it always works ... except for the Crystalline Waterfalls." Her eyes twinkled with amusement. "I'll never forget that."

"You always bring that up!" he huffed. "How could I know it was the 'pool spirit's' sacred outhouse? It was just a waterfall, for God's sake."

"It never moved, Barrackus, that's why they called it 'Crystalline.' And the thing they worshipped was buried inside the falls. It was no trapped god, but one of those Magi serpents that got buried when the falls used to be liquid, God knows how." She jabbed him with her finger playfully. "But I did at least recognize what it was."

Barrackus shook his head in bewilderment. "Those falls must've been hit by some wayward sorcery from the time of the Ancients. I hear the Core's infested with it."

She was grinning. It was a rare sight these days. "The locals didn't know that."

"I didn't either."

"You soon did when the thing actually woke up, broke free, and bit you on the ass."

They laughed.

"I still have that mark, you know," he said.

"Sometimes it's nice to know you're fallible like the rest of us." She was still smiling, yet the gentle barb did not go unnoticed. The soft sound of pumping machinery filled the space. Sheyna's look hardened. She was a literal walking war machine. With a shake of her head, she beckoned Gorlan over. He was closely followed by another fighter.

"Private Gorlan, Private Dayla, scout ahead. Check the place out. I don't want us to be ambushed again."

꠸ · ꠸ · ꠸ · ꠸ · ꠸

Gorlan and Dayla nodded and left the group, hugging the walls as they moved. There was a palpable flickering, an almost imperceptible glow of distant light. An octagonal entrance faced them at the far end of a long corridor.

Dayla stopped wide-eyed in her tracks. "Shh," she hushed. "I think I saw movement in the far corner."

Gorlan laid his sweat-caked head against the immaculate wall, straining for a better view. The sweat on his slick, black hair misted the surrounding metal into a wispy halo. "I don't see anything."

"It was up there, I swear it."

"Dayla, I was looking the whole time. I've seen shapes just about every turn but only mind tricks."

She shot him a fierce glance. "Don't patronize me; something was *definitely* there."

He held his hands up, keeping his voice as controlled as possible. "It's this place. It's so claustrophobic it's doing our heads in. Jumping through oxygen-starved worlds and fighting overly hirsute bone-crunchers has brought us close to the edge."

"Anything's better than Wirral, even this hole," Dayla said, shuddering. "They're just so goddamned vicious."

"I'll go and check it out," he whispered, eyes gleaming. "If you say something needs checking; that's good enough for me."

Her smiling response was brutally sarcastic.

Gorlan stuck one finger up in her direction, then winked. He approached the doorway and gingerly peered round the side, staring for what seemed like an eternity. An odd helplessness rose in Dayla. Her knuckles went white against her hilt.

Gorlan disappeared.

Dayla felt her stomach lurch. Without thinking, she crashed down the passageway, stave raised. Gorlan faced a voluminous room, his open jaw slack in quiet awe. A giddy plethora of translucent tubing, blighted at sporadic intervals with dripping green fluids, ran past their heads into a staggeringly complex matrix of glass repositories. Beneath twists of interwoven silver pipes, lay a vast, translucent tank. Dayla had the sense of a metallic leviathan feeding through its metallic, tubular mandibles. A soft, background thumping permeated the cloying air.

She whistled. "God's teeth—I never realized they had such technology."

He flicked back his hair dismissively. "It's primitive under the surface. Look at that archaic pumping system and those phials next to them. Simple pressure mechanics, probably from those volcanic vents down there. Explains why they need this spot. The only reason they're here at all is this secretive portal network, and that was built by the Ancients and not these assholes."

She wasn't remotely convinced. "I don't know, Gorlan. We're behind this sort of thing—our specialty is—"

"We'd better get back. Sheyna'll want to know about this!"

"The Ascendancy will *never* make it to the Core. No one has since the Interregnum." Dayla suddenly flinched. "*There*! Did you see it? Over there."

He spun around and scrutinized the direction she indicated. This time, his voice was more measured and respectful. "Honestly? Nothing!"

She shook her head. An indescribable cold had descended despite the heat. "Stay here and worship that thing by all means, but I'm out of here."

Clearly deciding it was best not to be left on his own, Gorlan hurried after her. Shooting furtive glances at the impressive ceiling, they hurried back, running into the others as they skidded around a corner. Sheyna regarded them bleakly.

"Trouble?"

Dayla could barely breathe. "There's a *vast* atrium ahead heaving with slush and tubes and an enormous transparent receptacle full of stuff, maybe fuel for weaponry."

"Breeding fluids," Gorlan corrected. "That's my guess anyway. Could be for Wirral, Proto-Goblin, or Mutant Class legions, or something equally dangerous."

Barrackus' eyes were dark slits. "We'll investigate briefly. I must caution that Central Command remains the priority here. What about guards?"

"We've seen no sign of sentries or barracks, but ..."

Sheyna leaned forwards. "What, Dayla?"

"I kept thinking I saw shapes darting around the corners above our heads. Probably hallucinating. This shiny catacomb is getting to me."

"Did you see it, Gorlan?" Barrackus asked quietly.

"Well, quite a bit going on there. Hard to say."

Sheyna stepped up to him and put an impatient, red face against his. His eyes popped with discomfort. "We *don't* have the time. Quit protecting her; she's not a child. Did you or did you not *see* anything?"

He didn't stand a chance. "Er, no, not really."

"Don't piss around with our valuable time next time I ask a question. Our collective butts depend on it. *Understood*?"

"Yes."

"Yes, *Major*."

"*Yes, Major!*"

Barrackus cleared his throaty. "Okay, good work. Dismissed."

"Sir." Relieved, they hurried back to the troops.

He faced his side arm. "Looks like we're going in."

❦ · ❦ · ☠ · ❦ · ❦

Outside of the chugging pumps and clanging hammers, nothing moved. The spaghetti conurbation of wiring feeding the glassy nucleus steamed and vented, but there was no sign of life. Barrackus' gaze roamed slowly and carefully across every kink and cranny, every razor-straight angle, before hovering on a mechanized panel of pulleys and gilded levers.

"See anything?" Sheyna breathed.

"Nope."

"Why don't I believe you?"

"Not sure. Why don't you believe me?"

She smiled grimly. "I don't know. The hesitation. The usual flickering of your lower eyelid. The fact that you sound as guarded as a pack of cloud hounds."

"Ha ... that obvious?"

"Give or take."

He shot her the darkest of glances. "Sheyna, if they've taken the trouble to squirrel this away in the most forbidden domain we've ever seen, it's not going to be deserted, is it?" She didn't answer, so Barrackus continued, "Something's not right. I don't think Dayla's being paranoid." He smiled wanly. "Sorry, you did ask."

"Won't make that mistake again." She twisted her lips into what could have been a grin or a grimace. "I wasn't brought up to handle this kind of stuff."

Eyes twinkling, Barrackus faced her. "You mean your aristocratic background?"

Her gloved fists clenched involuntarily. "Oh, come on, Commander. Despite what Andromedus thinks, the Asthen are *not* a class-obsessed society, and you know it. My kin might be an old, established family, but there is no 'heritage' power that gave me my skills."

He was smiling openly. "Sheyna, I'm kidding. As you say, it's our beloved Tracker who has that shoulder chip."

She inhaled deeply, then lowered her head as if embarrassed. "Off I shoot again ... the older I get, the harder it seems to be. No idea why. It only takes a fraction of a moment to kick off my anger again."

Barrackus smiled, then waved at the unit to move. A series of shouts filled the corridor as Adira and Lars ushered them in. "Your passion has felled whole Goblin units and laid waste to munitions dumps infinitely larger than this gleaming cesspit. I wouldn't change a thing."

Sheyna's face went a peculiar peach. Her eyes filled with a rare and vulnerable softness. "Did you know they put me on a martial counselling programme, Barrackus, a spiritual discipline course for excessive emotions like anger? They thought it would temper me. I was expelled."

He leaned closer. "I didn't know. Why?"

"Too much anger."

Barrackus bit his lip, trying not to laugh. His eyes welled with tears. She whacked him hard but playfully on the shoulder. Adira, who happened to be passing, stopped and frowned. Sheyna swore him to silence, then scanned the room again, her dispassionate demeanour already back. "Give me psi warfare and the Asthen fighter that wields it any day. Technology is peeing in the wind when it comes to harnessing the atomic vehemence of what holds the floors, walls, and stars together. The sort of power *we* deal with."

"Agreed." Barrackus shot her a wry glance. "Isn't it somewhat ironic that the Ascendancy seems to see eye-to-eye with Imperial military diktat?"

Her brow creased in consternation. "What does *that* mean?"

"They both hate your temper."

Against her instinct and entire upbringing, the major threw back her head and laughed.

⚉ · ⚉ · ☠ · ⚉ · ⚉

Barrackus approached the transparent, foaming tank at the centre of the capacious space. He tried to focus, but the heady atmosphere was triggering something he'd gone out of his way to ensure was buried as deeply as a basilisk's corpse.

He shut his eyes, but it did no good. Above the footfalls of his unit, he could almost hear that voice from the past drilling into the recesses of his skull. His Temporal Mechanics tutor was berating him again in from of the entire study lecture. Everyone knew he was different, but he could cope with that, just about. What he couldn't stomach was being summoned in front of everyone to be belittled by this arrogant, self-regarding, highfalutin caecilian, time and time and time again.

"Let it go, Barrackus. *Release* the gift inside you," he had said. People were smirking. He was odd, and it made everyone feel a little better about themselves to point it out. His strangeness made them look normal, and helped them fit in. "Everyone else can do it, but why won't you? It's okay to be different. Use that complexity inside you and the pain it causes. Channel what's inside; don't fight your life's purpose."

"*I can't.*"

"You mean you *won't.*" The tutor's voice was hoarse, hard. "There's nothing to be afraid of but the imagined shadows of your own mind."

He tried, but he couldn't. The twins were sniggering at him. With their long, flame-blue hair, the girls stood out. Once, he'd thought he could impress them, but with powers as wan as his at the time, he had failed spectacularly. Gregorian, the student with the patchy growth on his chin and eyebrows the size of giant earwigs, had effortlessly overshadowed the loner.

"Ignore everyone else. Forget the laughter. Name-calling only has power if you allow it to. It's just empty words from people who lack self-worth. Look inside, feel deeply inside."

"I can't."

Another round of sniggers.

The man grew angry. It was disconcerting, as this was a lecture about the virtue of discipline under stress. "Look at me; don't listen to the others. Do you think that out there in the cold void as legions of Proto Goblins come baying for your pitiful scalp, there'll be sufficient time to think? Do you imagine you'll have the chance to sit down with a parlay pipe and commune with the star spirits? When you fight, Barrackus, you must be prepared to do it day or night, awake or asleep. You must not question yourself as you do now over barbs that cannot do you harm if you do not permit them to. You must be prepared to act with only a fleeting moment to harness the *astonishing* puissance of the elemental firmament, in everything around you. Do you understand?"

The young Barrackus was scared. Though he nodded, he felt the terror twist his mind.

"Do it, boy, you're twelve now, nearly an adult. Use your stave; don't watch it." The tutor's hand rested on the boy's back. He didn't like it. The man had done it before. Though there were sympathetic glances, many were laughing. Even in Asthen society, humiliation was sometimes used to bond a class. Ahead, the flickering facsimile of a massive, armed Imperial Goblin faced him. Behind the image lay a target practice wall, pitted over the years by the successful strikes of those that had gone before.

"Fire the damn thing, Barrackus. *Fire!*"

He felt himself losing control. Whenever he attempted something of this magnitude, it ended up controlling him. Sometimes, he felt sick; other times, he fainted. This time was no different. Instead of power, there was a sickening sensation around his thigh. His left leg began trembling as a growing wetness bathed it in sticky warmth.

The other students were openly laughing. He was crying, but the man didn't seem to notice. Without warning, he smacked the youth across the head.

"Keep trying!"

"I'm a *freak*. If I let it go, I'll go *raving mad*."

The tutor leaned close, his eyes burning with fervour. Those fleshy lips were speckled with foam. "Don't let the envy of others sully your vision, Barrackus. Don't be held back by the delusions of an ego that either says you're too good for others or not good enough. Recognize the purity of your sight *inside*, rather than the deluded narcissism of the self on the outside."

The hand pressed intently. People were calling him names. A boy stood up and threw something hard. It whacked him on the back of his already sore head. The tears were welling feely, but the tutor still didn't seem to notice. Wiping the moistness from his eyes, he pushed to get away. "There's *nothing* inside but the thaumaturgic sickness that's always stalked my family."

The tutor grabbed him by the shoulders. "They are gone, young man. Dead. You have to move forward. If you don't, you'll be tending the grain in a farmer's poop yard. I know you have it in you. Use their laughter; *use* their mockery. Draw in the pain. It is only energy, Barrackus, and energy turns suns into nova if managed correctly."

Something was welling inside his chest. Barrackus tried to swallow it back, terrified of what it could do, but the man shook him so hard it was almost impossible.

"I can't!"

"You must!"

The tutor had slapped him with some force. Inside, a gelid singularity erupted in the confines of his young skull. The firelights in the room suddenly blinked off as cracks zigzagged along the ceiling, throwing dust and fist-sized chunks of mortor across the class. Amid the terrified screams and the slamming doors of those already running for safety issued the rending din of howling sorcery. Jagged cracks webbed violently through the floor. A plasma trail of neon whorls gored out a design of fiery ziggurats in the wood of the desks. Chairs and tables rose, then went spinning as students fled. One of the vast crystal chandeliers crushed a table with a deafening crash. The image of the Goblin and the entire wall behind it had been atomized.

The boy wasn't listening. The tutor had straightened, his face pallid, and he looked in horror at where his arm should have been, then back at Barrackus.

♀ · ♀ · ☠ · ♀ · ♀

"*Watch out, Commander!*"

A thunderous whump jolted Barrackus back to the present. Though he had instinctively raised his Magi shield, the Raider found himself sprawled out amid a maze of transparent wiring, a throbbing pain between his shoulders. Around him, shapes blurred, sounds hissed, and muffled screams erupted. Frantically, grabbing a nearby strut, he yanked himself upright and slammed his back against a metal wall for cover.

Someone cried out.

A white corona of light flared brightly toward him, striking him in the centre of his chest. This time, he skidded along the floor until he crashed into a blue-white panel. Gasping haplessly like an out-of-water fish, Barrackus flailed uselessly for his dropped staff. A dark blur sheared across the periphery of the ceiling then shot towards him. The figure of a Raider leaped suddenly into the air, sword swishing. With a cutting swipe, Sheyna sliced the assailant across the middle, sending body parts spinning with pieces of her shattered blade. A fine mist of black blood pattered over them. Barrackus exhaled, then once more tried to stand. Sheyna, visibly irked, brusquely helped him up. He leaned on her, drawing shallow breaths.

"Your mind was leagues away, but thank the devil that wards you, your Mage shield wasn't."

Barrackus could barely breathe. "Hell, the thing turned your sword to confetti." Blood bubbled between his lips.

She grimaced at his pain-stricken face. "I have another!"

Pandemonium flowered above them. The ground shook from the whumps of Asthen tannin fire. The electrified cracks of the staves were deafening. Barrackus scrambled, despite the pain, to retrieve his mace but was rudely and violently floored for the third time as two shapes skimmed past at breakneck speed.

"You alright?" Sheyna yelled. She carpeted the flying forms above with voluminous plumes of Mage fire. A dozen detonated mid-flight. "They're targeting *you*, Barrackus. Seems you're their number one guy."

Wisps of acidic smoke rose from two burn marks on the front of his breastplate. Blood had formed a gunk in his throat. Something went somersaulting across the space, leaving a smear of tarred murk in its wake.

Another hit. Damn, she's good.

Though she was giving them hell, her Magi energy barrier was depleting. As ever, she was overdoing it. His own shield was in even worse shape. They were pinned down, separated from their people, heavily engaged with blowing creatures out of the sky. With a huge effort, he coughed up the blockage and spat it in a messy splodge against a steel pipe. He slumped to the ground; his arms heavy as lead.

"What are they?"

Sheyna ducked. Searing charge flew overhead. "Can't see ... too quick. Some kind of Imperial chiroptera, but huge. Each one's two-thirds the size of a fully grown adult."

"You mean bats."

"I mean giant, flying shitheads of muscle, skin, stubby hair, and teeth the size of falchions." The tendons on her cheeks tightened. "Give me bats any day."

Adira barked orders. Volleys of light arched upwards as Asthen shooters immersed the horizon in streaming crescents of white-hot shot. Cascades of twirling, winged shapes struck the ground in a riotous succession of thuds. Some flapped around shrieking; most lay still. There was a pause before a bristling mass rose from another side of the glimmering cavern with a low-level hum. With well-drilled precision, the Raiders turned and baked the approaching swarm with a grid pattern of coruscating firepower. Smouldering carcasses piled up in charcoal-like mounds on every surface. Despite his injuries, Barrackus was overwhelmed with a sudden surge of pride. His people were wreaking havoc on the things, simultaneously keeping them at bay. The pitiful sight of two prostrate fighters lying against a wall, however, swiftly brought him back to reality.

There were muted curses as another haze of writhing shapes emerged from a hidden duct at the end of the glinting room. It formed a squall of shifting patterns above the glass sarcophagus of slopping fluids and the maze of silver tubing serving it. Without hesitation, Sheyna bellowed at the crouching fighters, gesticulating furiously towards the gathering host.

"Maces high! ... blind nova! *Prepare for a blind nova!*"

The Raiders raised their weapons and waited.

"*Fire!*"

A combined plume of spitting plasma raced across the room. It struck the centre of the vortex, creating a continuously spinning fireball of brilliant intensity. Barrackus and Sheyna instinctively recoiled. The thaumaturgic super-weapon, or blind nova, was whispered to be hotter than the surface of a new-born star and brighter than a quasar. They had no reason to doubt it. The fireball jerked then quickly swelled, jets of light cannoning in all directions. The Raiders continued to pour their combined strength into it, feeding it all the time.

"Duck!" Adira screamed.

The entire company hunched frantically behind their Magi shields. There was a soundless, white flash, then a basilisk's breath blast of searing heat. Shards of metal and shattered tubing rocketed in spinning wheels over their heads as debris crashed around them with loud thuds. The room drifted into unnerving quiet. Somewhat gingerly, the Asthen looked up, heads streaked with grey. Dirty snow layered the watchers and busted pipes with an ashy carpet of grisly festivity. The once airborne assailants formed a charred quilt of carnage around the transparent monster dominating the room.

"Bullseye!"

Barrackus rose uncertainly, his legs already gaining strength. Clouds of ash flowered down his front in flushes. "Never fails."

"Don't count your wyrms before they've crawled," Sheyna warned. "We seem to have a little more housework to do, and there's no time to re-join the others."

Barrackus' good humour vanished. "More?"

"Hell's udders, Commander, we've only managed to irk their pals. The entire hive's woken up."

His mouth bone dry, Barrackus looked up. At first, there was nothing, then, he heard a grating whine. Something massive was blotting out the light at the very purview of sight. Squinting hard, he could just make out a hovering tsunami of darkness heading their way.

"Maces ready!" Sheyna ordered.

Raider fire crisscrossed the approaching mouth of the storm, but it was haphazard, unregulated. Barrackus caught flashes of knotted flesh dive-bombing anyone that fell out of line. Though staves and tannan guns blazed furiously, the speed of the attack had radically distorted the accuracy of their targeting. He could tell Sheyna was livid. There was nothing she hated more than not being able to do anything.

"Regather. I said, regather! Can you hear me? Adira, get Lars and Skyron to marshal the lines. Stop firing. Converge your weapons for a single burst. Unify your fucking fire."

No one was listening, or perhaps no one could hear.

Glimmering shot raked the boiling supercell of darkness now directly above the Asthen position. The strikes were rebuffed by the shimmering barrier of the collective Raider shield, but a dislodged fighter was thrown backwards, the top of his skull a sluice of blood. A distraught Sheyna began barking orders at her troops with more urgency than ever.

"Lars! Tighten your positions!"

His weak voice came back. "Can't hear ... repeat!"

"Try and concentrate our strength."

"Impossible; too close ... can't get a lock. They're all over us!"

Another voice piped up, further away. "Major!"

"Adira!"

"There's no way of regrouping! The things won't let us!"

Sheyna swore royally. Every time she tried to join them, creatures swept past, keeping both commanders separated from the troop. She shot back with everything she had, igniting an entire batch mid-flight, but fresh assailants took their place. The constant hum was deafening.

"Captain, you must try! I can't reach you."

"Fat chance!" Skyron cut in. He was on the near side of the group and much closer than the others. "They've closed us out. Can't move. Lucky to get more than two shots in a row."

Sheyna's eyes glowered with loathing. Rounding sharply on Barrackus, she grabbed him by the shoulders and shook him violently. Despite the deep shock from the necromantic burns, he managed to stay standing. "You may be top of the menu, but, with all respect, Commander, you better get your shit together, *right now*." Her nose was almost touching his. "Injured or not, we need one of your little party tricks very soon, or those rabid devils are going to fillet our entire company." Her voice lowered. "Don't go too far, Barrackus. You know what I'm talking about; don't think I haven't sensed it too."

Barrackus regarded her numbly, then tried to coax his stave back to life, but a slew of creatures immediately swerved to attack. Before Sheyna could move, they were bombarded by blinding detonations and jags of flying shrapnel. Barrackus, along with his depleted Mage barrier, was effortlessly tossed against a bulkhead. After a long, stunned moment, he raised a shaking hand and fumbled a healing blue flame over the gory left side of his face. Sheyna quickly knelt to help. Lose tendon and bloody tissue began to reconnect as the fibres in his flesh melded together.

"They *really* do hate you, don't they, Commander."

He tried to smile reassuringly, but the still bloody mess gave the unsettling impression of a lunatic clown. "It's okay. I can finish my jaw off later." His eyes rolled towards the tumult of overhead shapes. "Mustn't make sharp movements. It gets them agitated. Time ... buy me some time, and I'll take all of them out!"

Sheyna's eyebrows came together as if doubting he could blink, let alone fight. "Every time you break wind, let alone move, they hit you with something. They're *scared*, Barrackus ... they can sense something in you that *really* freaks them out. Explains why they isolated us. I'll bet every vicious, hairy, armoured sadist I've fed the ground with that they're going to wait till the rest of us are butchered before they risk taking you out.

"Above." He indicated the struts overhead. Winged forms with red eyes were collecting. They watched every move with beady famine. "Some of them have Mage wands. That's how they've been hitting us."

Sheyna closed her eyes and gripped her stave. "Not for long" She turned and scoured the startled things with sparkling hellfire until they were fused to the metal they were perched on. Dark, sleek devices lay smoking nearby. Wiping her face with her filthy sleeve, Sheyna flopped against a bulkhead. "Magi weapons for sure ... Imperial too! Man, this takes it out of me."

Ignoring stabs of pain, Barrackus grabbed a strut and, again, attempted to stand. His jaw was raw, though the bleeding had stopped, and the skin was back. He regarded the slain forms with bloodshot eyes. "Elite troops ... must be sorcerer class, or those sticks wouldn't work. This place matters to them!" Giddy and uncertain, he fumbled at his mace. The harder he tried to force his theurgy through the weapon, the worse it seemed to be. Staggering forwards, his vision pixelated and he sank downwards into warm oblivion.

❦ · ❦ · 💀 · ❦ · ❦

Someone was shouting his name. Barrackus' eyes flickered.

Had he been gone a long time, or was it heartbeats? Death and ruin surrounded him. He had to act. Everyone was dying. He didn't want to. He didn't want to go down to that place again, the place he hadn't touched since he was young.

I have to!

Unrequited puissance rose in a riptide of irresistible force from the base of his skull to the front of his consciousness.

He froze.

The crystalline purity of knowledge, the training with his tutors, the illicit scrolling through forbidden texts; all of it came back. It was an infinite stream of malachite chaos flowing to a white-hot point on a lost horizon. He was a silvered crest of searing thought, sweeping irresistibly to an achromatic sphere beyond, glowing with an unfettered threat. With a horrified jolt, he realized he was flowing into the open maw of his subconscious mind.

"We need one of your little tricks more than ever."

He breathed Sheyna's name, but it came out inaudible.

Her face rippled pallidly in front of him, mouthing the same thing again and again.

"We need one of your little tricks more—"

"Than ever!" His eyes oscillated like opaque oyster pearls in a storm front. "You *hate* my tricks."

Sheyna's face ruptured into cracked lines, then clouded into crinkled parchment before blowing into dust.

Another scream.

Too many. Too many of the things this time.

His mind reached out to Lars and Adira, but they couldn't hear him. The butchery was coming; the cloud was too vast. Staves fired continuously, mutilated creatures fell in droves, but the buzz was growing louder. Where was Skyron? The swarm was descending, the group shield radically weakening.

Time sheered, stopped in its tracks. His consciousness arched. The vortex of people around him smeared into a kaleidoscope of blurred molecules, his prostrate form at the epicentre. Something was emerging, scraping its way out from the deep. He heard his one-armed, Temporal Mechanics lecturer scream. Choice was irrelevant; it always had been. He had to go with it, play his role. The thing that lurked inside wanted to take him over.

Another tutor had replaced Sheyna's voice with his own, "Let it out. Be who you always *had* to be."

A lunatic?

He was going to let it run free. It'd be okay at first, but one day he would be the shadow and the power would control him. A new saviour or another tyrant?

Take your pick!

"Don't," Sheyna whispered, her face swimming into view. "Don't." She was scared. His irises dilated with scarlet ruin.

"Can't ... control it this time. *Get out!*" Blood flowed freely from his gaping mouth. He wiped it repeatedly, but it didn't stop. The major's eyes were moist pools in the fug. He'd never seen her look so distraught.

"Barrackus, look at me. *Look.*"

He focused on the urgency in her face, even as the titan within smashed against his fraying reserve.

"You were out a while. Things have changed. Adira is moving the unit past *that* bulkhead, to the corner. There's proper shelter there. The attack vector of the creatures is *infinitely* more confined. Not only does it take pressure off the shield, but our people can concentrate their fire. The things will be decimated." Her face was deeply furrowed. He could see her struggling to find the right words. "There's something I don't understand; it's inside you. Every time you flirt with thing inside you, it takes more. It's thaumaturgic psychosis, Commander. It's a recognized phenomenon with those especially gifted. You're becoming sick. You need help."

A Raider luckless enough to be outside the protective barrier was whisked airborne. Wounded creatures flopped and flipped like manta rays across the floor as though it was a hot frying pan. Barrackus pushed himself forwards, but Sheyna grabbed his shoulders.

"You are injured, Commander, and dangerously overexposed to all that wild sortilege inside you. Over the years, it's been gradually torching your brain and your wits with them. Why don't you ever listen?"

"I always listen; just not today."

He doubled over, consumed by thrusts of rampant theurgy. She shook her head. "If you weren't so pig-headed, you'd let us do this. *Think* of the mission, Barrackus. We can't do this without you. I can't do this without you!"

The internal volcano went dormant, and the monster fled back into the darkness.

☠ · ☠ · ☠ · ☠ · ☠

Through the fog of burning machinery, Adira could make out the two figures isolated under the gathering cloud. "The commanders won't make it," she hissed at Lars. "What's left of the horde's turning towards them. I think they know we're stuffed without them."

"Big mistake," he hummed excitedly, a gleam in his eye. "Don't you see? We can triangulate *all* our firepower on those things without worrying about supporting the energy barrier at the same time. *Pow!*" His palms smacked together to emphasize the point.

Adira didn't need to be told twice. She waved her hand furiously at the company. Every veridian gun and staff quietened to a spitting fizz. Eyes stared blearily at the sudden withdrawal of the horde.

"Blind nova mark two! Raise your maces and converge your fire ... *now!*"

Again, Asthen Magi firepower combined at a point amid the writhing flurry. The detonation was soundless. The devastation was shocking. A shredded handful of creatures fled back to the ducts, leaving a wake of charred vapour. The vast majority had become a rain of cauterized carnage. From within the grey snowstorm, two figures smeared with dirt staggered out. Adira flashed a triumphant smile as they reached the harried sanctuary of the group, but her stomach lurched when she saw Barrackus' eyes. The once-green slits were now red, an unmistakable sign of sorcery pollution. Sheyna shot her a warning look. Doing her best to mask the fear and her Asthen senses, Adira finally allowed herself to breathe.

"Sir, you alright? Can you walk?"

He regarded her grimly. Adira shivered as though something fell had crawled across her grave.

"I abandoned all of you." Barrackus put a dirt-streaked hand on her arm. "Won't happen again. I don't care what it takes."

Lars scrutinized them wearily, then apparently decided that a somewhat breezier approach was called for. "Last one at the Fat-Eyed Centaur buys the biggest round of frothing tankards this side of the Abomination Goat's ass! We've taken bigger scalps, but if this doesn't warrant a round, nothing does."

Barrackus' eyes gleamed with friendly malice. "I know the place—the Centaur's one of the inns run by our allies. I thought our people were discouraged from visiting their dubious watering holes—they don't trust our gifts!

Sheyna snorted. "They seem to forget that without us, they'd already be dirt-tilling thralls under the Abomination's boot." The knotted sinews twisted into a sudden grin. "Sod 'em. I'm so spent, I could drink their slop."

"It's a deal then." Adira laughed. "And if they ban us for being sorcerers, I'll shove the inn sign up their—"

"Point made!" Barrackus reached for his water flask. After a long swig, he wiped his mouth and deeply sucked in the acrid air. "Dare I ask, but has anyone seen our goodly Tracker?"

"Here." The voice was right next to him. It was oddly unnerving. Andromedus stood alone and quiet. He had a habit of appearing when someone was talking about him.

"Ah, good. Okay?"

"As well as it can be, considering the circumstances."

"He's working on an exit," Adira said, eyes flitting uncertainly between the two. "Skyron just took a small unit to scout a way out. With a bit of luck, we could be home in weeks."

Barrackus said nothing.

Adira stepped closer, swallowing back a gulp. "Commander, we've been discovered. We can't go on now; we *have*—"

Barrackus waved her off. "This is just a sentry army left behind to rot, certainly for years, perhaps for decades. They are not a crack Proto Goblin legion or Wirral, even. By the time this killing field is discovered, we'll be long gone. Andromedus will have the time to cover our tracks."

"We can still sneak our way forward," Andromedus agreed, eyes furtive. "By the time the emperor hears someone's busted into this forbidden nightmare, I'll have laid a false signal back home. Trust me, the *last* thing they'll expect is us going in further, let alone an attack on Command Central—far too deep. Plus, that would be insane."

The commander fixed him with an intense look. "So, what's the plan?

The Dust Tracker fidgeted impatiently with the straps of his kit carrier, then scanned the room. "From my own rather skilled reckoning, I'd that say that far exit leads us to an omphalos. It's a hyper connection linking the main control area with all the relevant inter-spatial conduits."

They looked blank.

"Never mind," he added heavily. "It'll do!"

"Guarded?"

"Count on it."

There was a series of loud thumps. Skyron's scouting party burst abruptly into view, spewing a cocktail of flame at something out of sight. The stench of dead blood accompanied them.

Skyron approached, his gaze red-rimmed with anxiety. "*Find another way!*"

"Focus," Barrackus growled with uncharacteristic pique. "Can we bypass whatever's chasing you?"

"We have to go that way," the Tracker spat venomously. "I nearly bust my innards open figuring out ways out of this industrial hellhole while those hairy fowl took potshots at me. I'm not going to do it again."

Skyron was shaking his head. "Something's coming. Something *wrong* is com—"

A grating sound. Tremors rippled through the walls. Everyone froze. Andromedus turned to look, but Barrackus spun him around as though his bulk was made of paper.

"Find another way! You're the only one who understands the scrawls in this glittering jail." The man's jaw flopped ajar, but Barrackus' hand shut it back with a soft clop. "Say nothing! There are still other exits and other choices—make one. *Now!*"

Something clicked. For a fleeting moment, the man's overly manufactured self-regard disappeared. The same man Barrackus had plucked from obscurity within one of the many frontier units was back.

"We can try ... there, sir."

Barrackus followed the pointing finger all the way to the other side of the giant space. "That tiny door?" he asked.

"Aye, Commander."

"Why not mention it earlier?"

Andromedus' glinting orbs were infinite diamonds of hard light. "Because it's tiny. Like all good Trackers, I always look for options. Makes me look like a miracle worker if I have a plan B, C and Z." He coughed when Barrackus' gaze darkened. "However, we'll have to dump the mounts; there's no way around it.

They are far too large for the small spaces ahead." Andromedus paused, peering at the shock on their faces. "They've all been nicked if I recall; surely, we can nick some more? If you're worried, the groom can take them back. He's a trainee Tracker; you know that. He only must sit out the static and trace a way out. It's going further in that'll be murderous."

As if on cue, a collection of flying attackers rose from behind the tank and sped away in terror. It was Sheyna's turn to grab Andromedus and spin him back on target. His irises were dilated with surprise and something else when he saw who it was. He stumbled, sliding a hand around her waist to steady himself.

"Forget being a miracle worker and the ego that goes with it. Will that hole get us out of here or not?" she demanded, then bared her teeth. "Take that clammy hand off me before I feed it to that approaching stink storm."

He swiftly removed the offending palm. "Yes..." he stammered fearfully. "I'm convinced the door can take us to the main controls."

Sheyna arched a brow towards Barrackus. He gestured at the small door, then at Andromedus. "Take us through, quickly."

The Asthen had again melded into a single Starburst formation. Under the side arm's direction, they began to beat an organized if hasty retreat towards the door, firing non-stop as they went. Their shot thudded with reverberating force into a hidden flank. The impacts were hot enough to melt lead. The assailant was completely invisible, though the shot etched out its contours in outlines of fading magma. Barrackus had fleeting glimpses at something that looked like an elongated, dark brain. Thanks to the shot, its surface was beginning to boil like an onyx star.

Barrackus pushed his way through and flung his perception across its nebulous form. He could taste fathomless necromancy. A coarse, infinitely malignant intelligence looked out, a dark pother of spite among the shiny machines. Barrackus unslung his stave. The long shaft unfurled, and the blades clicked sharply into view. Summoning all his strength, he fired. The shape paused and gave off a high-pitched shriek.

"By the gods, hit it again before it cracks my skull open with that din," Sheyna called.

"Can't." Barrackus' head slumped.

"No more tricks?"

He shook his head mutely. Sheyna swore and beckoned at the group furiously. "Fall back to the door over there. Continue firing as you go; it's clearly hurting the thing."

The Raiders needed no encouragement to move, and neither did the Dust Tracker. Somehow, he crossed the room cluttered with dead creatures and thrust his bulk against the door, then stopped. Adira, her eyes wide and hands shaking, hurried up to him. "What's the matter?"

"We have to try another approach." His ample fingers ran up and down the gleaming contours of the tiny exit.

"We haven't the time, Andromedus. You haven't even opened your tool kit yet."

Andromedus glanced round at the rapacious void of thrashing theurgy. Despite signs of serious injury, the creature was closing. The Raiders had formed a half-crescent around them. Their firepower was slowing it down, but not enough. Turning back, he threw himself full force against the doorway before sprawling back onto the floor.

Adira stared at him. "What the bloody hell are you doing? Just get your tools out and open the damn ... wait a minute, is that even a door?"

What had seemed like a door might have been nothing more than decorative indentation close up. His fingers fumbled desperately along the immaculate surfaces. Occasionally, he'd bash his hands and, once, even his head against the panel.

"What are you doing?" Adira repeated, all attempts to stay calm abandoned. "Get your damned stuff out and open it."

"No time."

A voice boomed above everything else. It was Sheyna again. She'd unceremoniously shoved half the Raiders out of the way to reach them, and she was considerably angrier than Adira could ever hope to be. "Oi, Mister Tracker, something back there wants to eat us unseasoned and very much alive! If you can't use your glow toys or your wandering hands to open that thing, stand aside, and I'll kick the grunting thing in."

"You can't kick this 'grunting' thing in, Major." He grimaced, calloused palms exploring every tiny crevice, every etched hieroglyphic. "Because if you even try, you'll break your highly commendable toes in." He stole a swift glance at her, trying not to show his fear. In the process, a great globule of dirty sweat glopped onto the same foot he had just praised. "Sorry," he muttered, suddenly more terrified of her than the creature.

Adira glanced back; the gossamer shadow of the monster now flanked the cordon of protective weapons. No light or reflected image glimmered on that formless surface. It was a shifting volume of living darkness, a null that absorbed everything but the floors. Objects in its path appeared to simply de-exist, their particles whisked from sight. Barrackus quietly joined them. He looked calm, but after years of soldiering with the man, Adira knew when he was. She knew him better than anyone. She wanted to put out a hand and stroke his cheek reassuringly.

"I know we've done this before, Andromedus, but this time it's critical," Barrackus said.

"It's *always* critical."

Barrackus nodded grimly. "Well, let's just say this time we've exceeded that."

Sheyna thumped her fist against the wall, but before she could speak, Andromedus looked up. "It's alright; we're in."

With a *thunk* of his heavy hand, a wall panel flung open, creaking cogs activated by hidden pulleys. He slapped his palms together, his face slackening in relief. "The work of a genuine artist, even if I say so myself." Andromedus grinned. "It's just a door. There's no Mage lock on it, in this nightmare realm no person ever visits. It would've helped if they had a damned fire key next to it or something."

"Did ramming it with your shoulder help?" Adira said, taking enjoyment where she could. "In fact, did hitting it with your head help?"

His stare was watery. "Yes."

"For the love of all that stinks, can we get the raving hell *out* of here?" Sheyna's face was puce. "I'd rather be gobbled by an underwater Goblin than devoured by that invisible stomach of stench."

Barrackus beckoned at the unit. The anxious fighters poured through the doorway readily, with just Skyron's rear guard maintaining any recognizable cohesion. Despite the smallness of the entryway, there was just enough room to stand even if only two or three could enter at a time. The last of Skyron's heavy carriers shot flaming arcs into the assailant before jumping inside. Barrackus had moments to slam back the hatch.

The inside was as pitch. Several Raiders instinctively transformed their staves into makeshift torches. Barrackus, wedged somewhere in the middle, tried to work his way back to check that everyone had made it, but he was stuck like paste in a tube, so he gave up and followed the flow. Sheyna powered on ahead while Adira did her best to take stock. Somehow, she did what the commander couldn't and gradually backtracked to the rear to join Skyron, counting heads as she did.

The passageway widened. It was more reminiscent of a tomb than a transit point. The arcane wall etchings were chaotic, wilder. While nerves had always haunted Adira, it was clear that feelings of unease plagued all the struggling starfighters. Unhappy murmurs began to spread like bushfire down the ranks. With a gruff mutter from the side arm, the talk immediately died off.

Barrackus, his tone far wearier than Adira had ever heard it, also cut in with uncharacteristic impatience. "So, we're in a spot of trouble! Nothing you ain't seen a hundred times before. Andromedus tells me we should hopefully find these controls ahead to work the statically dead portal we came through. It's either that or spend days waiting for the static to clear, and no one wants that."

No one said anything, though uneasy shuffling broke out in the dark.

"It'll probably be a while before the Core even learns we're here. It won't even occur to them that we want to go deeper because, normally, that's suicide. So, not all hope is lost, at least not yet."

CHAPTER NINE

WHY DOES IT FEEL SO BAD?

M *abius!*

The name ran down the back of Ayilia's spine like liquid lead.

When she'd been a child, tales of his infinite fury and blighted magick were told the length and breadth of the city by those hired to tell such tales. No one was spared in those days, especially the unruly child at night.

"Best be good, Leif, or the renegade Dragon Lord will get you!"

The stories were enriched by ribald tavern talk and fantastic exaggerations. By the time she'd reached her teens, Mabius had more legs than could fit on any respectable torso and wings that stretched half a continent. With the febrile gossip came paranoia. Even adults were pleased when the official storytellers, the chroniclers stopped their prattling when the coin ran out. Sythians were indisputably powerful. Obsessed with the purity of violence, their souls were as degraded as they were strong. So highly thaumaturgic was the sinew of their flesh that they left molten steps in the naked rock when enraged and froze the life from prey with their gelid gaze. The fact no one had seen such things did nothing to dispel the fierceness with which the tales were told, which was only tempered by the fierceness of the liquor that went with them.

Agelfi knew. He understood. Leaning forward in his creaking chair, he'd murmured that Sythians were the ultimate reapers of the sublime maelstrom of atoms in every plant and in every stone. Like master composers, they summoned the quantum sonnets to their will, twisting and manipulating the hidden lights of the firmament as they saw fit. A true thaumaturge could heal, grow, meld, and mend, but they raided the earth round the soles of their puissant feet for power, sucking out the atomic rind until there was nothing left. They violated the energies for what they hungered, with the boundless maleficence inside their unbeating hearts.

Ayilia recalled it clearly; Agelfi had collapsed back in his chair to think, then throw some more imaginary logs on that imaginary fire of his. Those were special times. In that tower, magick and tales were a welcome antidote to confinement. In that safe and secure world, with Jarrak snoring flat out in one of the many copious corners, all dreams were possible, all nightmares real.

As far as Sythians, past and present, were concerned, people were sub-humanoid. The rest of creation was "plasma infertile," barren, a damning verdict on every doyen of Empire and beyond.

"They're not people," Agelfi had whispered, the dancing flickers of the flames splaying in shadowed cobwebs across his gaunt features. "Don't think of them as people. They are a cosmic spore of ruthless intelligence, of unfettered cunning, obsessed with their survival and nothing else."

She'd hugged herself in delicious terror in that tower of his, even as Jarrak finally dropped the mug his sleeping hand had been clutching. Its clattering had made them both jump out their skins, yet it didn't once cloud the beaming gleam in her mentor's eye. Stories were his blood, and once he'd started, which was most of the time, he hated to be cut short. It was a shame Jarrak had found them insufferably farcical, but sleep always claimed him swiftly, as it did the two guards in an adjacent room, a room decorated with over-comfy sofas and sleep-inducing incense candles. Agelfi had also made sure they were extremely well-fed. They hadn't stood a chance.

"You must think of them as living seed, Ayilia, an interstellar genome harbouring their malignance within the husks of countless generations of unwitting hosts. They're just a cosmic parasite, a hex on the flesh of the unlucky, patiently awaiting a distant signal to emerge."

She'd snorted in delight. He'd simply refilled his pipe amid brows so wild they threatened to crawl off his face and begin again as a new form of life. "The Sythian spore is conscious at *all* times, my dear. Existence as sentient DNA is their true state of play. Sythians only take humanoid form when their collective consciousness receives the clarion call to arms, and by that, I mean people. Or, more clearly, a particular threat posed by people. It is people that they hate, for it is people who they truly fear," he leaned forwards for dramatic effect, "it is people and only people that, through time and space, hunted and destroyed them!"

She'd flinched.

Imagine that... a scared Sythian. I can hardly believe it.

Whack.

The sword came down with a jarring thud. Wooden splinters exploded in all directions like timber bullets, sending alarmed birds squawking through the peaceful glade. Images of her mother lying on her bed, white as a spectre, her wrists bandaged and bloodied, flashed through the backs of Ayilia's retinas in angry streaks.

Whack.

A shaft of wood engrained with burls, knots, and ancient swirls ruptured off the shuddering trunk with a deafening crack. It dislodged another image, this time of Jarrak, iron features wrought with grief as though his face had been on a rack, kneeling to tell her of the news of her father being stricken for the first time.

Whack.

The hefty broadsword split the desiccated stump asunder with an almighty crack. Ayilia swore loudly and tugged at the handle. It was stuck fast. Furious, she slammed a boot on the trunk and dragged it free with a herculean heave. Another scroll of memories cartwheeled through the contours of her mind's eye. It was like someone had opened a chest of all the significant things that had ever happened, and it was impossible to close it. One of them was a younger Kemet, eyes red and watery, telling her that Jarrak had finally given into the cancer that had eaten his mind inside and out.

Muttering venomously, the lone figure made to strike again.

"Regent?"

Enraged, she froze mid-strike. "What?"

Kemet's eyes were wide with concern. "Has the tree done something to offend you?"

She cursed and whacked the trunk one more time, covering herself in a spinning welter of lightweight shards. "Everything's done something to offend me!"

"I see," he replied quietly. His eyes scanned the small forest on the edge of their camp. The evening sunlight spooled through the lush canopy. Outside a glowering regent, it was picturesque. "Seems a shame to take it out on an innocent tree, though."

She swung around, eyes blazing. "Tree's been dead years, like Jarrak. Our city's been dead for days, like my father. My mother ..." She choked, desperately holding onto her tears. It did no good. Her cheeks were shiny and wet. Her tunic was drenched at the neck. Kemet didn't need a course in counselling to see that she'd been upset and angry for quite a while.

He waited, gathering his thoughts. "You know, your mother was a good person. She did her best. It's not her fault she couldn't cope."

"She had problems, Kemet, and you know it. It ran in her side of the family. Her sister had the malady, and she died alone because of it. She did her best, I know, and I still love her, despite her leaving me so young."

Kemet sighed. It was a gentle, caring sound. She imagined he used it often with his children. "It's indeed tragic she felt there was no hope."

"Especially tragic for those she left behind." Ayilia went to strike the dead wood but decided against it. Instead, she sheathed the blade with an angry thrust. "Every goddamned person I've *ever* gotten close to has been taken. The only thing I ended up caring about was that city, but it died on me, too. I was going to give them *everything*."

Tears flowed freely. She cursed, then gave the trunk a thwack with her boot for good measure. "Everything I touch goes to shit!" A well of fury overtook the grief. Screaming with pent-up angst, she kicked the trunk again. "Agelfi's barking mad if he really thinks someone as blighted as I can carry the marbles of some feathered fire goose."

Kemet slowly approached and laid her head against his shoulder. The sobs came more readily. Both knew they had to come sooner or later. The weald was warm and safe. Butterflies enveloped the clearing in a flurry of sumptuous colour, getting ready for the coming twilight. Beetles with shiny, black-blue, chitinous scales munched happily on the wood she had so generously supplied them.

"Jarrak became my surrogate father, Kemet. I loved that old man as much as my real one, who was stuck on that bed, *rotting*."

"I know," he replied softly. "He did a far better job at fathering than me."

"You were too young at the time. Besides, I needed a best friend."

"You couldn't have done better, either." He smiled mischievously.

Though her face was as puffy and red, she gave him a mock slap. At that point, Aaron wandered into the scene, swearing at a butterfly that had accidentally upset the bangs he had so gingerly restyled.

"Firewood."

They looked at him blankly.

"Firewood," he repeated. "Just what I came here to look for." He took in the chopped-up trunk, then shot them a perplexed glance. "How the devil's udders did you know?"

☠ · ☠ · ☠ · ☠ · ☠

The next day, Ayilia, Aaron, and Kemet stood on a dark grey ledge, facing a broken tooth horizon of volcanic peaks smudged by a misty spangle of dawn rays. A miasmic squall of moiling steam rose from a succession of gently coughing vents half a league below. Shale crunched underfoot as they shifted positions for a better look.

Kemet explained how the elements had sculpted the limestone summits into definition, eroding the soluble rock into the hardened splendour standing before them. Like a wizened unit of retired soldiers, the craggy, gaunt, karst pinnacles stood serenely in small huddles. In the distance, a far-off rim of puffing cauldrons smoked in the periphery of their sight.

"Zeinkarst!" Aaron grunted. "Who'd have thought?"

Ayilia wiped a chilled brow. It had been a bracing night, and she wasn't used to the temperate coolness of the northern ranges. However, undeniably, she felt a little more positive. The pain was as red-raw as ever, and it wasn't going away anytime soon. Regardless, venting so openly somehow made her feel that she had a little more ownership of it than before.

For the time being, she had to focus on the job at hand. Once they'd found that cursed moon and hopefully the welcome protection of Agelfi and his Heretics, she could afford to process things as they should be.

Of course, she didn't believe a word of it. Not only was she unsure if she could hold on, she wanted to rip the collective scalp off every new government member and burn them in the nearest fire.

If the Imperium hadn't done it already.

Her fists started clenching again. She had to stop doing that.

"Didn't take too long—only four days," she said.

"And not a Lifeless homicidal maniac in sight," Kemet breathed. "However, they might've still taken the main road to cut us off in the ranges ahead. They don't need rest like us, after all."

Aaron rubbed his elbows. He'd slept awkwardly and wasn't in the best of moods, even by his challenged standards. "Maybe; they haven't even reached the open roads, let alone those Godforsaken, hog-eared, bovine-haired paths in that hell-damned series of rises coming up? I doubt the stiff's had the time. From what we witnessed, most didn't seem to have Prowlers!"

Kemet's brow creased thoughtfully. "Agreed—this was a lightning strike aimed at Agathon and you, Regent. It would appear that they banked entirely on surprise."

"And the betrayal of the Provost!" she muttered venomously.

"Without that quill-pushing, rube-loving, slop-sucking pantywaist on fungi sticks, they'd have *never* got in, not without a whole legion of onagers anyway," Aaron added unhelpfully. "You know what they say—even an antlered hog learns new tricks."

There's no such saying." Kemet smirked.

"Well, there should be." Aaron winked.

Ayilia pushed back hair as knotted as root bark. "Regallion was no better than an opportunist, an odd-job hatchet woman. *This* was a systematically planned invasion, even if it was on the hoof."

"It's incredibly baffling," Aaron muttered. "If any of this Kimiya stuff is true, I'd have expected more, to be frank."

Ayilia's breath clouded against the rumbling, grey backdrop. "More what, exactly? Undead murderers?"

"Why not?" He shrugged as he absentmindedly scuffed some shale over the ledge. It went rattling down the precipice in a crackling shimmer of gleaming puce.

Ayilia was thoughtful. "Worked though, didn't it? Barrik's treachery robbed us of a city, while most of the X Gemina were out in the deserts, bonehead-monitoring. Had Agelfi not tipped me off in the nick of time, we'd have been sitting ducks."

Aaron hmphed. "Well, they're still a bunch of inbred bone butts and *nothing* will ever change that."

She laughed loudly in that bright morning light. Aaron mock-bowed. Kemet was grinning from ear to ear. He slapped the commander energetically on the back. "On that highly insightful note, old friend, let's get cracking."

They turned and began making their way down the slope to the grassy plains below.

☙ · ❦ · ☠ · ❦ · ☙

The weather-eroded, circular gap in the centre of the rocky rise facing them was fittingly entitled Moon Hill. It stood alone among a swirling mash of russet grasslands swishing gracefully in the fresh wind. The jutting crags of the Zeinkarst were on the far side. Absolutely no one went there without reason. For the first time, Ayilia found herself marvelling at the astounding, monastic beauty, all the time trying to shake a sense of slowly growing dread that seemed to come with the place.

They bypassed the tranquillity of Moon Hill and wordlessly moved on. A narrow valley floor parted wide enough to support both the river and the deep reed-covered banks on either side. The fronds softly bristled amidst the chuckling of the waters, as ivory butter-bugs flitted among the feathery cones of the stems. The air was sharp and invigorating. A splash of brooding cloud drifted into view. It had been so hot before that there was a sense of relief that the suns might not show in strength after all.

The company trod quietly, unwilling to disturb the achingly meditative feel of the place. Inevitably, after a while, Aaron began to fidget, the impulse to disrupt the maddening echo of silence reverberating inside his overworking skull proving too great. He leaned close to Ayilia and Kemet.

"Blast this peace. This place might be pretty, but its solitude is bloodless!"

"Better start praying then." Kemet grinned.

"We certainly need it," Ayilia whispered. "Even if we do find Elder Maroukish and his gate, I'm not convinced we'll find this moon Agelfi's waiting on. If the gate connects to the entire portal net like I hear they often do, we could end up anywhere, maybe some giant troll's gut or something."

Kemet's face turned grave. "If I recall, the purple highlands are well inside Krayal territory. The X Gemina never go that far. A display of military might would likely cause a war, such is their historic mistrust of us."

"Great." Aaron shook his mane of mustard hair. To his surprise, a cloud of midges shook free and started to buzz relentlessly around his face. "In that case, shouldn't we attempt a more circular approach in the Ranges, rather than the *one* direct valley through this rock pile of grief?"

Kemet tilted his head in thought. "Aaron might have a point—we're almost certain to encounter Pit activity somewhere ahead, considering the river valley is the only traversable route in these parts. This is pure borderland for all of us."

"Been thinking that all morning." Ayilia waved off an enormous blue bug circling her head, looking for cuts to feed from. "I also thought, who's going to know we've been deposed all the way out here? They probably don't even know the Pit's been reactivated."

Aaron had an intense expression on again. "The Imperium could've told the Pro Consul's rabble to block every escape route *before* they retook the Pit ... *Wham!*" He struck the palm of his hand with his fist.

Ayilia snorted in amusement. "Confiding in the Pro-Consul's rather relaxed regime is like spitting into a gale with a blindfold on. You never know where it's going to hit. I think they trust him even less than us, and that's being generous." She reached for her water pouch. "These newcomers are the real deal. They almost got us in our beds."

"Not me," Aaron said, beatifically placing a hand on his chest, eyes as innocent as a nun caught with her hand in the collection pan. "I was too busy hunting down some quality mead, unlike my dozy pal here and the rest of the mutts behind us."

Kemet burst out in laughter, followed immediately by Aaron. Ayilia waited patiently as they exchanged ritual male mock hostilities. "If we *do* encounter Pit ahead, they'll think we're just an unscheduled human patrol doing its duty as stipulated by Treaty. They'll puff their chests out, and we'll insult each other, but no one will bite, because that's the way things have been done since the Pro Consul was ossified into his throne."

"Amen to that," Aaron exclaimed, finally satisfied.

☻ · ☻ · ☻ · ☻ · ☻

The quiet summits were softly adorned by a glimmering necklace of birds circling in search of food. Some of the more enterprising Gemina unstrapped their halberds from across their backs and started spearing oily fish from the choppy currents. Though not as large as the coastal varieties, it was welcoming.

The clean breeze freshened their burdened spirits. A sense of newness permeated the camp. The Dreamveldt, a vast delta stretching into the distance, felt invigorating and alive. However, not once did they let their guard down. In the Zeinkarst, visitors ran the risk of being ambushed by unregulated soldiers hardened by conflict with Krayal. Or, if especially unlucky, wayward, embittered cutthroats from the more belligerent Krayal tribes on the borders. Hardly surprising, their weary eyes continuously scanned the crags for movement or the flash of an incoming spear. Somehow, underneath the rocky spires of two overhanging karst pinnacles, they managed a fitful night's rest. Aside from those assigned watch, one person stayed awake, however, thinking. Ayilia's eyes were closed, but all she could see was the past.

The ochre blaze of the morning suns bejeweled the Zeinkarst's stone turrets with glittering bangles, the hue of bloody rose. The delta had forked into an infinite weald of cobalt tributaries within a cavernous gorge. Spoiling it all, on their side of the river, was the stark sight of an Imperial watchtower.

Ayilia could see the company's spirits were sinking.

Five stories high and perched on thick wooden struts, the building resembled a many-legged demon. Ragged and unkept, the worn cladding had seen intermittent action, usually involving fleeing criminals and stray Krayal. Grisly skins hung from a series of hooks; their green scales almost faded to white in the harsh light. Sentries skulked behind darkened observation holes, eyeing the troop beadily. Broken ramparts ran like cougar teeth along a sagging roof made of cracked slates. Thin fingers of acrid fug rose from a metal flue. Each strut was a large, outstretched talon, deliberately fashioned to intimidate any visitor by giving the impression of a vast bird of prey frozen over an imagined kill.

Stone carvings around the side heralded an obsolete age of fantasy and belief. As they drew near, a stack of low-level outhouses became visible, along with the dirty flames of a campfire. The terracotta roof tiles were brushed with beige fungus, the beneficiaries of frequent mists. The surrounding slew of sharp blades, shaggy hides, animal skulls, and greased industrial equipment added to the threat. A series of tiny settlements on the other bank, also Pit, were connected by an old stone bridge.

No one breathed.

The Gemina crossed a dilapidated ring of half-broken wooden rails and rusted gates and entered a threshold of iron spikes and shattered amphoras. Eight to ten guards stood facing them. Another three-score emerged from outpost doorways and the ramshackle buildings adjacent. Ayilia's senses were firing on all cylinders. There were probably a hundred or more border guards in total, most of them inside. Usually, they'd be spitting at pots, rolling dice, or lost in slumber more human than the kind favoured by the life inert. Today, they appeared overtly hostile.

A shadow approached. It merged with Ayilia's on the dry, russet grass. The Lifeless spoke in the Pit vernacular, not the more militaristic war tones the off-worlders used.

"Where are you going? What business do thralls have here?"

The speaker was a scrawny but powerful centurion. His bony, nicked head was a taut convolution of dereliction and spite, his voice a garrotted rasp. Calcified ridges flexed within a thick skull every time he spoke, a characteristic manufactured to intimidate. It was, Ayilia had to admit, effective. To him, organics were an aberration, a virus to be subjugated. To witness humans operate unfettered was an absolute violation of universal law and it stuck in his craw.

These were the good guys.

Still, he was unusually coherent for this world. The Pit soldiers, for the most part, had stopped caring about subjugation. When she inspected the Pit, some even invited her and her guards in for a tavern drink and some ribald singing. She'd never admit it to the council, but she had even made friends among them. She'd never seen Vespasian out amongst his rabble, in fact, she'd never seen him at all, though for the Lifeless to tell it, he wasn't much fun.

"Don't you know me, soldier?" Ayilia asked, almost insulted. Though he was eight hands taller, she walked up to him and squared her shoulders. "I am the Sovereign Regent of the city of Agathon and authorized supervisor of the Occupied Territories. We are conducting border inspections, as stipulated by Treaty between the Unholy Nethergeistian Imperium and aligned human principalities. I carry old Imperial chrysobulls granting us uncontested passage. The texts within have been ratified by your lord and Sythian master, the Pro Consul Vespasian himself, years ago."

The thing spat but said nothing. She wasn't sure if it was the Treaty or the mention of the Consul that irked him the most. She ground her teeth. "I *insist* on passage without hindrance or question. The X Gemina are solely authorized to authenticate Imperium diktat under the aegis of the Pit and, by association, the Empire itself."

The centurion regarded her with undisguised venom. It was hard to believe a local soldier took his duties so seriously. For long heartbeats, Ayilia couldn't pinpoint what was so different, then it struck.

The Lifeless looked motivated.

"What, and who, passes here is up to me and me alone. I hold no value in obsolete papers, signed by the remnants of a subspecies on borderline extinction. Your regency has no jurisdiction in this border zone. Test our magnanimity, and it won't just be the pelts of wayward Krayal geckos hanging from those hooks."

Ayilia stared into his scarlet gaze. To flinch in the presence of a 'live one' was lethal. They weren't common, but they certainly made up for it when it came to trouble. The centurion's burning pathological malevolence was unexpectedly unnerving.

"It's authority you want?" Ayilia fumbled in her pack for a stubby pencil and some battered parchment. "Go on."

The thing fidgeted almost imperceptibly, but it was a start.

"I'm going to need your serial number, the name of the unit here, and the operational records of your outpost." She furrowed her brow. "Bear with me, as I don't tend to visit the dumps up here much. I was reliably informed that the only sentient life up here were your so-called lizards."

Some of the guards fidgeted wearily. The centurion's jostled ego knew it had to reassert dominance and swiftly. "That scrap of paper is not fit to wipe the residue from your liquid-filled rumps, let alone dictate policy!" He leaned in close, too close. A stink of rancid oil and dead blood, probably Krayal, nearly made her gag. "However, you might find the reeds around here more than sufficient *should* the need strike. Existence is hard up here, hume, and I am concerned that your gut is not up to it."

There was a cackle of dry laughter behind. He had regained prestige. To lose hers now might end in bloodshed.

"Actually, the reeds aren't a patch on the ones back home." She flashed a smile. "Just like the personnel in your guardhouse. I'm looking forwards to sending my report to the Pit. I've personal experience of just how seriously they take inconvenience." Matching him movement for movement, Ayilia leaned in close. "The last time I complained, someone more senior than you got hurt, terminally. Your mutt-slaggers behind will almost certainly join you ... or replace you."

The Lifeless held her gaze for far too long. Then he did something she never saw them do. He smiled. The manufactured Ossein could barely cope with the movement. "Perhaps you haven't heard? The holy brothers are *here*, in the Pit. You know what that means don't you, Regent? You, your 'mutt-slaggers,' and that sterile Sythian on his feckless throne are finally finished." A messianic lustre grazed the grainy peripheries of his irises. "We're going back to the old days, hume, when your kind and Krayal were crushed at will beneath the Imperium's hobnailed heel. Instead of hunting the sinewy thew of the lizard for sup, when our lust for meat consumes all reason, we'll exterminate them instead. Then we'll flog your people into the helots they've always been. The days of watching the Sythian quisling pick his ear lugs are finally done."

These border Lifeless are carnivores.

Her exterior was granite, but inside, she had turned to quicksand.

Even the Imperium hated Lifeless flesh-eaters. The industrial sludge the Lifeless consumed was mixed with additives to minimize dissension. They weren't raised on meat; it was too barbaric, too akin to the Imperial bestial footsloggers of yore. Slippage was viewed with naked horror. It was odd to think of the Lifeless as vegetarians, but there was good reason to. Flesh-guzzling led to disobedience, infighting, cannibalism, and outright anarchy. The meat of the living poisoned them. Perhaps it defiled the Goat's life-giving Ichor inside. Soldiers going feral was the ultimate nightmare. The centurion could be capable of anything. Aaron and Kemet hovered close at hand, but Ayilia could imagine undead archers taking position behind those bleak walls.

"The rules apply as stipulated, Centurion. I'm guessing the brothers will loathe inconvenience even more than the Consul. Kemet?"

"Aye?" Kemet growled.

"Make a note. Our good friend here thinks Mabius' very sibling, our beloved ally the Consul, is a, what was it again, a 'dotard?'"

Kemet nodded. "He won't like that!"

"Don't forget the 'quisling' part," Aaron piped up a little too merrily. "Pretty sure Mabius won't like that either."

"No, I imagine he won't. Makes him look weak as hell," Kemet added.

Ayilia frowned. "In fact, I don't think any of the brothers will be pleased, for that matter. I mean, they are related, right?"

The Lifeless was nakedly riled. Nevertheless, it had visibly recoiled. "Go ahead, attempt to pass. We've had Krayal think they could do the same." He gestured towards the outhouses. "See for yourself. Their disembowelled carrion still filths up our pots in the sculleries and makes poor-grade sheaths for our weapons. You, howbeit, might make handy additions to the guardhouse furniture."

If the stiff could sweat, he'd be a fat hog on a spit. He clearly knew nothing of the fall of humanity. Just another bone-face relying on aggression for currency. Ayilia let the silence hang for one or two heartbeats. In the background, a gaggle of hacksaws clanged in the cool breeze against rusted cutters leg irons.

"Centurion, I'll get to the point. If you enjoy a personal rapport with our Sythian overlords then, by all means, let's spill our collective guts across your cozy wilderness. If you don't, and you start a war they don't want between our peoples ..." Ayilia shrugged and smiled winsomely though her throat was as dry as a desert shrub. "Obstruct our path, and a dozen arrows will pulp your face into the back of your anemic skull," she hissed. "After dispatching the halfwits outside, we'll kick those dilapidated doors in and finish the sots inside! If we should fall, several hundred Gemina will take our place in a day or so—we hardly came here unaided. You can tell Mabius himself why you thought this was worth it."

Ayilia's eyes glittered. After a long pause, she returned to her horse and swung herself back into the saddle. As the mount moved forward, it accidentally jilted the centurion's shoulder. There were muted curses and agitated bristling within the outpost's ranks. The centurion stiffened. Kemet quickened his pace until his mount was next to hers, shield and sword ready. Aaron fixed the leader with a blistering stare as he passed, imploring trouble.

Guards blocked their path, regarding them through unmoving eyes. The centurion gave them a furious nod to stand aside. Grudgingly, the silent killers slowly gave way, and the humans continued on. A row of butchered Krayal came into view, their fronts slit open from neck to naval. Wicked, jagged blades lay to one side. Flies and feeding insects buzzed in spinning clouds around the black-red gore at their feet.

Gemina eyes scrutinized every movement in the outpost, fully expecting the command to be barked and a hundred skeletal hulks to break out of the fort. Ayilia shot a furtive glance backwards. Their line was exposed on all flanks. Her bluster was the best weapon they had. Aaron was grinning wildly, clearly unable to handle the overwhelming surge of testosterone rushing through his system.

"Well," he jibbed at them. "Where's the might of Nethergeist now then, hey?"

Ayilia gestured at him to shut up. If the centurion considered killing him on the spot, the fear of Mabius held him rigid. Ayilia thanked the gods for that and beckoned the troops to pick up the pace. The gates ahead were firmly closed. Mindful that there was still a seething medley of armoured watchers in the background, Ayilia slid off her horse and kicked the sodden wood. With a flurry of splinters and cracking boards, they collapsed. Clearly, the guard had little need for fortification.

She returned to her mount, but not before catching sight of a lone sub-commander, a flagon of brown liquor in his boned fist. The Lifeless gaped at her, their jaw twerking rhythmically. They were mouthing obscenities in standard Nethergeistian, but not getting far. Looking back, Ayilia could see the centurion talking animatedly to his troops. Three shapes bustled over to a large wooden barn and came back with the gargantuan forms of huffing Prowlers, the beasts' red eyes clearly visible. They mounted the undead beasts and thundered in the opposite direction.

"Nicely done, Regent." Kemet beamed. "They had us outflanked. Not a good time to pick a battle."

Aaron seemed completely unbothered. "At least we skewered their superior sensibilities. You can't deny it felt good."

Kemet grimaced. "I've rarely seen Pit so belligerent. In fact, I've rarely seen them belligerent at all. Mabius has given the stiffs a reason to live, if you see what I mean."

"I bet most of the boneheads on this world will be *aghast* he's back. I think the vast majority quite like their lives now," Ayilia muttered as she urged her horse to pick up the pace.

Aaron sniggered. "I'd love to be a bug on the wall when Commander Stiff back there blows his spleen when he discovers he could've owned our organic hides after all."

Fatigue weighed on Seftus when he arrived at the hidden subterranean caverns, but he went straight to the meeting all the same. A scout had appeared out of nowhere a day ago and insisted he dropped everything to attend. War had returned to the edges of their bitter, windswept homeland, and the Krayal nations were in emergency shutdown.

The cave was vast. Shimmering struts of shiny crystal arched in great, belvedere vaults throughout a system of underground corridors, more akin to a glowing tomb than a shelter. The rock was a gossamer orange. The semicircle of stone seats facing Seftus were malachite fists of naked power. The surrounding auditorium was empty. Only the crescent of seats immediately opposite was populated, though the immobility of the silent watchers could have been mistaken for Lifelessness. A menagerie of reptilian statues armed with bows, blades and shredded quills signifying betrayals lined the far back wall.

There was a long silence. No one took their eyes off the Krayal chief.

Finally, the leading elder spoke. Her voice was scratched tin in the dry air.

"Seftus, you are heralded among our people." The words hung in the air. He almost rolled his eyes when he knew what was coming. It was always a feature. They just had to let him know their disapproval, no matter what the occasion or how much they needed him. "This is despite whispers that you are a warrior who prefers the company of other warriors, male warriors." Not quite a crime then, but something that still caused severe disquiet in such a conservative society. "However strange this is to us, the real question is *why* have you ignored our summons up to now?"

"Not warriors, *a* warrior. A man no longer with us, not that is anyone's damned business." They always got under his skin. They wanted, of course, to show him up. Seftus breathed in, trying desperately to keep his tone controlled. "In regard to ignoring the summons, it's war, Madam Elder. I had urgent duties to attend to."

"Meeting us is the most urgent duty you could attend to, especially in time of war." Her lips were cut lines in a withered roll of velvet cloth. An emaciated hand gripped a ceremonial spear with concealed strength. "I have seen more invasions than you've had years to live. This is no different. Our mountains held out then, and they will now."

Seftus' mouth worked feverishly, but the words were hard to find. "My lady, this is different."

Her face was a scowl. "How so? For the people who came to me then, it was different, yet the stain of atrocity is always the same. The soulless then behaved in the same way as the soulless now. You do not belong on the fronts; you belong here."

There was a long silence. Then she spoke again. "Seftus, we are the nomad council, and we do not have the time for schism. You think Empire is not interested in us; the universe of the soulless is after the hume city south of our mountains." She leaned forwards. "You think they want the female stooge, the one without power?"

Seftus looked away.

Her eyes widened. "You mock me with silence?"

"No." Seftus' eyes were needles in the dim light. "I think they want her, yes."

Her tone was pure scorn. "Because the gossips believe it? Everyone knows the back-bladers and their cheap tongues value fecklessness over intellect. Do not place faith in the changing opinion of such base personalities."

"No," Seftus bit back a little too defensively. "I do not listen to the prattle of others unless they have something worth saying, and that is almost never." He shifted uneasily on his feet. That sounded arrogant, and he knew it. "Jarong, my associate, had word from his scouts. Using their Krayal tracking skills, they succeeded in eavesdropping on the off-worlders at their nighttime campfire, like scouts used to do, in the early days."

"And?"

"Though details remain sketchy, they did discern a group of elite X Gemina soldiers had fled Agathon. They also discerned that these renegades were the object of the hunt. The Lifeless were griping about false trails, how their time was wasted on this remote world at the end of all things. They seemed to believe their quarry has now headed north, up here." Seftus regarded the watching faces sternly. "The Gemina would never desert the city like this unless their leader was present with them."

She waved her hand disdainfully, the veins a tapering network of worms across tight tendons. "Unless, perhaps, a member of the government was with them instead."

"The Gemina *hate* the new government. They would not desert their regent. No one in the Imperium would give a murmel's skull for the city's toothless political regime." He swallowed back acid bile. "My gut says it's the woman—she's been implacably opposed to the rule of the soulless all of her pitiful life."

Her glower in the half-light was a lemon hue. "You did not think to pass this on to the council?"

"I wanted to."

"*What?*"

Someone coughed in the hushed quiet.

"It makes no sense." Seftus gave a hapless shrug. "We sit on the edge of forever, of nothing. Not only are our people insignificant, so is this entire world. What could the most powerful tyrant in existence want with her, the puppet leader of escaped thralls?"

The woman regarded him for long moments. Her gaze missed nothing. "They do not want what little we have, or they would already be here. The whole desert crawls with them, but we see only the shadow's shadow." She closed her eyes and breathed in deeply. "Seftus, we are of different clans. In times of need, the leading figures of all tribes come together as the nomad council. You know this, but you do not know me. I am Amatashtar of the Ahiram."

Seftus fidgeted. "I know your name, my lady. My own clan is on passable terms with yours."

"Then you know of our friendship with the representative of the Resistance, First Gryphon Sceptre Agelfi Bil'Hazen? You also know that he used to traverse our lands to monitor the hume city directly? The regent's well-being was the driving force for his visits. I can tell you the Resistance and, unfortunately, many amongst us, believe that he has lately misplaced his wits, but we let him pass all the same out of respect for our friendship."

Seftus' clenched claws dug so deeply into his palms that they bled. His teeth were tight with venom. "I don't know what's worse: humes or that mad, old Heretic that visits them."

She rapped her stick on the floor. "Disapproval of us, Seftus? Recall our history, and how friends are priceless and rare. When we find them, we cherish them!"

The individual gazes of the circle of anhydrous faces bored into his own unflinchingly.

"I dislike outsiders and the tendency of our people to criticize those of us who get things done in times of difficulty."

Amatashtar paused to reflect, then stood up on bones as old as the rock supporting her, yet he was surprised at the cat-like vigour of her gait. Standing before him, she rapped the stick suddenly and violently against his shin. Startled, he found himself swearing colourfully.

Her brow arched. "Angry?"

"I ..." He bit back the words bubbling with fury to the surface.

She did it again.

Indignity and bruised ego swirled together, but he said nothing. She regarded him for several heartbeats.

Seftus inhaled again. "What is the purpose of—"

Amatashtar took her stick and slapped it so hard his temper flared out of all control. In a flash, his hand whisked the object from her grasp and smashed it against the wall, where it splintered in a series of reverberating cracks. The circle rose with a collective hiss. Nevertheless, Seftus' red face was thrust against her own.

"What the hell are you doing? I came here in answer to hail, not to be humiliated by some obsolete council's mummified harpy. I did not come here to be humiliated for choosing war over a hot-aired party or for being in a relationship where neither of the participants has a womb."

She was smiling, a spring crevice breaking through arctic permafrost.

"So, there is life in there, after all?"

His features were a milling knot of unfettered tendons. "What did you expect to find? Dust?"

"I don't know ..." Her voice trailed off. "Perhaps, the spirit of one of those soulless bone people skulking at our borders? You speak of choice! Do you choose self-regard over community, because only such people care about minor slights? Ego is the desert warrior's most crippling foe, Seftus. You know that. The blow was well-timed and, trust me, well-practiced."

Silently seething, the Krayal chief watched the elder shuffle back to her seat and then slowly sit. The observers sat too. Shame mixed dangerously with outrage and a searing sense of injustice. He was still furious that his personal life was up for judgment. He would never forgive that.

"Good," she said. "Let's start again." He gave no response. "I understand your distrust of off-landers. It is common enough amongst our people. But your boundless contempt of our *living* compatriots on this world shocks even me."

Seftus took in the silent expressions and realized he had nothing to lose. "Humes came to this world as star refugees that had scraped their way across the face of the night sky for centuries. We gave them land and trade. When the Imperium followed, we lost everything. I talk of a world where we once stretched from one horizon to the other. We live in the Zeinkarst and other assorted rocky rises of desiccated dumps. They, the free ones albeit, still have their rich and fertile coast. Their help, historically, was sometimes adequate, but mostly intermittent, and often only for selfish reasons."

He bared his teeth. "There is that Treaty, of course. Without it, we might have kept some of the lowlands. After they signed it, we lost their armour. Who knows what we might have kept if they had thought of us as much as themselves!"

"I see," she replied. He wondered if she did. "Your feelings are ubiquitous amongst our kind, Seftus, but amongst many of the learned, we understood that the humes had less choice than you might think. Signing the Treaty allowed the

Imperium to vacate our world and combat a renewed Heretic push. Had they stayed ..."

He could only scowl.

"Very well, Seftus, your bitterness is your guide, but also your burden, your corrosion, and yours alone. One day, if left untreated, it will consume you and all those that might still love you. All that remains are your orders."

His eyes narrowed. "My orders?

"You command great respect among the clans, especially the young bloods, a rare thing in this godless age. Your skills in the wild and your ability with that merciless blade have seasoned your instinct, some would say a little too much." She hesitated. "With regards to the Gemina, we know about them already; their tracks were sighted some days ago. In a universe of the soulless, it is essential that those who feel the song of the suns on skin co-operate."

The truth struck him with the force of a diamond arrow shaft. He almost spat with horror. "You want me to liaise with them? Gemina humes? The only ones who are dangerous?"

She leaned forward. The light refracted off a gaggle of rings on her hand in carmine splashes. "Not just liaise with them, Seftus. I want you to take them north; I want you to take them through a tiny, spatial doorway only the elders know of. I want you to go with them and find that 'mad, old Heretic' as you call him, so that he can do what he believes is right." She shrugged. "Maybe that puppet regency really is of use to what is left of their Resistance."

Seftus could scarcely believe his eyes. He spluttered, "So, I *was* right. You knew all along. It's all about the regent! You want me to help her? You want me to be her mountain guide?"

Amatashtar fell back against her seat, and the shadow reclaimed her features.

Two Krayal guards came up to Seftus and put a hand on his shoulder. The meeting was over, and there was nothing he could do about it. All he had left was the stark company of his disbelief.

❦ · ❦ · ☠ · ❦ · ❦

The air blew sharp but refreshing. The tension finally began to ease from taut muscles. The group of outcast humans were in the Zeinkarst proper now. Ayilia, who had been lost in thought all day, looked up. "Roots!"

Kemet and Aaron looked back at her, startled.

"Roots ... you know the big fat potato roots on the merrirand bush, seasoned with J'Lampa berries. There's plenty of merrirands round these parts; it's an ideal growing climate. They seed most of the year round so we should get plenty of fat, juicy tubers if we find a thicket or two. Time to celebrate, after all."

"What exactly are we celebrating?"

"We did it, Kemet, we're in! Unless they invade Krayal territory outright, the only thing we've got to worry about are hunting parties of human-hating reptiles and no water at all. Might as well enjoy ourselves while we can."

The next day and night passed swiftly. They saw no other sign of life, or non-life, in the Zeinkarst borderlands. Her dreams involved undead death beneath the majestic crannies of the karst summits, but she said nothing.

The next morning saw the suns immerse the gnarled crags in watery pyres of gold. After a while, the peaks began to drop away to a gravelly tundra of wispy shrubbery and sparse grassland. Undulating steppes strewn with grey slate ran towards walls of Karsk monoliths interspaced with meandering rivers in a complex web of glinting ribbonry.

The valley facing them was a spacious cauldron of mountainous molars and winding deltas the colour of smelted bronze. Ahead, a minor settlement of thatched circular roofs crouched beneath a pall of chimney smoke. They could make out livestock and mules grazing among moving figures. Rusty lines tapered from the hulking mounds of ore mines, almost at the edge of sight. Their copper hues refracted bloodlessly against the grimness of their watching features.

Muffled shouting broke the peace. Armed shapes were gesticulating in their direction.

"Bugger!" Aaron shook some wayward hair from a grimy forehead. "That's blown it, already."

Ayilia raised her arm. "Relax—if that lot back there didn't know anything, it's more than likely this rabble won't either." Balancing very carefully, Ayilia leaned back on her saddle to address the others. "If I remember rightly, this area is saturated with ore. We're an 'inspection unit'—if the border post was clueless about recent events, they'll be *entirely* clueless."

Kemet was frowning. "And if they resist?"

"We slaughter them. There can't be many. It's not a fortification; it's a poorly run, drone-work village with the only rules being to make money." She paused. "These things pop up everywhere."

Aaron shrugged and chewed his lip a little bit too vigorously. "Repeat—we get to kill them if they so much as break undead wind, right?"

"Something like that."

"Suits me."

Kemet kicked his stirrups and pushed forward. "Let's get to it then."

"Hail. Who violates Imperium territory? Speak, hume." A single soldier addressed them as aggressively as the centurion at the border. By the dialect, this lot were as local as the outpost. Legionnaires were swiftly appearing from doorways and sentry posts. Behind them, the village hummed, but it was a village of humans as well as drones. A market was in full swing. Chickens pecked at the shale, goats bleated by fences. A row of blacksmiths forged tools for the mines. Steam, smoke, and dust from the movement of feet, wheels, and hooves swathed a settlement that was surprisingly virile. A stocky figure burst out of the barracks, knocking aside some startled legionnaires as he did, and strode up to face Ayilia directly.

"You are the female administrator?" the Lifeless centurian barked.

"Last time I looked." Ayilia took a deep breath. She'd done this a thousand times. "By the powers granted by historic covenant, I demand access to both your records and subjects. In addition, I demand the right to inspect the health of your organic workforce using whatever measures I deem necessary. Under the terms and specifications of Treaty—"

"For the love of the undead god, just do it, hume; I don't give a damn!"

Ayilia's brow furrowed.

"Once you're done with the prattle, you can stay if it suits. The fields are brittle but they produce an acceptable Mustum, though the lora could strip the rind off a long-dead whore. It's more like Posca, our local vinegar, than wine! Howbeit, your arrival is impressively timely as tonight the villagers celebrate Newminia." Noting their uncertainty, it added impatiently, "It's an annual ritual unique to this desolate yard. It celebrates the farming solstice, or something like that. Personally, I just get stormed." Again, he noticed their blank expressions. Exasperated, he lowered his voice. "In these scum-forsaken borderlands where no one, but *no one,* ever visits, this forgotten garrison has developed rituals based on productivity, not corruption."

He hawked across the grit.

The humans looked at each other, astonished. Ayilia tried to speak, but there was no interrupting the tirade. "The Pro Consul can shove it up his skull sockets if he likes! Oft we double the quota they set, but they don't care, and they don't visit, so here I am, emperor, and here I get hog-washed whenever I can."

Ayilia heard sniggering behind her. She shot two of her soldiers a stare to curdle blood.

The commander noticed and flashed a bony smirk. "Believe me, this place runs just fine." He flicked some unfathomable debris out the ear gap from his chunky skull with a stubby digit. "And it's the cleanest hole on this planet!"

Ayilia turned to the Gemina. This had to be the most loquacious stiff she'd ever met. "Alright, you lot get checking—we're out of time already, so I don't want to take long."

She turned back to the figure and slid off her horse. "Trust me; we'll be out your hair ... *head* before you know it. I'm Ayilia, from the House of Kira. Do you have a name?"

"Of course," he replied, irritation mixing unevenly with bemusement. "Talorous, at your service. Stay or go; it's no skin off my socket. Newminia is only twice a week, so feel free to dive in." He turned and began to push through the watching troop.

"Wait!"

Talorous stopped and turned back, surprise in his arched brow. "Problem?"

"No. I'd like to talk to you in private, and maybe inspect your personal documents. If that's all right?"

"Whatever." Talorous shrugged again. "This way. This is where my ... office is."

Ayilia gingerly made her way through the watching crowd after Talorous, followed by Aaron and Soren. After they'd entered the office, the heavyset Lifeless slammed the door shut with his foot, upsetting an amphora and a number of glass bottles in the process.

"They should be over here. Somartise keeps the records. He has a strange fetish for figures." He threw open some drawers and yanked out yellowing ledgers. "If you see the Consul, tell that son-of-a-he-witch we're fed up with rancid slop for repair and resource. It's not a cut on the off-world models we saw the other day. Mother of all hells, they looked freshly stitched, mean, and keen."

Ayilia's blood froze. He'd answered her question before she'd even had a chance to form it. She turned to a gobsmacked Soren before he could say anything. "Okay ... right. Soren, take a rundown on these figures." He looked dumbfounded. "*Soren.* Please check the figures."

"Okay." He opened some folders and was immediately immersed in a cloud of dust. Keeping her eye fixed on Talorous, Ayilia went through the motions of giving a damn about figures no one wanted to see. "Start with the virgates, Soren, then scan the holds and hides, then any demesne you can find. Remember, we are short on time."

"Rest assured, there's no exploitation here," interrupted Talorous. "The villagers give us ore, crop, and barely, and we give them peace and the dubious benefit of our fireside wit. Out here, without trust and the grape, we'd go completely batshit."

Ayilia nodded to Soren, who made an appalling pretence of reading the folios aloud to Aaron, who was equally appalling in pretending that he was listening. Rolling her eyes, Ayilia sidled up to the embittered supervisor as he rummaged through the ramshackle contents of a drawer. "You're not the usual type of soldier we meet here."

"It's the paradox of a Lifeless universe—we are just as caged as you."

Ayilia didn't know what to say. She looked around the room uncertainly. "So, you mentioned outsiders?"

He swirled on her, eyes a deep shade of ruined amber. "Don't take me for homesick roadkill, hume! These lands are as exciting as a caulker's plums, and yet here you are, the top hound in a pack of obsolete armour. Mayhap we have a most unlikely convergence of accidents here: off-world head-hunters engaged in some kind of archaic venery and the head herself of what little's left of her freedom, both on the same road at the same time. I don't buy happenchance or mysticism—give me a soothsayer, and I'll give him a good boot up his crooked joints over coin, any time."

Ayilia's mind raced. Talorous' eyes glimmered with an intellect only sated by a glowering hunger to be treated with respect. "These are sown and hammered beings of death, hume. They march like machines and kill like jackals. They think they own the place—hell, they do. Pit people are their peons, not their kin. They are the scab-sucking scobblelotchers of the universe, so what's the point?" He slammed his knuckles into the wall with so much force that plaster detonated in alabaster missiles across the room. Everyone froze in their tracks, except Soren, who was still fighting with the dust.

"So, they treat you with as much regard as us." Her voice was dry. "Doesn't seem just to me, Talorous."

"No such thing." He growled, still facing the battered wall.

"These troops, could you tell me where they were heading?"

Talorous fixed her an acidic glare, his thick brow crunched with suspicion. "Now, Regent, I thought *you* would know something about that?"

A pregnant pause. Carefully, watching every word, she replied levelly. "I don't, because it's me they are probably after!"

The thing nodded but didn't answer. Ayilia's eyes were fixed on his powerful skeletal frame. In the confined space, the one saving grace was that his weaponry would be of little value. "Talorous, the Pit has fallen. I don't think the Pro Consul is in charge anymore; his rabid family is."

"Whatever." However, he paused in thought for long moments, then turned to fully face her. "There are two routes ahead. They took the left. If you take the right and take it swiftly, it is possible you will miss them—for a while. I understand the Gemina are the only organics capable of fighting such things. Never once forget; however, you are still physically inferior."

Surprising herself as much as anyone, she went over and put a tender hand on his shoulders. "I'll not forget this." She turned to go and stopped with a wry smile. "I want you to know this is the best run centre I've ever seen in all the Pit's lands."

Talorous hunched his shoulders but looked pleased, nevertheless. "Whatever."

♀ · ♀ · ☠ · ♀ · ♀

Grim, impassive faces of ruin regarded the road ahead from beneath chafed hoods. Occasionally, a Prowler would snort hunks of glacial mucus from un-breathing nostrils. A pair of eyes regarded Vespasian intently before looking away. It was clear that Stilgen was thinking judgemental thoughts that the Lifeless weren't programmed to think. Vespasian wondered, not for the first time, how long Stilgen had been doing it and why he hadn't noticed before.

"The Gauntlet Clasp, the tail end of the Zeinkarst this side of the Agathon Stretch," Stilgen muttered, joining him. "These peaks are actively volcanic, unlike the Zeinkarst itself. They are also considerably more varied—low-level mountains, valleys, craggy hills, that sort of thing."

"Essentially, an excellent place to hide!"

Vespasian took in the panoramic vista. The main thrust of the Zeinkarst shouldered off to his left. Smouldering calderas and red-rimmed pinnacles col-lectively crafted a skyline of outstretched, rocky fingers. To his front and right ran the Gauntlets. Here nestled the borderline tribes, some of the most warlike Krayal going.

The Krayal!

Despite their spears and cutthroat demeanour, they refused to live off the butchered flesh of anything with a pumping heart or a discernible face. It was an astonishing custom, as it made their scratchy existence in the rises bitterly tough. It was also another wedge between their holistic society and the more 'barbarous' human settlers down south. Some swore the lizards hated the humes more than the Lifeless, another paradox in a universe permanently upside down.

The Sythian warlord rubbed the porcelain veneer of his almost non-existent skin, deep in thought. It folded like crisp pastry across his unforgiving skull. "According to chroniclers' tales, the Imperium once believed the earth of this world was rich in ore. The more they conquered, the less they found. By the time the Goat's minions had learned their mistake, the Krayal bordered on extinction, and the humes were helots."

Stilgen's whitened, minutely cracked brow furrowed. "It is almost tragic."

Vespasian shot him a glance. Stilgen's calcified features shone dully in the harsh light. Skin equalled status, an absurdity considering the disgust their kind felt for the living. Unlike his Sythian master, however, Stilgen had not been ripped from a living womb and had none. Mabius' off-worlders were even starker. Nevertheless, the failed warlord found himself envying their shiny, diamond-hard bone, the rasping violence of their voices, and the abusive intensity of their scarlet orbs. The 'Pitters' were an underground rabble of nobodies in comparison.

"What's tragic?"

"That such a heroic and proud people were forced into the austerity of the rises, after once dominating the plains behind."

Vespasian shrugged. "Indeed, but they are the proverbial 'hopper in the gale.' Sooner or later, they will be blown over."

Stilgen looked down briefly. He was scrubbing the weapon with a sudden, feverish intensity, using a portable blade stone. The noise was jarring, intrusive.

Vespasian's gaze narrowed. "Problem?"

Stilgen grunted.

"Speak freely. We have no secrets!"

"Isn't it premature, going in like this?"

The warlord regarded him carefully. The suns were irradiating his rampant, unkempt hair with a bushfire of golden hues. It looked like a dark, dilapidated cornfield had taken root on his skull and been left to moulder for centuries. "You're worried that Mabius is sending us to certain doom, outnumbered and surrounded by an enemy who's nothing left to lose?"

"I think we're the rodent in a trap." He gestured to the watching troop behind. "I mean, look at them. They're hammered together from poor quality manure and rancid Ichor—they can hold a desert plain but give them a hill and they'll have a hernia." Stilgen was animated now. The arcing contours of his eyes gleaned with resentment. "Why do this? Your brother intends us to expose Krayal positions and the hume female with them, by using us as bait. In a day or so, our sightless skulls will be lying facing the skies amid the cacti and murmel waste, while vultures will nest in our brain cavities chewing our fingers."

Vespasian laughed. "By the undead god, I had no idea you'd developed such a healthy imagination." Slowly, carefully, he turned to the dour being whose presence he had taken for granted for so long.

"Stilgen?"

"Aye."

"Did I hear you correctly? Are you implying mutiny?"

Stilgen stopped rubbing a sword, now superheated by friction. "I merely suggest your brother's going to kill us."

Vespasian stepped closer. "You hate them, don't you: the off-worlders and the Imperial beast that sent them?"

Stilgen took the blade and swished it through the air two or three times. It glinted in fleeting arcs of silver.

"I think they're self-centred, arrogant, and bloodless. If it were not for us, the Resistance would have made this world a deadly and resolute base. As reward, the Imperium crucified you—you cannot walk without a limp and your left arm is fractured. You are scarred and pitted and your coordination is pitiful. I think they should be butchered where they stand, with extreme prejudice. I would like to get my cutter and ..." Stilgen checked himself mid-track. The light spangled around the two friends in soft shimmers as though embedded in a nebula of blazing cotton. There was a black urgency in his gaze. "Flee; don't fight. Once they have her, you're irrelevant and the off-worlders will kill you if the Krayal don't."

Vespasian looked away for long moments, then faced Stilgen with a hint of bitter mirth. "I would like to be a bug on the wall when the Unholy Ass at the centre of all things realizes the regent's a dud."

⚉ · ⚉ · 💀 · ⚉ · ⚉

The Lifeless and hapless troop from the Pit were sitting half-bored on armoured Prowlers. Feathers of dust rolled in sandy breakers across the sparse flora, refracting the void inside the necrotic non-soul of each. Vespasian took a deep breath before addressing them.

"We are going into Krayal territory. The Clasps are just over there. All those on point maintain close watch. Tugor, you wait with the mounts at our agreed meeting zone: take two guards for security. Reena, gather the others—adopt battle formation Virpon and follow myself and Stilgen. The lizards haven't seen Pit forces for decades, so any response is hopefully going to be ragged and intermittent, at least at first. Don't forget that from now on we're on our own." He lowered his voice. "It is the terrain beyond that makes the heathens within such a threat; treat it with respect."

"Sire?"

He inhaled. "Tugor?"

"I still don't think I can read the map. I might lose the Prowlers."

"It was upside down, remember? Make sure the inscribed 'arrow' is pointed upwards!"

"Er, okay. Arrow."

"Sire?"

Vespasian swallowed a surge of irritation. "Yes, Reena?"

"Once the Imperial off-worlders invade the Krayal and get the hume renegade, what happens to us?"

"Happens? Nothing! We go back, or, if Tugor doesn't learn to read old maps properly, we die. Then the local rodents get to see how tasteless our manufactured gut really is."

"But, sir—"

"But nothing—get the others and form the Virpon. In case you were unaware after all these years of stupefaction, it's like a sand snake; handy in the winding passages. Anything square and we'll get stuck in the gorges."

He didn't blame anyone for asking questions. None of them had realized their relatively small and under-equipped unit would venture alone into an armed mountain wilderness without support. In fact, none of them had been told they'd join him at all. The few witless saps too dumb to disown him on the spot were permanently fused to him.

Bad memories surfaced like floating corpses from the depths of an onyx lake. His compost heap gut went caustic. Mabius humiliating him in public again and again as they reached the emotional rage of puberty. Those gruesome displays of thaumaturgic tantrums, as the superbeing battered his elder with bolts of crimson abuse. The fury that grew in direct proportion to the increasing realization he was largely theurgically sterile. Mabius revelled in an audience, especially when the great and the not-so-good from the Senate came to gawk at the thrilling brood of thaumaturgic demi-gods being reared at the periphery of civilization. To have discovered one was extraordinary enough, but to have a family of them was astounding.

It seemed perfectly logical to renegotiate the Treaty with the Regent of the House of Kiya, Harden, Ayilia's father, based on peaceful coexistence after Sulla and the Imperial forces left, the infamous Abandonment. For a while, peace and harmony ruled a place defined by conquest. By the time of the second decade, this policy was taking him nowhere with the Imperium. For a universe of the soulless, good governance had brought him nothing short of anathema.

Reena was barking at the lines. She loved barking at the lines.

"Oi, you worm-sagged dolts! Get into line. There's going to be a little bit of friction ahead and because it's unlikely to be hand-to-hand, you're going to have to keep your beady, slumber-sprained peelers well and truly sharpened. The geckos like to fight from above, on their high hills, so make sure you use your pilums and keep your shields raised. Do not, I repeat, do not elect to expose your bony asses, or anything else you regard as precious, as these fellas will take that as a special invite for some in-depth target practice." She smiled. "Let's face it, they could hardly miss!"

Pilums were heavy-set javelins with a pyramidal iron head on a long shank fastened to a carved wooden handle. Not only were they capable of piercing heavier armour and light shields at short-range, they were ideal for picking off Krayal on low-level overhangs. Despite this, Reena had to keep yanking the weapons out of dilapidated hands to demonstrate how even to carry them. Through gritted molars, she repeatedly bellowed at them to be careful when tossing the shank and to release the rope on those that still had rope. If the point didn't turn on penetration and the rope was snagged on the hand, the weapon could become permanently embedded. "Imagine that!" she cried, loving every moment. Imagine thrower and victim meshed into a collective pirouette of grotesque destruction as the enemy on both sides hacked them to pieces in a frenzied melee.

The troop dismounted.

A reluctant Tugor and two others began to lead the Prowlers off for the agreed rendezvous. The rises were far too steep and constrictive to bring such powerful beasts.

Reena began shouting at their backs: "Stop fretting, you rundown old hags; we've had worse." Then, under her own breath. "That was before I was breached-birthed into existence from some mouldy old tank, of course."

Vespasian led from the front. Stilgen wasn't happy about the formation, but the Consul was adamant. If there was to be any hope of rehabilitation, a spot of artificial courage couldn't hurt, assuming they weren't killed.

It was easy to see why the Krayal had taken refuge here. The tracks ahead had become tightly sandwiched between alleyways as emaciated as battered ribbon, so the troop elected to clamber over the rounded hillocks instead. Stilgen's furrowed frown deepened to trench proportions. Archers kept their crossbows cocked while a small vanguard scrabbled to higher ground. On the summit, they instinctively formed a barbed semi-circle of armaments and shields, the Porcupine. A forbidding row of stark rises emerged on the line of sight. Not as lofty as the majestic Zeinkarsk, they nevertheless formed the spine of the Clasps. The rises tapered off to infinity, combined into a flank of broken-toothed summits of all sizes.

The look on Reena's puckered face said it all. Before she had time to speak, Vespasian chipped in, "I know. Far from ideal."

"An optimistic assessment," she grumbled sardonically, always happy to forget command structures when the mood took her. "That's going to cost us legs going up there and arms *and* probably heads!"

"Moderately suicidal then," he said, wryly amused. "We're not in the Gauntlets for the view, no matter how spectacular."

"I thought as much. We're bait."

Stilgen glowered at her. "Then we'd better keep our eyes open."

The heat was intense, the surrounding rock hotter than a recently fired stone oven. After an hour, the group came to an abrupt and undignified stop. The Miniature Mountains were almost impossible to cross in a straight line, or any other kind of line for that matter. There was little choice but to descend back down to a labyrinth of winding, constricted passes below.

Vespasian held his hand up. "Looks like the Virpon again. Please keep it tight and minimize the target. Show the shields to the peaks and return any incoming with everything we've got. Also, please, keep it down."

Reena needed no encouragement. "To reiterate," she spun aggressively to the troop behind, "*Don't* say a bloody word. One witless wisecrack too many, and we could have every single scale-rump scuttling up our collective snouts." She jabbed her finger at the nonplussed rejects. "Another thing. If we happen to be surrounded, form the Shellfire. Attack formations like the Virpon and the Porcupine would leave us lethally exposed, especially the tail."

The Consul nodded wearily. Almost every waking moment, he was using what little Magi ability he had to soothe those of his wounds that they couldn't heal in the Pit. Stilgen looked like he was severely constipated. Vespasian, feeling tense himself, leaned closer. "I know what you think," he whispered. "Things must be bad to even contemplate using the Shellfire, a formation of last resort." There was no reply. The silence said it all.

A single soldier, literally saying what everyone was thinking, came forwards and tapped Rena on the shoulder. "If we have to use the Shellfire, that means we're going to die, right?"

"It also means a lot of lizards are going to die. A two-way thing!" Stilgen barked.

Another soldier was shaking her cranium, unconvinced. Vespasian noticed, for the first time, that she had decorated her face with an ochre shade of rouge. He was astonished. Since when did Pit soldiers start wearing face paint? "This whole outing is one big death sentence," she said. "We wouldn't need a Shellfire, otherwise."

"Aye," came a chorus of muffled grunts.

"Don't want rats up me bits," said a strangely robust soldier. It was odd, as Pit soldiers were not able to gain weight like humans. Again, the Consul was taken aback. His people were not only aping the organics, but somehow, they were beginning to look like them.

Another round of approval followed the soldier's utterances. A mob mentality was sinking in, and mobs would clap for anything.

A soldier named Bastubic stepped forward. "We're built for desert flatlands, not that high-rise mausoleum of spite. They'll hit us with everything they have."

"Aye," said the face-painted female again. Her name was Stagen. At least, Vespasian thought she was. He was more interested in the fact she had ear jewellery, an impressive feat since they didn't have ears; she'd implanted hoops into her skull somehow. "We don't get repaired often enough, we don't get oiled often enough, we don't get kissed often enough, in fact, not at all, and we don't get the best materials often enough. In fact," she thumped her rusted armour with a dirty thumb, "we don't get anything often enough, except Pit manure."

Kissed? Vespasian's eyes were moons.

"Unlike the new arrivals, the Imperials. They're gold standard they are," Bastubic shouted angrily. "They'll also be right up our ass!"

Stilgen had had enough. "Pity's sake, stop this whining. Either we go on and probably die or we go back and *guaranteed* to die." His thumbed towards the way they had come. "Would you rather fight geckos or Mabius? He doubts your resolve and your courage, and he regards you as no more than Prowler feed. Don't give him the satisfaction of being right."

At the mere mention of his brother's name, everyone immediately went quiet.

☠ · ☠ · ☠ · ☠ · ☠

After some time had passed, visible waves of relief began sweeping through the ranks at the lack of enemy activity. The rocky alleyways they'd vacated had become as constricted as a choking man's throat. A breathtaking array of ridges, crags, and undulating pinnacles haloed within the dying light now lay before them. Deep crevices cobwebbed the sides of every slope. Soft twilight and crisp darkness vied in huddled, menacing shapes.

Vespasian exhaled softly, but the alveoli of his lungs were as useful as deceased dust mites. He stopped and turned to Stilgen.

"Perhaps the Krayal haven't got wind of my kin's imminent arrival and aren't expecting us? Look at it from their point of view. I mean, what could they possibly imagine Mabius would want with *this* weather-tortured place? Still, if they are aware of our force of grumbling mannequins, it'd be best to wait until our intentions are clear." He gave a brief chuckle. "We're just as likely to break our necks getting there as getting ambushed, after all."

"Then let's pray they have grown toothless since their last hiding at the Imperium's hands." Stilgen's eyes narrowed. "I can see it now, historians and scribes of the future recording this as the Battle of the Imbeciles."

The warlord smiled. "Things must be bad. That was your first joke in years."
Stilgen's impassive face furrowed with confusion. "Joke?"

Chapter Ten

KILL JOY

The thick, beige-white strata towering above the human renegades looked more like an otherworldly cake than a rock face. Gaunt, alabaster trees perched precariously from disjointed ledges; their exposed roots gripped the precipices with desperate intent. Though the X Gemina had come to meet the Krayal, paradoxically, no one wanted to attract attention. Not one of them could recall the last time anyone had had a face-to-face meeting with the elusive reptilian humanoids.

The historic alliance had decayed into a historical drip-drip of relentless negativity. Everything became the Krayal's fault. Humans blamed theft on them. Humans would curse them for a rise in crime, for an unexplained rape outside the city walls, or for the disappearance of a citizen somewhere in the desert. The news pamphlets even claimed the 'saurian cutthroats' ate unwary travellers despite their aversion to flesh. What would they, the Krayal, make of her petition for aid now? For a heartbeat, she hated Agelfi for even suggesting she come here, on doomsday's door.

They stopped for an early afternoon meal. Lightly salted, dried fish seasoned with dashes of Beech helm spice and vengah (thick, luxuriant green vegetables found in damp climates) were mixed with potato root from the Merrirand bush. Then, it was off to be immersed in a forest of rocky spires that gradually replaced the ledges and imposing rises. The spectacular array of natural skyscrapers semi-circled upwards to the horizon. It was a silent city, one devoid of life. Late afternoon became evening.

Aaron joined Ayilia and Kemet at the front. His skin was soft strawberry, a perfect match for the faded red-blonde, somewhat silver, thatch always warring with his scalp. She leaned over and released a wry smile.

"This still beats addressing the new Panchayat."

He returned an amused scowl. "Right. The ingrowing toenails wetting their entitled britches down some Imperial thrall-pit right now, digging for salt. Wonder if it went the way they thought it would?"

Ayilia grinned openly but stayed silent.

The place seemed to concentrate thought. Everyone was retreating into their own insular cocoons. She found herself drifting back to a buried time, a time when Aaron had made her feel she was the only person in his world. It had been a long, hot summer. She'd been young and inexperienced.

Because everyone had warned her, she'd made a point of ignoring them. She had done a lot of that then. As the years slipped by, she'd come to see Aaron as an arrogant pig. He eventually found a kind of bickering contentment with a stubborn spear woman from the regs who had a penchant for earrings made of mouse skulls and body piercings the size of ships' anchors. Ayilia, on the other hand, had found that things only got more complex.

That was, of course, life.

The other two important relationships in her life were a definite improvement, which, compared to Aaron, was hardly difficult. One was Jacob, a person with dwarfism, that ran the city's main apothecary. He also specialized in racing pigeons. She caught people laughing at them together, but he was the gentlest, most emotionally aware person she'd ever met. He was mugged one day, walking home from his very successful business. The thieves, expecting a wallet of gold coins, only managed to steal a silk kerchief and a bottle of perfume he'd specially made for her.

He died six days later in her arms.

The other was Lorelai Milandra Kelcrest.

Lorelai had been the closest she'd come to real love. They'd been together a decade. At one point, Ayilia had told the then Provost she'd marry Lorelai once her father succumbed to the necromantic phage, as at the time had been becoming increasingly likely. After a period of mourning, she'd chuck everything in and hand her regency over to the Doge.

In those days, the government was mildly tolerable.

Even then, the city was forgetting its loyalty to her father and didn't seem to notice that she'd persuaded the Panchayat to tax the rich and distribute the wealth, among other things. If anything, some were more concerned that she was romantically involved with another woman, especially the landed interest, the kind of people the regency historically relied on. As time went on, she became increasingly desperate to throw the whole thing in the political bin and settle down on the spot.

Instead, her father hung on.

Ayilia was glad. She never gave up hope. Agelfi regularly sent herbs and assorted medicinal tinctures his people thought might help, but they never worked, and no one knew what mephitic enchanter was responsible.

Ayilia would've married her at any point, but Lorelai refused to commit to a legal arrangement while she was regent. Unfair perhaps, but she had a hatred of the ways things were done, the way some in the city treated their woman puppet, while Ayilia couldn't resign until she became regent proper. The law was specific, and she refused to leave her helpless father like that anyway, no matter what the cost.

One day, Lorelai just left.

There was a brief note on the side dresser when Ayilia came home. There were even kisses the morning of.

They had been arguing for some time. The pressure of the acidic judgements from the city's back-bladers, the behind-the-scenes scheming, and the venality of the gossip pamphlets were corrosive. All the time, waiting for a good man, the regent, to open his eyes or die. It ate at everything.

Lorelai went south to the same safe place Kemet's family had fled.

Ayilia didn't trust people, not because of who Aaron, Jacob, or Lorelai were. She didn't trust people to share her fading ideals with because she *knew* nothing or no one could stay. It was the way it was. She didn't know why or how or who or what made these decisions, but she felt it in every particle of her soul. Until something happened somewhere, she was destined to be isolated and bitingly lonely.

In some ways, it was almost a relief. It meant she didn't have to wed some self-obsessed sycophant, people who could offer only a relationship of three: them, and them, and her. The low-key scandal of her 'inconsiderate' single status was almost worth it. Nothing epitomized society's definition of what being a good woman was more than a cooperative womb.

She'd certainly put Aaron out of her head until the day he'd shown up, rejected, at the doors of her very own unit. She could've kicked him out as the regs had, *should've* kicked him out, but he was a good soldier, and she'd put the service first. Also, life had taken his machoistic arrogance and levelled it a bit. He was almost likeable.

"Ayilia?"

"Umm?"

Aaron cleared his throat and brought his horse closer. Kemet followed suit. She felt outflanked and outgunned. Damn, they were ganging up on her.

"I still don't get it. Normally, I wouldn't bat a lid at Imperial double dealings, honest. As I'm supposed to be the second-in-command and Kemet the third, I, *we*, were wondering when you'll spill the beans!"

Mock indignation. "I thought I'd had."

"With the greatest of respect, you've told us enough to skin a ground murmel. They want you *real* bad, but what do you mean He's 'seen' you in dreams? The Great Dolt, I mean? Makes Him sound like some cosmic stalker!"

"The emperor thinks your ... unique perspective can help Him?" Kemet added, also clearly unhappy. Like Jarrak before him, he'd spent years keeping the rumours of her apparent 'witchling' curse secret. Now, even the Goat had heard of it. "Hell, Regent, folk will see you more a freak than a fugitive."

Ayilia shrugged. "I think the Dolt has got Himself all soiled up over a bunch of shades that don't exist."

"They must be the liveliest bunch of shades in the universe to get the Goat *this* riled." Aaron scoffed. "Come on, Ayilia, we've all been through too much for secrets now. If we can't trust each other, what's the point?"

She filled them in, again. They listened politely. Given his sour expression, it still remained utterly incomprehensible to Kemet. Aaron was predictably more robust. Every other paragraph, he sounded off about something. "The Goat's senile, it's official! Well, *sod 'em all*—we'll give this Resistance whatever murmel lunacy might be stored in your brains, assuming that old Heretic pal of yours hasn't gone totally la-la, then we'll go down fighting."

She nodded. "Go down fighting, indeed."

After some intense debate with Ayilia, Aaron trotted back to join Kemet, who had fallen back. Aaron's little finger was all that touched the bridle, betraying long years in the saddle.

Kemet slouched on his mount. "Still no luck, hey?"

"What do you think?"

"I'm assuming that's a no, Aaron!"

"As I said, it should've been you who tried to push the point! I *did* warn you!"

"And as *I* said, I already tried days ago. She's too stubborn."

Aaron patted his horse absentmindedly. "You've been her personal guard for more years than I can be assed to remember. She tells you things no one else hears."

Kemet grunted. "Maybe. But considering your distant past together, there have been occasions she felt *you* were the best to confide with over certain matters."

Aaron chortled. "Do I detect some rebuke, old friend? Be honest, you never thought I was good enough for her even though, of course, I'm talking of events that happened in Jarrak's day."

Kemet arched his brow. For long moments, he said nothing. "The regent's private life was always her own, officially." He frowned. "But I will say you're the *last* person I thought I'd be friends with all these years later."

"That makes two! Doesn't take away from the fact you still thought I wasn't good enough."

"Goes with the job." He grinned. "It's what I do—keep her away from undesirables like you. Shame she didn't listen to me then. In fact, shame she doesn't listen to me now."

Aaron snorted with mock outrage. "My God, Kemet, are you telling me you *don't* object to me anymore, you pompous, relatively-old git?"

Kemet slapped him. "I object to you emptying my family house of every speck of spare grub we might have had every week!"

"*Me?*" Aaron gasped, putting on his best-injured look. "Nessan and Kofi were always there when I turned up. Who the hell invites them?"

"No one. They're even ruder than you!"

They both broke out laughing. The sound reverberated off the dry walls and bounded down the passageways into rocky oblivion.

Kemet rubbed his glistening dome mournfully. "If this little jaunt isn't just one big wizard wind-up, I don't what is. I always wanted Ayilia to stay away from that Heretic Agelfi, but Jarrak never listened. He never saw magick as harmful."

Aaron scratched his brow uneasily. "To be perfectly frank, I used to loathe that clapped-out goat, coming off-world to check on her, too." He leaned over his saddle and spat across the ground. It sizzled lightly on some rocks. A tiny lizard scuttled over and began licking it up. "I heard Jarrak swore the Heretic had a calming effect on Ayilia's issues; kept her safe. Heck, they swore the old man believed Agelfi was protecting her."

Kemet fumbled for his water pouch and sucked in deeply. Water splattered down his legs and across the ground, where it was immediately consumed by more lizards. "Jarrak never got it wrong, but if this is one big wizard paper chase, I'll take out that Heretic-that-really-isn't-a-Heretic and run him through with Mr. Faithful here." He patted the hilt of his weapon.

Aaron spat again, to the delight of the reptiles. "Come on, Kemet, this is bud-to-bud talking, so tell me truthfully. You don't think there's something in Ayilia's skull worth it to either Goat or the Heretic outside a fevered imagination?"

Kemet chewed his lip but said nothing. Satisfied, Aaron rode on quietly next to him.

$\bullet \cdot \bullet \cdot \bullet \cdot \bullet \cdot \bullet$

The dying light gave one final dance off the gilded armour and polished shields of the silent riders. There was only the muffled sound of creaking saddles and the soft chinking of spears. Ayilia ruefully massaged an annoying ache at the top of her buttock, not caring how undignified it looked. *Too much time on horseback.*

She yawned and gave up scanning the uneven landscape. Under the darkening twilight, both her vision and her spirits were dipping fatefully into shadow.

What was that?

Ayilia jerked to full consciousness.

There it was again. An impression was flitting across the mound of rocks to the right. Her tired eyes were treacherously feeding a mind addled with sprites. She scrutinized every contour in pinprick detail.

An unfocused humanoid stood slightly abreast of the rocks facing them. Kemet had already caught up with her, sword arm poised. She heard the clacking of sharp flints thrust by calloused hands into cross bolts and archers prepping their bows.

"No," she hissed, waving her left hand fiercely. "Don't alarm them—they're an extremely paranoid culture."

Aaron gestured the others down with his palms, then shot Ayilia a fierce look. Nessan followed suit, calming those at the back.

No one cursed or challenged the silent watcher.

"Right, here goes," Ayilia muttered a little louder than she intended.

"Wait, you can't do this alone."

"I have to, Kemet. More than one appears aggressive, and aggression will upset everything. Their cooperation is crucial."

"I don't like this," he spat.

"Nor do I."

Ayilia dismounted and approached the figure slowly. The temptation to reach for her shield and side arm was irresistible. There were more of them now. The watchers had gravitated to open space, though they were still camouflaged by the dim light and craggy overhangs. She swallowed rising apprehension. These people, as far as she knew, hadn't sent an honorary representative for longer than she could remember, though illicit trades used to take place. Once Agathon's markets had heaved with trinkets, batiks, emblems, thick pelts, precious stones, and dirks fashioned from Krayal forges. Now it was rare to see anything bearing their mark.

The Krayal stood as still as the stone they perched on, like hawks eyeing the scurry of rodents. Ayilia stopped a dozen hands from the rocky outcrop. She resisted the urge to speak, sensing it was appropriate to await acknowledgement on their turf.

"You are unwanted here, human!"

The sibilant rasp rattled off the rocks like dry chaff. She fought to keep her face calm, mildly impressed that it knew her tongue.

"My name is—"

"I do not care. I will not repeat myself. Leave. Now!"

She glanced at Kemet, then back at the speaker. He was male and stood over six feet, gaunt, and coiled like a hangman's knot. Wild skins, taken from already-dead bush life, covered a rusted, light breastplate the shade of wine. Their face remained obscured by darkness. Ayilia waited, trying not to press too hard, desperately thinking. They had to be at least curious.

"There was a day when we were allies," she replied evenly, letting that settle in. "But that's gone, as is our city. There's no reason you should care what's happened to us, but reflect on this: you'll be next! Historically, the Lifeless had less regard for your people than ours—trust me, negotiation is not an option."

The Krayal bunched his hands. Dry veins ran in frayed networks across scaled arms. "I submit a final warning—if you don't go *now*, we shall fire. The accord is dead. Gemina or not, we will grind you down with the advantage of our positions and anger sharper than a cutter hewn from barbed wire."

Damn Agelfi. He was utterly, completely wrong. Maybe he hadn't even made it or warned this tribe; Otho has done us all in with his timing. Agelfi is already the only card I have left.

Ayilia held her position, letting the Krayal stew for long heartbeats.

"Agelfi Bil'Hazen told us to come here, that you would accept us. He talked to your seniors. They agreed to help. I believe he means the nomad council." Silence. That was a good sign, as they went. "I believe the council is also the collective voice of the Krayal!" It was a statement, not a question. Still, there was silence. "Good, so you have heard we were coming. You've been instructed to assist us too! Whether you like that or not, *I* don't care. What I care about are the consequences if our peoples don't cooperate. I'm talking about genocide, not another raid in the good old days when you only lost barren desert." Silence.

"A dilemma whatever way you look at it," Ayilia half whispered. "Risk the wrath of the Lifeless to help us or get wiped out if you don't."

She expected a quivering shaft to smash through her chest.

"You come here entreating for help, hume, when, at this very juncture, your dead allies have encircled our domains. What do you think we are? Ignoramuses with no will to fight? You flaunt the name of our Resistance friend, even as your co-conspirators violate our people, rob our lands, and spit on our bones. I was instructed to help, but this treachery changes everything. If you don't turn back, *you* will become our priority! Hume 'values' ... they make us sick."

She was stunned. It must have showed, as the dark figure was scanning her face. Perhaps he'd noticed?

"You mean the Empire *and us*? You think the Gemina took up arms with the dead?" She took a deep breath, seeing she had the speaker's attention. "We knew *nothing* of this. My House fought with your people once, but we are not spies or decoys. We've been running for our lives through the Zeinkarst, evading pursuit from the same people raiding your lands. We are only here because Agelfi sent us to you. Trust me, throwing ourselves at the mercy of a people who hate us as much as the enemy was the last thing I would have done."

There was scuffling on the rise. With a degree of dexterity, the speaker leapt down and padded towards her amidst motes of swirling dust. There was an immediate series of clanking as the Gemina raised their weapons. Ayilia didn't flinch, though the Krayal was a good four hands taller than her.

"Why?"

"Why what?" She frowned. "Why should you trust us?"

It didn't answer. Her gaze flicked over features as sharp as wrought flint. Like her, he was bipedal. Deep-set, red-veined eyes regarded her among the shining malachite scales. His jaw was slim but strong; his nose was both bent and oddly aquiline. Two ridges ran back under a rust-green, wispy mat of hair that was cut short at the nape of the neck. His eyes were pickled balls of burning hostility.

"First, Lord Gryphon Agelfi was a childhood mentor and one of my closest confidantes," she spat. "He was my friend, my guide, and my guardian during a youth spent hiding from critics and nebulous devilkin that haunted my nights."

There was no change in the Krayal's expression. "We are here because Agelfi's Krayal friends are going to help us leave this world. I have their details, here."

She fumbled out a piece of paper and shoved it into a join in his half-hidden breastplate.

"He believes we can still help the dying Resistance, the *only* people who can defeat the walking carrion at your door." The figure didn't move. She tried to mask a rise of irritation. "To be brutally honest, I don't trust you any more than the stiffs. We can bend to Nethergeist's will and beat the shit out of each other right here, right now, or we can do what the council has asked you to do. Join forces."

She looked at darkened shapes watching from the high rocks. They watched back. The one facing her exhaled abruptly. "We don't blaspheme here, hume—there is no greater insult than to breathe the name of that benighted place. Refrain at least from profanity."

Ayilia exhaled sharply. "Listen to me." Their faces were practically touching, which was almost comical considering their height difference. "I might be bringing the only hope you have left!" A cheesy end to a resolute argument. She cursed inwardly.

The Krayal paused, then snorted in derision. "What you bring is the very Abomination and His forces to our hearths!"

"Do you think they ever left?" The Krayal froze. *Got him.* She pressed the point home. "If they had, would you still be living here in ranges so desolate it's hard to grow crops? Would the Imperial outposts at your border be displaying the skins of the Krayal they hunt, *for meat*?"

The creature's breath was hot. It smelled of herbs and burned wood. Though he was clearly unsettled, the scowling warrior wasn't done. "All this because you are apparently so valuable to the Resistance?"

"Because Agelfi, your people's life-long friend, thinks our *information* is so valuable to the Resistance!" Ayilia stabbed her finger into his unflinching bulk. "Surely, that's worth a conversation?"

He sniffed the air acidly, then fixed that jet gaze back toward her. "Our elders indeed guide us, but I still have operational control on the frontline if there are complications, and there *are*. You're concealing something. The stink of lies permeates you. A terrible, unseen threat haunts your every step. To admit you might bring the end of my people forward by centuries."

Trembling with unexpected rage, Ayilia scowled openly. Their noses were practically touching. "Your elders have invited me in, and in I'm going. What will you do? Fight the boneheads, or fight us and do their work for them? Make your choice!"

The shape regarded her darkly. The air was tense. With breath-taking agility, he sprung two dozen hands up to a low-lying ledge and disappeared into the gloom. Panic, fury, and desperation clouded her vision. She'd ruined it.

Time slowed. She felt like someone else. Before she knew what she was doing, Ayilia stepped forwards and cupped her hands to her mouth to shout at the Krayal's disappearing back.

"They think I know where the Al Kimiya is—they think I know where the Phoenix is."

The effect was like lightning. Instantly, three scaled figures thudded down in a semi-circle twelve paces from her. The Krayal she'd just spoken to landed barely three to four hands opposite. Unsheathing his blade, Kemet rushed forwards, followed by three Gemina. She screamed at them to hold. The Krayal speaker curled his hand around the hilt of his blade, a glint in the jade arc of his eye.

"Al Kimiya—insanity! How? Lie, and your tongue is cut loose, and I care not if it will cost my life. The winged champion is the prophecy that sustains us in our time of need, the only thing that sustains us."

She cocked her head and bared her teeth. "The actual truth is I don't believe a word of any of it, but that's what Agelfi thinks." She smiled coldly. "And he's not the only one. Seems he's got some august company."

The Krayal visibly stiffened. "Who?"

She took a deep breath. "The Emperor Goat!"

The shock was palpable. No one could move. The silent figures above were stiller than the rock they stood on. The shadowy form of the leader loomed over her. When it came, the voice, however, was quieter.

"Tell me more."

Ayilia motioned her men back. The air was hot and grimy. All she wanted to do was slip into a volcanic pool of fizzing water with a glass of something dangerously alcoholic.

"Agelfi says that the emperor thinks this flying myth, I mean the Kimiya, has put something in my head." She shrugged uneasily. It wasn't so much the Krayal that bothered her, but her own soldiers. Still uncertain themselves, they edged in and watched with beady, disbelieving expressions. She felt like a fraud. "It's apparently some kind of chart, a guide perhaps, to the Al Kimiya's alleged spawn site; maybe its egg. I'm not sure exactly, and I don't care. I want it out, the map. I want it gone!"

Ayilia looked at each glowering, scaled face in turn. "I'm hoping what's left of the Resistance can take it out of me, assuming it's even inside, find this wild animal, and get it to stick it to the Goat once and for all."

She explained about the Sythian attack and the plans for escape. Krayal and human, in that heady, insect-filled air, listened intently, their differences fleetingly forgotten.

"The stiffs are here now. You think giving the Goat whatever nightmare's in my head is a good thing for both the universe and you?" She scrutinized the watching figures furtively. "I know things are bad between our peoples, but you stand on the brink of a decision that could be catastrophic for all life, everywhere."

The leader's eyes were the size of liquid moons. He began conferring with the others in urgent whispers. Eventually, he faced her.

"You leave me no choice but to admit you, but you will do exactly as I say, and you'll do it when I say! The terms are not negotiable."

"You will help us, and that's all the terms will be," Kemet growled from beside her.

The Krayal ignored him. The air was dangerously balmy. "You mentioned the Sythian bastard Otho. Know this. A force led by the Pro Consul of this world himself approaches rapidly. We thought you might be aiding him."

As a unit, the Gemina gaped. Nessan blurted out, "*Vespasian?* He never goes *anywhere.*"

The leader seemed pleased, enjoying their discomfort. "Clearly, something has him by the craw, or else he's developed an uncharacteristic taste for violence." He shook his scaly, dark head. "In spite being at the centre of all things, you truly seem to know nothing." As an afterthought, he added. "By the way, my name is Seftus."

Chapter Eleven

Hate and Perdition

"*Silence!*" *Jarrak thundered.*

Unsurprisingly, the crowd milling on the ramparts went as quiet as a derelict boneyard. The collection of ornate officers stared at Jarrak and then back at Ayilia. They were resplendent in their battle garb. Golden tassels, freshly pressed green tunics, and rich, black belts crisscrossed breastplates freshly bossed with spit. Some even wore rare Dresprei feathers. Behind them milled a crowd of civilians who'd come to gawk at the host of Lifeless figures outside the city walls, and there she was in her everyday clothes. Because of the meeting with Regallion, Ayilia hadn't had the time to change.

The whole thing was incongruous. A girl ordering them to resist the Undying Nethergeistian Imperium. A youth leading those who knew better against the greatest power the universe had ever seen. The Provost himself had been persuaded to throw the whole weight of the government behind her. She had full authority for the duration of the crisis over the state regulars as well as the mysterious X Gemina, who were elite and effective undoubtedly, but small in number.

The First Agathon Defence General Schornhamel sighed, failing to mask his disdain.

"Ayilia, I mean, Regent, what makes you truly think we can resist these thugs without your father?" He gestured at the host of pitted skulls and metal baying below the ramparts. *"They are Imperial legionnaires. They fight on land and sea we haven't heard of. The Empire they represent could quash us like a beetle. Why provoke them further?"*

She swallowed and replied in her high, youthful voice, one commonly found in the playgrounds in the city below. *"Regallion is a nobody in charge of a ... um, Prefecture, on the edges of their realm. Agelfi knows of her because he's mentioned her before. Regallion's trying to get power on the chance! We all know,"* she waved her arm grandly for the benefit of the other officers present in the way Jarrak had shown her, *"If this was okay with the emperor, there'd be* six *legions at the gates, not a badly-armed rabble of really badly trained guards."*

Gazes flittered from one to another, followed by some polite coughing and anxious shuffles. It fell on the general to address the young upstart. He straightened his battle dress and ruffled his grand whiskers.

"With all due respect, Regent, this is the Imperium. Should we prove victorious, their Senate will descend on us with such thunder that we will be driven further into the ground than we already are. We either treat or we sunder our rights to any meaningful understanding of the word existence!" He cocked a wizened eyebrow at the horde. Muttered whispers rose in weak agreement driven by fear.

Ayilia felt the same.

"Yes, good point; thank you. So, you know, I asked my contacts to do some research into Regallion." That was Jarrak, of course. He had simply asked one of the bored boneheads outside. *"It turns out that this dead woman's due for retirement soon. So soon, in fact, I think her replacement is on his way now. I think they live in the grandly titled Federal Exterior X11... Nethergeistian Demarcation."* Damn, she cocked that up. She had rehearsed that. *"My contacts say she's just a chancer. She's desperate, even for someone meant to be dead."*

Jarrak prodded the general. He didn't want to, but the army had to have a say. It was the law. By the extremely vigorous nature of the prod, the man could tell that Jarrak was not on his side.

"Regent Elect, we are dancing with death here, and the lives of the last human city. I have to say, this smacks of astonishing impetuousness."

Scorn and patronisation. The man verses the child, the man verses the woman. She should've just agreed. Yet something inside, something that was a bit scary, wouldn't let her.

"There won't be a free city after she's finished, General. It's just the mad gabble of a badly promoted corpse looking for a new job. Look at her troops; they're auxiliary people from a far-away sector. They're not soldiers at all."

Did she get that right? The general was shaking his head anyway. He looked distinctly unhappy. Everyone looked distinctly unhappy. He was the general. He knew everything.

"How can I put this diplomatically? With all the respect in the world, you are just a child waiting for her father to get better. It's nothing personal, just a fact. The sole duty of Agathon's safety rests with my officers and me until he recovers. I have the experience, the maturity, and to be frank, the right, which counts for everything. I'm sorry, but that's the way it is."

Jarrak spat and clenched his fist, but Ayilia furiously gestured him back. The general had a point. He knew about the places where the great and the good shook hands and did deals that had to be done, who to bribe. Everyone nodded. His tone demanded acquiescence. Spittle flecked the lips of those that wanted solutions that required no courage. Each applauded with clammy hands. All drew themselves up to watch the quiet satisfaction of another's disquiet, even if it was a child he was rebuking.

"Thank you." She drew herself up to her full diminished height. That inner certainty was talking for her.

Had her senses abandoned her?

"Was that a passionate plea for the destruction of our freedoms? A new era of slavery and mines? When you say 'we' can treat, do you mean only the rich?" The watching throng seemed uncertain, so she tried to sound imperious. "I have temporary permission to defend this city, from the Provost and the Doge, and that's what I'm going to do. I'm going to defend it for everyone. *When the day comes when I'm regent, I'm going to give everything to the people, even maybe my job."*

She swirled on the army officials. Mouths gaped.

"Jarrak says you know about the positions the army takes along the walls and towers, so we'll leave that part to you!" She drew breath quickly. The inner clarity was dissipating. "I think you're also familiar with Kemet. He's the man who's going to be the go-between between you and Jarrak. He'll help, too."

That sounded stupid. Her mind was clouding. There was a surge of panic as no one was moving, but a man sure of himself, albeit only ten years her senior, appeared at her side, brown arms folded.

They looked at Kemet, and he looked back.

"You heard the lady," he said, smiling. "If the officers present don't deploy themselves in approximately three heartbeats from when I finish, and the civilians don't get the uddering hell away, Jarrak and his spare Gemina are going to kick you all there personally, butt by butt!"

He placed a reassuring hand on Ayilia's slim shoulder and the other on the haft of his blade. "By God, forget Jarrak; I'll do it myself, you bunch of horses' asses, if you don't hurry up!"

Jarrak's head popped back into view among a crowd of disappearing people, after having already robustly 'encouraged' the shocked general to take position. He looked at their pallid faces as they scattered, then rubbed his hands in quiet satisfaction.

"What do you know? You did it, Ayilia! Look at them go!" Jarrak wore the brightest of grins. "It seems Regallion's men aren't even good enough to be guards. They're just auxiliary, logistical support mules." When he saw them looking at him blankly, his beam grew even wider. "They dig trenches!"

Kemet tipped his head back and began to laugh. It was so infectious that even Ayilia joined in.

Rows of dilapidated phalanxes of the soulless formed outside the suns-drenched city walls of Agathon. Like a bee swarm, they bristled and buzzed, but the lines were ramshackle and chaotic. Clouds of dust drifted in beige shrouds over the makeshift army, only partially masking broken armour that barely fit the wearers. Their pockmarked helmets were too large, while their shields were as ruptured as drought-blighted soil. The calcified troops of ossein and ligament looked emaciated and broken, their proud gazes as rheumy as a tavern sop.

A menagerie of captured lubber kin—giant, hairy, bipedal creatures—dragged and scraped an assortment of ancient war machines of rust and wood, each creaking and cracking. Bits continuously tumbled off as they trundled, leaving a colossal snail trail of debris and rubbish in the desert funnels they created. The patchwork army of delinquents and abject rejects staggered its way through the sand and scrub, whipped frenetically by thick-armed thrall-drivers while the regular forces of the city watched on.

The general had joined Ayilia, Jarrak, and Kemet, and he was not happy. He kept moaning that now was the time for talk while they still had a chance, that was, until Jarrak dead-legged his thigh with a curt introduction of his knee. No one had noticed, but the general turned to give him a piece of his mind. The old warrior was too quick.

"Compose yourself, man," he hissed so vehemently the other's jaw immediately clopped tight. "You have a teenager leading us, and she hasn't complained at all." Jarrak put his hand on the red-faced man's grandly decorated shoulder. "Would you like her to give you some classes in courage, my friend?"

The man could only splutter. Jarrak coaxed him back to position, then spoke up so Ayilia could hear. "The general and I think this is a perfect time for the catapults to give our official response to that bonehead's demand we hand over our people. Would that be agreeable to you, Regent Elect?"

Ayilia looked over, face lightly sprayed with dust. She nodded as regally as possible and turned back to regard the horde below. Jarrak nudged the general again, a little more gently this time, and the man shuffled over to the scared-looking horn blower and gave the signal. The man inhaled nervously and then gave a blow. Nothing came out but a strange, strangling parp. The assorted dignitaries, those that had the courage to return, looked embarrassed, so he cleared his throat and tried again.

The noise rang hollowly across the battlements, the waiting crowds in the city, and the yellow and black-teethed beings below. For an instant, no one moved or said anything. Then, the weapons of death thundered and growled so loudly that the ground shook, and a ballistic wall of shot cannoned into the air and the figures below.

There was a terrible, hideous cry of fear and pain as ugly chasms erupted among the witless soldiery, opening great flumes among their ranks, eviscerating shapes into dark, twisting mishmashes of cartilage and alloy. Abandoned jaws, pumping fluid, white gutting, and jagged fingers protruded from heaps upon heaps of unrecognizable ruin. It kept growing as more shot pummelled the soulless into the anhydrous dirt. If that wasn't hellish enough, the city's archers fired in unison, turning the battered army into a dying hedgehog of quivering shafts.

Within moments, the survivors let out a scream and ran into the desert, discarding all military equipment as they did. Many were without limbs, and others dropped them as they fled. There was no sign of Regallion. The Lifeless left behind a grisly field of sickness and rapine bloodshed.

Tears in her eyes, Ayilia turned to Jarrak. "Please, stop the guns."

He nodded gravely and, ignoring a now white-faced general, gave the order himself. The firing quickly stopped, and the city emerged to gape at the destruction below. Jarrak and Kemet came over to stand each side of the young regent. Together, they stood upon the stars-kissed fortification and stared ahead, no one able to say anything.

☻ · ☻ · ☠ · ☻ · ☻

A volley of Pit arrows sang into the dark. A Krayal vaulted backwards, a shaft juddering from his midriff. By the time he reached the bottom, he was already dead.

"Again."

Stilgen gestured, and another blast of shot hissed towards the inky silhouette of stone.

Visibility was appalling, but his Lifeless sight saw dark shapes recoil. Something airborne whined past Stilgen's ear. The Krayal arrow shaft splintered to bits against a rock wall and clattered to the ground. That had been close. Several more ricocheted off the surface to his left, and another thwacked into a soldier's chest, killing them. However, the Pit troops were too quick, something of a revelation, but then it was their own hides they were fighting for.

Stilgen brought his arm down again, and another volley hummed away. Casualties lay at unnatural angles along the rocks and blood. Lizard men bled quickly and died slowly. Without a doubt, he loathed them, but for some reason, he didn't enjoy butchering them. It felt empty.

The bands of reptilian marauders melted back into the craggy gloom. Fluid ran down the sides of a large rock in dark tributaries. Vespasian joined him. He looked lost, even by his standards.

"How many?"

"I would say a few hundred. We got a dozen or two, perhaps."

"Nice to see someone's taking us seriously."

Stilgen grunted, amused. "Astrid lost an arm just cocking her weapon. It's being stitched up, but if she had any less Ichor, she'd just be a head on a tin of soup. Fortunately, the geckos fled."

"I don't get it," Vespasian muttered, his tone uneasy. "We're outnumbered. We should be dead by now; I mean, really dead!" He beckoned to Reena. She'd just returned from inspecting the Krayal bodies. "Anything?"

She looked pleased with herself. "Two wounded, which we quickly dispatched, of course."

"Dispatched?" Stilgen rasped. "What will we do for information now when our very bones depend on it?"

"Err ..." Stumped, Reena scratched her cranium.

"Go."

"Aye, sir. Apologies."

"Don't be too hard on her, Stilgen," Vespasian whispered. "It's their first proper battle. The scaleheads never talk anyway. I remember hearing of the old wars when I was young, before Abandonment. They fought like those old Imperial Proto Goblin legions of yore. They can feel such rage, such intensity: their minds disconnect from their very nerve endings, even under mistreatment. Otho seemed most impressed. He quite liked stuff like that. Even then."

Stilgen snorted. "Otho's a psychopath." He turned and walked towards the bodies.

His commander remained where he stood, frowning.

♀ · ♀ · ☠ · ♀ · ♀

"My name is Seftus!"

"Set-what?"

"Sef... tus!"

The Krayal chief didn't look happy. Ayilia didn't blame him either. For some reason, Soren had a problem with names. In fact, Soren had a problem with everything.

Soren cleared his throat. "Seftus? Are we close yet? We've been going ages, and the night's getting as worn as me—"

Impatience flooded the Krayal's face. He turned on the man before he'd finished. "Time is our master, not our serf. We regard it as our ally, our friend, the warden of our journey—we will get there when we get there."

Soren shuffled his feet. Ayilia jabbed him with her elbow.

"A bit touchy," he muttered to Kofi as he re-joined his friend. He had a soft spot for the man. Kofi was a noble fighter but, and this was the most important part for Soren, he found he had a healthy respect for the finer arts of fear. Ayilia's promotion of him was the best thing ever, as far as Aaron was concerned.

Kofi swept the area with his gaze. "You were at the parliament chambers that night, Soren. You even saw one of the evil ones; I mean a Sythian, Otho!" He leaned close so no one could hear. "Surely, you learned something else that night in between loosening your guts?"

Soren winked. "Funny! Clearly, you'd have been behind me all the way. Trust me, all I learned is that they want her. The Phoenix that doesn't exist because it's a myth now exists."

Kofi shook his head. "The lizards are taking us in because of that? Hell, what a bunch of superstitious dolts."

Soren nodded. "When they find out this is baloney and they're a bunch of superstitious dolts, what then?"

Kofi choked.

The group trotted on in strained silence. Krayal scouts brought extra mounts for Seftus' people. They were very similar to the horses that humans used. Seftus led the way, and Aaron partially slumbered in the saddle. Ayilia felt a sense of something akin to relief. Agelfi's plans were in motion. There was not much more she could do. The nomad council were, effectively, in charge now. Kemet was glaring at what had been three Krayal warriors. They had disappeared into the blackness without comment. Concerned, Ayilia caught up and addressed the hard, cold face next to her.

"Seftus, my troops are getting tense, and so am I. Your people come and go unannounced, and it's unsettling. We are a healthy distance from the Pro Consul's forces; we should do this in daylight."

No reply. She waited a long time. His wilful reticence was becoming infuriating. It didn't help they were exhausted. "Seftus! We've been going most of the night on top of a day already spent riding. Failure to pace ourselves lessens our capabilities." Then, perhaps a little too insistent, "All we ask for is a guide up north. The longer this takes, the more the Imperium will circle and cut us off. Time is *too* much our master."

The Krayal stopped and turned on her, eyes flares of disdain. "That's the problem with humes—you can't see beyond your immediate needs. The fact that cultural requirements might factor in is of no consequence to a race irredeemably self-entitled." He spat across the ground. "Time cannot hurt or harm you. We used to travel once, extensively. Did you know that? To your blighted eye, we are wretched nomads, but in an eon past, we were renowned as astrologers, chartists, and many other things. Once we sifted through the sky tunnels like sand through fingers. We learned how time is illusory, how it is bound to the physical. We learned how it changes and flows differently on worlds massive beyond reckoning. We learned it is also a fake construct created by a mind self-colonized by its own self-imposed limitations. To know the universe, to really understand it, an adept must extend beyond the constrained prison of thought and upbringing and reach." He took a deep breath. "Time is only what you make it. You will find you have the *time* to do what you must do, but only after we see what *has* to be done."

Despite a desire to ram him through the neck with her blade, Ayilia resisted a sudden, sly chuckle. This Krayal was clearly bad for her health! Though it felt as if the balmy night was running out of oxygen, it was still unable to shut him down.

"Listen, Seftus, rested troops equals effective troops. I'm still calling for a break."

"Huh," he growled.

"Problem?" Her tone was a clear warning.

"Not really," he replied scornfully. "I was led to believe the all-powerful Gemina could march for days without a break, fight armies with their eyes shut, and dig trenches leagues wide with nothing but their genitalia. Obviously, that particular chronicler told his story with a belly full of spiced rum."

There was a sudden commotion. Aaron had decided it was time for a spot of his special kind of diplomacy. "I'll show you exactly what passes as genitalia in my world, gecko."

Ayilia barked him down as he reached for his sword. She smiled acidly at Seftus. "Perhaps, it's more a tragedy that the mighty Krayal now spend much their time telling stories about humans." She turned to face her troop before the chief could answer. "Okay, dozy heads; break."

A Krayal soldier took issue that the command hadn't come from her chief.

Aaron squinted menacingly at her: "Go on, have a pop, but let me warn you, I get in a *bad* mood if I'm forced to sit on a horse longer than half a day and must listen to a pile of drivel at the same time. By my reckoning, it's been *triple* that."

"He gets in a bad mood if he even has to *mount* a horse," Soren whispered, though everyone heard. One of the Gemina laughed.

The agitated Krayal glanced at one another, but Kemet wasn't having it. "Don't even think about it, folks. He may have atrocious hair, but I've seen him use bonehead's voiceboxes as flutes."

"Not bad," Aaron admitted. "Normally, you have to think first."

"I'm rather pleased myself," Kemet replied, smiling.

Seftus lifted a hand, and the accompanying troops stopped. A horizon of white sand and gentle, rippling dunes faced them. "You can have your rest now, hume. We are, in fact, close enough that the sand seas ahead are free of dead filth."

He made to depart.

"You're just leaving us here?"

Though his voice dripped venom, he now addressed her with some kind of respect, albeit grudgingly. "I sent word of your approach. You are not alone for long." Then, cryptically, he added, "Learn the sand viper's patience; he kills by becoming the desert."

"That didn't help," Soren grumbled as Seftus vanished into the brightening dawns. Chalky dust swirled as the Krayal chief merged into and became one with the vista. Another Krayal came up and tapped Ayilia on the shoulder.

"Hume?" The tone was brusque, typically condescending.

She ignored it.

"Hume!"

Ayilia rounded impatiently on them. "I have a name—*use it.*"

He stared back, nonplussed. He was surprisingly stocky for what was, according to the human stereotype, a lean, mean, and desperate species.

"Apologies, hume leader," he said, this time with genuine respect. "I've not talked to one of you before. All I wanted to say is that there is a stream with clean, cool waters beyond the other side of that overhang. It's why the scavenger lord brought us this way."

She frowned. "You mean Seftus? Is he of some seniority in Krayal society?"

"God help us." Kofi winced.

"Yes and no. No, in the sense that he's not a politician or a nomad representative. To be honest, I would say, um, it has little translation in your tongue, but he has a proud reputation among our people, but only with the young. He represents a new way of life the elders believe undermines our culture. In fact, well, I represent that too! Seftus unites the young across the range of our peoples, which is a good thing as there is also a considerable void between our tribes these days."

Ayilia nodded pensively, not wishing to dig too deep into reptilian politics, then scanned the area. The light was now growing. "Are we being hunted right now?"

The Krayal smiled shyly. "It's hard to say, hume leader. They are close but not imminently so. All, or at least most, are being tracked."

"Reassuring. Well, we could do with a wash and a snack. Let's find that stream."

"Excellent—I'll take you there straight away." He propelled forwards, looked back at them, then almost excitedly continued: "My title's Jarong. Jarong G'laith at your service. I am his second. I am pleased to meet you."

He led them off without a further word.

"Damn," she sighed.

"Eh?" Soren gave her a quizzical look.

"I think I like that one. That'll confuse things if they turn on us, and we must kill them!"

♀ · ☻ · ☠ · ☻ · ♀

The slaughter was small-scale but shocking. Broken figures were draped over rocks, impaled against inclines, or left hanging gaudily from a set of stark ridges in grotesque positions. Ground hogens picked unwittingly at shreds of Krayal, as hungry, feathered shadows pirouetted overhead. Hardly anything gnawed at the Pit's deceased, however. Even when officially dead, nothing and no one wanted to know, not even nature.

Scavenger bows lay among the Krayal. Their slain seemed to outnumber the legionnaires. Arrows speckled the field of war with stunted spreads of what seemed like badly-kept stubble. Spears and halberds added depth and scope to the forest of lethal bristles. There was blood of all shades. There was no discrimination. The dead of both sides were equal now, despite rank and pretention, as they lay putrefying amongst the rodents.

A soldier swore.

Stilgen raised an eyebrow at Zeamus, one of the more outspoken legionnaires in the group. "You wish to share an observation and use hume profanity while you're at it?"

Zeamus gulped. "No sir, I..."

"You what, trooper?"

"I didn't know the Imperium had dispatched other legions here!"

"You apparently don't listen to mission briefs either. If you consulted whatever constitutes as matter in that skull of yours, you would recall we are to be relieved after we have distracted the target."

"No sir, I mean ..."

Stilgen held up his finger. "What do you mean?"

"I mean, they had no hope of capturing the female either, not with so few against so many!"

"Thank you for stating the obvious." Despite his tone, Stilgen was impressed. It seemed there were still working brains in the Pit. "Re-join the rest."

"Aye, sir!" The man was gone.

"He's right," Vespasian said softly. "Hard to believe, but Zeamus actually has a point."

"Indeed."

"That unit was Pit, not off-worlders. The commander lying diced over there is J'Lusian. He's just an ordinary soldier; nothing special, usually loyal."

"A decoy, like us."

"Brutally expendable. My presence will probably soak up more of the Krayal, but we are expendable, too." He stroked his head ruefully. "The deeper we go, the angrier the lizards will get." Vespasian removed his Mage staff from its sheath. He regarded it with a crestfallen gaze. "Hell, I haven't used this for ages. It's got rust where there should be crystals and slug trails where there should be symbols." He smirked. "I'd more likely blow out what's left of my innards than the foe's if I used this."

"Then please don't aim it my way."

The other laughed, then put the object away in a cloud of flaking dust.

They surveyed the patchwork mix of canvas tents, mobile huts, and smouldering campfires in the process of being smothered. It had been a few days since they saw Seftus. Jarong G'laith managed a wry smile. "Soon, hume leader, there'll be nothing left here to show that we ever visited, that we ever lived. It keeps our enemies guessing and the lands unsullied."

Ayilia eyed him quietly. "I was hoping to meet some of your leaders."

"Umm, nearly there." Jarong nodded. "You must appreciate our people's extraordinary level of worry, especially at this time. Betrayal among our kind is, well, unknown. Yet, all they talk about is how we have been betrayed."

They turned at a shout. Seftus walked nimbly towards them. He had that familiar scowl that Aaron had quietly threatened he'd cut from his face if he had the chance. The Krayal's mood hadn't improved. He gave Jarong a displeased glower as he approached.

"You're late."

Jarong was wringing his hands apologetically. "Seftus, it's my fault. These people have come a long way. I wanted them to enjoy some extra respite."

"The Kleingarts are too harsh a place for arcane niceties. You know that." Seftus faced the visitors. "Your presence is a herald bad of things, predictably. Reports of invisible legionnaires have gripped the fevered imagination of my kin. There is open hostility toward you. There'll be plenty of blood spilled, and I cannot guarantee who will do the striking and at whom."

Ayilia flexed her hands impatiently, trying to fight back her irritation. "Look, I'm sorry, but they'll take your people out the moment the Heretics have been crushed anyway."

He spun on her. "If I had my way, I'd give you *and* the Heretics to them, the good you have all done my people." He took a deep breath, perhaps slightly shocked at his own response. "There is a senior elder present back there, one that chooses to see you. Trust me, she is not what you had in mind when you schemed with your off-world wizard. We have a circle prepared. They will converse with you now."

"Finally," she muttered. Before she could move, Seftus put a firm arm out. "Just the female! Not the guard."

Kemet frowned. "Guard or not, where she goes, *we* go."

Aaron nodded at his side. Seftus seemed to automatically bring out the worst in him.

Ayilia put a gentle hand on Kemet's arm and shook her head. "It's okay, really! If anything happens, I'm sure I can demonstrate just what a cornered Gemina can do." Then in a softer voice: "Besides, we need them." She turned back to Seftus. "Incidentally, as already explained, the *female* happens to have a name. If you don't want to use it, don't call me anything."

She pushed past the Krayal commander. He watched her darkly, then followed. Jarong joined them, a dejected expression darkening his face.

☠ · ☠ · ☠ · ☠ · ☠

Distant peaks jutted precariously among a hodgepodge of smoking caldera on the far horizon. Ayilia, Seftus, and Jarong were standing before a small, outdoor circle of important-looking Krayal. Opaque crystal stones and salt pots were arranged around the periphery of the space. Herbs smouldered in blue jars at twelve points along the circumference. What appeared to be a spiritual leader had just finished an incantation. He walked away when he'd finished.

An older Krayal with thick veins the texture of burned bark faced her. A story of survival was etched into her face and neck like chiselled letters on a chipped tomb. Ayilia waited patiently.

Eventually, the woman focused a piercing, withered gaze on her. She used the common tongue of the Imperium, Nethergeistian. The whole universe seemed to speak it.

"Welcome, Ayilia, of the House of Kira. I am Retari of the clan of the Ahiram. It is Amatashtart who was to meet you, but the threat of invasion now demands her attention on a full-time basis. Perhaps it is unfortunate for you, as she is known to be, how shall I put it ... the most progressive of the elders."

Ayilia's blood chilled.

The woman went on. "Amatashtart is the nominal head in times of strife, but as events move ever more swiftly, it has fallen to me to deliberate on regional matters. Forgive the brevity, Regent, but circumstance demands that we forego pleasantries. All we ask is that you speak from your soul and do not use the words of politics. What do you want from us?"

Ayilia braced herself. "You are aware, of course, that we are here because of your good friend Agelfi?"

No response.

"The Imperium has just sacked our city. I estimate after a year or so of entrenchment they will enact penance. After all, our people are escaped thralls, and they hate that more than anything."

The older woman's irises darkened.

Jaw set defiantly, Ayilia continued, "You'll have heard that the Imperium want me, and you'll have heard why. You'll have also heard Agelfi wants the Heretics to extract the information this Al Kimiya apparently put inside my skull. He feels it could be the last hope for all of us. The Heretics don't believe me because I am theurgically sterile and incapable of receiving what is essentially a product of sorcery. They have far more suitable candidates for hosting Al Kimiya, genuine Magi who are infinitely more qualified. Agelfi is, basically, the only one who believes this has happened to me, and he's not highly regarded by the Resistance anymore, to say the least. Whatever the truth, if Agelfi is right, you could lose everything by throwing me out."

Nothing.

Ayilia scanned the space and the faces. She shot Seftus a glance, but he was looking directly at the woman. She returned her stare to the elder. "Apparently, you know Agelfi well."

"Apparently." The woman's face was implacable.

"Seftus probably told you all this himself anyway?"

The woman arched a brow. "Probably."

If anything, Retari was even more irksome than Seftus. Her silence made Ayilia sound weak. Her teeth clenched. Jarong was beginning to fidget while Seftus stood stoic. The wind was light, but in this enforced stillness, it chilled Ayilia. "Well, can we talk about this?"

Unsurprisingly, Retari continued to withhold her council. Ayilia couldn't hold back a frown. "I hope to return and recover my city and maybe even the Occupied Lands if this Phoenix, which isn't really a Phoenix, can be harnessed. This alleged creature is why the Imperium doesn't give a murmel's claw about anything else until it's found and butchered."

The woman's face cracked into a dry smile. "So, you are saying we should hand you in? Because if we did, the Imperium would cease to care about our desiccated mountains."

With incredulity, Ayilia glowered at everyone, one by one. "Listen, maybe I haven't been clear. If there's one thing I've learned, the Lifeless hate you as much as they hate us. Not helping us is the equivalent of signing your own death warrant, not in your blood, but the blood of the people you pertain to represent. Help us and have a chance of living. Do nothing now and die for certain later."

The woman became suddenly animated, hostile even. "Why not hand you in? You come here after decades of silence from a people *you* pertain to represent, who formed a pact with an ancient evil you do not represent. Our lands had been lost, and without your aid, we did not have the strength to take them back. Your people grew prosperous off the back of a highly selective peace that favoured only them. These same people not only require our help, but their presence has brought the very killers who crucified the Krayal's freedoms in the first place to our door. If that wasn't enough, embedded within the ranks of the soulless are the most feared of them all, Sythians." She pointed a finger. "We honour guests as a rule, but you are uninvited and unwelcome!"

The acrimony and rage reflected in Retari's irises burned into Ayilia's heart, and she was taken aback. Her faith in Agelfi was so deep that she had been naïve. The Krayal's response was inevitable. Even so, she couldn't help but notice Seftus' natural scornful demeanour was directed at the council, not at her. They had a history, apparently, and a sour one at that. Nevertheless, the whole thing was catastrophic.

"I'm not defending our people, but I do know without the Treaty we'd be slaves again, and not even here. The Imperium told our scouts that they were going to relocate the whole population halfway across the galaxy, back to the vast work camps they escaped from centuries ago." Despite her genuine sincerity, her hands instinctively twitched for her hungry blade. She hoped the Krayal didn't notice. "Indeed, my people have gotten rich trading with the Pit and the Occupied Lands. I know many of them didn't care about you or our historical alliance. We've finally harvested the soiled fruit of our own greed and disinterest for all those years. Know this: when the Heretics and we are defeated, they're not going to let you live. Handing me in will bring that day in all the sooner. Would your cooperation with the Lifeless now, and in that I mean literally handing us over, be so much worse than what we did?" It was desperate, but it was all she had. "None of us have the time for this, elder. Unless you bind me now, I'll take my troops and we'll go north and find this gate all by ourselves and take the Imperium with us."

Fighting anger, despair, and disappointment, she turned to go. It was blatantly apparent that asking, even begging, wasn't going to change the old stout's lifelong, if deserved, prejudice. The woman didn't seethe like Seftus. She stewed like the coldest of dead stars in the deepest void.

"Wait." It was Jarong.

Ayilia flinched.

"Respected Elder, can we not help? These people specifically are not responsible for the past. Maybe this is a good step, to um, mend things?"

"Jarong!" Seftus hissed. "Matters of state do not rest under your purview."

"It is of no matter," cooed the elder to the chief. She seemed to quite like Jarong. Retari fixed her stare on Ayilia. "Understand one thing, *human*: I have never met Agelfi, and I have never comprehended how he inspired this trust among scatterings of my learned friends. I *do* know one thing, however," Retari continued, a distinct threat in her voice. "I know that you are trouble. As night follows the day-time trail of the three suns, you bring with you a miasmic malodour. Maybe you are one of the chosen acolytes of this sky warrior, the Al Kimiya, but with you, I can sense something dark. No matter how much we revere this creature, there will *not* be peace for anyone where your footfalls tread. Do not judge us, Regent, for respecting the scalp harvester more than the bitter taste of the treacherous ally, the human chameleon."

"She's right, Regent," Seftus added. Ayilia had the distinct impression he was trying to convince himself more than anyone. "I admit you're not as expected, but you defend a people who are coin-grabbing, self-obsessed turncoats who'll hawk their birth parent to the highest bidder. Your friendship brings blood to a race already saturated with it. I won't hand you in, but I want you off our lands within one day."

Ayilia swivelled on him. "You know, my one regret is Agelfi. He was so wrong about your people. He was always far too soft."

"This is how you plead for your skins?"

"This is how I argue for yours."

Mouth working feverishly, the elder rose to her feet. "Sense the mood against you, Regent, and your people. It is in *everything* around you—the trees, the coldness of the rock and stone; even the wind is hostile. The human race wanders through existence trampling on all that doesn't serve it, consuming the flesh of anything that has a face. You have no connection to the earth anymore, or your souls."

"Maybe, but what good is having a connection, Elder, when you are dead? You just don't know it yet."

Three Krayal entered and strode briskly up to the elder.

"Elder, apologies, we have disturbing news." The head speaker was leaner, gaunter than the rest. Though Retari's features flashed irritation, she fleetingly looked vulnerable.

"Speak, quickly."

He bowed. "A column approaches by stealth from the northeast. It intends to cut us off and bring us to the attention of three more approaching from the southwest."

"*Just what we need,*" Ayilia muttered to herself sarcastically, furtively flicking Seftus an intense stare. The Krayal's facial features had condensed into something that she recognized as war lust.

"Their intent?" Retari asked.

"We do not know, Elder, though it's fair to imagine that they are targeting this gathering. Their Seers are either first-rate or they are informed as to our movements."

The elder's face remained impassive, yet her eyes betrayed uncharacteristic disquiet. She waved him away.

"Seftus, I want you to move your units southeast, then cut around and back toward that single force. Deploy decoys in every direction—sow confusion between their legions; frustrate their intelligence. I want you to understand one thing above all else—there is no ground here worth keeping. All that is precious is in our blood. It is the only position worth holding. It is a position that can shift with the same ease as the sand dunes in dry storms."

Seftus bowed curtly and strode off. Retari walked forwards until her small but vital figure was standing directly before and beneath the lone human. "You are undoubtedly brave but deeply foolhardy. Do not be mistaken, Regent—the only reason I have not sent you back already is the soft kiss of the sky spirit, the Kimiya. Why it might have chosen you among the Magi of the Heretics, a person of no sorcery, makes no sense. I suspect you are more likely a decoy than a challenger. The Al Kimiya has its reasons, and we have our pain."

Retari beckoned towards Jarong. He stumbled over tentatively. "Jarong, take them with you and Seftus."

Ayilia recoiled. "Wait!"

The older woman looked up, eyes as diluted as a blood-red river. "You expect more?"

"Agelfi wanted us to meet with Elder Maroukish of the purple highlands, or was it the lowlands? Actually, I don't remember, but it's all in the paper Seftus has." The chief thrust a ragged piece of parchment over. "No disrespect to Seftus, but it's fair to say we've had our fill of each other."

The elder stared blankly for long moments at the tattered paper. Eventually, her tight fist scrunched it up and let it drop to the floor. She brushed sand from her garb and sniffed in the direction of Ayilia's aghast face.

She looked at a horizon scarred with dark clouds and jagged peaks, then back at Ayilia. "No one will take you there today, Regent, because they are dead. You are too late. A small Imperial hit squad, one of several, intercepted them as they made their way here. They wiped them all out before we could destroy them." The older woman leaned in very close. "You are completely alone now. I will give Seftus instructions to get to the portal. But know this, Regent: Seftus is honourable, but he is also very angry. A slow bitterness against the soulless and the betrayal of your kith eats at him, and almost everyone is to blame." She shook her head. "I told you before, everywhere you go, only blood and strife follows."

CHAPTER TWELVE

RETURN TO THE PAST

I t was a day later, and Seftus was still complaining. "I still don't know how the Imperium did it," he spat.

Kemet winced. "They ain't the biggest, baddest bunch of bastards for nothing."

"This is our *land*, our *home*, our *lives*. Where did the soulless learn to sneak us from behind like that? It isn't possible. Hell's teeth; there's treachery here!" His finger jabbed the air repeatedly, emphasizing each already emphasized point.

Kemet thrust a dusty arm in front of the slimmer, but equally broad, Krayal, flashing a dangerous smile as he did. "I hope that doesn't mean what I think it does?"

Snorting, Seftus pushed his arm brusquely away. "It means that you are all advised to stay the hell out of my way, hume, if you want me to help find that hidden gate."

Kemet's hands moved to his battle axe. "I'll bear that in mind, friend. Be advised that the Gemina, and myself particularly, don't take kindly to threatening behaviour."

"Then you are not alone." Seftus also reached for his weapon.

Ayilia crashed across the gritty slope to reach them. "Wait!" She was panting, but also furious. "You two shut your holes up and fast, or I swear I'll have the both of you sent home in pieces. This is precisely what they want."

Seftus and Kemet froze. Ayilia put a restraining hand on the Gemina while she held the other up in the Krayal's direction. Kemet reluctantly re-sheathed his axes as Aaron approached, eyes eager for a fight. Ayilia ignored him. "Two grown men acting like tavern thugs when our joint fates hang by a thread. Make your choice, Seftus, fight us or the Empire, but understand that you can't fight both. Feel free to take your pick, right now, because my diplomacy is all burned out."

Seftus slid his weapon back. Despite his fury, he appeared somewhat embarrassed. Kemet was rubbing his glistening dome. He wouldn't show chagrin, but she knew he felt the same.

After a few moments, the Krayal quietly muttered, "Follow me, unless your Gemina friend prefers to meet the Pro Consul alone. Vespasian may be a runt, but he can still pack quite a necromantic punch." He walked off.

Irked, Ayilia jagged a finger into Kemet's chest. "You shouldn't have done that."

"Oh, I think I should. There's been too much loss already to put up with someone who can't decide whether he's our friend or wants to gut us."

"If those scaled terrapins are our friends, I'd hate to meet our enemies," Aaron added.

"Do you two *always* have to stick up for each other," she smiled despite herself. It was too surreal to frown. "Out here, friends and enemies are the same thing. Let's not push it, eh? If you don't wise up, I'm going it alone!"

Most of that morning was spent tracking. Lunch was wheat rusks and dried meat on the move. Powdered, somewhat lemony herbs picked from the unforgiving scree of Agathon's hinterland helped the flavour a bit. The day passed, and the stone shadows on the flatlands grew imperceptibly longer. Faint dust devils twisted mischievously off to their right. The undulating rocks and crevices had vanished entirely. The Gemina were accompanied by a unit of Krayal marauders armed with scavenger bows, sharp blades, and round shields that they called targes. Their armour was light, but of the toughest material. None of them seemed able to relax or feel the slightest weariness.

Kemet and Aaron conferred in whispers to the left of Ayilia. She was, as usual, lost in thought, probably in a vortex of self-blame for a people that, to a degree, didn't want her.

"What do you reckon?" Aaron's eyes darted.

"About what?" Kemet scanned the horizon, confused.

"Them—those ... lizards."

"Not much."

"That's it?"

"What do you want me to say?"

"Well, I think you could manage a little more, considering you nearly rammed your sword arm up his gizzards!"

"Humph—a misunderstanding."

"Right. Tell it to the jury."

"Why do I get the impression that I'm winding everyone up today?"

Aaron couldn't resist a chuckle. "It must be your charming personality."

"I'll take that as a compliment."

Kemet glanced at his long-time friend. Aaron's eyes were squinting hard at something ahead.

"Aaron?" Kemet, now a little unnerved, couldn't see anything. It was hardly surprising. Aaron's eyesight was unmatched; it was common knowledge. "What's there, old bud?" He felt a tinge of foreboding.

Aaron went rigid, hand instinctively on his sword hilt. "Holy teeth! Follow me." Visibly agitated, he marched to where Seftus happened to be conferring with Jarong.

"Hey, Krayal?"

Both looked up.

"I thought you said this morning the Imperium was behind us?"

Seftus replied with his usual sarcasm, though it was noticeably less acidic this time, "What have you seen? A pack of hunting voles?"

"Oh, nothing. Nothing, apart from that humongous, piss-off army heading into us, *right up* our collective cherries!"

Everyone froze.

A dozen eyes scanned ahead, following Aaron's outstretched hand. Seftus still didn't appear impressed.

"Nothing! The desert can be unforgiving for hume perception," Seftus said.

Aaron wasn't having it, though. "Your desert eyes must be based in your rear friend, look ... just there. See that black line? Those tiny sharp points, that's armour and weaponry. The *only* ones who give off that ochre burnish at this angle of the suns are the same good folk who confined your kin to this cesspit in the first place."

Seftus shielded his sight from the harsh light. Eventually, he muttered, "I see nothing ... wait." His eyes widening, he swung around and started barking at his group in native Krayal. The resulting rush and clanking of armour was deafening.

Ayilia approached, grabbing the Krayal chief by the arm. "I thought you said they were behind us!"

"They are. That must be another unit, but they're slightly larger than the legion chasing us."

"Slightly? How much slightly?"

"Very, *very* much slightly."

"How is it possible that they can encircle us like this?"

"As I said, treachery—no one gets past our scouts without being noticed. Since you arrived, it's been happening a lot." He strode off, shouting orders ferociously at his troops.

"Damn," Aaron said unhelpfully.

"It seems we are," Kemet muttered.

Ayilia snapped. "We're not done yet! Aaron, how many did you see? We've a fully armed Gemina unit and an extremely bad-tempered Krayal battalion. I'd say that attack force has got the fight of their lives at hand."

"Seemed sizeable enough."

"Kemet, align the troops to the right of our allies where our armour and training are going to be needed. Aaron, throw the crossbow and slingshot sharpshooters behind the mobile artilleries. Make sure they wait for my mark. Our archers will deplete the fronts, but if we can also eradicate the commanders, the rest will be murmel meat."

"Aye."

"Nessan!"

The blonde Gemina ran up. "Yes, ma'am?"

"Get our supplies and mounts; make sure they're all strapped in and ready to ride back to the rises for protection. Only take a maximum of two fighters—I need everyone out here."

"Aye." She hurried off. By now, the Krayal had adopted a crouching attack posture, their numbers divided into three groups interlinked together. The humans began gathering on their right in a flurry of cusses and clinks. There was no way the Krayal were letting them take the centre even if they tried. Fights almost broke out between the allies, even as the Imperials approached. Behind, archers and catapult flint cannons, each powered by a taut pulley, were setting up. Ahead, the dark line had thickened into a black wall, thundering toward them leaving a prodigious wake of dust. Kofi reached behind his back and pulled out the jagged halberd strapped to his back. Everyone else did the same. Soren was next to him. Both dug their swords into the soil and raised the jagged spears at the advancing storm.

"Soren, look at Kemet. He's got those hammers out again. I bet he *loves* this."

"Loves it a bit *too* much. Maybe his subconscious is trying to say something."

Their eyes scanned the horde with considerable alarm. It filled their eyesight from end to end.

"By all that's holy," muttered Kofi through gritted teeth.

Most of the fighters stood transfixed. Ayilia, next to Kemet in the vanguard, hissed, "They can't be what I think they are."

"Looks that way," Kemet replied gravely.

"How come? How can they be here?" Panic rose in her. She quashed it. Panic tried to rise again. She could smell her own sweat and sense the dread grip everyone.

Kemet looked pensive. "Kommandos ... definitely Stormkomers. Shit!"

Ayilia swallowed quietly. "Imperial elite; we've had worse."

"Aye, we have!" Aaron shouted so everyone could hear. "Soren's backside blowing off every time he has sprouts."

There was muffled laughter. It helped diffuse the tension, though Soren and the Krayal didn't look impressed.

Ayilia waved at the troops for quiet. "Everyone listen! Those things are a long way from home, and they're not packing artillery. Despite appearances, there aren't many—they're lined up to maximize our fear, but this is a strike unit, not an army. Remember, their specialty is hand to hand, so halberd them hard and keep them at a distance. Let the shooters have them instead! I repeat, *never* engage them less than spitting distance because they'll always be stronger and deadlier."

"We can take out the Prowlers," Kemet suggested, his tone almost merry.

Aaron nodded with enthusiasm. "When the survivors try to regroup, we hack them to death."

Ayilia hollered as loud as she had ever done in her life, "Take position!"

The armoured host pounded toward them in a tempest of swirling grit. Bits of stone ricocheted into the shields of the crouching fighters from the cumbersome Prowlers. A collective howl from the skeletal leviathans hammered into every cell, pore, and dirt-encased cuirass, human and Krayal. As the cyclopean storm front swept in, the cry was reinforced by a jarring blare of hell-horns and clashing drums from deep within the ranks. The urge to flee was instinctive, even for the veterans.

It was terrifying.

People were shouting, many at her, for clarity, action, and purpose. The whirlwind of flying sand produced a mirage of flaming wings and claws. She gripped her broadsword tightly.

"Fire!"

A barrage of Gemina shot slammed into the leading ranks, shredding ribs and churning guts into ruin. Figures flipped over before being pulped under a forest of behemothic hooves. A thick arrow hail of Krayal shot joined the ballistic flint barrage from the human mobile artillery. Their levers clanged shut with jarring bangs, cutting down the enclosing ranks with the efficiency of corn threshers. Skinned bone erupted in flowers of white flakes as the flint rammed into the force, opening great gaps in the centre.

Sappers scrambled to shove handfuls more flint into the cylinders of the weather-worn machines before slamming the doors shut and yanking pulleys back to wind up the firing mechanisms. Nessan strode among the melee shouting orders. She paused and looked up. There were shadows arcing towards them. She screamed at a group of cross-bolt archers and gestured skywards. Lightning darts of sharpened stone impacted something moving too quickly for her to make out clearly.

On the ground, all hell broke loose.

A wave of organized loathing slammed into the allied lines, propelling ranks of soldiers back against their comrades in a roil of tumbling Prowlers and splintered spears. The disciplined Gemina phalanxes were thrust into reverse as

Lifeless riders were diced upon their halberds. Imperial soldiery had to struggle into a sea of spears as the momentum of their attack faltered. Prowlers snorted yellow liquids, spitting and dying, despite being as impervious to pain as they were to life. As the charge became a slowly circling vortex of primal butchery, units of horseless Kommandos sprinkled the air with a driving rain of pilums. A line of Krayal collapsed, scythed chest to neck by bloodied javelins. The cries of the living mingled with the chanting, cursing, and yelling of the undead. A row of trampled human and Krayal bodies lay at the front, covered by Prowler hoof marks and deep gashes.

Ayilia could barely see their allies, her human compatriots nearby slashing at the now slow advance. It was the striking appearance of the legionnaires themselves that floored her. They were horrifying.

These off-worlders were a far cry from the bedraggled flotsam the Pit had churned out since Abandonment. These were magnificent, astonishing. They cut at the pikes with abandon. Had the shot not been careering into them, the organics would've already been butchered. The allies were doing their best to maintain distance by keeping their bristling spears up. Whenever a Lifeless pushed through, they quickly hacked the wielder to death. Ayilia thanked the heavens the shot was pulverizing them into flying particles where they stood, fought, and even screamed at their terrified foe.

These were the best soldiers of Imperium she'd ever seen, the one percent used for specialized missions. They splintered open the toughest of sieges, chanted the loudest during the tributes of triumph, and were the first to storm a barricade. They slaughtered until they were slaughtered. There was no mercy once they were deployed.

Flee or fall.

Ayilia went to shout orders but didn't get far. Something airborne whacked her so hard that her vision shattered into a knot of bright lights that wriggled like worms across the back of each eyeball. When her sight returned, she found herself sprawled unceremoniously rump-over-head on the dry turf, her weapon several paces away among scattered armour.

A sudden hiss.

She instinctively ducked, catching a rush of talons, acidic irises, and a shrivelled shuck within a riot of neon veins and a viscous mouth where a head should have been. As she lay there, stupefied, hand clawing for her blade, they swung in for another strike.

As Ayilia's arm scrambled hurriedly for her shield, Kemet lurched into view and swept his battle hammer into their startled front, smashing them into the ground. They lay unmoving. The broad grin of satisfaction immediately vanished as a soup of the thing's entrails washed over his feet. Aghast, he kicked the splosh of rufescent gore over the creature's hairy thorax.

Somewhere, Aaron chortled mercilessly.

Ayilia wanted to heave. She also wanted to laugh, but two mounted soldiers lunged from the battlefield fog as she rose. Kemet kicked himself free from the sludge and thwacked both hammers through the shield of the first. Their thick clavicles snapped like twigs. They fell in the path of their comrade, allowing Kemet to drop his weapons and hack the other's leg off with a sword whisked hurriedly from its scabbard. A still-winded Ayilia somehow managed to bring her blade repeatedly crashing against both their skulls.

Flint and bow shot struck the attacking ranks in singing volleys from archers and sappers at the rear. The Gemina were falling back, their spear lines helping to bring the attack to a chaotic standstill. The Kommandos were unable to advance. They could still destroy the organics, but the rain of incoming projectiles forced them back or felled them outright. With Imperium fighters stuck in a scrum of bodies, pikes, and mounts, the most immediate threat to the living shifted to the shapes pirouetting above. At intermittent moments a victim was bulleted skywards and eviscerated by a squall of movement in a macabre snowfall of metal shreds. Somehow, Ayilia managed to bark out commands to Aaron, Seftus, and Nessan. They began hustling human and Krayal sharp shooters toward the new threat. The effect was staggering.

A creature disintegrated mid-air. Others began falling around them, back-flipping across the ground peppered with shot. People cheered loudly. The struggle took on renewed vigour as hopes rose. The odd sight of Gemina and Krayal coming together was uplifting, despite the losses. She watched, stunned, as the Lifeless struggled remorselessly under the onslaught, sluggishly wading through a mass of ruin. Every time a Stormkomer threatened to overpower an allied soldier, which was frequently, they were cut down by eagled-eyed shooters. Nevertheless, the living were under critical pressure.

Ayilia gritted her teeth and pushed her way to the front, swiping at the giants with loud grunts. Many were wounded, flint and halberd wounds forming welts and wicked gouges in their sides. Yet, they slashed back with shocking strength, killing Krayal and Gemina too, despite their amour. The troops at her side were now huffing with every parry, tiredness and fear stretching their features into pallid caricatures of their rivals. Soulless faces spat vitriolic obscenities at them even as their heads hit the dirt, arrow shafts protruding in all directions.

To Ayilia's immense relief, it was apparent that she had been right. They were a rapidly deployed spearhead unit, not a proper force, and their numbers were easily smaller than the allied units combined. It was terrifying, however, to see that they were nakedly after her alone. Skulls turned towards her mouthing brutal insults. Jagged incisors flashed. One threw an axe, and it narrowly missed taking part of her skull off. She wondered if the Lifeless were simply trying to knock her out. Others lunged at her on sight, but the damage from the bombardment had given rise to a cumulative effect.

An Imperium soldier thrust a group of the living aside like they were dolls, but then fatally stumbled on their broken spears. Ayilia barely succeeded in ripping the Lifeless' steaming, alabaster-coloured gut out from beneath her ribs before she impaled her. As she staggered back into position, a human trooper grabbed her shoulder and pointed her towards the Krayal lines to the far left.

Her mouth dried for the hundredth time.

Hot yellow flashes of flame were tearing them apart. Burning fighters were falling quickly; the lines were concaving. Brief thunder cracks followed each fire burst moments later.

"Holy God!"

She prodded Kemet urgently.

"Ayilia?" Kemet only used her name in emergencies. "Something's happened?

"Over there ... a Sythian death machine!"

"The Pro Consul?"

"Can't be. His line's *behind* us, apparently, and I don't think he's that powerful anyway!"

Kemet's face dropped. He forged through the soldiers until he reached a frenetic Aaron, who was doing a heroic job obliterating any shot-damaged crack troopers trying to drive wedges into allied positions. The man visibly winced when he saw the mammoth, hulking shape hammering into the Krayal flank with soul-destroying speed. Flailing arms and glittering weaponry blurred as everything standing in the Lifeless' path was vaporized by sporadic plumes of flame. A boiling ruby aura, a vivid super-shield of thaumaturgy, blocked any buckshot that came his way.

As if sensing her, the giant paused and looked directly at Ayilia.

He smiled and she felt sick. This had to be Mabius. He was nothing like Vespasian or even Otho, either in the terror he exuded or his stature.

Impervious to the missiles twanging off his Magi shield, the Lifeless sorcerer strode directly toward her. He was the only one moving without restraint. She watched him with her 'witchling' awareness, transfixed to the spot. Kemet, after felling an imposing fighter who had literally whacked one of his men a dozen paces across the ground, whirled around again.

"Go!"

"No, we make a stand, here."

Kemet regarded her gobsmacked. "*How* can we stop him? *Look at him.*"

She couldn't take her eyes off the behemoth. He was coming in almost slow motion. "No choice!"

Kemet's mouth was as round as a moon. "We'll have to have a talk sometime, Regent—I've not seen you do this before."

She grimaced. "A one-off, I promise."

Mabius closed in, flickers of venom trailing from clenched fists. Ayilia studied his capillary-studied mutt of a head, half hidden by the fug of conflict, with almost ghoulish fascination. Rows of jagged ridges and stubby spikes jutted through his shoulders and upper back. No one interfered with his trajectory; no one could. She motioned the others to back off. A few heavy-set Imperial troops not puckered by arrow or sling shot also backed away. Without a word, Mabius aimed a burning index finger at the point of her breast where the heart lay, embers sparking off the end.

She stiffened then, and, without warning, blacked out.

An ivory storm of static and disjointed simulacrums ransacked the recesses of her mind. The 'witchling curse' immolated the inside of her retinas like nova and moved like lightning up her veins in streaks. A wooden house in a black-gold, copper cornfield, framed under speeding cobalt skies, shimmered fleetingly into crystal clarity. She sensed something inside. The vision imploded as rapidly as it had appeared.

Mabius' Satanic face grinned with his Sythian supremacy, but rather than quake at his menace, all she could do wonder was why his thaumaturgic field had collapsed. *His Magi shield is gone.*

Kemet's shield thrust between her and an incoming charge of Mabius' heated energy. It atomized with a sharp crack in a maze of sparks. Kemet was back on his feet in a heartbeat with a shield ripped from a fallen soldier, yet he seemed unable to move properly. The blow had clearly stunned him. Waking up fully, Ayilia screamed for the artillery to fire.

Nothing.

Where were the bloody guns?

On cue, collective cannonshot struck the warlord full force. Sharpened projectiles skewered his body armour and ripped into the muscle beneath. His upper torso a red stew, he reeled just as the second Gemina gun hurled its load into both chest and face, sending parts of him exiting in crimson gouts. The giant staggered, then fell backwards onto the prostrate forms of the dead.

Everyone was looking at her.

They all looked at her, the imposter, the politically impotent pup. The child that dared to sit on the throne, the same fraud who dared to fight the corruption and clean the city's streets. She was the imposter that lost a kingdom because her ego had claimed she could do it as well as any of them. Yet now they looked at her as though she'd done something.

"He let his guard down," she explained, glaring especially hard at the Krayal who, like the few Lifeless still standing, were gaping at her like some kind of freak. She'd done nothing at all other than blackout.

She couldn't remember.

What little was left of the battle took over but there wasn't much left to fire at. Aaron joined them at a full-throttle run, grinning wildly.

"That dunderhead Sythian ain't doing anything now. We wasted him; we actually wasted that asshole." Associated Krayal stared at him blankly. "All respect to you, gal. Next stop the Goat, eh?"

Soren and Kofi just laughed. They had to; they were trembling. Ayilia had noticed the warlord move. The giant's personal aura, his thaumaturgic shield, had flicked back on, and she had no idea what had flicked it off in the first place. Flight was the only option.

Ayilia turned and cupped her hands to her mouth.

"Back! Back! Battle function Gamma!" She waved desperately at Aaron's quizzical face. "Aaron, get Nessan. Keep the Imperium bogged down. I want distance between us and Mabius. Meanwhile, someone *please* start the shooters up again. Cover our retreat ... we're done here."

There was a mad rush of armour and grimy bodies. Arrows and flint fire hit confused enemy soldiers as aghast legionnaires stared at their still-grounded warlord. Yet, no one went near his twitching body. No one was foolish enough to approach the devil in his rage.

The living rapidly evacuated the battlefront.

Battle function Gamma, orderly retreat to new support positions under covering fire, was somehow working. Archers still gave support fire as they went, significantly slowing the pursuit of the few unscathed demons. The carnage was over as quickly as it had begun. The heavy guns fired one last time, creating a cloud of bone and armour as the handful of pursuers were scythed down. At that point, the Imperium seemed to realize that they were now on the defensive. The remaining handful of Lifeless, their glares scarlet suns in the smog, stopped. Despite the impacts, they remained majestic and impressively dangerous. A huge centurion headed towards the fallen leader, his sizable frame seemingly rippling like overboiled ham in a crosswind.

Ayilia led the allies as they rushed in the direction of the protective rises, Kemet always at her side. Human and Krayal ran together, carrying as many of the wounded as they could. The silent, exhausted troop darted among rocks and rise until the destruction was well out of sight. Ayilia exhaled and scrutinized the columns, making for the horses ahead. It was obvious there were missing people, especially among the Krayal.

She hung back, checking the rear, making sure that there were no stragglers. Feeling overwhelmed, she closed her eyes and inhaled. She could hear the light but powerful weapons disappearing into the ridges. It was surreal and blissful. For once, she'd given Kemet and Aaron the slip, and a moment to herself was invigorating. A soft wind blew particles across her grubby boots. The silence was astonishing, beautiful.

As such, it was especially surprising when she found herself spitting desert dirt from her lips, the ground level with her face. She rubbed her head. Her fingers were wet with blood. The right side of her torso was taut with shocking stabs of pain. She sucked in air in huge, heaving gulps, mouth gaping like a landed cod.

It felt oddly ridiculous.

Ayilia struggled to look up. To one side, Kemet was motionless on his back—he must have come back looking for her. Others were approaching rapidly, looking fearful at something behind her. A flash and one abruptly collapsed, smoke coming from his mouth. She tried to get up but was too stunned to move.

"Aargh..."

The voice was hers! How embarrassing. A wave of agony swept up in a rush from the small of her back. With an undignified grunt, Ayilia pushed herself over and focused.

Stifled laughter and shuffling feet. The suns' light was stained by a group of murky figures. They seemed to be staring.

"I have you! It's over!" a deep, rumbling voice crowed.

Gemina forces were collecting, taking new forward positions. Nessan was shouting, but Ayilia waved her back. No point watching them get slaughtered too. They were no match for the warlord and his handful of bulky, elite troops, each protected by Mabius' shield. She cursed bitterly.

I'm a fool!

A wall of fire forced her people back into the growing darkness. It formed an impassable ribbon between her and them. Mabius leered over her, his features a gruesome mess of peppered gun-flint. Intertwining muscles and knotted tendons slowly curled back into shape under a sheen of crimson Mage charge. It was reforming the outlines of a face that was already looking like his psychopathic mug.

When the odd feeling inside her arose once more, she let herself black out completely, consigning herself to whatever fate had in store.

❦ · ❦ · ❦ · ❦ · ❦

Dank mists coiled around a motley collection of glossy rocks that lay scattered in all directions like colossal, sable marbles. Broken rows of Doric pillars circled piazzas and venerable buildings partially visible through wealds of silent spruces. Reclining water fonts, cobbled pavements, and chipped archways darkened under the daily deaths of the three suns.

Two dozen crack Imperial troops packed supplies, cleaned weapons, and dug in. Not a word was said. The giant figure of Mabius walked purposefully among them. The wind rummaged through discarded robes and the hanging tassels of stored equipment. The ground was dry; the exposed ruins austere and desolate. Sand rivulets drifted in gentle spools among the hobnailed boots of the soldiers.

A pair of Lifeless whispered together in awe. They were slouched against an ancient wall running along a red horizon.

"The lizard skins built this once?"

"So, they say—being Krayal meant something here."

"After today, it only means slaughtered cattle."

They snickered. They were more sophisticated than regular off-worlders.

"They said this rabble once travelled the network between all things!"

"They say a lot of things."

The other shrugged. "Well, that's what they say."

More laughter, practiced laughter, not like the organics. Perhaps they urged to feel alive, but they couldn't. Nothing would fill the pathological cold within.

"You're all a bunch of rat-infested dolts," cracked the giant without warning. "Look at the scrawls. Look at the designs ... this place is *Imperial*. If the Krayal built this, they built it under the lash."

No one dared reply.

"The lizards did things once, but such cities were not their work! Watch your throat boxes; I don't want careless talk here."

There was silence. Then the gang of whisperers began again, unable to quell the need to gossip. It sent Mabius into seething fits of impatience, but he said nothing.

The breeze panned through the ruins, before sifting up a row of stone stairs split into spiderweb cracks and patterned whorls. The vista was painted in cobalt brilliance as half-moons rose into the sky. Additional sets of cracked columns interlinked with dark firs led to lichen-dusted thermae. Though neglected, the terracotta walls were in good shape despite a decayed roof. Arches held arms over the remains of empty public baths, next to abandoned rooms where forgotten inhabitants once gathered. A dry river and a disused aqueduct ran into a star-speckled distance. To one side, a small pool of water with the hue of mercury glinted like a silver dirk.

The Sythian wasn't interested in the carcasses of lost towns. He was pacing the perimeter defences of the camp, growling orders. He stopped when he spied figures riding out from drifting dust clouds towards them. Dismounting and carefully picking their way through weather-sculptured rock spires, they made a bee-line for his position. The emerald spheres of other worlds were popping into view in the sky next to Nero KaSeti, the companion planet, the dwarf brother of the larger world. For Mabius, it was a hugely inauspicious sight. It hung like a vast burnished plate in the dark, its shadow vying with the turquoise equivalent thrown by the watching megalomaniac.

Mabius spat venomously. He turned and walked away.

Vespasian strode after the disappearing back of his brother, though the hulking warlord paid him no mind. Mabius stalked through the columns and shattered buildings until he reached a natural rock pathway running through a smattering of desert shrubs and sage. Two soldiers sprang to attention, but he carried on, oblivious. Beyond, isolated eucalyptus trees tapered off into a circular formation surrounding a voluminous depression in the dark. As Mabius approached, the blackness receded, revealing the lip of a copious, empty amphitheatre. Stone seats ran down in concentric rings towards a half-visible stage shrouded by night. An eternity of history and knowledge was packed into the powdery mortar of a lost realm.

Mabius loved it.

He loved the haunting, timeless quality of a frozen life caught in the 'amber' of the soft white stone and overgrown frescos: an entire culture imprisoned in petrified harmony on a world as barren as an eburnean moon. He could almost taste the stillness, was almost content; perhaps the only time he was at peace in years.

He regarded Vespasian with a languid gaze.

"Hard to believe how such ancient splendour can be so eviscerated by the unforgiving bitch of time. What a mistress she would make, Vespasian. No one who has ever strode these paths lives this day. The builders are dust, their woods and crafts termite fodder, their bones minerals for insects. Such lives as we may live are wrought in the furnaces of our own personal hells, yet they are just sandy islets in the murky ocean of time. What point the faithless puerility of endeavour, when there is nothing and no one left alive to decipher and record the strains of passage?"

Vespasian, however, did not seem to care. "What in hell's name did you want me out there for? Only once did they engage us, only once was I given combat. My guard have been riding in circles pursing shadows while all along you tracked the target, then took her into custody."

Mabius turned and cast a wolfish smile. "I wanted you for exactly that."

"Stilgen was right then. A decoy! I take the lack of resistance means you bribed quite a few of them."

"I don't bribe dog meat. They were poisoned."

"How?"

"A particularly nasty Magi insecta introduced in the ranges by other compromised Krayal in case the female escaped Otho's predictably disorganized assault. The minds of those infected were fused subsequently to my will. I knew where they would be and when before they did. The X Gemina, alas, fled before I could infect them, too."

You could have still trusted me!" Vespasian whined. Mabius had to refrain from slapping him.

"What's the problem, my little pariah? You got to play soldier, to look all big and mighty to the islanders on this world." Mabius' weighty tongue licked his teeth. "They swarmed over your backside like flies, allowing me and the compromised scouts a direct and unwatched path right up their blind side. I had a clear shot, Vespasian, and I took it! She didn't even know I was on-site until battle. I smelled her desire to find that portal in the Arctic climes, the one we could never find. I knew that old Heretic would compel her to use it, too."

Mabius' lip stretched in vainglorious delight. "What a distraction you were. Even with the Krayal drones and my disinformation campaigns, your witless presence shook them from head to foot, and sucked up their watchers. A tiny, rapid penetration unit guided by my lizard scouts slipped right through. Don't fret too hard, brother; it is as futile as a hopper bug in a gale!" Mabius' triumphant grin dissipated into a devilish gleam. "Let me put it this way. You're *Sythian*! That means something around these parts."

The giant warlord straightened. After all, the regent's capture was a great victory, and he was in a magnanimous mood. "Despite being neut, you are still more powerful than any gutless, vat-bred Magi in the highest-class Imperial unit in the Core. You could've made a difference."

"A ... difference," Vespasian replied weakly. Already, his anger had evaporated into automatic meekness. "What to? The desert rats in the um, desert?"

"You lazy, self-obsessed, stench-encased mafflard. There's a huge horizon out there—cities and stars and thousands of hundreds of portals in this sector alone! The only thing holding you back was the incarceration of your own mind. You could've attacked the Imperium's enemies off-world, created new ways of mining critical minerals, occupied nearby Heretic-infested moons. You could have built beautiful cyan-glass domes near dying suns or soul-crushing castles that reached to the blue above. You could have *really* impressed Vice Roy Myrian or even the Undying Himself," he paused for breath and spat in disgust, "You've squandered your inheritance, Vespasian—you're a failure."

It never changed. The younger had always usurped the gentler elder, berating him endlessly until all that was left was shame. His mouth went as cold as a locust's corpse. Mabius, physically, seemed to drain the heat from the rocks and anyone unlucky enough to be standing nearby.

Huge angelic statues, thirty times his height, arced majestically over the amphitheatre. Frozen wings caught the moons' light as their eroded fingers grasped toward one other across the central divide. Rain trails washed down their cheeks in sad, grey runnels. It was the kind of beauty you'd only truly notice when faced with the belief your existence was nearly up.

"My ...?"

"What?" Mabius shot back impatiently, still glaring into solitude.

"My people! I take it they now no longer follow me?"

"They haven't followed you for the last two decades."

"I get it," Vespasian murmured. "The primary reason for your anger is the fact my failings cost you your dreams. Without me, there aren't enough of us in our family to do what you really wanted against the Goat!"

The mephitic gleam in Mabius' eye as he faced his brother again was a razor-sharp diamond. "You are seeking insight?"

"The regent? Why?" Vespasian asked, realizing it might be prudent to change the subject. "What possible use could she be to an Empire of a million suns and worlds? An Empire that defeated the Asthen Ascendancy, the Interregnum, the Heretics, and even the first Al Kimiya. Is it *really* because the winged insurgent put a chart to its birth site inside her sorcery-neuter skull, even though there is a powerful range of Seers at the Heretics' disposal who certainly received it?"

Rather unexpectedly, Mabius looked amused. "So, you want to know how it all really works, brother, do you?" He chuckled. "Is that it?"

Mists around the silent edifices swelled in thickness and intensity. It felt like the world of the dead, the real dead, was watching. Mabius regarded him malevolently. "I represent our family now. It should have been you, but you screwed that up.

"In the impossibly short time we were given, I've prepared a half dozen attack forces, poisoned the Krayal scouts, and bribed the already morally impaired humes of influence in the city. The latter was immensely easier than the geckos who, at the very least, possess a superior, ethical culture. If it wasn't for that old Heretic's warning, Otho might have succeeded at capturing Ayilia." The warlord sighed wistfully. "All He wants is the female, Vespasian—alive. He believes the Seers might be decoys and she the true recipient."

The mist had thickened to pea soup. Mabius' frame was pitch-black, his shape framed only by planet light above.

Vespasian steepled his fingers. "So, the greatest terrorist this universe has ever seen chose a person usurped by her own people. This person happens to be incapable of sortilege and therefore incapable of even carrying the map in the first place, as it's made entirely of thaumaturgy. It defies belief."

"The credibility of the story depends entirely on the chronicler telling the story. Perhaps that's all it is." Mabius laughed.

Vespasian went as close as he dared to his brother's imposing presence. For all his strength, Mabius was being shockingly naive. "Do you believe this fairy tale?"

"Did you ever read the parables, Vespasian?"

"What parables?"

"I'm taking that as a no." The giant was an onyx executioner in the blackness. "They're integral to Magi lore. The Al Kimiya is not a being of legend or of mythology, no matter how many times it has been rewritten about in the degraded, plagiarised scriptures of the organics as some Phoenix. This being never entirely died—it *hibernated*. It's a fiery killer, of *science*, not folklore." His eyes were boreholes. "As with this Kimiya, we believe if the knowledge of an individual of immense learning becomes too great, they attain the Ji'naa."

Dread gripped the Consul. He'd wanted to hear his brother's true thoughts; now he regretted it.

"The Ji'naa? Good God, Mabius, I haven't heard that since we were young. This surely is as much myth as the Phoenix."

"How would a fool like you know? You can barely stroke life out of the mottled soup that you mistake for brains, let alone tease the quantum firmament in every physical thing and steal its puissance to make flame."

Mabius steadied himself, though his hands were flexing. "It is a time when the soul-mind of a Magi attains the purest clarity *before* death, not after. Do we enter Ji'naa with the most absolute understanding of the universe, its knowledge, its essence. Everything is understood; our petty failures and successes, why we chose to suffer before we are born, why we chose to fight or cower, and why we may choose to hurt the energy of another when they did not merit it. Or most likely did! At this point, and only at this point, the dualism of an existence is gelded together by the cosmic forge of an enlightened soul. They become something else, something beyond all ken—a being with the soul-mind of a *god*! Such a being would have galaxies for irises and a supernova for a heart, yet we might not know them as we passed in the blood-stained streets, throwing discoloured coins into a beggar's cap." If Vespasian could sweat, he'd be in overdrive now. Mabius' titanic presence overpowered every Lifeless neuron in his body.

"*Think*, Vespasian. The newfound purity of such a consciousness would merge with the quintessential mind of the universe. The electrified RNA in its cells would match the building matter of every sun in every dimension, in every cosmos, everywhere." Even by his standards, Mabius had a severe dose of passion building. It was times like this anything could happen.

"By the undead god, Vespasian, I swear you would become the key that fit into any cosmic door. Open that door, and the universe is yours. Moons would be your playing dice; comets could be hurled like flaming rocks into the terrified earth!"

Vespasian knew it was coming. The brief but intense high, the popping of the bubble and its immediate deflation; the cursing and the anger spiralling in giddy circles out of control. That's when it got nasty. Eventually, the giant would walk away, his fists and feet covered in someone else's blood, the savage void never sated.

"What the living hell do you think the Goat *is*, you cretinous dolt, Vespasian? You can't build an organization this big and hold it indefinitely without knowledge, without attaining Ji'naa. The Uncertainty Paradox *forbids* it—it states quite specifically that the entire structure becomes unsupportable and ultimately collapses." Mabius shook his brother like he was a doll made of stitches and bone. "*For some reason, not for the emperor!*"

There was merciful silence. It hadn't been as serious as Vespasian had feared. The Consul had no doubt they were still using him, cloaking their intent. The feeling of doom was powerful. Nevertheless, Mabius began to calm. Somehow, it was even more unnerving.

"Vespasian, the Unholy One has made the destruction of the Al Kimiya egg the highest and only priority." His voice was a demonic purr. "The egg will remain hidden until near the apogee of the hatchling's emergence. At this point, the Kimiya's increasing power cannot be camouflaged, and the Goat's thaumaturgic eye will spy it." The giant moved menacingly close to his brother. "Make no mistake, no one knows if He has the time to dispatch it before the creature escapes."

The Consul kept his face impassive. The mists were so strong that it was becoming hard to see, feel, or even hear. "Mabius, if the regent's map can really pinpoint this egg, it could win us this necromancer's war, especially as the Goat can't see it until it's nearly ready."

"Hence her utter, indescribable, priceless value." Mabius smiled. It was almost impossible to see directly but somehow, he could detect the gelid contours of his smile. The giant shook a finger in front of his brother's face, eyes sparkling dangerously in the vapour. "The elder of our family isn't quite as thick-headed as I feared. You finally begin to understand."

The Consul hissed through cracked teeth. "So, the Goat will extract the sorcery from the woman's mind directly." It was not a question.

"It's not a war of armies anymore, brother; it's a war of the Arch Magi, of the very soul, a war waged in the very firmaments of existence itself!" Mabius sucked in the cold nighttime air. His stare was gently messianic within the wisping folds of grey whiteness. "Can you also envision what damage the Heretics could do if this hume had given them the wherewithal to find and enrol this beast? Can you imagine just how powerful this creature will be the second time round, after all it has learned in the void?"

Mabius put a reassuring, planet-sized palm on the other's shoulders. It was just as much a threat as a placatory gesture.

"Vespasian," he cooed. "You've seen enough of life to know things. You can appreciate that no ordinary soldier, or group of soldiers, would have a whore's chance in hell to get to the egg remotely in time if this hume does not work out." Mabius' finger pointed at the space between his eyes. Vespasian nodded, resisting the impulse to shove his brother back.

Fearfully, he mumbled. "The Goat requires a champion."

"All or nothing, brother Consul, either way. The Al Kimiya must be destroyed before it breaks out and this champion must be the one that does the destroying, if all else fails. Even if we have had our fill of war." His fingers closed around Vespasian's throat. "I am that champion, brother! If the female has the chart, it is a win, as I brought her in. If she does not, I will still kill the winged terrorist. Either way, it is glory for me." He let the Consul go and abruptly clenched his elder brother in a tight hug, pointing at something with his left hand. "The humes are tied over there. You will not touch them; you will not approach them; you will not lay eyes on them for the entire duration of the ride. She's dangerous, but she might not know this yet. We will decipher her potential at the Pit, see if we can use her first before the Goat gets His bloody claws on her.

Maybe she's a false prophet, or maybe she is a sensitive, but trust me, if she's of no use to anyone, I will personally smash her mind-guts on the nearest stones and use them for belts."

Silence.

"*Understood?*"

"Yes."

"Good."

Mabius almost crushed the smog, such was his sudden haste to re-join the camp. He left the other staring mutely at his disappearing frame.

The giant warlord shouted for his centurion. The skeletal chieftain thundered up.

"Felm, pack the equipment and mobilize the troops. We leave."

"Yessir. Sir?"

"What?"

"The hume's Gemina unit is only two leagues off; a perimeter scout spotted them—evidently, they are attempting recovery of their leader. This is our chance to take out the rest. I doubt the lizards will interfere so far from the rises in open territory. Forewarned, we could decimate them and their guns this time round."

"Felm understand; my *only* concern is the delivery of the female and her companions," Mabius growled, trying to keep his voice level. "Get her ready!"

Heavily armoured shapes clanged and thudded through the cloying vapour, their weapons clinking as they broke camp. Mabius moved among them issuing orders. His brother followed silently. Struggling figures in sackcloth and chains were lifted and bundled onto spare Prowlers. Vespasian walked back across the camp, a little queasy inside. He mounted his frothing Prowler and turned in the direction that the battle unit was riding.

Chapter Thirteen

PRISONER OF THE PIT

V ultures circled.

They moved languidly, choosing where to go and when, a freedom unavailable to the mindless denizens struggling deep below the acid-yellow skies. They eyed the suns-radiated desert, the wind-blasted sand drifts, the occasional stunted tree leaning like a broken-backed man. Only a knot of guards grouped against the vast gate betrayed any indication of apparent intelligence, though most only managed blank stares at an unchanged horizon.

No change there.

The birds and guards had been doing this for years.

Staring.

Through the doors of the Pit and down its cantilevered throat, under the vaulted ceilings and its clinging shroud of manufactured nothingness, the new prisoners were embraced by an army of ramshackle cogs and creaking pistons. Each mechanism strained to churn out Lifeless only a little less animated than the machines berthing them. In endless cycles, the life of the obsolete outpost continued with as much change and meaning as the baked tombs of the desert above.

Except today.

The Pit had a purpose again. The Imperial base thrummed to the martial message of its founders, energized into feeding a war most had never seen, producing items of quality that could deliver oblivion to the living in a hundred different ways. Through the intricate array of intermingling walkways, brooding viaducts, and contaminated waterways, the new arrivals walked. The river of machine oil and broken parts had blossomed into a labyrinth of tributaries and deltas, each with a miniature ecosystem of bank-side fungi. Insects and microbes swarmed within the choppy toxins, digesting the supine flows, as a low-level perma-mist hugged the murky surfaces above. On the banks, squatting reptiles hungrily watched wriggling shapes in gaudy waters filled with chemicals.

It was an unusual day. The Pit had received guests for the second time in just a matter of months. Things must be looking up.

One shape moved slowly within the hum of unorthodox excitement. No one spared a glace in his direction as Vespasian shuffled through the corridors to the reaches below. The most powerful person in the Pit barely existed. He'd never been so alone, despite a lifetime of it. A new cavern appeared, one he hadn't visited for longer than he could remember. Green, rusted iron doors waited at the end of an abandoned corridor. Etched onto their eroded surfaces were hands wielding nailed clubs and helmets shaped like wolves.

He kicked them open.

Beyond, metal walkways hugged the curved walls, circling the central dais like polished neck clamps. A handful of Kommandos patrolled the route ahead. They regarded him disparagingly. A spear was thrust against his breast.

"No one passes."

The takeover was as simple as that.

"Do you know me?" he rasped, desperately demanding respect.

Silence. Then, "As I would know a ghost."

"Then that's a yes."

It didn't move. With surprising ease, Vespasian applied a spot of thaumaturgic thought to the spear. It showered into sparks. The Pro Consul walked on. To his amazement, the Kommandos didn't follow. He walked into the stricken vaults below. The guard at the main dungeon door stepped aside, though the entry remained closed. A voice broke the quiet.

"Wait!"

He swirled around. Stilgen sprinted after him, past the startled guards. Vespasian couldn't quite stifle a lurch of gratitude toward him.

"I want to come, too," his lifetime companion said breathlessly.

Vespasian smiled, then hammered on the doors. Long heartbeats passed, then two more guards pulled them open. He pushed past wordlessly, then walked with tentative steps down hallways decorated with intricate whorls forged into the stone centuries before he'd even been born. A maze of patterns graced the inner walls, mixed garishly with a riot of fearsome faces. Femurs sporadically erupted into star-burst patterns at tasteful intervals in between. Whoever carved them had clearly been ... artistic.

Stilgen regarded him carefully. "You look perturbed."

"An understatement."

They faced a dark but spacious hall with at least six floors containing nothing but closed prison rooms. During his time, they'd only been used to cage delinquent Pit.

"The prisoners will be in the main clink," he mumbled.

"Is this wise?" Stilgen whispered. "Even you have been forbidden access."

"This is still *my* Pit, after a fashion, so they technically also belong to me. They've been here two weeks, yet he hasn't touched them. He just talks to them, prods them like hapless livestock."

"We aren't exactly versed in the arts of torture. It's something you showed no interest in, so we never did it. What can you hope to learn if Mabius' sheer presence isn't enough?"

"I just want to talk. The Imperium can boil my bones later if they have a problem."

They'd entered a private annex decorated with the long-dead remains of past enemies. Vespasian hesitated at an iron booth. Again, two non-Pit legionnaires faced him. Without saying a word, they parted and let the pair through.

Out of earshot of the guards, Stilgen hissed. "Mabius hasn't barred us from here; it probably didn't even occur to him."

Large wooden gates with colossal metal bolts slammed behind them. Three routes beyond led to three cells. Vespasian took the middle. Someone here had taken the trouble to carve words and inscriptions in the old Imperial dialect, replenished with obsolete scrawls. The last door automatically swung open.

The Consul nodded in remembrance. "Seems we've a few old incantations remaining in the locks. They forgot to change them. They're the only thing that still recognizes my authority."

He walked through.

The atmosphere in the Pit's prison was dense and foreboding. Manacled like beasts, several silent humanoid figures stared up at the Lifeless warlord and his side arm. Though neither group betrayed anything in the way of emotion, the grim fierceness on the captives' faces said enough.

Wordless, Vespasian cast his eyes over the scene. The room was intricately laid out with red pennants and long scarlet batik hangings. Ruby glow stones shone from the corners.

A placard proudly announced, *Make yourselves at home, filth, before we take your bones.*

He looked directly at the captives again. One face, with a bald head, looked back. That had to be the ever-loyal Kemet, the regent's favourite hound. Three other humes, fellow Dragoons, were apparently titled Soren, Kindred, and Kofi.

They had been in the group attempt to rescue the regent and had been stunned by Mabius' fireballs.

Join the club.

His bitter gaze swept over the ragged forms and unexpectedly found itself hovering over the captured geckos. The chieftain named Seftus glowered back resiliently. Astonishing to think he'd also hurried back to rescue the regent. Vespasian knew enough about the cold bloods to understand just how shameful it was for Krayal to be captured. The other, a slightly hefty Krayal companion called Jarong, perched quietly beside. During the journey, he was said to have talked nonstop until an impatient boot or two put an end to that. Now, he didn't talk at all.

Finally, the source of all this trouble herself.

She wasn't even looking at him.

This dismayed him. Even the humes regarded him with disdain! By God's breath, they were hardly masters of destiny stuck on Etherwolde's dust bowl. He ground his fingers into his palms, swallowing back the sense of worthlessness. She was no Mage; that was obvious. From a sensory necromantic point of view, it was like she wasn't in the room at all.

She spoke first, startling him into reality. The clinking of manacles suggested it startled nearly everyone.

"So, *you're* the Pro Consul."

He stared at her blankly. She finally turned her eyes to him. Though grimy from the dungeons, her face was poised in menace.

"In all these years, we never met." She inhaled deeply. "Perhaps that was a mistake, but I was under the impression you were fused to the stone of your chair."

He couldn't be seen to respond to her lead, to let her take the initiative or humiliate him in front of everyone. "There was nothing in your micro-world that interested me. I was busy." *A bit too defensive, perhaps?*

"Busy rotting."

That hit like a slap in the face. The tension was claustrophobic. Even the Krayal's vexed look stilled. Was that pity? Stilgen was frowning so deeply, rivers could have formed permanent ravines on his forehead.

"Maybe then, you'd prefer the company of my brother?" Vespasian said.

As expected, no one replied.

Encouraged, Vespasian continued, "Perhaps, the apparent inactivity of my administration seems more to your liking now?"

She wouldn't be quite so uncooperative next time. He gesticulated at Stilgen and turned to go. Already, he'd had enough; this wasn't going to get him any answers.

"Not looking good, is it?" she said.

He halted, brows raised. He found himself responding again, participating in her manipulation. "Meaning?" The menace in his voice was unmistakable, though the scorn in her own was more than equal to his toothless threat.

"Didn't all this belong to you?" For a fleeting moment, Ayilia seemed to have read him like a dilapidated tome, half-decayed into the mildew of its own disuse. "What happened? Your family showed up. You know what that means, don't you?"

He was trying not to snarl, though now more with trepidation than anger. He stalked up to her, looking down. She met his gaze. "Enlighten me."

"It means you don't have long."

He leaned close to the sweating face taunting him and growled through exposed teeth. "I'm sure you're going to tell me. Exactly what *will* happen to me?"

"Umm ..." She smiled. "Don't know." She averted her gaze. "Yes, I do. He'll cut your throat wide open. I give you days, at most."

"Regent?" Kemet asked, his tone protective.

Vespasian turned her face back to his with a thumb and forefinger on her chin, then pressed his forehead firmly against hers. "You don't know the first thing about how things are done. I'd advise you to observe your tongue with the same scrutiny as a blood hawk. Be ... very ... quiet."

He held her head steady. She stared back and did not flinch at the smell of death, the one that threatened them both. The warlord withdrew his head very slowly and inched away. Both knew he was incapable of threats but, for once, she said nothing. Perhaps, she really was a witch, albeit one without power.

"She's right, dead man!" a sibilant voice called from across the room.

Vespasian let out an exasperated splutter. "A comment from one of our strapped-up *geckos*? It's Seftus, isn't it? What makes you think this is a forum on me, cold blood? *You* are the ones under discussion. I wouldn't want to be in any of your boots right now!"

"Nor I yours! The hume talks sense."

The regent's bodyguard smiled darkly. "You can have all our tongues any time you want, Consul, but you still have to face the fact you're in as much trouble as we are."

Vespasian was starting to feel foolish, and in his own dungeon. "I suppose *they* said that, the Imperium?"

All exchanged furtive glances.

"Something like that," Kofi said.

"'Something like that!' That's sewn that, then! This conversation is over."

"*I* said it." Ayilia gazed at her feet. She seemed embarrassed.

The warlord rolled his eyes. The whole thing had gone completely out the window. "I don't have the time for any of this." That was a lie. "Think what you think; it's irrelevant anyway. Coming here was a mistake." Yet, he still couldn't make himself walk out. What really held him fast was the realization that he *wanted* to hear what she had to say.

"It's in the dreams I have."

He snorted, masking the cold sensation creeping through his chest. "Was this the flimflam that ensnared the entire hierarchy of the Imperium? I give you this: you are a top-quality trickster, the best."

"Your brother is in one of my dreams, Consul."

Vespasian froze.

"He's watching something at his feet. I recognize who he was now, but I didn't at the time." Her voice was low, each word chosen carefully. "He had someone or something writhing helplessly by his boots. Mabius was standing in the rain, grinning wickedly. He was taking it all out on this individual, and his soul was just a massive hole filled with self-loathing." The woman shivered at the memory. "In the background, I saw the egg, the Phoenix's egg. Something powerful was about to come out in piercing light." She fixed him a searching gaze. "The ... hatchling will be at the utter mercy of your brother, Consul."

The lakes of fire that were her eyes shone with reckless disregard. For the moment, *he* was the captive. "Somewhere, somehow, in all that well of hate, I sensed an ultra-strong vein of bitterness aimed at *you*. He's waiting for permission to kill you, Consul, perhaps from off-world. You should've died baiting the Krayal with your obsolete troop trapped in those canyons, but you didn't. You should've died and taken the Krayal army with you, but you didn't do that either, did you? Whenever he gets to kill you, the one thing that strikes home is the fact he is looking forward to every ... single ... moment of it."

She was staring hard into the back of his skull.

"It's probably why you came here, whether you realize it or not. Face it, you're not one of them!"

Everyone watched. Their eyes glittered in the darkness, their apprehension hostile. Stilgen was silent behind him.

Finally, Vespasian managed a bloodless whisper. "Your deceit is why I hate your kind. You call us dead, but it's your race that sheds skin, and it's your hide that stinks non-stop. You pollute just by existing, whereas we are clean and dirt-free. I don't believe you, and I don't believe the things the Goat ascribes to you. You survive through manipulation, back-stabbing, and cunning, like all humes. Your concept of nobility died long before the Imperium enslaved your people."

Vespasian stared at Ayilia, eyes as intense as a child's. Kemet strained uselessly against his chains, perhaps petrified the warlord would batter her to death, but Vespasian wasn't intending to harm her, Ayilia knew; instead, he was transfixed, waiting for her reply. Ayilia understood the dilemma pounding through his Lifeless veins.

The knowledge gave her control.

"I understand your terror," she continued, then swallowed hard. Her calm was maddening. "The Lord Goat wanted me because he *actually* believes I can find this Phoenix egg, even though I'm about as magick as a budgie."

"Budgie?"

"It's a bird people keep caged!" Soren blurted from the gloom. "A really nasty thing to do to a bird!"

Vespasian was completely lost. "Why? Has it done something wrong?"

The other shrugged. "Don't know?"

"*Soren*," Kemet hissed.

"Aye!"

"Shut it."

"Aye."

"They came here with humans," Kofi muttered. "But you probably assumed that, Consul."

"They came with humans through the stars when we were nomads," Kindred added. "Some of them, like the rat, never seem to go away."

"Rats!" Stilgen's features hardened with deep contempt. "Those things eat everything. We leave an arm lying around ready for attachment, or a spare adrenal gland, and the scum have already taken it. We declared a great war on them, but it was fruitless."

"What happened?" Soren asked, his tone fascinated.

Stilgen shot him a murderous look. "We nearly lost the Pit."

"How?" Kofi exclaimed.

"One day, they broke into an Ichor tank and drained it completely. Within weeks, they'd turned into four-headed, swine-sized ogres with giant cullions. We eradicated most of them in the end, but they gnawed an entire platoon of poorly-stitched Pit to death and destroyed our beetroot scullery. Even now, the survivors occupy the lower levels where the guest latrines are kept."

"You entertained guests here?" Seftus hissed, unable or unwilling to hide his amazement.

"No," Stilgen growled, rubbing his knuckles defensively. "*No!*"

Ayilia cleared her throat.

They looked at her, nonplussed.

"Help us, Pro Consul. If the Resistance finds the Kimiya, we all benefit."

Vespasian attempted a sardonic smile but made a complete hash of it.

"It stupefies me people on so many worlds have adopted the Kimiya. They think it some kind of spiritual freedom fighter, a pan-planetary sorcerer, a space-aged legerdemain. You are simply witness to a mirage heralding false dawns, a shared myopia that reassures only the condemned."

"Don't take my word for it, Consul," Kofi retorted. "Your great pal Stilgen knows time's just about up too."

Stilgen's nasal cavities flared. He thundered over, arm raised. Kemet lunged against his restraints, but Ayilia was ready for the Lifeless.

"The Consul's turned from the Imperium, like you, Stilgen." She gasped. "I felt it when you came in. I saw your hate for the Goat flame like a burning bushfire, *both of you!*"

She thrust forwards. Her chains rattled and shook, but she paid them no mind. "It's rare, but it happens. People like you can go renegade left on their own too long."

"You bag-sacks of stinking vulture kills! I should ram my—" Stilgen's words strangled off. He turned, as did Vespasian. They were not alone. A broad, hulking figure flanked by a phalanx of guards regarded them through the shadowed door.

"Vitallius!"

The shocks kept coming. Poleaxed, Stilgen and Vespasian stared bloodlessly at each other.

"Correct, Stilgen, faithful Pit side arm. It's good to see you again and, of course, my dear elder brother, Vespasian. I would respectfully counsel against mixing with the Imperium's captured thralls. It seems our infamous siren has quite wound the both of you up." He nodded at Vespasian sternly. "Time to go."

"Go? Go where?"

"Trust me when I say this gives me no pleasure, but it's out of my hands."

Vespasian gulped. "What's out of your hands?"

The other looked pained. "You are to face trial with the prisoners. They are already waiting for you."

Stunned, the Consul approached the dark Sythian form, but the guards immediately blocked his path with spears. "Brother, what have I done? What am I charged with? I did everything demanded of me and more."

The other sighed, regretfully. "You'll see. Perhaps, it's more for what you are than what you've done."

As the guards grabbed Vespasian and Stigen by the arms and started to drag them away, Vespasian could hear the regent's words rebounding through his mind.

Face it. You're not one of them.

A cheer erupted with shocking ferocity, rebounding off the marbled halls within the catacomb-shaped chamber. Such noise hadn't been heard since Abandonment. The floor had been lately polished, revealing a mosaic of fighting demons and one-eyed giants. Another cheer shook dust from arches above, sending things with impossibly segmented legs scuttling to even darker spots under the gaunt stonework. Giant firepits ringed the amphitheatre. The place looked almost presentable.

Vespasian was pushed into the centre, hands in chains.

The reaction of the sea of faces threatened to bring the roof down. If that wasn't sobering enough, it was even more sobering to realize that many of them used to be his people. An irony of ironies that it was the lash, a weapon he'd himself refused to deploy, being used on him now. An armoured ogre with a spikey collar flicked the wicked tongue of the whip against his back, releasing a mist of sepia-coloured blood and peels of grey skin. Looking around the nebulous atmosphere of charged loathing, he spied the ethereal portal that had brought Mabius back. He could see it through the great doors, separating its room from the voluminous space he was being flayed in now.

The watching Pit among the crowd will regret what they're doing once the new order sets in.

His lips spread wide. Delusion felt good. Fluid trickled down his arms and over his hands. In the flickering half-light, it formed grotesque deltas around his body. The din died down, but lips were openly licked in the caliginous stands. They wanted more.

"Brother, come."

The beast grabbed him by the neck and thrust him toward Mabius.

"Don't be afraid, Vespasian, high lord of the low Pit."

Muffled laughter and sporadic jeering rippled through the crowd. Their collective features were garishly stretched by the fluttering lights from flaming torches on jade plinths brought in from God knew where.

"Traitor scum," the crowd intoned.

Vespasian stared at the wall of jeering features as the masses seethed as one. He hadn't asked for this, and had done his best.

"The moment of truth, *Pro Consul*." Mabius could barely say the title without sneering. "Do you meet the challenge?"

The crowd broke out in ear-shattering noise. They were here to see a killing. Mabius, suddenly the showman, acknowledged the crowd with raised hands.

"Bring out the Haruspex!"

The drones tasked with bringing on the Pit's forgotten soothsayer looked decidedly apprehensive, shifting uneasily on their feet.

"Can't, my liege," said the nearest in an oddly nasal whine.

Mabius raised his brow. "Why not?"

"Haruspex's dead, my lord."

Exasperated: "What happened to him?"

"Fell in a barrel of wine. Didn't foresee it, apparently." Haplessly he added, "Died happy, though!"

"This place is the hole of the universe!" Mabius grunted quietly before raising his arms again. "Then accept the Auspice."

When no one responded, he nodded vigorously at a wriggling skin satchel nearby. A plethora of sentries scrambled to bring it to him first. He held it up for all to see.

"The Auspice is a tried and tested formula for the assertation of spiritual purity. Because the Pro Consul is blessed of Sythian stock we, tonight, get a chance to reaffirm his *astonishingly* rich heritage, while determining that his precious gifts haven't drifted with criminal disuse." Mabius looked around accusingly. "Should he fail the test, then he can be no Sythian. Should he fail, he is but a charlatan, a fallen slum-devil not worthy of the necromantic god status of our breed."

A lie.

He was here to be ruined.

The charade was to disempower him of that same heritage, so no one could say 'here tonight died a Sythian!' It wouldn't do if such mighty beings were seen as fallible, not if you were hewn from the same DNA.

"Failure," Mabius paused, "is not an option! The Auspice assails any sorti-lege-gifted miscreant who has slipped from grace. The potency of the Auspice is set previously, in this case by myself. The incumbent will use his gift to resist. If he is successful, then he is worthy. If not ..."

"Get on with it!" a voice called.

Mabius nodded sagely at a Pit drunk in the crowd, as though he welcomed the intrusion. Immediately, people applauded. They didn't notice the drunk being relieved of their head by burly guards. An inscrutable Stilgen sat nearby with some hapless Pit loyalists. They were clearly prisoners as well.

Vespasian glared at his brother. "Leave my people out of this—this is not their conflict."

"Conflict?" Mabius' huge frame edged closer. "Is that what you think?" There was a disturbance. Thousands of faces looked around in unison as though part of some sports tournament.   "Ahh, our guests!" Mabius' veined head leant lower, his voice soft. "Believe me, brother, what awaits you is clemency compared to the fate prepared for her. Count your blessings that underneath it all I am graciously magnanimous!"

Why couldn't he at least shut up? He could never shut up!

The prisoners were herded into the circle with chained hands. The two Krayal had been beaten severely. Vespasian, despite himself, was shocked. What was it about the geckos that ignited such a reaction within his kind? The other captives tried to walk proudly, but Soren looked terrified and Kindred walked stiffly. Even the regent seemed to have been struck, despite her welfare being of apparent paramount importance.

Vespasian almost felt pity for her.

One of the guards gave Kemet a wallop with a spear. With a loud curse, he shoved back, destabilizing the guard, who promptly struck him to his knees. Within moments, the humans were tied like animals to iron benches, except for the regent, who appeared to be in some kind of stupor. Triumphantly, Mabius held up the squirming bag containing the Auspice in thick, sausage-fingered hands. The crowd roared with delight.

Vespasian had never seen an Auspice before and tried not to panic.

On cue, the bag spilt.

To his quiet horror, it was pitch black inside. Mabius broke into a feral grin and flung it at Vespasian's chest. A frozen, invisible weight gripped his dead heart, paralyzing his torso. The shocked warlord tried moving his neck and arms, but they hung uselessly by his sides. An echoing croak sent the confused audience into euphoria. Looking around in the middle of an oscillating vortex, he spotted his brother's wolfish grimace superimposing itself across his vision. He felt he was at the bottom of a long spyglass where colours and shapes kaleidoscoped into a fairground craze, with a single, distorted image at the centre.

"They're inside you, brother. Perhaps, truth will expel them, or perhaps it will expose you as the catch-basin swine you always were."

"Kick them out!"

That desperate cry was his voice. He wondered if this would be at least quicker than being crucified.

The audience exploded with primal satisfaction. Their mother was a rusted, industrial womb while their father was a flop. They mindlessly mimicked everything their ex-lord said.

"Kick them out! Kick them out!"

With a neck of lard and his brains army ration soup, Vespasian caught flashes of jawed millipedes inside his chest. They pierced the tough pelt of parched skin with ease, hiding the mungs of flesh within. Heart, lungs, and gut melted into a wilted mesh of arthropod spines and legs. The swarm of chitinous shapes moiled vigorously against each other, devouring anything not strictly bone.

That didn't leave much.

Legs buckling, the Sythian fell hard on his knees with an audible crack. Gore liberally slopped out the rent, spilling over the floor. The crowd let out an enormous cheer as Mabius proclaimed him a traitor, with expertly rehearsed lines practiced long before the trial had begun.

Was this death? Could a dead man die twice?

The whirling inside the lost warlord's head shuddered into a dot, then winked out into infinity. Darkness replaced what was left of his mind.

As if in response, there was a splash of colour and a vision of grass and white fences. It was utterly incongruous, so he lay there, quiet. There was rustling, and a light pattering too. When the softest wind ruffled what should have been thick, healthy hair had he been allowed to live in the first place, the Sythian shot to his feet like a startled rabbit. Turning in repeated circles, Vespasian took in a riot of yellow corn fields and trees bordering rippling grasses. A modest path with white stones led to a hume-styled, wooden house. Paint curled in peels down the front of the creamed walls. Half-raised slats revealed only darkness within. The place was a veneer of rustic gentility and ruin.

He spent some moments gathering his wits.

It started raining. An effervescent spray, almost imperceptible to the senses, sheened the plants in freshness. Dazed, he walked around, unaware that half his face was dirt from his time lying in the rich soil. He looked like a bohemian, plaster-cast scarecrow to anyone who might be passing in a place where no one ever passed. Ruby poppies and wildflowers tinted with dashes of blues, yellows, and golds bobbed in russet crowds in meadows near the crops. He could see the approach of a slowly-circling storm in the distance.

With a lurch, he noticed a figure standing at the gate to the seemingly abandoned property. So much for his senses. How had he missed it, or her? The woman stood there staring at the deserted porch and the overgrown garden. He tentatively made his way over.

"Beautiful, isn't it?" She sighed.

He didn't answer, didn't know what to say. Did she mean the house or the weather or the fields?

"All of it," she replied. "So beautiful!"

Surprised, he looked at her. Her face was impassive, but the corners of her mouth attempted a smile. *Why are you here?*

"I don't know," she whispered. "Don't really care either. So free and safe here."

He nodded and looked around. He seemed to appreciate the absolute solitude, the sheer invisible energy that swept through the fields. Looking back at her rain-speckled head he had a realization. *I know who you are.*

She shot him a look. He recoiled but held his stance. She looked different. The hard lines on her face were softer, and her eyes no longer registered that keen, burning intellect within.

"You know you're dying, don't you, Consul? *Right now.*"

Vespasian spoke this time, "I'd guessed as much." He shrugged. "Why are we here?"

Ayilia paused. "No idea. Usually, if I'm taking refuge in some make-believe place like this, I'm chasing off some nocturnal sprite invading my sleep. This one's new to me."

Her hand rested on the gate. His shot out, slim but powerful, and pinned hers to the wood.

"Don't go in."

She looked at him blankly. "Why not?"

He shuddered. Didn't answer. She made to enter again, but he held her back.

Her eyebrows came together. "You can't stop me *here*. This is *my* head, and you have no powers in this place."

"It's dangerous," he blurted, quickly releasing his grasp. "Outside, it's all beautiful— even someone like me can see that—but inside ... I *feel* it."

"How can you know? You're as good as dead in that chamber; you can sense nothing."

"I sense that whatever's inside there is ageless."

The woman rounded on him, eyes black with suspicion. "How the hell are *you* here anyway? Do you make a habit of gate-crashing other people's heads? Don't tell me that house is evil, not in my head. It's all I got left in this underground hole outside *your* underground hole!"

His head begun to swim. His consciousness was retreating now, being sucked somewhere else. Her frame, and all the moody beauty behind her, was shrinking, though he could still see her staring at him. He watched it all recede to a bright pinprick, one that abruptly winked out into blackness. A din exponentially increased in volume until it became a cauldron of noise. The faces returned, as did the outlines of the halls he was sure he'd just died in. His body contorted, but there was no pain.

The Auspice was ravaging his guts. His skin rippled and bulged as they spread out. Through the periphery of his bastardized vision, he spied Stilgen and the others being herded towards the centre. The baying intensified. Vespasian could barely move. It felt as though every ligament had been gnawed to oblivion. There was no self-pity. All he could think about was saving the few friends he had left.

Crash.

A shape broke past the mortified guards herding it. It leapt directly at him, skidding across the floor. She hadn't been tied like the others, perhaps because she had been drugged. He blankly watched as she slid to where he lay before thrusting her mouth against his ear, whispering quickly. As the regent was dragged backwards, they administered sharp kicks. Ayilia didn't resist. She sank into a limp dream-state again, cutting herself off from the pain and the hate.

The Auspice worms were hitting peak frenzy. His tissue was shrinking, revealing mounds of bone underneath. The cracking of femurs mixed disjointedly with a dull gnawing. The entire crowd, the worms, his brother's contempt, the whispers; nothing really mattered. Everything was swept uniformly under a mental carpet of sudden peace.

Only her words concerned him. "*That was no dream fool. Get up or die.*"

An urge to laugh swelled. Could it be the only person who had faith in him was his human adversary?

Another blow to the back of his skull sent a spare tooth chiming across the floor.

The crowd spat and growled, sharp incisors bared, red eyes refracting loathing; the one emotion the Lifeless were comfortable with. Cranial ridges formed furrows across shiny but nicked foreheads. Guards with thick arms of bone and even thicker armour placed hobnailed feet on the exhausted regent. They thrust chains so tightly around her that she practically stopped breathing. *What was the point*, Stilgen thought venomously. *Kill her and be done.* He regarded his ex-lord quietly. Had he been anything but Sythian, he would have been gone already.

"Get ready, you dead idiot."

Vespasian's eyes flickered open, but he couldn't identify who'd spoken. All he could see were savage-looking guards and that woman again, staring at him through the spit and blood. Did the drugs wear off? Did her witch curse neutralize them? Mabius was shouting vaingloriously at the crowd and thoroughly enjoying the reverence. The fallen warlord felt a rush of indignation.

"I said, get ready, Consul!"

The voice shook him more than his death. It was *inside* his mind. She was staring at him. She then gestured at Stilgen, until a guard kicked her. Immediately, she returned that piercing gaze. It bored into his mind, kept his consciousness pinned to the body he couldn't feel.

"It's time."

Shit! She could talk to his very brains. At least the things consuming him hadn't found those yet, small wonder.

He inhaled sharply.

Something was happening inside, something triggered by that human. He couldn't believe it.

She was taking control.

A fire welled up inside him like a boiling, orange geyser.

Shit.

The crack was deafening, the sparks blinding. His chains sundered in a cloud of spinning debris. The room recoiled from a blinding light that blazed off every surface. He raised his arm and fired venomous plasma through his fist. An astonished guard was vaporized on her feet.

The woman was actually in his head.

He concentrated on the chains holding the others. They buckled and flung open in a series of loud cracks.

Get out of my mind!

Electric-white flashes arced in dancing spirals. A row of dumbfounded guards back-flipped into the crowd in fiery spews of skulls and bone. Alive with flame, Vespasian sensed the swirling Auspice millipedes turning to blackened particles. Tendons twined and wrapped furiously around the re-emerging gristle of his tissue and lining. Even the deep wounds from his crucifixion healed. Every Auspice was reabsorbed atom by atom into the energized guts of the Sythian. He felt astonishingly whole as the kiss of the swathing fire did its work.

People were running in all directions over prostrate shapes. Without even trying, he'd got every cutthroat warding them. Mabius, assuming the assault was external and that his idiot brother was dead, had his back to the Consul. He looked around, bewildered, his mouth gaping, finally turning around.

His gaze met his brother's.

Before the giant could react, a jagged flare lashed into the face of his disbelieving sibling. Mabius staggered back in a cloud of smoke, flickers of corrosive puissance hissing through his eyes and fingers. As the ambushed warlord crashed to his haunches, Vespasian witnessed himself swivel to greet an oncoming company of off-world soldiers. He also registered mild surprise when a plume of super-charged heat turned them into spitting bonfires, prompting a number of low-grade Pit guards to scurry into the dark like frightened strays.

There were groans and fading sighs. He'd butchered just about every guard who'd so much as looked at him, in addition to members of the belligerent audience and the ogre. Gravely weakened and traumatized by the transformation, the warlord slumped to a sitting position on the ground. Around him lay a vast killing field of carbonized skulls and burning bones.

•.♥.♥.♥.•

Stilgen shot an anxious glance at a sightless Mabius, who was still alive and mouthing obscenities as he furiously attempted to heal his broken face. Vespasian, meanwhile, despite his discovery of Sythian fire, was clearly spent. There were raised voices. He swung around. The woman and her companions were overpowering some newly-arrived Pit guards using the weapons of the fallen. Stilgen and the Krayal quickly followed suit. As the living despatched them, he couldn't help notice just how expertly the humans moved.

"Impressive," he muttered darkly.

Stilgen was deeply reluctant to fight with the humans. His brow was puckered with conflict. A decision had to be made rapidly, one way or the other. He paused, then grabbed a discarded blade and made his first kill, sweeping the head from an unsuspecting Pit sentry as it forced Seftus back. The sentry's two companions turned. In a flash, Stilgen brought the cutter across a skeletal throat and plunged it effortlessly into the startled neck of the other. Both crashed simultaneously. The other Lifeless prisoners were following suit now, fighting their own kind with as much self-loathing as he.

Before they knew it, the crowd was gone, the arena empty. Pools of fluid flooded the floor around everyone's feet. Among the clumps of hacked, burned forms stood a tense, edgy non-alliance of humans, Krayal, undead outcasts, and one huddled Sythian.

Mutual foe bonded by mutual defilement.

Stilgen's head shot up as an alarm horn sounded. To his immense dismay, battle-hardened collections of more organized killers steadily poured into the vast space.

He swore.

A Lifeless unit approached in serried ranks; blades, pilums, and javelins steady, bossed helmets barely concealing carmine eyes within. Horns were sounding throughout the Pit—an army would soon arrive. The motley group of renegades backed further together until they formed a tight circle of shared animosity, both to the foe but equally to each other.

Rattled, Stilgen confronted the only person he sensed had any control at all. "What invidious trickery did you use on the Consul, Regent?"

Clearly equally rattled, she spat, "What would you have me do, Pit Man? Would you rather die like a piece of chopped wood?"

"I trust, then, that you have another of those tricks up your sleeve. If you can light him up again, maybe one or two of us will survive!"

Before she could answer, Seftus pushed through and grunted at his undead counterpart, face contorted with centuries of pent-up Krayal fury. "She has *nothing* more up her sleeve, armour or anywhere else, dead skull, can't you see?"

Stilgen scowled. "Keep out of things you know little of, gecko, unless you've cooked up a solution in that green catch-basin you think a mind."

The Krayal swore back, weapon raised, ready to kill an accidental ally than the foe.

"Stop."

They froze instinctively.

Ayilia barged in between the seething warriors. "*In case* you've both forgotten, we have a *real* enemy about to fillet us on the spot. Afterwards, *by all means*, slaughter yourselves in some hormonal, primal blood feud because I won't care, but for now, hold your shit together!"

The Nethergeistian unit charged with a battle cry that was part scream, part hiss.

They crashed into the escapees, armour on armour, sword on sword, in a ringing clang of violence. The group fought viciously, but the off-worlders were superior in strength and speed. Immediately, they were on the back foot. Ayilia fought to concentrate. The Lifeless were stronger, but not always smarter. She drew on every childhood sword skill to keep that strength at bay.

Ramming her stolen shield against the horde of skulls, metal, and broken teeth, she chopped and parried against the flashing weaponry, all wedged together in the super tight throng. Only occasionally would she jab her blade through the crush, barely digging a gouge in the ox-sized torsos. They were losing ground, running out of space. Had the newcomers time to prepare, it'd be over already.

One nearly cut her head with the tip of their blade. With a lightning reflex, she surprised herself by running her sword into their exposed gullet. Ghoulishly, the head lolled backwards into the crowd. As the Lifeless fell, two more brought down a double blow on Ayilia's battered shield, sending waves of pain into her calves and up her strained spine. With a cry, she thudded the shield into an unwarded, mailed shoulder and followed with a swift thrust. The thing stepped back, angrier than ever. A centurion appeared from the scrum to organise the melee into an ordered fighting force, mirroring the formation their living opponents had takenShe was suddenly worn to the core.

"They're too strong," she said, defeated.

Kemet shook his head. "We make our weapons *part* of our bodies and keep them boxed in. They cannot use their physical advantage to the full."

She shook her head in return, panting heavily and nodded towards the centurion. "Not when he's finished with them!"

Kemet regarded the situation with grave eyes as the ranks pulled away on command. Before he could answer, a couple of over-zealous, badly repaired, and noticeably shorter Pit soldiers made use of the room to abruptly rush them, oblivious to the bellowing expletives of their company commander.

Ayilia automatically crashed to her knees and severed their legs at the exposed area just above the calves, taking both down. They crawled across the ground, a fluidic gore of stumps, trying to find their lost parts. Another Pit soldier paused in surprise, giving Kemet just enough time to batter their raised shield with an axe. As they warded off the blow, Ayilia lunged forward and cracked the unguarded helmet open with a hefty grunt, as though it was a silver walnut. As bone imploded into the greyness of their mind, she swore their face was still mouthing obscenities. Gunk scattered on their feet. She forced back a lurch of nausea.

"Some Pit got through," she whispered breathlessly to Kemet. "Contaminating the overall cohesion."

"Not enough to save us, though!"

A Lifeless rebel soldier called Gleck had failed to hold onto his throat, which had come out on the back of an Imperium pilum. That now lay clattered on the ground along with his body. The trained off-worlder had twisted the shank after the strike, so that the pyramid-shaped head remained inside the victim's neck, tangling the inner tendons and the bones into a twist. The knight Kindred had tried to save Gleck in an immensely heroic act. The onslaught had simply been too violent, and the undead powerhouses had left Kindred flopped across his undead ally to Kemet's anguished cry.

Standing above them, Stilgen fought like a dervish. Ayilia made a mental note, even if it was a rather academic one at that point, that he was someone you could use in a tight spot if you could overlook the fact that he was just as likely to skewer them as the enemy.

It was hopeless. Seftus' eyes flashed scarlet-black desperation.

"Regent," he cried. "God's teeth ... do that thing you did again!"

"*I'm working on it!*"

"Don't work ... just do!"

Kemet grimaced almost affectionately as he finally crushed to death a brute. "Man, that felt good! Where's Aaron? He would've loved that."

Immediately, another rammed Kemet's shield with their own, the vehemence of the Lifeless' assault nearly knocking the human senseless.

Ayilia crashed her blade against another, grunting heavily with the exertion. "At least," she gasped, "they didn't get their show!"

Stilgen snorted derisively. "Superb, humes die proudly in failure. I get to die beside you. If I had the strength, I would arch my brow in wry amusement."

Kemet let out a guffaw. "Then we're *all* happy, dead man. But you've got to ask yourself, why are *you* dying for the wrong side?"

There was no response except a muffled "ha." Heads briefly turned in Seftus' direction. "Ha!" the Krayal exclaimed again.

"Problem, coldblood?" Stilgen's brows arched as promised, but not in mirth.

"*You think*?" Seftus' shield clattered against a terrifying, red-eyed mountain of metal and bone. "Stuck fighting alongside an escaped morgue of walking bodies, fighting an even bigger morgue of taller, walking bodies," he bashed back the death machine again, "and next to me, also fighting, are some low-life humes and the benighted and magic-stunted ex-ruler of this cesspit himself! *Ha*—bring on death before I die laughing!"

"Umm, folks?" Soren asked, wide-eyed.

"The archers—already seen 'em," Kemet muttered back, ignoring the new threat. "Can you not just die quietly!"

"You're Aaron all of a sudden."

"What is it, Soren?" Ayilia broke in, suddenly attentive. Something in his voice alarmed her.

"Nothing really, except over there. What's the Consul doing?"

"Eh?"

Mabius' clam-like hands had encased his face with healing fire, like a demonic absolution. Being without sight, he hadn't noticed his wayward brother. Vespasian had laid his hands on the shoulders of the hunched hulk as he crouched on his knees.

Suddenly, his dark gaze was on Ayilia.

Despite being moments from death, it chilled her to the bone. The Lifeless host cutting at them surrounded them in a slow-motion death dance, jaundiced incisors flaring. She stared back at the deposed figure, but in that glare, she saw only nothing.

His eyes closed. A flaming shroud of power flowered from the stricken giant into the arms of his ruined sibling.

It seemed that a dozen suns silently went off. It came from their direction.

The room ignited in a retina-splitting flash. The fighting instantly stopped. A violent tsunami of plasma swept the room. The crowd immediately scattered, stamping on each other in feral anarchy, somersaulting down steps in confused piles and scrambling across the roasted bodies of the many slain. Thin, grey wisps of smoke rose from Stilgen's still-standing fighters in swirling patterns of foggy talons. Kofi, Soren, and Kemet wordlessly joined the two Krayal who were despatching survivors. It was apparent that most were hollowed forms of crackling embers.

Soren stood and rearranged his armour. "Maybe next time, you'll all listen when I say I see something?"

Kemet pushed past him, toward Ayilia, voice creaking with exertion. "You alright, ma'am?"

She carefully flexed her arms, then her shoulders. "No, but I'm glad to see you all are."

Kemet shot a look at the allied dead. She shook her head sadly and whispered, "If we get out of this, we'll have a memorial."

He nodded and looked at the Consul. This time, the warlord was completely out, lying on the floor like a drunken starfish. Mabius, now protected by a halo of Magi power, was close to recovering his eyesight.

"How?"

"The Consul? God knows, it has nothing to do with me." She paused to think. "I suspect he picked up one or two tips when I used him the same way, but all that matters is getting the hell out of here. Mabius is almost back, and we're totally cut off."

Ayilia searched the faces and realized that they wanted guidance from her alone. She looked back. "Actually, a suggestion would be quite helpful right now."

No one said anything. There was nowhere to go and nothing to say. The corridors were already resounding with the sound of footsteps. Even if they had the strength left, they were still no match for what was coming, and there was only one way out.

Seftus spoke first. His voice made them start.

"The only reason we are still breathing is lying on the floor, bereft of whatever cursed sortilege he had left!" He regarded them beadily. "No way out—so let's die well and be done with it." As an afterthought, he added, "It's what Krayal have been doing for centuries."

Ayilia gestured at the Consul. "Soren, please give him a hand. He deserves to die on his feet with the rest of us."

Soren looked pained. "He scares me." When no one looked sympathetic, he added, "Well, outside the fact he's terrifying, he keeps blowing up. Sorry, but got my looks to think of."

Kemet snorted. "As Aaron used to say, the only ones bothered about your looks are the beasts of burden in the barrack yards."

"In that case, I hope you save some for me."

"Gentlemen!" Ayilia barked. "Soren, *please*. We may as well get diced on our feet than our rears."

Stilgen cursed and strode over to the ruined warlord. The Consul's bones jutted against skin pulled as taut as waxed paper. As Ayilia watched, an unthinkable thought surfaced from somewhere very deep. It rose as unwelcome as a love-struck demon bursting through the puckered mantle of her soul.

She was gripped with a venomous, cold despair.

"Shit!"

Without warning, something powerful pulled her deep within herself. Her mind was propelled towards a giant, imaginary oval sea the colour of soft eggshell, a neural ocean harbouring a nexus of silent intellect within. It was a placid, briny surface bathed beneath a titan perimeter of hidden suns, a place of silent sanctuary. It reeked of knowledge. It was a personified ossuary, a sanctified bolt hole, an illness of the psyche created by that 'witchling' curse, or more accurately, the Kimiya's uninvited and seemingly sentient map.

She gasped at something so blindingly obvious she'd never noticed before.

Were they one and the same thing?

When she was nine, she was horrified when other people denied, clearly lying through their teeth, that they had similar seas. It was the earliest point that the child implicitly understood that she'd only be safe if she shut up and said only what they wanted to hear. Even the keep staff began to shoot glances reeking of judgment. When she kept her jaw shut, people eventually began to relax. To her, it was the opposite of growing up. To become an adult was to sacrifice the gift of an unthinking connection with the subconscious and all it promised.

"Never trust your eyesight," Agelfi had said. "Your heart is as good a place as any to work things out."

Fat good it had done her.

She came to, mind as sharp as a freshly cut gemstone.

Dear God! She was going to say it.

For a fleeting moment, her sight wavered. Yet, there it was, that thought again; the solution to staying alive.

Die now or die later?

Damn it, die later every damned time!

Stilgen hurried back over to the humes. "Consul's finished. Nothing left. He might be able to tie his laces, but that's it." He regarded Ayilia with a steely eye. "He's going to need a lot of rest before he can even light up a candle, let alone those thugs."

Soren was red-faced. "*Rest?* We don't have the time to piss in our boots, let alone kip in a sodding four-poster, pal. Tell him he either gets up or we all get barbecued."

Seftus nodded reluctantly. "Unfortunately, the whinger's correct."

Stilgen flinched as though slapped. "This is *exactly* why my people believe the living are so defeatist."

Kemet seemed to see the loose alliance disintegrating and spoke quickly. "This can wait. For now, we form a combined unit and body-ram our way through to the desert above, setting this mechanized armpit of an outpost on fire on the way *before* that Sythian meat grinder, the big one, gets his peelers working."

"Eh-bloody-men to that," Kofi said. "Meanwhile, can I say: *what the hell are we even standing around talking about it for?*"

"Because taking them on is *suicide!*" Soren's voice hit a high pitch.

"I, er, agree," Jarong said. "It's really, er, pointless to throw ourselves into the middle of that!"

Seftus snorted. "Perhaps you think they might somehow miss us if we stay here?"

Soren gulped and spoke in frantic tenor, "It's the dying bit that bothers me! Perhaps I'm being pedantic."

Kemet slapped him across the shoulders merrily. "We're going to die anyway, Dragoon! Die with honour and die tearing the calcified heart out of the people that took Agathon. At least some!"

Ayilia looked up slowly. "No."

The others stopped, gobs open like slacked-jawed marmosets.

Seftus shook his head. Parts of the ceiling were coming down in motes of swirling dust as the tremors of the approaching reinforcements. He regarded her as though she was in absolute need of being sectioned on the spot. "We must *go*. Time's up."

"Not that way. Even with the Consul firing, we've no chance."

Soren was in full agreement. "Exactly."

A crowd of vicious scarlet orbs was milling in the distance. Not a single person watching didn't feel fear. The host was hollering. Their bloodlust was up.

"Why stay for dinner when we're on the menu? At least charge them and give them some serious indigestion." There was gruff applause at Seftus' defiance. He was pleased that he was getting better at humour, though he regretted it came at the point when it didn't matter.

Ayilia shot a glance at the horde, then looked back. "Wouldn't you rather live?"

"Yes, oh yes. Let's do that!" Soren jabbered eagerly.

Jarong's head was bobbing up and down fervently, eyes bright with childish hope as was Kofi's.

"Regent," Kemet whispered. "Your plan?"

She breathed in pensively, then indicated over their shoulders.

Gaping wordlessly, one by one, they turned to see where she was pointing. The air seemed to die around them. Eyes widened in complete disbelief, almost horror.

Someone dropped their weapon.

"If I live, I'm blaming Soren for that," Kemet muttered.

"We can't go there!" a voice called out.

"Why can't we?" Ayilia growled. "Come on, what's stopping us other than our own lack of courage!" She looked around. "Fear is only an emotion. Agelfi told me that; an emotion the brain creates when it's overwhelmed, but a mere emotion anyway. It's how we deal with it that counts, not the false cage that emotion creates."

Without waiting for a reply, she turned to the one person still calm. "Stilgen, get your lot to bring the Pro Consul; we have about ten heartbeats. If I shut the doors on the way, that'll buy us another ten heartbeats."

Stilgen nodded and moved toward the direction of her gaze without question. She'd counted on that. The others remained frozen.

"We'll never get back!" Soren wailed, unwittingly arguing for the original plan of death.

"Stilgen knows the system, and so does his men. We can go wherever we like, as long as it's unofficial and off the beaten track." She jabbed a finger at them, suddenly angry. "You idiots, I'm arguing for your *lives*. We're so far out in the void on this world, what chance we're going to run into any guards, let alone an army."

They were staring at the object, wide-eyed. She pressed on trying to keep the rising urgency pinned back. "Think it through—we're effectively inside the Empire already, so there's no ring-fenced border on any scale, and there's pretty much nothing at all in the entire sector than bleached sand. We'll return later with the Heretics' help. Agelfi'll get us back. Our plan was to meet the Resistance anyway; who's to say we wouldn't have had to do it like this?"

The screaming was ear-piercing. The sand glass was empty. She couldn't quash the swelling panic anymore—she had to act.

"I'm going." She wiped the gore from her sword. "Come and do something useful with me. Those that love blood, witless ego, and the needless sound of their own demise, stay, and look noble even as they wipe your guts from the floor."

Ayilia turned towards the Pit's portal, clearly visible between two heavy doors in the adjacent room, and ran.

A sea of armed hatred was boiling towards them with visibly more speed than the last. She heard the others follow without argument, scant surprise considering how feral the new arrivals seemed to be. Stilgen and his soldiers were already there, carrying the sorcery-ruined warlord with ease. Without pause, Stilgen lowered the slumbering Consul and threw himself at the controls. When the last of the witless allies had crossed into the space containing the silent, interstellar iris, Ayilia gave a cry and heaved the doors shut, kicking the bolts into place with her boots in one go, just in time. The doors instantly buckled as the host slammed into them.

Turning around, she noticed some chunkier doors on the other side. Though she didn't know it, they led to the Pit's Forbidden Chamber, where Mabius had interrogated his hapless brother. As the others hovered by the portal, she sprinted over and furiously hacked at the joins, but they were locked fast. She didn't need to be a carpenter to work out it would take them half a day with the weapons they had to cut their way through.

Frustrated, Ayilia scrambled back to Stilgen, practically falling over him in her haste.

"Can you work it? Will it take long? Hell, we've got heartbeats."

Stilgen's brow arched as though charting a course while under threat of being eviscerated in the process was child's play.

"Already done; Imperial channels open. I have codes, old but active, codes that lay dormant in the Pit's archives but are still valid. If I've miscalculated, Imperium security will detain us the moment we step through, but we hardly have a choice. Invisibility is the only defence!" His gaunt but strong palm rested on a complex circle of hieroglyphics. She wanted to scream at him to hurry up, but his demeanour kept her in check. "I have triangulated a target—there are numerous possibilities: it's a below-average portal, but we'll still have the range of most of the nearby worlds of our local Prefecture. We can piggyback covertly on Imperial signals anytime. It's how the Asthen Raiders used to do it.

"Connecting the target mouth here. We're there now," he gestured at the yawning construct, "just jump."

"Where?"

He smiled thinly. "Where it will take you."

The group surrounded them in a bundle, all reluctant to plunge in, despite the melee now starting to spill through growing rents in the doors. The portal arched gracefully over them, dominating their line of sight. Close up, its skin was pockmarked, worn like a leathered glove. Fraught, Ayilia gestured at the others, pointing directly at the opaque surface.

"God's sake, jump everyone!" Soren hollered, racing forwards, knocking Kofi off-kilter as he lanced into the howling quantum lake of horizontal puissance. He was bathed by an intense flash of venomous brilliance, his silhouette imprinted on the faces of the damned, the walls, and the mephitic corners of the Pit.

Then there was nothing, not even a ripple. The lake was dense, unblinking.

The pursuing soldiers stepping through the collapsing doors halted in genuine disbelief, their features unintentionally mirroring that of the rebels. No one had counted on Stilgen's mastery.

"The effect is different with each jump," Stilgen added nonchalantly like a bored tourist guide. "Rest assured, while these controls remain triangulated, you'll end up in the same spot as Soren. At least, I trust so. I can't vouch for the time ..."

A piercing screech electrified the huddle as the skeletal butchers surged forwards again.

"Go!"

The rest of the group banged unceremoniously into each other in a desperate rush toward the waiting mouth. Seftus was uncharacteristically the first, along with Jarong, who moved with impressive speed, followed by Kofi and the undead soldiers. A mute Vespasian was roughly grabbed by Kemet, leaving only Ayilia and Stilgen. The approaching orbs blazed collectively, almost in slow motion, like an army of fireflies in the gloom.

With so many people entering at once, the great portal iris was a churning, bubbling vortex gyrating towards infinity amid a howling wind. In the maelstrom of flaring, rampant energies, Stilgen gently smiled down at her, a neon angel in the harsh, cobalt blaze. He indicated upwards. One of his soldiers was hiding in the rafters. He must have clambered up the moment they entered the side room. With all eyes on their group, no one would see, or assume, he was even there.

"Once the hubbub has died down here, that soldier will sneak out of the Pit and round up those still loyal to the Consul and you. I have already given him all the information he needs about meeting again one day out there!"

She gasped. "What good does that do? We'll be out there, and this gate will be a permanent no-go zone."

"Who said anything about *this* gate?" He smiled again. "Ready for eternity?"

The portal mesmerized her, even as Stilgen bustled the gobsmacked woman into the swirling tempest of crystal cyan. Their outlines were a billion tiny flashes as he held her firmly with one hand and spun the controls out of sync with the other, preventing them from being followed. The funnel jerked after they jumped, as its far exit helter-skeltered across an entire universe.

A dozen Lifeless skidded into the dials to brutally grapple with the retro-styled panel while the rest threw themselves at their disappearing backs. The arc's flat waters engulfed the escapees immediately, and any sign that they had ever existed was eradicated, as was their direction, even their lives.

They could not follow!

Stilgen was a genius.

As they atomized into gyrating flecks of plasma, Ayilia heard his fading words in the frothing fuzz surrounding them.

"Trust me, he will send word to your men. They will know of this."

If only she could believe it.

Within the briefest of moments, her atoms became void.

She became void.

EPILOGUE

W elcome. Let me re-introduce myself.

I am the all-seeing, all-conquering ruler of charted space. My legions call me Imperator, the Asthen necromancers called me Abomination (though one wonders where those Magi pond scum are now), and the crushed call me God. Through the gilded arc of time, one name, a nickname from the docile and oppressed at that, sticks neck and skull above all others. For them, I am the Goat, the Emperor Goat, and that suits me just fine.

Well, I am a god, aren't I?

Enough of my triumphs. Something's happened, something that hasn't happened in a very long time, something that beats even the demon invasion from an underworld universe. Today, I stand above the stricken form of the Al Kimiya, the Al Kimiya mark two.

You have oft heard of it. The thing first came for my scalp a forgotten epoch ago, flaming suns of terrifying puissance angling for my Imperial gizzard. It, of course, failed. Now it's back, but this time, it displayed startling ingenuity. I am almost impressed.

While I slowly harvest its dying puissance, while I slowly become the *real* god, let me tell you its story, one that begins with a baseborn hume, a ruler of a dying city at that. Who would have thought such a meagre, gut-crawling speck of nullity from a species with no thaumaturgy, no powers, no magick foresight other than a strange, feral cunning could have been chosen by the beast, this

Kimiya, but she was, and she fooled me too. While my intellect crossed space like the scarlet spores of a cosmic orchid searching for this debased predator, it was instead grooming her, can you credit it, to find and protect *it*.

Her!

A hume loathed by her sorcery-sterile species, chosen instead of the Magi Heretics and other assorted sorcerers to find the *only* being that could stop me! The Kimiya!

Astonishingly blasphemous.

As I grow into the numen of all things, let me tell you the story about the Kimiya and this female ruler. Let me tell you the story of my imminent takeover of not just this existence but all that has gone before. Let me tell you the story of a winged terrorist and that human midwife that dared to deliver it.

It is the story of a powerless hume that dared come at me with a dirk aimed at my everlasting throat, the blade the glinting form of the Kimiya itself. It is the story of a witless witch despised by her hume populace, a woman who came close to changing the fate of a universe that belongs to me.

Do you remember the bright, blinding light, the destruction, the sheer annihilation? The skies were burnished with flaming, blood-red fury as large and multitudinous as those on the bruised corpse of a giant. I remember the armies, the self-righteous horde gathered outside our very walls. I remember the sea of skulls for decades to come, all that was left of them, plus some rusted cutters.

There is little time before the Al Kimiya, my foe of eternity, perishes for the second and final time. I wish to state my intent.

I wish to explain what I am, to give context to the bloodshed.

I wish to explain that what I do is good, not evil.

I have been so misconstrued!

If neither the arch Magi of the Asthen could not withstand me nor the Interregnum in ancient years, then what hope for the Heretics? My hard men of steel and bone move as remorselessly as a parasite on the caustic lungs of the

Resistance. For those who resist, the future is pitiless. For those who cooperate, life is a glorified hegemony of liquor-covered grog shops.

Can you imagine the life in my realm inexorably swapping places with the soulless within the ceaseless paradox of the Imperial gyre?

It makes me chuckle to see the taverns of our age brimming with inebriated legionnaires, as they mix mindlessly with my living subjects. Logistics auxiliaries, factory workers, bright smiths, journeymen, wainwrights, quarry handlers, pigmen, neat herders, malenders, snob scats and draymen all swilling together with the killer bones and tendon that are my army as the alcohol kills off what little life both have left. Imagine them being beadily watched by gargantuan proprietors, each more than willing to pinch the sovereigns off the moori and those full of tangle-foot for a shifty half-quart.

Envision the fattened burgomasters, bucket-eyed crowners, court tipstaffs, barristers, Imperial leeches, bailies, and magnates. Imagine them among platters of dry meat for the living and mulched gruel for the dead. By the last order, grimy women too addicted to gin to leave are chased by feisty soldiery of bone too addled to stand, hunting them with the pointless fury of long-deceased lotharios. With the imaginary act fulfilled, the bemused targets are back at the bar for a last sniff of liquid toxin, with the coin their untroubled wombs have earned. Shame this tale of the living and the Lifeless has to end, but it does. For a little longer, the circle continues where the robbed end up ripping off the robber in a pirouetting dance of spectacular futility.

Gone are my soldier-beasts of antiquity and their questionable discipline. This is the age of the Lifeless, and I would take my legions of killer bones any day. Undead don't run, undead only intermittently feed, undead cannot experience anxiety and undead do not panic. Their armoured predecessor beasts of yore were as likely to spear their own as the foe. Not anymore.

The soulless don't spoil. They can't; they are already spoilt.

My search for this warrior of spite and darkness, this insurgent of fire and loathing, took all my thought. There are moments even I knew despair, such was my inability to find this Kimiya. Even the demon apocalypse did not detract me from what really counted: the second and final return of the thing now dying at my side.

Goodbye to a past that only lasted forever.

Welcome to an undead universe whose million suns will never sink.

Welcome to eternity.

The second book in the *Nethergeist* series will be releasing March 2025

ACKNOWLEDGEMENTS

Outside my dad, who never lost faith even when I often did and this despite his illness, and also my mum, I would like to give a heartfelt thanks to everyone on the Rising Action team and especially Tina and Alex. No matter the concerns/fears/paranoias with what can be a sobering process, all terrors were always met with warmth, patience and understanding.

And also a special thanks to Nuno for the classiest cover design I could ever imagine.

ABOUT THE AUTHOR

After graduating from university in history, social science, and politics, Nick Stevenson began work as a magazine editor. After putting in his time at a desk, adventure called, and Nick became an extensive traveller. After years spent in south-east Asia, China, Australia, New Zealand, and Australia, Nick returned to the UK and took up a career as an editor and writer of various e-zines. Fifteen years ago, Nick left the online world to run an English Language School to focus on crafting the Nethergeist books.